HOW TO BE A STAR

A SURVIVING HIGH SCHOOL NOVEL

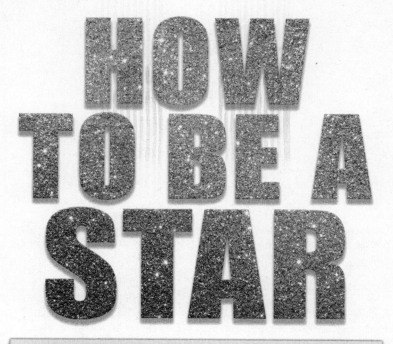

HOW TO BE A STAR

A SURVIVING HIGH SCHOOL NOVEL

BY M. DOTY

poppy

LITTLE, BROWN AND COMPANY

New York   Boston

ALSO AVAILABLE

SURVIVING HIGH SCHOOL

Poppy

Hachette Book Group
237 Park Avenue, New York, NY 10017
For more of your favorite series and novels, visit our website at www.pickapoppy.com

Poppy is an imprint of Little, Brown and Company.
The Poppy name and logo are trademarks of Hachette Book Group, Inc.

The publisher is not responsible for websites (or their content) that are not owned by the publisher.

First Edition: May 2013

ISBN 978-0-316-22017-0

10 9 8 7 6 5 4 3 2 1

RRD-C

Printed in the United States of America

TO EVERYONE
ON THE SHS TEAM,
ESPECIALLY K.L.

PROLOGUE

Kimi prepared herself to face the music.

Darkness surrounded her as she waited onstage. There was no way out of it now. She would have to go on—on *national* television—and sing a song she could never pull off. The audience would hear her voice—her *real* voice. And they would laugh in her face. Worst of all, it was her own fault.

When she was younger, Kimi had a recurring dream where she lost the ability to speak. In the dream, she always tried to hide the problem, nodding and smiling as her friends made conversation, but inevitably she ended up in a class where a teacher would ask her to name a state capital or solve an equation out loud. The worst thing was, Kimi always knew the answer—she just couldn't say it.

Then, standing in silence, she waited there stupidly as

everyone around her started laughing. It began as just a light chuckling, almost like whispers all around her, but soon the laughter grew louder and louder until her ears rang. She'd always wake up sweaty and stressed—yet relieved that it had only been a nightmare.

Tonight, though, was no dream.

Nearby, a spotlight turned on, illuminating the show's guest host, who smiled widely as he introduced her. Then, slowly, purposefully, the light moved through the darkness until it settled at Kimi's feet. Looking up into it, Kimi felt hot and blind.

Her mouth went dry.

The music started.

She wondered if she'd sing even one word.

CHAPTER
ONE

Kimi Chen shivered in the crisp January air. Despite the fact that this was California, winters were still cold, certainly no time to wear a thin silk top. Yet she was doing just that. The winter air pricked at her bare neck like a thousand tiny needles. *Pain is the price of beauty,* she'd read in the November issue of *Vogue.* Now she believed it.

Kimi had sewn the silk top herself after watching a winning contestant on *Project Runway* craft a similar look in the show's most recent episode. Of course, she'd also added her own flair, accessorizing with a flower pin placed just above her heart and adding a strip of lace around the neckline.

The top hid all of Kimi's worst features: her too-thick waist, her too-wide hips. Her mother called Kimi's extra weight "baby fat," which didn't help. Was there a worse phrase in the English language? Guys didn't write love poems to fat girls, and they definitely didn't date babies.

The top had required hours of painstaking labor to sew, but she had no other option. Thanks to her lackluster report card for the fall semester, her parents had lowered her allowance to subsistence level—not that they'd let her buy anything so trendy anyway.

Naturally, Kimi had hidden the shirt from her mother, burying it beneath a green-and-white school hoodie until her mom's minivan disappeared from sight. What did her mother know about fashion? She still wore the same blue-gray pantsuit every day—she'd picked it up at Sears three years ago for her job interview at the district attorney's office.

Kimi shuddered to think that she herself had worn a similar outfit on her first day here at Twin Branches. She'd been going for a sophisticated look, but no one seemed to get it, and it took months before the popular girls stopped joking that she dressed like a Realtor.

Before heading into the cafeteria, Kimi paused for a second and removed a compact from her backpack, quickly checking her skin for breakouts and applying just a little blush—unnecessary, since her cheeks were rosy from the cold. At least her skin looked okay.

And she had a pretty face. Right? She exfoliated, applied whitening strips to her teeth, and plucked her eyebrows regularly. She had also just updated her haircut last night, cutting her own side bangs to take the focus off her too-round face.

Bottom line: She was doing as much as she could with what nature had given her.

Of course, the most popular girls at school tended to be skinny, and rich, and effortlessly beautiful. They were born with petite noses and full, pink lips that framed teeth that had never needed braces. But that's how life was. Some things the universe gave you; the rest you had to earn.

As Kimi passed through the double doors leading to the cafeteria, a wave of warm air rushed over her. The room vibrated with bits of laughter and conversation and smelled of toast and hash browns. During the winter, everyone hung out here until the first bell rang. At the center of the room, she spotted her best friend, Emily Kessler, sitting at a circular table, surrounded by the more popular half of the school's cheerleading team and their football-player boyfriends.

Of course, even among the popular girls there were three who composed the true social elite of Twin Branches High. Kimi would have given anything to be friends with them. The Big Three were:

1. Amanda Applebee. A wide-eyed, very cute red-head. Dumb yet adorable, she was friends with everyone, simply because she didn't know any better.
2. Nicole Black. Generally considered the hottest girl at school, she'd already dated most of the guys at Twin Branches. Her hair was currently

5

brown, but no one, including Nicole, quite knew what color it had originally been.

3. Maria Gonzalez. The school's head cheerleader and queen bee. She'd been spotted in the presence of celebrities, including Justin Bieber, Ryan Gosling, and Snoop Lion (back when he was Snoop Dogg). Rumor had it that she aspired to extend her reign beyond Twin Branches and take over Hollywood.

Of course, Kimi knew Maria hadn't *always* been so popular. Up until Maria was in fifth grade and Kimi in third, the two girls had been neighbors, hanging out all the time despite their two-year age gap. They'd played endless games of checkers, built pillow forts, and argued over which Pokémon they wanted to be.

There was no single event that ended their friendship; rather, Maria had slowly grown apart from Kimi after she left for middle school. Halfway through sixth grade, she had already started faking her parents' signatures to get piercings and sneaking out with boys, as if overnight she'd turned from a child into a woman.

She'd still hung around with Kimi on occasion over that year, but less frequently, and never in a way that felt as close. Soon she was saying things like "Once you get to middle school, you'll realize that..." or "That is *so* fourth grade."

After Maria hit seventh grade, Kimi barely saw her at all. The next summer, Maria's family moved across town, and any lingering excuse they'd had to hang out had disappeared.

By the time Kimi was in sixth grade and started going to middle school, Maria hardly even made eye contact with her when they passed in the halls, as if any memory of their friendship had disappeared.

So what, though, right? People changed. Kimi couldn't fault Maria for that. She'd worked hard for her popularity—and sometimes that meant leaving old acquaintances behind. Plus, by then Kimi had moved on and made a new best friend: Emily Kessler.

Kimi smiled. That's right. There was technically a fourth member of this prestigious "most popular" list. Over the past few months, ever since Emily had risen from social nothing to celebrated athlete (and likely future Olympian), she'd been the most-talked-about girl at school, literally. Kimi estimated that at least 10 percent of all conversations in the hallways centered on everyone's favorite swimmer.

Unfortunately, Kimi didn't share Emily's popularity. Her social stock had fallen drastically, thanks to last fall's "rate the guys" debacle, in which Kimi's written assessment of every guy at the school had become public knowledge.

These days, the popular guys shot her dirty looks, and the popular girls barely tolerated her. If she hadn't been Emily's best friend, she probably would have had to go into permanent exile. As it was, she had to be content with the role of sidekick.

Today, though, Kimi was hoping to get noticed. *If nothing else*, she thought, *the popular girls should respect my keen fashion sense and skill with a sewing needle, right?* She knew for a fact that Maria watched *Project Runway* religiously.

As Kimi approached the table, Emily caught her eye and smiled warmly, scooting over to make room. Maria, for her part, didn't seem to notice Kimi was there.

"Nice haircut!" said Emily, checking out Kimi's fresh side bangs. "You look so different now. Like, sophisticated, you know? Older."

Across the table from them, Lindsay Vale smirked. "Yeah," she said. "Now she looks like she's twelve instead of eleven."

Lately, Lindsay's star had risen. Before, she'd been nothing but Dominique Clark's minion, a pretty blonde with a bad attitude. But Dominique had left shortly after losing several races to Emily at Junior Nationals. Rumor had it that she was training under mysterious circumstances in some foreign country, but no one really knew exactly where she'd gone. Cameron, for his part, said nothing about his sister's whereabouts, and no one wanted to ask.

Since then, Lindsay had secured a spot on the cheerleading squad, befriended several of the most popular older girls, and made out with Marcus Jones after a football game. Other than Emily, Lindsay had become the most popular freshman at school, and she'd even taken on a follower of her own, a tiny yet pretty girl named Shannon, who agreed with everything Lindsay said. Kimi couldn't have despised them more.

"I *like* looking young," Kimi said, forcing a smile. "When I'm thirty, I'll probably look twenty-two. Guys'll be all over me."

"That's just sad," said Lindsay. "Even in your imagination you're going to be thirty and single."

"Yeah!" said Shannon.

A few of the cheerleaders around the table laughed, but most of them weren't even paying attention—which was arguably worse. Instead, they were all looking at Maria, who was showing off her new iPhone. Holding it out, she snapped a picture of herself next to Emily.

"Awesome," said Maria. "I'm totally posting this in my 'Pics with Celebs' album on Facebook." She looked closely at the photo and then at Emily. "Did I mention that I love your top?"

Kimi grimaced. Emily was wearing a fairly standard gray shirt that Kimi had helped her pick out at Anthropologie a few weekends back. Sure it was cute, but it *definitely* wouldn't have made the cut on *Project Runway,* and Emily *definitely* hadn't stayed up all night sewing it.

Emily's face turned bright red as she looked down at her chest.

"It's...it's just a shirt," she stammered. "It's definitely not as cute as what Kimi's wear—"

Her sentence was cut off as the first bell rang and the girls stood, picking up their book bags and purses without even glancing Kimi's way.

As Kimi left the cafeteria, Deependu Mahajan, who, she'd learned, went by the nickname "Dex," approached her from the side.

"I couldn't help but notice you hanging out near Nicole Black just now," he said. "I don't know if she happened to mention me at all?"

He looked at her hopefully.

Dex was one of the nerdiest guys at school. But since he was best friends with Kimi's pseudo-boyfriend, Kevin, she'd gotten to know him pretty well—and as impossible as it seemed it would be to get him together with Nicole, Kimi didn't want to shatter his hopes.

"I, uh, don't think so," she said. "But she may have glanced over at you once or twice."

"I knew it!" he said, suddenly beaming. "Every once in a while I catch her looking. Put in a good word for me, okay?"

"I'm not sure it'll mean much coming from me," said Kimi.

"You never know," he said. "And I can use all the help I can get."

"I'll do what I can," Kimi said, shaking her head. Like it or not, people at the bottom end of the social totem pole had to stick together.

As she turned away from Dex and started walking to class, Kimi couldn't help but think about the stupid smile on Lindsay's face as she'd hurled her insult.

Even in your imagination you're going to be thirty and single.

Whack. Kimi imagined smacking Lindsay in the face. Why hadn't she kept up with her kickboxing lessons? Kimi's gloves and pads were still hanging in the hall closet, right next to her aikido orange belt, her fencing mask, and her tennis racket with the broken string—each object a testament to her inability to stick with an activity longer than two minutes.

10

"Are you okay?"

Kimi looked up to see Emily now walking by her side, a worried look on her face.

"Yeah," said Kimi. "Fine."

"It's just…you look kind of, uh, ready to murder someone. And I'm guessing that someone is Lindsay?"

"I just don't see why she has to go out of her way to be mean to me, like it's her job or something," said Kimi. "And the worst part is, all those other girls laugh right along with her. I know I'm not exactly the most popular girl at school, but that doesn't mean they can just—"

"Hey, it'll be okay," said Emily, putting a hand on Kimi's arm. "Popularity comes and goes. One day you're everyone's best friend. The next day they hate you. Then they love you again. I definitely know what that's like. You can't let it get to you like this."

Kimi couldn't help but smile. Emily was a good friend, always looking out for her, optimistic, hopeful—and all that despite the brutal last year Emily had endured, first losing her sister, and then nearly giving up on her swimming career.

Of course, Emily was also naive. Popularity had arrived at her doorstep, practically gift-wrapped, without her having to lift a finger. She'd never had to try.

"Thanks," said Kimi, giving Emily a brief hug. "I'm sure you're right. Things'll get better."

CHAPTER TWO

After a brutal morning of pop quizzes and enough note-taking to make her hand cramp up, Kimi was looking forward to lunch. She approached the center table, prepared to vent to Emily immediately, but her best friend was nowhere in sight.

Maria cleared her throat. "If you're looking for Emily, she's off with her boyfriend," she said, acknowledging Kimi for possibly the first time in years.

"Speaking of boyfriends, I think I see yours watching us from over there," added Lindsay, pointing to the far reaches of the cafeteria, where the nerds sat. In the distance, Kevin Delucca waved for Kimi to come over as his friends Dex and Amir Singh focused on an intense card game.

"He's not my boy—" started Kimi.

"Whatever he is, it seems like he wants to talk to you,"

said Maria. "Don't worry. We'll tell Emily where you went if she comes back."

And just like that, Kimi realized she was not welcome at the center table. Without Emily to stand up for her, she had no choice but to leave. Grimly, she turned and walked toward Kevin's table, trying to stay calm. If she blew up now, that would be it. The popular girls would giggle about the story for weeks, and any chance she had of ever returning to the center table would be gone.

"Nice haircut!" said Kevin as Kimi sat down next to him. "You look…beautiful. And the shirt is…Wow."

Kimi blushed. She'd hung out with Kevin pretty regularly ever since their homecoming date, and she'd really started to care about him, but she still wasn't sure if she liked him as just a friend…or something more.

Kevin was definitely handsome. Tall and thin with messy brown hair, he looked a little like Liam Hemsworth from *The Hunger Games*, though not as dour. But he didn't act like the other guys she'd dated. Kimi and Kevin had sat through a half-dozen movies together at the local theater, and he hadn't so much as tried to hold her hand, much less kiss her. And now here he was, saying she looked beautiful.

Dex snorted and muttered "Get a room" as he turned three of the cards in front of him sideways and then announced "Fireball."

Amir rolled his eyes.

"Thanks for nothing," Kevin said to Kimi. "You distracted me."

"Don't blame the girl," said Dex. "You were going to lose anyway. Besides, this is the perfect chance to switch out the card games for a little role-playing."

Dex reached into his bag and took out a book titled *Monster Manual*.

"This edition isn't necessarily compatible with the new rule set I've been working on, but there are some really excellent crossbreeds of dragons and—" He stopped for a second to catch his breath. "The point is, we have enough players now. Kimi can be a healer, and we can finally start a real campaign!"

"Say the word *dragon* one more time and I'm eating lunch in the library," said Kimi. "Let's get one thing straight. I may be sitting here for now, but it's temporary. So don't count on me sticking around for any of your *campaigns*."

"Wait," said Kevin. "Don't leave. He'll be cool. Right, Dex? I'm sure we can make it through a lunch or two just, you know, having a conversation."

Dex shook his head and reached down for a pair of oversize headphones. "Fine," he said. "Go ahead, then. *Converse.* I'll try to amuse myself on YouTube."

"Look," said Kimi, smiling—playfully, she hoped. She knew Kevin was trying. "I like hanging out with you, Kevin, I really do. But let's keep the *Magic* talk to a minimum if we're going to keep eating lunch together, okay?"

Across the table, Amir had cracked open a sci-fi novel, and Dex was snickering to himself, watching videos on his phone. A few seconds later, he started softly singing, "*Monday, Monday, gonna skip school on Monday…*"

"Are people still listening to that song?" asked Kimi.

"Just Dex," said Kevin, shaking his head. "He tends to keep thinking things are funny for a *long* time. He still makes references to *Tron*.…"

"Guys," Dex was saying between chuckles. "Guys, you have to check this out."

In the distance, a different sort of laughter arose from the center table. Kimi wondered what joke she had missed. Just this morning, she and Emily had been sitting there, privy to every last comment and nugget of gossip. Now she didn't even know what they were laughing about. A few seconds later, she heard Lindsay and Maria giggling yet again. Kimi resisted the urge to look.

Dex started singing a new song, and Kimi exhaled, trying to stay calm.

"You seem tense," said Kevin. "Did something happen?"

"Nothing *happened*," said Kimi. "It's what *hasn't* happened that's the problem. Everyone loves Emily because she's an amazing swimmer. No one makes fun of her hair or her clothes. They scoot over for her when she wants to sit down. But me? They think they can just ignore me and I won't exist anymore, and you know why? Because unlike her, I'm not *good* at anything."

"You're good at lots of stuff!" said Kevin. "You're always designing cool outfits, and based on what I saw during our brief time at homecoming, I'd say you're the best dancer I know. Oh! And you nailed 'Poker Face' when you sang it at Amir's karaoke party."

"I'm *okay* at a lot of stuff," said Kimi. "That's different from standing out. Lots of people are good at stuff. I want to be great at something."

"I think you're great," said Kevin. "Who cares about the rest of them?"

"I do," said Kimi, looking back toward Maria and her friends.

"Oh, man," said Dex, taking off his headphones. "I started following links from that 'Monday' video. Do you realize how many girls our age make *horrible* music videos online? They can't even sing, but their videos have over a million hits. Ridiculous! Especially when my *Doctor Who* podcast only has a few hundred subscribers."

"That's it!" said Kevin.

"What?" asked Kimi, completely sarcastic. "You want me to be on Dex's podcast?"

"Not that. Listen. You're a way better singer than most of the girls who make those videos," said Kevin. "Not to mention cuter. If you recorded one, you could show everyone how great you are."

"Are you kidding me?" asked Kimi. "Those girls probably get laughed at all the time. I wouldn't be caught dead doing a stupid YouTube video."

"Don't be so hasty," said Kevin. "Honestly, success is success. Even if you get famous for doing something stupid, you're still famous. Plus, I bet you could make something way better than most of these songs. And I haven't even gotten to the best part. I've got a cousin over in the city who works at a recording studio. He could definitely hook us up."

"I don't know," said Kimi. "People would think I'm a total loser."

"No offense, but look what table you're sitting at now. You have nowhere to go but up," said Kevin, smiling. "Of course, if you're happy here with us, we're more than glad to have you."

Kimi picked up Dex's phone and looked at the video that was playing. In it, two blond girls were singing some kind of anthem about how much they liked BeDazzling their iPhones.

"I'll think about it," she said, shooting one last glance back at the center table. It looked hopelessly far away.

CHAPTER THREE

"More chicken?"

Before Emily could say a word, Kimi's mom heaped a huge portion of stir-fry onto her plate.

Typical, thought Kimi. *Half the time, Mom is taking food off my plate.*

Of course, if Kimi ate the same portions as Emily, she'd bloat to the size of a whale in a matter of weeks. Not that Kimi resented Emily—she knew that the amount of time Emily spent in the pool meant she needed to replace eight thousand or so calories a day. Still, it was hard to watch Emily polish off plate after plate of delicious food without feeling a twinge of resentment.

"Kimi tells us you set *another* record," said Kimi's mom,

leaning over to set a scoop of rice next to the chicken on Emily's plate. "Your parents must be thrilled."

"I don't think my dad will be *thrilled* until I'm wearing a gold medal," said Emily. "But, yeah, I guess he's pretty happy with my progress."

"You know, Daniel is in the same dorm as Jenny Lodge over at Stanford," said Kimi's dad. "Silver medal last summer. Very impressive."

Here we go again, thought Kimi. *I should have known they couldn't go a whole meal without mentioning their precious son and the fact that he's at Stanford.*

It wasn't that she had any problem with Daniel per se. Five years older than she was, Kimi's brother was a complete enigma in her mind. Even when he'd lived at home, he'd spent hours hunched over his computer. Most of their interactions had consisted of him focus-testing various computer games on her, then berating her for breaking them or failing to follow the tutorials.

"We're thinking of signing Lily up for swim lessons," added Kimi's mom. "Not that she can put in as much time as you, of course. She's too busy with piano. Her teacher thinks she might be the next Lang Lang."

"Who's that?" asked Emily.

"Some pianist," said Kimi.

"The best in the world," said a small voice from across the table, and Kimi looked up to see her younger sister, Lily, staring at her. Just eleven years old, Lily was already playing complex Mozart and Rachmaninoff pieces that gave professional pianists fits. Kimi was proud of Lily's accomplishments, but hearing their parents constantly praise Lily also stung. Kimi couldn't remember the last time they'd bragged about anything *she'd* accomplished.

"The best *for now*," said Kimi's mother, shooting Lily a smile.

Kimi sighed and took a small bite of chicken, trying to savor every last bit of its taste. Meals like this, with fresh-cooked food and the whole family sitting around the table, were rare. Most nights, it was either takeout or leftovers, with her parents, both exhausted from long hours at work, sitting in front of the TV, their eyes glazed over.

Tonight, though, they had "company," and that meant pretending that this sort of meal was normal. Her parents even cooked differently when guests like Emily came over, softening the spiciness of the food and forgoing the usual bok choy and Chinese broccoli for more American-friendly fare that Kimi hated to admit she preferred.

"Lily is also an A student," added Kimi's father after a pause. "Of course, they say talented musicians are often good at math, so—"

Emily looked up between forkfuls and made eye contact with Kimi. She must have sensed some kind of frustration on Kimi's face because she interrupted, saying, "You must be really proud of Kimi, too. Have you seen the latest outfits she's been sewing? They're pretty impre—"

"Outfits?" asked Kimi's mom. "I thought you were just borrowing my sewing machine to patch old jeans."

"Exactly," said Kimi, trying to think fast. Her mom had never approved of her fashion choices, calling them frivolous and distracting. "A couple patches and Emily thinks I sewed the pants myself." She laughed awkwardly and shot a look at her friend.

For a moment, Kimi's mom regarded the girls suspiciously, then, not wanting to make a scene, she reached forward and calmly poured herself a cup of tea.

"I'm just saying, she's talented," said Emily after a second, giving Kimi a meaningful glance. "She should be proud of herself."

"Of course I agree," said Kimi's mom, sipping her tea. "But one needs to make the distinction between talent and accomplishment. The world is full of talented people who end up accomplishing nothing with their lives. Only when natural ability meets hard work and perseverance do people become exceptional. Think about it. How many 'talented' swimmers do you know who've lost races to you for lack of conditioning?"

"A few," Emily admitted, looking down at her plate.

Kimi felt her face getting hot. It was bad enough that her mother clearly preferred Daniel and Lily over her, but did she really have to make it so obvious in front of Emily? The shame of it ate at Kimi's stomach, making it feel empty despite the full meal she'd just eaten.

"I think we'll skip dessert," she said, trying not to let her anger show.

After dinner, Kimi and Emily hung out in Kimi's room as the sound of a muffled Chopin piano sonata wafted through the closed door.

"You okay?" asked Emily as Kimi stared blankly at her computer screen. "Your mom was being—"

"Herself," said Kimi. "She's right, you know. I'm not *exceptional* like you are."

"Well, maybe you haven't found what you really care about yet," said Emily. "Honestly, most people at school don't exactly know what they want to do with their lives. That's the exception, not the rule."

"Not for you," said Kimi. "And not for my family." She took a deep breath. "Look, I don't want to spend our one sleepover a month moping about this stuff. This is supposed to be fun. Let's grab some popcorn, sneak into the den, and watch *Friday Night Showcase*. Zac Efron is hosting, and Jessie J is the musical guest. I've been looking forward to it all week."

"Sounds good," said Emily. "Classic girls' night."

"Perfect," said Kimi. "The show starts in twenty minutes. In the meantime, you can tell me about your love life with Ben. In vivid detail."

Now it was Emily's turn to blush.

"We didn't—" she started. "I mean, we haven't—"

Kimi laughed.

"Come on, give me something," she said. "It's been months since I made out with Phil."

"But what about Kevin?" asked Emily. "I thought you two were—"

Kimi let out a strangled groan. "Does *everyone* think I'm dating him?" she asked. "I mean, yes, we've been hanging out. But he hasn't made any moves. And honestly, I'm not sure I want him to. He's a nice guy and all, but I'm not sure I feel that extra...spark, you know, when I'm around him."

"Too bad," said Emily. "Ben and I definitely have that. Kissing him is like..." She trailed off.

"Like what?" asked Kimi.

Emily flushed red again.

"Well, you know what it's like," said Emily. "Don't you? When you really care about someone and you start kissing, it's like the world disappears."

"Oh...yeah," Kimi lied. She'd certainly felt *something* kissing Phil, and a couple of other guys, but nothing quite like what Emily was describing. Suddenly, she wanted it more than anything.

Imagine having an amazing guy whom you loved so much that touching your lips to his erased the rest of the world entirely. Unfortunately, getting an awesome, totally hot guy like Ben Kale to fall madly in love with you didn't happen to girls like Kimi. Only to superstars like Emily.

She thought back to Kevin's suggestion earlier that day, the idea that she could record a video and become some kind of Internet celebrity.

"I've been thinking about writing a song," she said.

"Cool," said Emily. "I mean, a little random, but cool. You should go for it."

"Yeah," said Kimi, nodding, trying to convince herself of the idea.

"So...what's it about?" asked Emily. "What made you want to write it?"

"I don't know," said Kimi. She hadn't gotten this far in her planning yet. That was right: Songs actually had to be *about* something. "What are all songs about? Like, thinking a guy is hot. Going to a party. Having fun."

"So...you're going to write a Ke$ha song?" asked Emily, grinning.

"No, no, no. Nothing that trashy. Maybe like *one* level classier. Like, Britney Spears or Pink or Rihanna or something."

"But not, like, Taylor Swift–classy," said Emily.

"Please. I'm not *that* much of a goody-goody," said Kimi. "I want to look *sexy* in the video, you know?"

"So now there's a video?"

"That's the whole point," said Kimi. "I—"

They were interrupted by a beep from Emily's phone. She pulled it out from the front pocket of her jeans and checked the screen.

"Who texted?" asked Kimi.

Emily frowned. "Ben."

"Aren't you usually *glad* to hear from him?"

"I know, it's just...I kind of forgot he was planning something special for us. For tonight. It's the two-month anniversary of our first kiss, and—"

"—you need to go."

"I don't want to be a flaky friend, I swear. I can just tell him to reschedule for tomorrow if you—"

"No," said Kimi. "Tonight is special for you guys. You should go."

"You won't be mad?" asked Emily.

Kimi smiled. "You'll make it up to me."

"You're the best," said Emily, leaping up to give her a hug.

Even as she wrapped her arms around Kimi, Emily was already texting Ben.

An hour later, Kimi was alone in her room, lying in bed, staring at the ceiling. Down the hall, Lily was still playing Chopin, the same piece she'd been working on for weeks. How did she keep it up, making her fingers trace the same pattern over and over again, without making so much as a single error? It seemed impossible. No wonder their parents were so proud of her.

Kimi got up and went over to her laptop. She pulled up Facebook, looked at it for a second, then aimlessly clicked to Polyvore, ModCloth, and a few of her favorite fashion blogs. Finally, she closed all her windows and started up a fresh Word document.

What's it about? Emily had asked. Well, what *was* it about?

Parties were a thing. Lots of songs had something about them.

There's a party at my house, she wrote. Then, as if by reflex, she continued, *and I'm standing in the corner.*

That didn't exactly sound like fun. Who stands in a corner at her own party? Maybe she'd have to go back and revise that later.

She wrote the next line: *Everybody's dancing, and I'm here on my own.*

Awesome. This was starting to sound like Goth poetry. At this rate, she'd have to change her name to Lucretia and start dressing in all black. Not her look.

Still, at least she was writing *something.* At this point, she might as well finish. She could always rethink it tomorrow, and anyway, it kind of felt good to write like this, putting her scattered thoughts into words.

An hour later, Kimi stopped typing, looked up, and realized she'd filled a page. It wasn't exactly poetry, but it wasn't half bad, either. She was halfway through rereading it when she heard her door open. She immediately minimized the window.

"What are you doing?" asked a small voice from behind her, and Kimi turned to see Lily peeking in at her through the half-open door.

"Just writing ... stuff."

"Like a diary?" asked Lily.

"A song."

"Oh," said Lily, looking down at her feet. After a few seconds, she added, "I'm sorry Mom was mean to you at dinner.

It made me want to throw out her jewelry box or set her clothes on fire or something."

Kimi laughed. Her sister was one of those quiet, seemingly normal girls who tended to say the craziest things. She looked so innocent that no one ever took her seriously.

"Uh, yeah, you don't have to burn anything. Mom is who she is. Tossing her necklaces in the trash isn't going to change her."

"Well, maybe I just shouldn't play piano anymore. She's always bragging about it, like *she's* the one who has to practice all the time and play at stupid recitals."

"I thought you *liked* playing," said Kimi.

"I do," said Lily, sighing and partially collapsing against the door. "I just don't like her saying that, or comparing us—"

"Hey, come here," said Kimi.

Lily walked over, and Kimi stood to give her a big hug.

"You just keep doing what you're doing, okay?" she said. "You let me worry about me. And about Mom. You're supposed to be *my* little sister, so I take care of you, not the other way around, got it?"

"Got it," said Lily, hugging her back. "And good luck with your song! I know it's going to be great."

Kimi wished she could share her little sister's confidence.

After Lily had left, Kimi opened her document back up and finished rereading the lyrics. They weren't quite as bad as she remembered.... Maybe they were even good.

At school on Monday, Kimi walked down the hall after the final bell, thinking over the lyrics to her song. She'd revised it a few times since that initial creative flurry, and she was liking it better and better.

But while she was excited about the idea one second, the next she worried that the whole thing was stupid. She could only imagine how the cheerleaders at the center table would react if they found out about some video she posted online. Would they actually think it was cool, or would they just ridicule her more?

Kimi spotted Lindsay and Shannon a few paces in front of her, laughing softly about something as they strode through the hall with total confidence. What was the difference between them and her? What had they done to win popularity, hot boyfriends, and spots on the cheerleading team?

"Did you see what she wore *today*?" she overheard Lindsay ask.

"No!" said Shannon. "Tell me."

"Jeans and a T-shirt," said Lindsay.

Kimi looked down, a sense of dread filling her. After suffering through the girls' insults last week, she'd decided to go low-profile and wear the least offensive outfit possible. What could Lindsay possibly have against her jeans-and-T-shirt ensemble? That's what *everyone* wore *all* the time!

"And?" asked Shannon, apparently also confused.

"I'm just saying," said Lindsay. "It's like she's either trying *way too hard* and dressing like some reject off *America's Next*

28

Top Model, or trying to be completely invisible. There's, like, no middle ground."

"Between train wreck and invisible, I'd prefer invisible," said Shannon.

"Luckily, it's a choice we don't have to make," replied Lindsay, and for just a second, Kimi was pretty sure she caught Lindsay looking back over her shoulder.

She knows I'm behind them, she realized. *She wants me to hear this.*

As they got to an intersection with another hall, the girls veered left, and Kimi headed right, where she wouldn't have to listen to them anymore.

Invisible? she thought. *Invisible?!*

For a moment, she thought about adopting her usual approach—a quick run to the bathroom followed by a short cry in one of the stalls. But that was what Lindsay wanted, wasn't it? For Kimi to be in pain and out of sight. Just…gone.

She thought about the song again. Yeah, making a video and putting it online came with a few risks. But at least she wouldn't be invisible.

She called Kevin. After only half a ring, he picked up.

"Hey! What's up? It's good to hear from you."

"I've been thinking about your offer," she said. "And I've been writing. Tell your cousin I'm ready to record a song."

CHAPTER FOUR

That Saturday, Kevin showed up outside Kimi's house a little after four o'clock. Despite the relatively early hour, the winter sun hung low in the sky, and Kevin's stout, ugly hatchback cast a long shadow over the street.

Kimi hated this time of year, when darkness came early. She was a summer person, the type who thrived on warm nights and days that seemed to go on forever. But despite the cold, she refused to wear a jacket—it could wrinkle her outfit.

"Nice dress!" said Kevin. "Is it new?"

Kimi looked down at the outfit she'd modified overnight. What had once been a standard floral-print dress that her mom had picked straight off the rack at Macy's was now completely customized, with one shoulder cut off and the hem slanted at a thirty-degree angle. It was a little eighties retro, a little postmodern, and all Kimi.

"Just something I threw together for the video," she said. "Thanks for driving."

"Anytime." He opened the car door, bowed slightly, and motioned for her to enter, like a prince inviting her into his carriage. He was certainly sweet, but Kimi was glad that none of her friends were around to see the gesture.

Stepping into the car, she thought back to a few months earlier, to the nights she'd sneaked out of the house to meet Phil nearby. Of course, in that case, he'd had to park down the block so they wouldn't get caught by Kimi's parents. She remembered the thrill of it: She'd slip into the passenger seat and kiss him as music blasted all around them; then they'd speed off to some hill or lake or beach to watch the stars and kiss some more.

They must have grabbed food, or sat and talked, too, but she couldn't remember those details. Mostly, she'd just felt excited to be there with him.

She looked over to see Kevin adjusting his mirror. When he started the engine, jazz began to play at low volume.

"What's this?" she asked.

"My 'blue' mix," he said. "This is *Kind of Blue* by Miles Davis. Next is *Rhapsody in Blue* by Gershwin. And then 'Blue Monday' by New Order."

"You know you're totally weird, right?" Kimi asked.

"I assumed that's why you like me."

"Well, I guess I don't *completely* despise you," she teased, hoping she wasn't flirting too much and leading him on. She was still evaluating. Maybe they really would end up together, but like she'd told Emily the week before, she needed to feel that *spark*. And she was still waiting for it with Kevin.

"Good enough for me," he said, pulling away from the curb.

As they drove, she listened to the soft music playing faintly on the weak speakers. It wasn't what she would have picked, but it did set a certain mood, a sort of relaxed, rainy-day vibe. In a way, it was perfect for right now: it helped calm her nerves.

She'd started the day with butterflies in her stomach, thinking not only of the recording session ahead but also of actually posting the video online for public consumption. What would people say?

Of course, the girl who had recorded "Monday" got some negative reactions at first. People thought it was dumb. But now that girl was famous, so *actually* she was kind of a genius: It was an idea so dumb it was smart. But what if, in Kimi's case, it was just plain stupid?

Flap, flap went Kimi's butterflies.

And the wing beats got worse when they reached the city. The car passed through an upscale area near the Ferry Building, where tall, glassy buildings rose all around them, and headed toward the warehouse district, an uninhabited swath of empty factories and graffiti. This looked like a good place to get mugged—not to record a hit music video.

"You sure you have the address right?" asked Kimi.

Kevin nodded.

"I used to come here a lot when my older brother was in a band. He was in our cousin's studio all the time."

Kimi locked her door.

"Don't worry," Kevin added. "My cousin just set up shop in this neighborhood because the rent is so low. There's hardly any crime during the daytime, and besides, you've got me to protect you."

Kimi gave Kevin a once-over. He didn't look qualified to protect her from much.

"Are you freaking out?" asked Kevin. "We can head home if you're freaking out."

"No," said Kimi. "I want to do this."

"Good," he said, pulling over to the curb. "Because we're here."

Walking through the doorway to the studio, Kimi felt like she was entering another world. While everything outside had been dirty, crumbling, even dangerous, inside, it was clean and slick. Burnished steel walls lined a narrow corridor, and Kimi's and Kevin's reflections shone in the polished black tile beneath their feet.

Several pictures of moderately successful local artists hung from the walls. None of them had necessarily hit it big nationally, but Kimi had seen their names in the local paper and heard about their concerts from her more music-obsessed classmates.

At the end of the corridor, they reached a door and

entered a large, windowless office, sparsely decorated with a glass desk and several metal chairs. Sitting in one was perhaps the largest man Kimi had ever seen. Well over six feet tall and nearly as wide, he seemed far too big for his small chair to support. His expensive-looking suit could probably fit two of Kevin in each pant leg. The man glanced up from his iPad as they entered, and smiled.

"K-Dawg!" he said, standing with considerable effort. "Good to see you. And this must be your girlfriend!"

Girlfriend? What exactly had Kevin told his cousin? And more important, did *he* think they were officially together? As if Kimi didn't have enough on her mind already.

"I'm, uh, Kimi," she said, as the man strode over. She shook his huge, fleshy hand.

"Alan," he said. "Kevin's cousin. Can you believe our dads are brothers?"

The idea that Kevin could possibly be related to this giant *was* hard to believe. They were complete opposites not only in terms of sheer size but also in everything else. While Kevin had dark brown hair, Alan had a slicked-back blond ponytail. Kevin had smooth, almost olive-colored skin; Alan was a rosy-cheeked Santa Claus, complete with a bushy beard. Kimi, never that good at guessing ages, couldn't tell if he was thirty or fifty.

"Come on," he said. "I'll show you the sound booth."

Kimi soon realized that Kevin's and Alan's personalities were as different as their appearances. While Kevin was calm and deferential, Alan was impatient and bossy. As Kimi walked into the sound booth, she handed Alan a printout of her lyrics. He set it down on top of a nearby speaker.

"I guess Kevin didn't tell you," he said as he turned on a sound board covered with hundreds of switches and knobs. "But I write the songs. Trust me, it's better that way. No offense to you, but teenage girls—they're not exactly a bunch of William Shakespeares, you get me? No one wants to know about your problems. Frankly, no one cares."

"So, uh, what am I going to sing?" asked Kimi.

"Glad you asked," said Alan, handing her a lyrics sheet. "This baby is called 'Three O'Clock.' As in the end of the school day. I've been saving this for someone special. I think you're her. The song is fresh. It's fun. It's relatable. Nail this, and it could be a hit."

Three O'Clock
By Alan Delucca

Yeah! Yeah-ah! Yeah!
Uh-huh! Yeah-ah! Uh-huh!
Yeah! Yeah-ah! Yeah!
Oooooh, hey!

Eight in the morning it's chemistry
Nine and I take another SAT
Ten and I want to climb a tree
Gonna be lucky if I get a C

35

```
Noon and it's lunchtime
Wish I had some brunch time
But it's not Sunday so I don't!

Three o'clock! Three o'clock!
When's it gonna be three o'clock?
I just can't wait for this day to
    ennnnnd!
(x 4)

One o'clock and I'm taking math
Wish I could be in a bubble bath
Teacher's mad 'cause he heard me laugh
Best friend got a cupcake, give me
    half!
```

It went on like this for a while. Reading the lyrics, Kimi wrinkled her nose.

"Are you sure about this?" she asked. "I don't think some of this makes sense. Like, she's taking 'another SAT' at nine… but she wants to climb a tree at ten. So is the test just an hour, or is the singer daydreaming in the middle of the test? And then, you don't get a C on the SAT. It's more like a number score, like a 2080, which would also rhyme, if we used that—"

"You're thinking about this *way* too hard," said Alan. "Is Britney *literally* in a circus in the song 'Circus'? Is Katy Perry *literally* a firework?"

"I think what she's trying to say—" started Kevin.

Alan glared at him.

"Give us a second, Kev," he said. "Go get a soda or something."

For a moment, Kevin paused. He glanced at Kimi, as if trying to gauge whether she needed a knight in shining armor.

"It's okay," she said. "Give us a second."

He got up and walked out of the room without another word.

"Okay, here's the score," said Alan. "You asked me to do a job, to do what I do well, to maybe, just maybe, make you a star." He stared at Kimi. "Now listen. If you want to do this on your own, just say the word. There are plenty of girls with guitars who make YouTube videos in their bathrooms, where they think the acoustics are best. You want to sit on a toilet and try to rise to fame doing acoustic covers of Adele, go for it."

"No," said Kimi. "No, 'Three O'Clock' is great as is. Let's do it."

"Cool, cool," he said. "Then we can sign the contract and get to work."

"Contract?" A wave of nervousness flooded Kimi's chest. If the movies she'd watched were any indication, most contracts involved some combination of the devil, a soul, and a wish that ends up a disaster.

"Just a bunch of legalese my lawyers make me make my artists agree to. Just a couple of details like who gets credit for what, how profits get split up. I'd tell you to take your time and read it, but honestly, we're burning clock. We should probably just get started."

He handed Kimi the contract and a pen. For a second, she hesitated, trying to skim over the details, but she couldn't understand half of the words, and honestly, she didn't care. All she wanted was to get this song recorded and over with.

Without another thought, she uncapped the pen and signed her name.

"Good," said Alan. "Now let's get you behind the mic. And while we're at it, let's change you out of that ridiculous dress and into something a little more 'high school.' We'll splice some shots of you in the booth into the rest of the video."

"Uh, yeah," said Kimi, looking down at her dress. "I guess I can wear whatever you want."

"Now you're talking," said Alan.

Before Kimi made her costume change, Alan played a version of "Three O'Clock" on a loop that featured himself as the lead vocalist.

"Just to give you a sense of the song," he said, as she tried not to get creeped out hearing a man, singing in a deep baritone, describe his day in high school. At least the music sounded okay.

Kimi wasn't thrilled with the whole experience so far, but sometimes you had to suffer a little to get what you wanted. Just look at Emily. How many brutal workouts had she gone through to get where she was today? It would probably be worth it when it was all over.

Half an hour later, Kimi, dressed like someone out of a JCPenney ad, stood in front of a microphone, the lyrics sheet for "Three O'Clock" balanced precariously on a music stand in front of her. Kevin and Alan stood on the other side of a thick, soundproof glass wall, though she could hear their voices through a pair of bulky headphones.

"Okay," said Alan. "I'm going to play the music. When I do, you just sing along to the melody with the lyrics in front of you. We can do it piece by piece, so don't worry about nailing it all in one try."

"Good luck!" said Kevin.

A few seconds later, the music began. Kimi had to admit that the song, synth-heavy and poppy, was growing on her.

"*Yeah! Yeah-ah! Yeah!*" she began, but even as she sang the words, she knew her pitch was off.

"Should I stop?" she asked as the music continued to play. "Sorry. I'm not sure what, exactly, Kevin told you. I can kill it at karaoke, but this is all kind of new to me."

"Don't sweat it!" said Alan. "We can just Auto-Tune out any vocal imperfections. Once I'm done fixing it up, it's going to be like Celine Dion, Mariah Carey, and Adele all had a baby together, and her name was Kimi Chen."

"I...I guess so," she said. "But I'm not even sure I was in the right octave for that last 'yeah.'"

"Like I said, Auto-Tune is a beautiful thing," replied Alan. "Don't worry too much. Just sing it the best you can, and I'll take care of the rest."

"So…it's not really my voice?" asked Kimi.

"Of course it is," he said. "It's you, just better. Trust me. *Everyone* Auto-Tunes these days. If Auto-Tuned voices aren't real, then half the songs you hear on the radio are fakes. Now, you ready to take it from the first 'uh-huh'?"

Kimi nodded. "Cue the music."

The song took less than two hours to record. Kimi was fairly sure she'd been off-key for most of the chorus, and she definitely hadn't been able to hit most of the high notes, but Alan had repeatedly told her she was doing great, even flashing a thumbs-up from time to time. Maybe he really was as gifted an Auto-Tuner as he claimed to be.

The video took longer, and mostly consisted of Kimi dressing up in various outfits and standing in front of a green screen, singing along as Alan's version of the song played in the background.

Occasionally, Alan would shout commands like "You're on a football field now. Give me 'cheerleader'!" or "Now you're walking down the hall and you see your friend over to your left. You're waving hello! Okay. Now you're walking again!"

By the end of it, Kimi was totally drained. When Alan finally turned the camera off and shouted "That's a wrap!" as if there were a whole crew around to hear him, Kimi practically collapsed onto the floor. Luckily, Kevin pulled a chair over to her, and she melted into it.

"Perfect," said Alan, looming over her. "Brilliant. My best directorial effort yet. You're going to be a star."

Kimi looked down at herself. She was wearing a green tracksuit complete with matching wristbands, and she was dripping with sweat. Not hot.

"Are you sure that looked okay?" she asked.

"Gorgeous. Beautiful. Amazing," said Alan, walking back to his camera to review some of the footage. "And that's just my camera work. I'm kidding! You looked great."

"It's true," said Kevin, handing Kimi a bottle of water. "You were amazing. Even better than I thought you'd be."

Too tired to do another take even if she had wanted to, Kimi hoped he was right.

On the ride home, Kimi was so exhausted that she didn't realize they were pulling into the In-N-Out parking lot until Kevin killed the engine.

"Your favorite, right?" he asked, smiling.

It occasionally left Kimi dumbfounded that Kevin knew stuff like this about her. Had she mentioned her love for Double-Doubles at some point or was Kevin a Facebook stalker? Probably both.

She looked up at him, dazed. Was this dinner or a late-night snack? Based on the waning moon in the sky, she guessed the latter. The whole day had passed in a blur. She hadn't even realized how hungry she was until this moment. Now, though, her stomach growled.

"Thanks," she said as they walked across the parking lot. "You didn't have to—"

"This wouldn't be much of a date if I didn't buy you a meal," he said, taking her hand in his.

So this was a date. She had to give him credit. The whole setup was very sneaky. Exactly the kind of trick Kimi might have pulled on a potential boyfriend.

She let him hold on to her hand. She was curious to see how far he'd push things—though she suspected hand-holding might be the limit.

CHAPTER FIVE

Before school on Monday, Kimi looked around the cafeteria for Emily, eager to tell her about the recording session and the "date" with Kevin. All Sunday, Kimi had tried to reach Emily by any means possible, but multiple calls, texts, and e-mails had failed to win a response, and Kimi was beginning to suspect Emily's dad had blown another fuse and thrown her into an all-day workout. Unfortunately, Emily was still nowhere to be found.

Kimi had just finished asking Amir if he'd seen Emily around when a voice behind her said, "She just headed off. With her boyfriend. To the roof, I think."

Kimi turned to see Cameron Clark staring down at her. He was tall, blond, and beautiful; Kimi had never even been able to talk to him in her dreams. Now, real-life hottest-guy-in-school Cameron was standing in front of her, looking cocky—and hot—as ever. And he was clearly waiting for her to respond.

"She, uh, with…her boyfriend…roof?" Kimi managed to ask. She'd already heard about Emily and Ben's secret spot on the roof, and Kimi certainly wasn't going to go interrupt their private time. The last thing she needed now was to catch the two of them making out—and thus be reminded that no one had kissed her in months.

Cameron nodded, then looked back at the center table, where his friends were waiting.

"I'll see you around," he said, and walked away.

Awesome. Kimi's first conversation with a popular boy in months, and she'd been about as articulate as a preschooler.

Even worse was the news that Emily had left with Ben *again.* If this kept up, Kimi would be down a best friend, and she'd end up spending the rest of high school playing Ogres & Elves with Kevin and his buddies. She shuddered at the thought.

She headed out of the cafeteria and had started walking down the hall toward her first class when her phone vibrated in her purse. She pulled it out and read:

Alan Delucca: Google yourself.

Kimi opened the Internet browser on her phone and typed in her own name. The top results were the same as they'd been for months—message boards full of nasty comments about Kimi from her "rate the guys" fiasco—as well as a nice website filled with praise that Kevin had created as a counterpoint.

The sixth result, though, was new—a video labeled "Three O'Clock."

Kimi almost screamed. *No way.* Had Alan already finished the video? And had he *really* just posted it online without showing it to her first? Kimi's heart pounded, the sound of her pulse filling her ears like a drumbeat. The bell rang and she ignored it. She had to watch this video. Now.

Pushing past the other students rushing to their classes, Kimi headed for the closest restroom, where she barricaded herself in a stall and clicked the link on her phone. As she waited for the video to load, a static image of the first frame filled the screen. It featured her in a poorly fitted cheerleading outfit, a stupid expression on her face. Not a promising start.

She took a deep breath, trying to reassure herself that it wasn't *terrible.* Just one slightly stupid-looking frame so far.

How bad could it be?

The answer, it turned out, was *very* bad. The image of her in a poorly fitted cheerleading uniform was only the tip of the iceberg. In the video, Kimi wore ridiculous outfit after ridiculous outfit, looking totally sweaty and messy-haired, dancing offbeat as nonsensical background footage appeared behind her where the green screen had been.

A second-by-second breakdown went something like this:

(0:00–0:15) Kimi is dressed as a cheerleader. In the background, firefighters attempt to rescue a cat.
(0:16–0:27) Kimi wears roller skates, short shorts, and a tight T-shirt, and rolls awkwardly around the screen. Fireworks erupt behind her.
(0:28–0:40) Kimi is bundled up in a fur coat. Bears fight in the background.
(0:41–0:47) A static image of Kimi midjump. Behind her, a star goes supernova.

From there, things only got worse. There were dancing babies. Cartoon unicorns. The Eiffel Tower, the Pyramids, and the Taj Mahal. Alan had even inserted a small segment of himself, performing a brief rap.

Why? she thought. *Why, why, why?*

And then another question crossed her mind: *How many people have seen this?*

She scrolled down to the bottom of the video and read:

Views: 7

She gave a sigh of relief. Six of those views were probably just Alan watching it over and over again, and she was the seventh. The video was a disaster—but at least it was contained.

She immediately wrote a text to Alan:

Kimi Chen: Take it down. Now.
Kimi Chen: Please!

Okay. Message sent. He'd take care of this. Maybe they could go back to the drawing board, figure out a new concept for the video, and shoot some new footage. Then they could post a video where she didn't look like a mental patient.

For the first time since she'd received Alan's text, she started to relax. The adrenaline that had surged through her a few minutes earlier began to dissipate, and her heartbeat returned to normal.

He'll take it down, she told herself. *He'll take it down.* Maybe, just maybe, everything was going to be okay.

As it turned out, at least one other person at school *had* seen the video: Kevin. He put up a hand when he saw Kimi walking toward him in the cafeteria at lunchtime.

"Nice video!" he said. "High-five."

"Put your hand down," she said, gritting her teeth as she sat across the table from him and Dex. "Is that thing still online? I told Alan to remove it. Like, ASAP."

"Why?" asked Kevin. "It's hilarious."

"We laughed," said Dex. "A lot."

"Do you think I shot this video to be *hilarious*?" asked Kimi. "I want to be cool, not a joke."

"Cool people can take a joke," said Kevin. "That's what makes them cool."

"Being cool is what makes them cool," said Kimi.

"A classic example of circular reasoning," said Dex.

"Can't you talk like a normal person?" Kimi asked. Her

eye had started twitching. Was it possible to have a stroke and a heart attack at once? At age fourteen?

"I *could* talk like one of the regular J.Crew clones around here," said Dex. "But why would I want to?"

"Don't be upset," added Kevin. "It really is funny. You should be proud."

Kimi stood up.

"I'm watching any potential of ever having a social life crumble before my eyes, and it's just a big joke to you," she said. "And here's a free tip: When a girl is upset, the *last* thing you want to do is tell her not to get upset!"

"Come on," said Kevin. "It's not that big a deal. Please... sit down."

Kimi shook her head. "I'm going to the library. So I can watch my stupid video on a bigger screen."

The second viewing did little to improve Kimi's outlook. Neither did the third or the fourth. By the time lunch was over, she'd watched the stupid clip eight more times, her anger growing with each subsequent viewing.

Every time she watched it, she noticed another wince-worthy moment. These included:

1. A segment in which her back was to the camera and her bra strap was clearly visible through a gauzy Roman toga
2. A scene in which she blew the landing of a cart-wheel (she'd insisted Alan use a different take!)

3. A moment where sweat flew off her and landed on the camera lens (so gross!)
4. Multiple scenes where her top rolled up, revealing her "baby fat"
5. Multiple cases of bad hair/makeup (too many instances to even count)

Luckily, the views counter at the bottom of the screen only read twenty-five, which meant pretty much no one else had seen it... which would stay true as long as Alan took it down. Now.

Stepping out of the library and into the hall, she called Alan.

"Kimi Chen! How's it going?"

"I guess you didn't get my text?" she asked.

"Yup. Got it. And promptly ignored it."

"And you did that because..."

"Because sometimes a producer knows better than a star."

"People are going to laugh at me," she said. "Take it down."

"No one ever got famous without taking a few risks," said Alan. "In this case, you have to risk looking stupid. Trust me."

"That's easy for you to say!"

"Do you think it was Britney's idea to wear that schoolgirl outfit in 'Baby One More Time'?" asked Alan. "Do you think Justin Bieber asked for that stupid haircut? Do you think Miley Cyrus picked out the name Hannah Montana? No. A producer did. And those stars probably all fought tooth and nail... right until the moment they got rich and famous."

"I...I..." She didn't know what to say. Alan clearly wasn't going to listen to reason.

"Sit back and enjoy the ride, sweetie," said Alan. "I've got this."

The line went dead. For a few seconds, Kimi stared at her iPhone and contemplated tossing it against the hallway's cinder-block wall. Only the fact that the cell had cost two hundred dollars prevented her from doing so.

Twenty-five views, she reminded herself. *Just twenty-five views.*

But it didn't stop there. Of course it didn't.

By the end of the school day, her mantra had become: *A hundred views. Only a hundred views.*

And by the time she went to bed, it was up to two hundred. Desperate for support, she logged on to IM and was thankful to find Emily online.

ChEnigma22: I'm freaking out here, Em! 200 views?! At least a few of those have to be from people at school, right?

EmilyK14: Don't worry too much. Remember that time last semester when I fell in the pool and my dad jumped in to save me? Someone put a video of that online. 5,000 views. And I look way stupider there than you do in your video.

ChEnigma22: 5,000? Really?

EmilyK14: For what it's worth, I think your video is pretty good. I mean, who else at school is even in a music video at all, right?

ChEnigma22: You think it'll be okay?

EmilyK14: You're going to be fine. Don't stress. That's my job. You're supposed to be the carefree one in our pair.

ChEnigma22: Thanks, Em... I'll try to relax.

EmilyK14: Trust me. This will all look better in the morning. Get some sleep.

CHAPTER SIX

"Do you know what time it is?"

Kimi looked up from her homework to see Dex standing gleefully in front of her, a pair of huge headphones strapped to his ears. By sitting alone in the cafeteria, she'd hoped to finish her work before school started without anyone bothering her. No such luck.

"It's, like, seven fifty-five," she said. "Leave me alone, okay? I have to finish these stupid geometry problems. My mom is threatening to cancel my Netflix subscription if I don't bring my C up to a B."

"It's almost eight o'clock, Kimi!" he said, a mischievous grin spreading across his face. "What happens at eight o'clock?"

"Lower your voice," she said. "It's bad enough for me to be seen talking to you."

"What happens at eight o'clock?" he asked again, his smile growing even wider.

"School starts?" she guessed, confused.

"No! *It's chemistry.... Nine and I take another SAT.*"

Kimi groaned. "I get it, okay. It's a stupid song."

Dex nodded. "Spectacularly stupid. Famously stupid."

A shiver went down Kimi's back. "What do you mean, famously?"

Dex smiled. "I saw the link on reddit this morning. Naturally, I reposted it to several of my favorite message boards."

It had been two days since Alan first posted the video online, long enough for it to accumulate a few hundred views, but until now, no one at school had mentioned it. As far as Kimi knew, no one else had seen it.

Dex held up his phone. On it, Kimi saw herself in the horrible cheerleading outfit yet again.

"Put that away!" she said. "Someone is going to see!"

Dex made a half-choking, half-snorting noise. Apparently, this was how he laughed.

"Sorry to tell you," he said, "but forty-eight thousand people have already seen it. The cat is kind of out of the bag."

"Forty-eight thousand? That's impossible. Last time I checked it was only a few hundred."

"News flash," said Dex. "A lot of people have the Internet. Like, almost everyone, actually."

"Give me that stupid phone," said Kimi, ripping it out of his hands. As she did, his headphones came loose, and music began to play from the phone's tiny speaker.

"*Three o'clock! Three o'clock! When's it gonna be three o'clock?*"

Kimi cringed and scrambled to mute the volume before anyone heard. It was a little too late, though. A few skater guys at a nearby table had turned their heads and were looking at her curiously. Her face burned red.

"After your last Internet debacle, I'd have thought you'd know when to quit," said Dex, laughing again. "I'm so glad you didn't, though. This is literally the funniest thing I've ever seen. I even forwarded it to my grandparents in India."

The image of Dex's elderly grandparents laughing at her was simply too much to bear. Her hands trembling with anger, Kimi handed the phone back to Dex, whispering, "You'd better take this before something *bad* happens to it."

Dex grabbed the phone and quickly deposited it in his backpack. Kimi took a deep breath, looking around the cafeteria. The skaters who had turned to stare at her had gone back to bragging about their latest injuries. No one else was paying her any attention. Maybe only nerds like Dex had seen the video. Maybe things were going to be fine.

Yeah, right. She was never that lucky.

Kimi packed up her books and headed to her first-period class—Biology. Stupid song lyrics. She wasn't even *enrolled* in Chemistry—it was a sophomore class.

As she settled into a desk at the back of the room, she noticed a young, very uninterested-looking substitute sitting at her teacher's desk. He'd written FREE PERIOD on the whiteboard above his head. Kimi took her geometry book back out, flipping to the set of questions she still had to answer for the homework.

"Calculate the volume of a cylinder five inches high and two inches wide."

Stupid video. Stupid Alan.

"If two sides of a right-angled triangle measure six inches and eight inches respectively, its hypotenuse has a length of _____?"

Stupid Kevin for talking me into this.

Kimi's thoughts were interrupted when she heard a loud *snap*. She looked down to find her pencil broken in half.

"Psycho," muttered Chad Davis from the seat next to her.

Kimi tried to remain calm. She looked up toward the sub to see if he had noticed what had just happened, but he was laughing at something on his computer. Something playing at very low volume.

"Three o'clock! Three o'clock!"

No. It couldn't be. Impossible.

"When's it gonna be three o'clock?"

The sub chuckled to himself, then looked up at Kimi and caught her eye.

"I just can't wait for this day to ennnnd!" came the last line of the chorus.

Kimi couldn't agree more.

As the next three periods rolled by, Kimi started getting texts from random phone numbers she didn't recognize. A few were from local area codes, but others were from out of state, and some were from international numbers:

Video = hilarious! What's up w the dancing baby in the background lol.

Can't get ur song out of my head!

Nice cheerleading outfit.

U R hot.

Call me, hot stuff. B my girlfriend?

She got three texts in second period, ten more during her History test, and then twenty-two while her phone languished in her locker during Gym. Given that her cell phone plan carried a limit of two hundred texts a month, she was starting to worry about this trend.

Call me back and sing ur sweet words.

I wrote a song. Will you sing for me?

U r sooooo ugly.

Nice video. Did you lose a bet?

Are you really as dumb as you look? Hope so!

I would totally make out with you. Call me back!

And those were only the PG ones. Most of the others Kimi had to delete immediately.

How had these people even gotten her number? She suddenly remembered adding her phone number to her Facebook profile in the vain hope that a guy she'd been crushing on would call. She needed to take that number down. ASAP. She tried to access the Facebook app on her phone but couldn't figure out how to change her profile info. In the meantime, the texts just kept coming.

Marry me.

Eres muy bonita. Hablas español?

Lose twenty pounds. Then call me.

Worst song ever. Thanks for making my ears bleed.

Stop singing. Now.

Is your album on iTunes?

Single?

Is this really Kimi Chen? If so, call me!

Kimi had to wait until lunch to race to the library and log on to Facebook. When she did, she finally realized how bad things had gotten. Four thousand friend requests, three hundred comments, and at least as many private messages. Even Emily's Facebook page hadn't blown up this much when her *Swimmer's Monthly* article hit.

When Kimi checked YouTube, a chill went through her. She was up to a hundred and eighty thousand views—quadruple the number from four hours earlier. This was getting out of hand.

As she stormed down the hall toward the cafeteria, Kimi couldn't help but notice a few people staring at her. One guy even pointed at her and mimed roller-skating to his friends.

Inside the cafeteria, Kimi spotted Kevin sitting at his usual table with Dex and Amir. As she crossed the room, she glanced quickly at the center table. Maria and Lindsay were laughing at something Spencer had just said, and no one was looking in her direction. It seemed like the video hadn't reached them yet.

"Kevin," she said as she reached him. "We need to talk."

"Heh. 'Talk,'" said Dex, pursing his lips to imitate his version of kissing.

"About the video."

"Heh. 'Video,'" said Dex, smiling even wider.

"And you wonder why you're single," she said to Dex, dragging Kevin by the arm over to the door.

Outside, a cold wind blew, piercing through the thin fabric of Kimi's dress. Seeing her shiver, Kevin took off his hoodie and held it out to her.

"I'm not wearing that," she said, trying not to explode at him. "I'm really freaking out. This is bigger than we expected. Way bigger."

"I thought this was exactly what you wanted," he said. "You're famous."

"For being totally stupid."

"So what? You went into this wanting to be the next You-Tube star, right? Well, you got your wish."

"But this is—it's different. At least other girls look *hot* in their videos. This one makes it look like I'm some unkempt ditz, totally oblivious to all the crazy stuff happening in the background!"

"I don't know…" he said. "I think you look hot in the video."

"You *always* think I look hot," she said.

"Well, yeah."

"This is pointless," she said, taking out her phone. "I'm calling Alan."

"Just—don't act too crazy, okay?" he said. "Calm down and take a step back, I think you'll realize that—"

"Shhh," she said, gesturing to her phone. "It's ringing."

"Kimi Chen!" Alan said, completely enthusiastic. "I was wondering when you'd call! Congratulations! You're famous! Do you know who called me before you? KNXG. As in the TV station! You're blowing up, baby! You're an official star!"

"I'm an official joke."

"You're the joke everyone's telling," he said. "Now it's up to you. You either let them laugh at you, or you laugh with them. Trust me when I say the second option is going to be more fun."

Kimi didn't know quite how to respond. As much as she hated to admit it, Alan was right. She had to play this *just right* and make people think she'd been in on the joke all along.

"Listen, I'd love to keep chatting, but I'm getting a call on the other line, and I'm sure *you* are going to be getting some attention, too. Just remember: For better or worse, you're on people's radar now. *How* they see you is up to you."

He hung up.

"Well," said Kevin, "are you okay?"

"I..." said Kimi, thinking about it. If she was going to be in on this joke, she'd better start acting like it soon. As in, right now. She took a breath and said, "I am. I'm great. The video is really funny, right?"

"Yeah," said Kevin, smiling.

"Yeah," she said. "It's...great. I...I guess I was just surprised by how fast it took off. This is...a good thing."

Kevin smiled again. "It's a very good thing."

"Let's get back inside," she said. "It's freezing out here."

As Kimi and Kevin reentered the cafeteria, the room went quiet and all eyes fixed directly on Kimi. Even Maria, Lindsay, and their friends at the center table were staring.

Suddenly, Spencer belted out, "*Three o'clock! Three o'clock! When's it gonna be three o'clock?*"

For a millisecond, Kimi was paralyzed. Was he making fun of her? Was everyone about to laugh? She wasn't going to wait and find out. It was like Alan had said. *She* was in control.

"*I just can't wait for this day to ennnnd!*" she sang back.

For a moment, silence followed. Then Spencer started clapping. Others followed.

"You rock!" shouted Zach Reynolds.

"You're hot!" said someone else.

More people started shouting out at random, so many that Kimi couldn't tell who was saying what.

"Sign my phone!"

"Sign my chest!"

"Do the skating thing!"

"You still haven't friended me!"

Kimi wasn't paying attention to the crowd, though. Instead, she was looking at the center table. Maria Gonzalez had turned fully around in her seat. And for the first time Kimi could remember in years, Maria was looking right at her. Not out of the corner of her eye. Not briefly or accidentally. No. Maria was looking *right* at her.

And she was smiling.

CHAPTER
SEVEN

Over the next few weeks, the video only got bigger. A cursory search on YouTube revealed not only parodies, but also reaction videos and live covers. Unfortunately, not everyone seemed to be happy about Kimi's success.

Cruel responses appeared in droves, mocking everything from Kimi's singing ability to her weight, her lack of coordination, her race, her clothes, her face, her everything.

"Don't worry, getting a few mean comments from strangers is par for the course, especially when it comes to a video like this," said Emily as they sat together in Kimi's room on one of Emily's rare Saturdays off from her training regimen. Outside of a few minutes between classes, it was the first chance the girls had really had to hang out since the video first hit the Web.

"I guess it's like they say," said Kimi. "'Haters gonna hate.'"

Emily laughed as Kimi clicked onto the next page of comments for her video.

"Let's see here," said Kimi, reading the comments aloud. "'Cool vid.' 'I'd hit that.' 'Not as bad as everyone says.' 'Can't get the song out of my head.' Another 'I'd hit that.' That's original."

Emily frowned. "The Internet is, like, the worst place in the world."

"Wait," said Kimi. "Look at this one." She pointed to a post from someone named DiamondGirl22 that read, "*Ugliest girl ever, and she was even grosser back in middle school.*" "There's a link to another site. Should I click it?"

"Maybe not." Emily looked worried.

"It was a rhetorical question," said Kimi, clicking away.

Several photos of Kimi appeared. The pictures, none of which she'd ever seen before, were from elementary school, when she'd gone through an awkward pudgy phase, dressing in too-tight clothes. The pictures were also taken pre-Invisalign, when her teeth had been at their most crooked.

"Oh my god," said Emily. "Who did this?"

Kimi's heart skipped a beat, and she had the immediate urge to look over her shoulder, just in case someone was watching her. Whoever had posted these photos wasn't just some anonymous stranger. It was someone local, someone she'd known for years. Half the kids at Twin Branches had been her classmates since elementary school. Everyone she knew was suddenly a suspect.

Wanting nothing more than to erase the entire website from her mind, Kimi clicked it closed.

"How did you do it?" Kimi asked. "When you had all those articles written about you, you must have gotten a few mean responses, right?"

"Honestly—I think there might be a Facebook fan page about me or something," said Emily. "And I'm sure there are people out there who posted mean stuff. But I just never went looking for it. I'd rather not know."

"Maybe I shouldn't have clicked on that link."

"The problem isn't that you clicked it," said Emily. "It's that a site like that exists. Who would bother spending so much time on this?"

"Someone who hates me," said Kimi. "Lindsay maybe? She's never been my biggest fan."

"That's not a bad guess," said Emily.

Kimi reopened Firefox and went back to the website, looking at the horrible photos again.

"So…what do I do?"

"Well, you *could* stop clicking that link!" said Emily. "It's like picking a scab. And…I think you just have to stick with what you said earlier. 'Haters gonna hate,' right? You just be cool, and things'll be fine."

"That was okay when it was just anonymous Internet people," said Kimi. "But this one…"

"It's hard," said Emily. "But it's just one stupid person.

64

And in the meantime, focus on the positive. There are plenty of people who *love* your video. Including me!"

"You really like it?" asked Kimi, feeling slightly better.

"Are you kidding? It's hilarious! And I love your song!"

"Aw...thanks." It really did feel good knowing that Emily liked the song. Even if Kimi hadn't exactly written it or anything. "I was thinking...maybe we could head out to get some celebratory frozen yogurt?"

"Wish I could," said Emily. "But I should probably get back home. Ben is picking me up in twenty minutes so we can make it to the movies in time."

"Oh, cool," said Kimi, suddenly feeling deflated. She remembered Emily's first state finals win in seventh grade. Afterward, Kimi had taken Emily out for burgers, and Emily had eaten, like, five. Now, instead of celebrating Kimi's big break, Emily was ditching her as usual.

Unless...maybe if she dropped a hint or two, Emily would invite her along.

"What are you going to see?" asked Kimi.

"Uh...I don't know. A movie. Ben's picking it."

"I hear the new movie *House of Vampires* is out this week," said Kimi.

"Cool," said Emily. "You should get Kevin to take you."

"Right," said Kimi, giving up. "I'll think about it."

Once Emily was gone, Kimi resigned herself to an afternoon alone. She *could* have given Kevin a call, but hanging out with him was starting to stress her out. How long were they supposed

65

to stay in this gray area? He was just always so *nice*. Maybe too nice. Like a puppy or something, cute and cuddly, but not exactly *hot*.

Kimi was getting ready to settle in for a day of Internet surfing, snacking, and watching last night's episode of *Friday Night Showcase* on TiVo when the doorbell rang. Who could that be? Kimi's parents never had company. And Lily wasn't exactly the most popular sixth grader in the world.

"Kimi!" yelled her mom from downstairs.

"Who is it?" Kimi called back.

"Kimi!" shouted her mom. "Now!"

Kimi peeked downstairs to see a familiar face at the front door, an attractive middle-aged blond man. How did she know him? A teacher at school maybe? Or was he the mayor or something? Or...

Trent Hillfer.

The name came to her all at once, as did the phrase *This is Trent Hillfer, signing off.*

The man gave Kimi a quick wave from the bottom of the staircase.

That's right, Kimi remembered. *Alan said he got a call from KNXG!*

"We were hoping to do a little piece on your artistic success for the local news," he said. "Would you mind coming down so I can ask you a few questions?"

Kimi glanced back at her reflection in the hall mirror. Her hair was a mess, she wasn't wearing a speck of makeup, and she was dressed in pajamas. This wasn't good.

"I'll be down in a minute!" she shouted, running back to her room and slamming the door. Frantically, she searched through her clothes for something *amazing* to wear. There was the dress she'd altered to look like one she'd seen Mila Kunis wear to the Emmys...but that seemed a little much. Maybe the short skirt she'd sewn back when she was trying to get Marcus Jones's attention—no, her mom would *flip* if she saw her wearing that.

A loud knock sounded at her bedroom door, and the knob jiggled as someone tried to get inside.

"Kimi Weiyun Chen! You get out here this instant and tell me what's going on!"

"Just a second!"

Kimi thought back to what Alan had told her when she shot the video. *A little more high school.* That's what people expected. She couldn't exactly dress one way in the video and then go back to her usual style when the local news showed up. Frantically, she dug through her bottom dresser drawer, looking for jeans and T-shirts that still might fit.

"Open the door right now or I'm telling your father to unscrew the hinges!"

"Okay!" said Kimi, zipping up a pair of jeans and pulling on an old Abercrombie T-shirt. Where had she even gotten this? She must have had to spend a gift card or something. Still, she had to admit she looked very high school in it.

Kimi threw open the door to find her mother fuming on the other side.

"Why are there *reporters* at our house?" she asked.

"Probably to ask me about my video?"

Over the past few weeks, Kimi had managed to avoid mentioning anything about the video to her parents. She figured it was best that way. They wouldn't have understood it.

Last year, when she'd tried to explain what YouTube was, her father had ended up thinking it was a cross between MTV and *America's Funniest Home Videos*. He even tried to find it by channel surfing on TV. As for Kimi's mom, she seemed to think the Internet was used exclusively for sharing spreadsheets and checking her E-Trade account.

"What kind of video?" asked Kimi's mom, her eyes wide.

"Just a—a song," said Kimi. "It's pretty stupid. But it's also kind of popular."

"Show it to me," said her mom. "Now."

"But Trent Hillfer—"

"Can wait."

"Fine," said Kimi, opening the video from the Favorites tab on her computer. "You can check it out while I put on my makeup."

Her mom watched the video as Kimi applied foundation.

"Yeah! Yeah-ah! Yeah! Uh-huh! Yeah-ah! Uh-huh!"

"So you are…going to help the firefighters rescue the cat?" asked Kimi's mom, trying to make sense of what she was watching.

"No, that's not—it's just—funny, you know?"

Her mom shook her head.

"I don't understand."

"Look," said Kimi. "You understand numbers, right?

Well, four million people have watched this video, so I must be doing something right. Want to know how many people checked out the video of Lily's recital I put up last year? Like, ten."

Her mother shook her head again.

"I'm sorry to say this, but this song, it makes you look… ridiculous. Four million people, and they're all making fun of you."

"I should have known you wouldn't get it," said Kimi. "Whenever Daniel gets another A, you call the grandparents. Whenever Lily shows up the other kids at a concert, she gets a trip to Baskin-Robbins. Me, no matter what I do, it's wrong."

"Kimi—" started her mom. "I'm just worried. Videos on the Internet. You didn't even tell us you were making—"

"Forget it," said Kimi. "Just let me go talk to this reporter, okay? I don't want to get upset and cry and smear my makeup."

"Okay," said her mom, relenting. "But later—we need to talk about this."

Outside, on her front doorstep, Kimi hoped Trent Hillfer would keep the interview quick. The sun was barely shining over the distant hills, and the air had gone from chilly to downright freezing. Kimi, of course, had refused to wear a jacket. This was TV. She was going to look good.

"With over four million hits, local teenager Kimi Chen's video, 'Three O'Clock,' is the hottest thing this side of the Internet. KNXG is proud to introduce the Twin Branches sensation in her first of what I'm sure will be many interviews."

Trent Hillfer stuck his microphone in front of Kimi. On TV, Trent always looked kind of attractive—at least, for a middle-aged guy—but up close Kimi could see the wrinkles peeking out from beneath his caked-on makeup.

"Uh, hi," she said.

"Before talking to you, we spoke with your producer, Alan Delucca, who called you 'the first of a new breed of singer-songwriters who are using digital media to make their unique voices heard.' Do you attribute your song's success to the fact that you've tapped into a larger cultural movement?"

"Uh…"

"Singer-songwriter"? Where did Alan come up with that? I didn't even write *"Three O'Clock"!*

Trent Hillfer smiled at her hopefully.

"Uh…yeah. I guess I am part of a new generation. Giving, uh, voice to issues that I think are important."

"Like wanting school to be over," said Trent.

Kimi cringed but answered, "Exactly."

After a few more questions, Trent finally relented and lowered his microphone, indicating to his cameraman that the interview was over.

"Great stuff," said Trent. "This is Trent Hillfer, sending it back to the main studio for now, but don't worry. I'm sure we'll be right here with Kimi Chen once her next song, 'Four O'Clock,' comes out."

Trent took a handkerchief and wiped his brow. His makeup left a deep flesh-colored smear on the white fabric.

"That 'Four O'Clock' thing was a joke, right?" asked Kimi.

"You tell me, kid," he said. "You're the singer-songwriter."

"Right," she said. "Yes. Of course."

Kimi's first instinct when she walked inside was to call Alan and figure out what was going on with this whole singer-songwriter thing—but she was interrupted by Lily shouting from the living room.

"Kimi! You're on TV!"

Kimi ran to the living room to find her little sister staring wide-eyed at the TV, where Kimi's video was playing. As the footage ran, the host joked about it.

"So *that's* who stole my roller skates," he said, "not to mention my cheerleading costume. Shut up. I pull it off way better."

"This show is...national," said Kimi.

"He's making jokes about you," said Lily.

"You're really not supposed to watch this," said Kimi. "There are a lot of bad parts."

"Duh," said Lily. "That's why I like it." She flopped back on the couch and continued watching the show upside down, adding, "You should totally call and ask him if you can go on. He had that Juggling Fratboy Fail guy on earlier, and he *still* couldn't juggle, even sober."

"Mom and Dad wouldn't even let me go see *Terminator: Salvation* when I was your age," complained Kimi, but Lily had gone back to watching the show.

71

Over the next week, Kimi tried in vain to reach Alan, even as the video spiked to five, six, and seven million hits. In the meantime, Kimi started to get calls from newspapers and radio shows—first local ones, then bigger ones in LA and SF, then finally national ones.

Trent Hillfer's segment had aired the night after he came by to interview her, and things had snowballed from there. If anyone at school hadn't heard about the video before, they knew about it now. She couldn't walk down the hall without at least four requests to sing the song's chorus, and at least six guys she'd never met before had asked her out. She'd politely rejected all of them so far. Getting asked out was fun, but that didn't mean she was going to grab dinner with a random stranger. Besides, none of them were that cute.

Of course, Kimi couldn't complain, because random strangers weren't the only ones who had seen the video. So had Maria and the cheerleaders.

As Kimi entered the cafeteria on Monday morning, she noticed a flurry of activity at the center table and realized it was directed at her. It took a second for the scene to register: Maria Gonzalez herself was gesturing to Kimi and calling her over. Trying to look confident, Kimi strode forward, stopping a few inches short of Maria.

"I never knew you were such a good singer!" said Maria. "I love, love, love your video!"

"Uh, thanks," said Kimi.

"It's so...creative. Were all the backgrounds your idea?"

"Well, not *all* of them. My producer, Alan, and I collaborated quite a bit."

Maria looked impressed. Especially at the words *producer* and *collaborated*.

"You've got to tell us everything," said Maria. "Here, you can sit next to me. Scoot over, Lindsay."

Shooting Kimi a look that could melt lead, Lindsay grudgingly slid to the side.

"So are you, like, superfamous now?" asked Maria.

"I guess so," said Kimi. "Er, at least semifamous. I'm not like Kim Kardashian or anything."

"Not yet!" said Maria. "But I bet you totally will be."

Kim Kardashian had never been Kimi's favorite celebrity (though Kimi definitely wasn't opposed to five-million-dollar rings or marrying an NBA player for a few months).

"I hope so!" Kimi said.

"Just don't forget your old friends when you make it big-time," said Maria, as if they'd been best buds for years. "I still remember when we all used to pretend to be ponies in elementary school. So fun, right?!"

Now she remembers, thought Kimi, trying not to let her anger show. She'd been dying to sit here with Maria and her friends all year. She wasn't going to let a little resentment get in the way now.

"We totally haven't hung out enough lately," Maria added. "Give me a call sometime, okay? We can go grab some frozen yogurt, or shop, or just whatever."

"Sure," said Kimi, trying not to sound *too* enthusiastic.

Inside, though, fireworks erupted. Not only had Maria acknowledged the fact that they used to be friends, but also now she actually wanted to hang out again.

Which meant…which meant that maybe, just possibly, Kimi was friends with the most popular girl at school. And that meant *Kimi* was cool. Suddenly, a text from Kevin popped up on her phone:

Kevin Delucca: Just heard Howard Stern make a joke about u!

Yeah, her social stock was going up. The question now was, just how high could it go?

After school that day, Kimi's video hit its ten-millionth view. It was an afternoon filled with milestones.

Later that night, she heard a joke about herself on *Conan*, and Jon Stewart on *The Daily Show* compared her to a Republican governor. She was glad she didn't know much about politics, so she couldn't be too offended.

Online, she found a small *Rolling Stone* piece calling her "this generation's least-expected one-hit wonder" (okay, so it wasn't exactly a glowing review, but still—she was in *Rolling Stone*!).

MTV News had also run a clip featuring an interview with Alan where he'd called Kimi "a once-in-a-lifetime talent. The best singer-songwriter since Jewel, if not Janis Joplin," which had caused the host to burst out laughing.

Huh. So apparently Alan had time to return MTV's calls but not hers. And there was that "singer-songwriter" thing again. Not expecting a reply, she called him.

"Kimi Chen!" he said. "How's my favorite pop superstar?"

"For such a big fan, you seem to have a lot of trouble returning my calls."

"A thousand apologies!" he said. "You know I love you. I'm just busy hustling, talking to the media—all on *your* behalf, I might add. Now drop the angry-lady act and admit it. You're loving this attention as much as I am. I saw it in your eyes when you walked into my studio. You were hungry for fame. How's it feel to be full?"

"You tell me," she said. "It seems like you've got experience putting words in my mouth. Mind telling me why *MTV News* thinks I'm a singer-songwriter?"

"Because according to a recent poll in *Spin* magazine, artists who write their own songs tend to make forty-four percent more money on iTunes!"

"But I didn't write—"

"But you *did*," said Alan. "It even says so in your contract. You create the songs. I do the production. Trust me on this. Don't you think I want the credit? Of course I do. That's *my* song getting millions of listens. But you know what I want even more than fame? Money. And packaging you as a singer-songwriter is our best ticket to making a lot of it."

Stupid contract, thought Kimi. *I knew I should have read that thing.*

"Think about it," Alan added. "If people thought some

middle-aged dude wrote that song, it would automatically take on a big-time creepy factor. But if people think it's coming from a fourteen-year-old girl, it's cute, innocent. We've got an image to maintain, you know? That's why your status as singer-songwriter is detailed in the contract."

"What *else* is in that stupid contract?"

"Right," said Alan. "The details. Well, for one thing, I'm your manager. That much should be obvious. I book all your gigs."

"Naturally," said Kimi icily.

"You should be happy," said Alan. "We're getting all kinds of offers. Leno wants you to perform. Colbert and Letterman, too. I even got an offer from *Friday Night Showcase!*"

Now Kimi was interested.

"*Friday Night Showcase?*"

"I *thought* that might get your attention. The producer is the cousin of a friend of a friend. She thinks you're hilarious. Perfect fit as a musical guest. Even better for us, the lead singer of One Direction just strained a vocal cord. The band had to cancel, and now *FNS* needs a replacement pronto! You'd be on in less than three weeks!"

"Wow," said Kimi. "Wow. Wow. Wow." The news was still hitting her. *Friday Night Showcase?* That was a *real* show. Meaning she was a *real* star. Then, suddenly, reality set in.

"Uh, one problem. I can't exactly actually *sing* the song. You Auto-Tuned the whole thing. I can't even *hit* half the notes!"

"Not a problem! We can Auto-Tune it on the fly. Trust me,

this stuff is standard. How do you think Usher can do all those dance moves and sing at the same time? A little electronic assistance, baby."

"You're sure?"

"I'm two hundred percent certain. So you'll do it?"

Kimi considered. All her life, she'd been the one sitting home on Friday nights watching *FNS*. Now, suddenly, she'd be the one performing on it. It almost seemed like a dream, too good to be true. Yet here she was.

"I'll do it," she said, and she could *hear* Alan smiling on the other end of the line.

"Good," he said. "Because I already told them you're in."

CHAPTER EIGHT

"Two words: talent show."

Kimi closed her locker to find Kevin standing on the other side of the door. He looked hopeful.

"Think about it," he said. "Everyone loves your song. You'd be a shoo-in to win."

Kimi shook her head.

"Come on," said Kevin. "Dex is running the lights and sound, and I'm helping out. But the whole thing is going to be a bust if we don't get at least a few popular kids to perform."

"Look, no offense, but I've got bigger performances in mind," said Kimi. "Like *Friday Night Showcase*. I'm on in less than three weeks."

"Wow." Kevin looked genuinely shocked but he recovered

quickly. "I mean, that's awesome. But it doesn't mean you can't do both shows, right? The talent show isn't for a month."

Kimi sighed.

"I'll think about it, okay?"

"Okay."

Kimi was just about to tell Kevin more about her upcoming spot on *Friday Night Showcase* when out of the corner of her eye, she spotted Maria and the other cheerleaders approaching.

"Hey, Kev," said Maria, stopping beside them. "Mind if I borrow Kimi for a couple of minutes?"

"She's all yours."

He took a few steps away before disappearing into a steady stream of students, all headed to class.

"He's *such* a nice guy," said Maria. "Very, uh, *sweet*, right? Are you really dating him?"

"Who, Kevin?" asked Kimi. "No way. We just hang out sometimes."

"That makes so much more sense!" said Maria. "A girl like you... you could probably be with any guy at school." The girls flanking her nodded.

"I guess so," said Kimi. "I mean... yeah. I dated Phil for a little while, but I kind of got tired of him."

"Of course you did," said Maria. "That just means you're ready for the next one. Of course, you'd probably get a *little* more attention with a new dress or two. And maybe a haircut. You should totally come to the mall with us after school! You could do a total makeover."

Kimi couldn't believe it. They wanted her to go to the mall. With them. It took everything she had not to jump for joy and scream yes.

"Yeah, sure," she said, totally calm. "That sounds good."

"Great," said Maria, turning to the other girls. "Nicole will drive you."

Nicole frowned and nodded, resigned to her orders. "I'll see you at the back lot as soon as school's out."

After school, Kimi found Nicole waiting impatiently for her in the back lot, standing by a small, silver Jeep. A pair of pink fuzzy dice hung from the rearview mirror, and the license plate read SUPR SXY. How had she talked her parents into letting her get that?

"What took you so long?" Nicole asked.

"School just got out, like, thirty seconds ago."

"Which is why I always make an excuse to leave early," said Nicole. "Come on. Hurry up. Let's get out of here before this place turns into a total nightmare. Do you realize I've been in three accidents in this lot? *No one* at this school knows how to drive."

Kimi cringed as she got into the car. She was starting to understand why Emily had always been afraid of driving with anyone but her dad. As she sat down, she found a tattered sci-fi novel on the seat.

"That's, uh, never mind," said Nicole. "It's not mine."

She took the novel out of Kimi's hand and threw it in the back.

They pulled out in a cloud of dust, nearly hitting a crowd of Goths who were gathered on the edge of the lot.

A few seconds later, safely down the street, Kimi gave a sigh of relief. "So you and Maria are, like, best friends, right?" she asked.

"Sort of," said Nicole. "As much as you *can* be friends with Maria, right? I mean, from what I've heard, you two were pretty tight once upon a time."

"Back when we were kids," said Kimi.

"So you know what it's like, then," said Nicole.

Kimi didn't exactly understand Nicole's meaning.

"You mean she's...guarded?"

Nicole laughed. "No, Maria's a megalomaniac."

Kimi was shocked. That was a much bigger word than she ever would have given Nicole credit for knowing. Maybe Nicole and Dex would have more in common than she had thought....

Nicole continued as if she hadn't just insulted her best friend. "But I mean, all cheerleaders are guarded. You have to be. Otherwise you get torn to pieces. Do you know how many head cheerleaders I've seen come and go since I got to this school? Four. And I've been 'best friends' with a couple of them. Of course, they always moved on to someone better. Or else freaked out and quit the team and never talked to me again."

Kimi adjusted her feet...and stepped on a comic book.

"That's...ignore that," said Nicole.

"So you were saying..." started Kimi. "About friends. About Maria?"

"With some people…you're friends until you stop being useful. Or it becomes inconvenient. After that, it's over. There's nothing wrong with it. It's just the way it is. Friendships are like boyfriends. Here today, gone tomorrow. You put in your time trying to work yourself into someone's good graces, and then, *bam*, some other girl comes along—"

Kimi cringed. Was Nicole talking about *her?*

"Listen," said Kimi, "if you think I'm trying to steal your best friend—"

"You don't have to *try*," said Nicole as they pulled into the mall parking lot. "It's already happening. You're already doing it."

Kimi frowned.

"I'm…sorry?"

"Don't be," said Nicole. "Maria will do what's best for her. She always does. Oh, and don't you dare tell people about that comic book. I've got a reputation to keep up."

Maria, Amanda, Shannon, and Lindsay sat at a table in the food court, sipping Jamba Juices and surreptitiously checking out passing guys. When they saw Kimi and Nicole, Maria smiled and stood, hugging Kimi when she got close.

"So glad to see you," she said. "I can't *wait* to get you into some decent clothes—and we set up a five o'clock for you at Salon 232."

It had been over a year since Kimi had visited a salon— she'd grown accustomed to cutting her own hair, carefully snipping bangs or trimming unruly split ends. The benefits of self-barbering were twofold: Kimi could carefully control her look while simultaneously saving money.

"Salon 232?" she asked. From everything she'd heard, it was one of the most expensive places in town—not good, considering all she had in her purse was eighty dollars and a credit card to use "only in case of emergency."

"I know, I know," said Maria. "How did I manage to get you an appointment, right? My sister went to hairdressing school with one of the stylists there. Normally, you have to book a month in advance, but I pulled a few strings. You can thank me later."

"Yeah," said Kimi. "That's so...great of you." She had to admit, it *would* be pretty nice to see what an actual professional did with her hair.

It looked like today's appointment at Salon 232 would have to qualify as an "emergency." Oh well. Her parents wouldn't see it on their credit card bill until the end of the month. Hopefully, by then she'd have thought of a way to appease them.

"So...what now?" asked Kimi. "Shopping? Maybe we could start at Macy's and then work our way down to Nordstrom?" She'd brought a full stack of coupons from the stash she kept in her locker—ten dollars off a purchase of twenty-five dollars or more, 20 percent off a total purchase, even a free bottle of Christina Aguilera perfume with a purchase of seventy-five dollars or—

"Macy's? Vomit," said Maria. "No wonder you look like a fashion victim. You're stuck in the wrong store! From now on, we're putting you on a strict diet of Juicy Couture and Bloomingdale's Juniors. No excuses."

Kimi could almost *feel* the money draining from her wallet. One piece of clothing from either of those places, and she'd be out of cash. It looked like that emergency credit card would be getting quite a workout today.

"Right," said Kimi. "No excuses."

Fifteen minutes later, Kimi stood in the dressing room at Abercrombie & Fitch as Maria and her friends threw dresses, skinny jeans, shirts, blouses, skirts, and scarves over the wall to her.

"You're a size three, right?" asked Maria from the other side of the wall.

"No way," said Lindsay. "She's at least a five."

In truth, Kimi *was* a five. But she wasn't going to admit that in front of Lindsay.

"Three!" she shouted back, trying desperately to squeeze herself into a pair of jeans. Why had she eaten *two* slices of pizza for lunch?

She willed herself not to look at the price tag but couldn't help herself. The number made her heart sink. A hundred and ninety-five dollars? These weren't even on sale.

Finally, with heroic effort and a lot of sucking in, she got the jeans on, buttoned, and zipped. Unfortunately, she was left with a *slight* muffin top. Stupid size three. Stupid Lindsay.

Luckily, she'd picked out a loose top earlier that fell just past her hips, disguising the bulge at the top of the jeans. And in the mirror, her legs *did* look pretty hot. A few weeks of dieting and she *would* be a size three, right? It made *complete sense* to pay almost two hundred bucks for a pair of jeans that didn't fit.

Of course not. But what was her other option? Leave the store empty-handed and lose any chance she'd ever have of impressing the girls on the other side of the dressing-room door?

She wasn't paying two hundred bucks for *jeans*. She was paying to impress Maria and the other cheerleaders. Who said you couldn't put a price on friendship?

Later, at the salon, Kimi sat in a cushioned chair as Maria and Nicole hovered nearby. The too-tight, too-expensive jeans Kimi had bought still cinched her waist, leaving her feeling pinched and uncomfortable, almost like that post–Thanksgiving dinner feeling—except she hadn't eaten anything since lunch. She hoped the other girls didn't notice her discomfort.

In the meantime, Chance, the stylist, a tall, thin man with meticulously gelled blond hair and well-kept beard stubble, gave Kimi a once-over. For now, he stayed silent, studying her as if she were a statue.

"The side bangs have definitely got to go," said Nicole. "But where does that leave us? A pixie cut? It's still a little 'alternative,' but at least it would be *slightly* less DIY."

Chance scratched at his stubble, looking concerned.

"I've got to be honest, girls, the look is pretty hot already. Who gave you your last cut? Leila down at Bellissima? You've kind of got an Asian Zooey Deschanel thing going on."

"That's exactly what I was going for!" said Kimi, but Maria shushed her.

"That's *exactly* what we're trying to avoid," said Nicole. "That whole indie-hipster thing. *So* played out!"

"If you say so," said Chance, turning on his electric razor. "Pixie it is."

He looked down at Kimi, a sad look on his face.

"You sure you want to do this, sweetie? Once the hair is gone, I can't stick it back on."

Kimi looked up at Nicole and Maria, who nodded their encouragement.

"Do it," she said.

An hour later, Kimi stepped up from her chair and looked at herself in the mirror. Her side bangs were a thing of the past, and the tresses that had previously fallen just past her ears now sat in a pile on the floor at her feet.

"OMG! Amazing," said Nicole.

"You look like Michelle Williams," said Maria.

Kimi laughed. "Michelle Williams is blond."

"Don't get caught up in the details," said Maria.

Kimi paid Chance—cringing as she signed a credit card receipt for two hundred and eighteen dollars—and then she and the girls circled back to the food court and settled in at one of the center tables.

"I just can't stop looking at you," said Maria. "You're totally hot now. This is some of my best work."

"Chance is a genius," said Nicole, picking delicately at a Cinnabon before pushing it across the table and out of reach.

"Uh, thanks," said Kimi, her face glowing red. "I do . . . like the new look."

Suddenly, without warning, several middle school girls from across the food court pointed at Kimi and screamed. Kimi's eyes went wide. The haircut wasn't *that* bad, was it?

Without warning, the clump of girls ran toward her, their cell phones in hand, snapping pictures and shouting.

"Kimi Chen!" shouted a short, dark-skinned girl with pigtails. "Is it really you?"

"Lily Chen is telling everyone at school that you're her sister," said a brown-haired girl. "Is that true?! I *usually* never believe a thing she says . . ."

"Will you sign my Trapper Keeper?" asked a third girl, a blonde.

"Can we take a picture with you?" asked someone else.

Lindsay rolled her eyes. "Middle schoolers think anyone with a video on YouTube and a couple of views is a celebrity."

"And they're right," said Maria, shooting Lindsay a cold look.

Before Kimi could even get a word in, the girls surrounded her, posing and smiling as they took turns playing photographer.

"Could you sing for us?" asked the blond girl. "Just a little."

"Uh, I'm not so sure," said Kimi, starting to get nervous. It wouldn't take more than a few notes for these girls to realize that Kimi wasn't quite the singer she was cracked up to be.

"Yeah," said Lindsay, sensing Kimi's nervousness. "Sing for them."

"I'm, uh...I have a little bit of a cold," said Kimi, looking back at the cheerleaders, praying for someone to jump to her aid.

"That's enough," said Maria, playing guardian angel. "She's a celebrity, not a jukebox. Go listen to her on your iPods. That's what they're made for."

The girls' faces fell.

"How about one more photo?" asked Kimi. "And I can pretend to skate, like in the video."

The girls smiled and posed. After a few more photos, they seemed satisfied and retreated to the far end of the food court, where they sat at a table and continued to watch Kimi and the cheerleaders.

"Pretty impressive," said Maria.

"They're just her little sister's friends," said Lindsay.

"Yeah," said Shannon, agreeing with her as usual.

"They actually seemed like her little sister's *enemies*, which makes it even more impressive," said Maria. She looked thoughtful. "So you've got your fans...and your new look...." Suddenly her eyes lit up. "All we have to do is set you up with a decent guy. Candidates?"

"Maybe Cameron Clark?" offered Nicole, immediately excited. "He's perpetually single."

"Interesting," said Maria. "But he'd eat her alive. It'd be like sending a baby deer on a date with a lion. No offense, Kimi. Just looking out for you."

"Uh, thanks," said Kimi. She supposed Maria knew what she was talking about. Cameron *did* have a reputation.

88

"Maybe Phil," said Amanda. "He's cute—and supernice!"

"I, uh, already kind of went down that road," said Kimi.

"What about Marcus, then?" suggested Nicole. "I heard you tried to ask him out in the fall."

"...and he said no," said Kimi.

Maria smiled. "That was then, when you were just Emily Kessler's sidekick. Now you're a star. And you know how Marcus is. Total model wannabe. If he hears an up-and-coming celeb like you is interested, he'll *beg* you for a date."

"Well—" Kimi thought it over. The idea of Marcus Jones begging her to go out with him *did* have a certain appeal. She smiled. "I wouldn't be completely opposed."

Later, after another hour of gossiping, shopping, and snacking, Nicole mentioned that she had to get home.

"Good hanging out, Kimi," she said. "We'll have to do it again sometime."

"Great!" said Kimi, still not quite believing she was really at the mall with these girls—and that they were actually enjoying it.

At the far end of the food court stood a wall of glass windows, looking out at a dark parking lot and reflecting ghostly images of the people inside the mall. Glancing at her own reflection next to those of the cheerleaders, Kimi couldn't help but smile. She looked just like them.

"I should go, too," said Amanda. "Hector has been texting for the last three hours."

Maria pulled out her own car keys and turned to Kimi. "You need a ride?"

Maria drove a Miata two-seater from the late nineties, a tiny car with a hair-trigger accelerator. Dwarfed by the SUVs and trucks driving past them on the freeway, the car seemed a guarantee of a quick death in the event of an accident.

"So, how does it feel?" asked Maria.

"What?" asked Kimi, as they flew across two lanes to pass a pair of semis.

"Being famous, of course," said Maria.

"Uh...good?"

"It's funny," said Maria. "When we were kids...I never thought *you'd* be the one to become a celebrity, you know?"

"I guess so," said Kimi.

"It's just...I worked really hard all through middle school, trying to build a certain image," said Maria. "I remember waking up at six AM so I could jog, take a shower, and get my hair and makeup ready....And then I'd walk out to my car and see you over at your place, looking like you had just rolled out of bed."

"I guess....I was in fourth grade," said Kimi. "I wasn't into that stuff then. But, uh, at least we can be friends now."

"I remember when I was your age. When I was a freshman, I knew I wanted to be *seen*," said Maria. "So I did the obvious thing. I joined the cheerleading team. The only problem was that there was always someone in front of me, you know? Someone else shoving me out of the spotlight."

She jerked the wheel left, and the car sped into the carpool lane, nearly clipping a motorcycle, who had to mash his accelerator to avoid them.

"I waited for *years*," explained Maria. "First there was Taylor Vale. The Fidel Castro of cheerleaders, running the team like it was her own personal dictatorship. Then, once *she* was gone I had to deal with Jessica Blaire. She was even worse. I spent a *lot* of practices on the bottom of the pyramid. Oh, and don't get me started on that goody-goody Zoe who took over after Jessica! She was the worst of all!"

She sped ahead, nearly kissing bumpers with the car ahead of her.

"Come on!" she shouted. "This is supposed to be the *fast* lane."

The car ahead of them merged right, clearing a path forward.

"The point is," said Maria, accelerating into the gap, "when Zoe left and I had my chance, I took it. Now I'm the head cheerleader, and I'll never be at the bottom of the pyramid again. Life doesn't give you second chances. If you're not ready when opportunity knocks, you might be stuck licking someone else's boots for the rest of your high school existence."

"Right," said Kimi. "That makes sense."

"I look at you," said Maria. "Someone who played second fiddle to Emily Kessler for years, finally getting a chance to make her own name, and I see myself. I just want you to make the most of this opportunity."

"Me, too," said Kimi, trying not to pay attention to the road.

"What I'm saying is, who knows how long this Internet fame is going to last, you know? You've got to strike while the iron is hot. Nail down a hot boyfriend. Do *everything* you can to solidify your social standing."

"How do I do that?"

"Well, hanging out with me and the girls was a good start," said Maria. "But you've got to think long-term. Get yourself invited to some sleepovers, like the one I'm having on Saturday night. You should totally come. But you also have to make sure you're seen with the right people in school, especially at lunch, and you should probably join the cheerleading team while you're at it."

"They'd let me join?" asked Kimi.

"Haven't you been listening?" asked Maria, swerving across three lanes toward a freeway exit. "There is no 'they.' I'm in charge. I saw your moves in the video for 'Three O'Clock,' and that's enough of an audition for me. I say you're in."

"Just like that?" asked Kimi, hardly able to believe it.

"Just like that."

CHAPTER NINE

"Awesome news," said Kevin, catching up with Kimi as her mom dropped her off before school the next day. "I just saw that *Troll 2* is playing next Thursday over at the Red Vic up in the city, so... I figure Bad Movie Club is in for a real treat."

"Oh, great," Kimi said, trying to feign enthusiasm. "I love, uh, trolls."

"That's the thing! There are *no* trolls in the movie. That's part of what makes it so epically bad!"

He paused and stared at her strangely, noticing her new look for the first time.

"What happened to your hair?" he asked.

"It's called a haircut. You should get one sometime."

He smiled awkwardly and raised his hands as if begging her not to shoot.

"Touch-y," he said. "It's just—not your usual style. Same goes for the jeans."

"Maria and her friends helped me pick them out."

"Well, you seem to be moving up in the world," he said. "Just don't forget about us commoners now that you're Twin Branches royalty. Speaking of which—have you made up your mind about the talent show?"

"I'm still thinking about it."

"Well, don't think *too* long. Dex and Amir have been bugging me to bug you, and—"

Kimi looked over toward the front of the school, where Nicole was waving at her.

"I should go," she said.

"Oh, sure." Kevin looked disappointed, watching her as she backed away. "So I'll pick you up next Thursday?"

"Right," she said, turning away. "Thursday."

Kimi was in the middle of a Geometry test when her cell vibrated in her pocket. She looked down to see the name ALAN DELUCCA.

"Mr. Carr!" she said, raising her hand. "Can I go to the bathroom?"

"I don't know," he said. "*Can* you?"

"Uh...yes?" she said.

"Yes, you *may*," he said, clearly exasperated. "But hurry back. And don't expect any extra time on your test."

Out in the hallway, Kimi quickly called Alan back.

"There you are," he said. "How's my favorite superstar this fine afternoon?"

"Busy," she said. "Trying not to fail Geometry."

"Geometry?" he asked with a laugh. "I wouldn't worry too much about it. You just worry about singing. I'll handle the math."

"Math? Does that mean there's money from my video?" asked Kimi, suddenly curious. Maybe she could just pay her parents back for the expensive mall trip with Maria and her friends.

"Just a little right now," he said. "But I'm working on getting the song up on iTunes...and monetizing the YouTube video with some ad revenue. The bigger play is long-term. We keep building buzz, get you in here to record a few more tracks. Then we start selling albums!"

"Isn't that...getting a little ahead of ourselves?"

"You're right," said Alan. "Absolutely right. We're taking this thing one step at a time. Which brings me to the purpose of my call. A week from Saturday. You've got a dress rehearsal for *Friday Night Showcase*."

"Next week?" asked Kimi, panicking. Up until this moment, the *FNS* performance had seemed far away, something she'd do *eventually*. Now, suddenly, the moment was fast approaching, and she was completely unprepared. "I, uh, wow. Should I be practicing or something?"

"Don't worry about it," said Alan. "Part of your charm is that you're an amateur. If we send you out there all slick and polished, it might actually *hurt* your image."

"I guess so," said Kimi. Alan had a point...but did she really want people to think she looked amateurish and in over her head?

"Awesome. We'll get you out there, get a couple of guys in to hook up the Auto-Tune software, and you'll be good to go. Oh, and try to wear something nice this time. Ethan White is going to be there, and I'd love to get a picture of you with him...providing you look halfway decent."

"Ethan White?!"

"Total diva," said Alan, adding an exasperated sigh. "The whole reason we have to rehearse so early is because he's got two concerts and a video shoot the following week. So of course *everyone* has to schedule around him."

Kimi was barely listening. She just repeated the name, trying to make sure she'd heard Alan correctly. *"Ethan White?"*

"It sounds like you know who he is?"

For a moment, every fact Kimi knew about Ethan White leaped to the front of her mind:

Ethan White. Age eighteen. Former lead singer of boy band Superteam. Star of four top-grossing films: *The Secret Prince, Undercover Kid, Fifteen Again,* and *Undercover Kid 2: Welcome to Japan. YouthBeat Magazine*'s 2012 winner of the coveted Sexiest Teen Alive award.

"Yeah," she said. "I've heard of him."

"Awesome," said Alan. "I'm sure you two will hit it off. Talk soon. I'll come by to pick you up on Saturday—but you're going to have to get one of your parents to come with you, too. Some sort of legal thing. Anyway, I'll see you then."

The phone went dead, and Kimi stared blankly down the empty hall. How was she supposed to finish her Geometry test after getting news like this? Less than a week and she'd be hanging out with *Ethan White*!

Taking a deep breath, she turned around and headed back to class, knowing full well she'd sit at her desk and daydream through the rest of the test. But it was like Alan said: Kimi didn't *need* to pass it anymore; she was a star.

"Hey."

Kimi looked up from her homework to see a pair of gorgeous green eyes studying her. Below them flashed a perfect white smile Kimi would have recognized anywhere: It belonged to Marcus Jones.

"Been a while," he said. "I wanted to let you know I saw your video."

"Yeah?"

"Everyone kept saying how funny it was," he said. "But I just thought you looked cute in it. Way cuter than I remembered from last semester."

Kimi blushed. "You thought I looked...cute?"

"I've always thought you were cute," he said. "Even when you were dating Phil."

"Uh, yeah, I guess Phil's still pretty mad I tried to ditch him for you."

Marcus shrugged.

"He's over it. It was months ago, right? Honestly, I was kind of flattered that you liked me better. I just couldn't take you to homecoming, because of the bro code, you know?"

"I get it," said Kimi. "There are certain guys I'd never touch out of loyalty to Emily. Like if she ever broke up with Ben—"

"Never say never," said Marcus. "The point is, you and Phil had your thing months ago. As far as I'm concerned, you're fair game. Plus, Maria *may* have tipped me off to the fact that you're interested."

Kimi blushed again. She'd have to thank Maria for this later.

"You really thought I was cute...all along?" she asked.

"Of course," he said. "Well, you look even better now. And trust me, I know what I'm talking about. I've hung out with plenty of models."

Kimi's mouth went dry. What was she supposed to say to that? She'd never been compared to a model before. She said a silent thank-you to Maria and her friends for the makeover.

"Speaking of modeling," added Marcus, "my agent hooked me up with a couple of tickets to this fashion show next Thursday. Some girls I know are in it. You want to come?"

Thursday...Wasn't there something she already had scheduled? Well, whatever it was, it couldn't be more important than a date with Marcus Jones.

"Sure," she said. "I'm free."

It wasn't until Marcus had walked away and returned to

flipping through a copy of *GQ* at his desk that Kimi remembered her *Troll 2* date with Kevin. Well, not a *date*. A hangout. With a friend. A friend who would have to understand if she canceled on him.

That night, Kimi logged on to her IM account, trying to get in touch with Kevin. Sure, it was a little cowardly to break the bad news online, but better to do it this way, where she could take the time to think before typing, rather than risk having the conversation in person and saying the wrong thing.

> *ChEnigma22:* Uh, hey. About next Thursday…

> *Kevinyourface**:* You mean Trollsday?

> *Kevinyourface**:* Sorry. That was dumb.
> What's up?

> *ChEnigma22:* I don't think I can come.

> *Kevinyourface**:* Everything okay?

Kimi considered her options. The easiest thing would be to lie, to tell him her parents had grounded her or that she was buried in homework. But that wouldn't be fair to him, and besides, she had nothing to hide. It wasn't like she was dating him. They hadn't even kissed.

She typed out a sentence and hit Enter before she had a chance to second-guess herself.

ChEnigma22: I'm going out with Marcus.

For a moment, the words just hung in the text box, waiting for a response. The silence was deafening. For once, Kimi wished Lily were downstairs playing her stupid Chopin sonatas. Then words appeared.

*Kevinyourface**:* That's cool. We'll hang out
    some other time.

ChEnigma22: Sorry I had to cancel.

*Kevinyourface**:* I'd better go...Talk to you
    later.

Kevin signed off, and Kimi stared blankly at the screen. She should have felt relieved—but instead, her stomach was in knots. Kevin had been so *nice* about it. It almost would have been better if he'd gotten mad. At least then she wouldn't have felt as guilty.

CHAPTER
TEN

Having taken Maria up on her offer from the other day, Kimi was curled on the head cheerleader's monster-sized bed with the rest of the popular girls on Saturday night. They were eating popcorn and fun-sized Snickers bars, and giving each other over-the-top glamorous makeovers.

It almost felt like they were getting ready for a dance or something—except that they weren't even planning to go out. The only people they were trying to impress were one another.

Amanda had her long red mane up in a set of curlers, Shannon was straightening Nicole's hair, and Nicole was using a thick curling iron on Maria's usually straight locks.

Kimi couldn't help watching them, missing her own tresses. With her hair as short as it was, there simply wasn't much to be done with it.

"I thought just the *cheerleaders* were supposed to come to this sleepover," complained Lindsay as she returned from the kitchen, a glass of orange juice in hand.

"Did I forget to mention it?" asked Maria, looking up at her coldly. "Meet Twin Branches High's newest cheerleader, Kimi Chen. She'll start coming to practices as soon as I clear everything with Coach."

Lindsay wrinkled her brow.

"Some of us actually had to try out," she said under her breath.

"*Some of us* didn't post an amazing video online and become overnight celebrities," responded Maria, glancing at Kimi.

With that, she returned to concentrating on her reflection in a hand mirror, and Nicole continued curling Maria's hair. In the meantime, Lindsay walked up to Shannon and whispered something in her ear as the two looked back at Kimi.

Ignoring them, Kimi tried to focus instead on makeup. As she stared at the stunning variety of powders and creams that the girls had brought along for the occasion, Amanda came up to her.

"What are you thinking?" she asked. "I say we've got to do something *crazy* with your makeup."

Kimi nodded. "Any ideas?"

"A few," Amanda told her with a sly smile. She pulled out an emerald eye shadow and got to work. A few minutes later, Kimi looked like a fashion goddess. With bright green on her eyes, a purple-hued lipstick, and a golden shimmer dusting her shoulders, she looked ready for a runway.

"I still can't believe you're going to meet Ethan White," Amanda said as she painted liquid eyeliner onto Kimi's eyelids.

The room had gone quiet, and Kimi tried to glance around without moving her face too much. She realized that all the girls had stopped what they were doing to give her their full attention.

"Well?" Nicole prompted before realizing she'd left the curling iron in Maria's hair for a few seconds too long. She pulled it out as quickly as she could, but a burning scent filled the air. She tried to fan the smell away before Maria noticed. "Are you going to try to hook up with him?"

Kimi blushed. "I don't know. I mean, we'll have a lot of time alone together in the greenroom, I'm sure. Who knows what might happen, right?"

"You are *so* lucky!" said Amanda.

"Ethan is *amazing*," Nicole said. "Why can't we have guys like that at our school?"

"You never seemed to have a problem with the guys at Twin Branches *before*," Maria said, giving Nicole a look.

Nicole gave a dramatic sigh. "They're not bad. Just not great when you compare them to Ethan White."

"All right, enough about Ethan White," Lindsay said. "I'm bored. Let's do something else."

"Truth or Dare!" Amanda squealed.

Maria nodded thoughtfully. "Not a bad idea."

"I'll go first," Amanda said. "Dare."

"We'll start with a classic. I dare you to stuff fifteen marshmallows in your mouth and call Domino's to order us a pizza," Maria said, snickering.

"I've never had more than thirteen at once," said Amanda, looking anxious.

"You said you wanted a dare. Now you have to do it," said Maria. "I don't make the rules."

Nicole ran to the kitchen to fetch the marshmallows.

"Fifteen?" asked Amanda, nervous, eyeing the bag when Nicole returned.

Maria nodded and smiled.

A minute later, Amanda stuffed the marshmallows into her mouth while everyone counted.

"Eleven, twelve..."

Just watching Amanda try to fit all the marshmallows into her mouth made Kimi want to gag. She was definitely opting for truth when her turn came around.

"Fifteen!"

Amanda dialed the number for Domino's and turned up the volume on her speakerphone.

"Mawo, Ibe lide bo orber a pibba," Amanda said, trying to stifle a giggle.

"Excuse me? Miss, I think your phone has a bad connection," the pizza guy said on the other end of the line.

"Mawo? Cab yoo hea be?"

Marshmallow goo oozed out the corners of Amanda's mouth. She was laughing so hard she was crying. Nicole ran to the bathroom and came back with a towel just in time to catch the gooey marshmallow lump as Amanda spit it out.

The girls dissolved into a fit of laughter, causing the pizza guy to hang up.

"Who's next?" Maria called out.

"I'll go," Nicole said. "Truth."

"Come up with a good one," Maria told Amanda.

Amanda cleaned a bit of marshmallow off her lip. "Ohhh... if you had to hook up with one of the nerds, who would it be?"

Nicole hid a smile. "That's easy. Dex."

"What?!" asked Amanda. "He's more into video games than girls."

"Exactly," said Nicole. "I like a challenge. Plus, if you really look, he has a hot face. Like an Indian Ryan Reynolds."

Kimi filed that away mentally. As hard as it was to believe, Dex had been right: Nicole really was kind of into him. Kimi would have to let him know.

"That seems like a little bit of an exaggeration," said Maria. "Anyway, all nerds are gross, so it's purely theoretical. Right?"

Nicole nodded sheepishly. "Right." She turned to Kimi. "Okay, since it's such a popular question, if *you* had to kiss one of the nerds, who would it be?"

"Ew," Shannon said, wrinkling her nose.

Kimi felt herself blushing. "I... um..."

Amanda elbowed her. "You're, like, always with that one guy," she said. "What's his name?"

"Kevin," Kimi said. "I mean, we're friends, but... yeah, I

guess I'd kiss Kevin." *If he ever actually made a move,* she added in her mind.

Nicole shrugged and smiled. "I've kissed worse."

The other girls exploded in laughter, and a deep sense of relief flooded through Kimi. She'd made her confession, and the other girls seemed to like her even better for it. Soon, it was the next girl's turn.

Kimi wouldn't have thought that Truth or Dare could be so much fun, but she spent the rest of the night torn between fits of giggles and shocked gasps. She never would have guessed that Amanda had a secret crush on Howard Wu, or that Shannon could stand on her head and recite the alphabet backward on the first try.

Eventually, though, Kimi found herself feeling tired. Emily always insisted on going to sleep at a reasonable hour, never wanting to throw off her schedule *too* much. The cheerleaders, it seemed, weren't as concerned about circadian rhythms.

It wasn't until 4:00 AM that Maria started yawning.

"Time to sleep," she announced, and the girls sprang up off her bed.

Kimi steeled herself for a long night ahead. Maria's family had a downstairs guest room with a bed and a futon. The girls had set them up earlier with pillows and blankets, but it was going to be a tight fit, and there were sure to be squabbles over who slept where.

But when Kimi stood up to leave, Maria stopped her.

"Kimi, you can stay on my couch if you want," she said, nodding to the cushy off-white couch in the corner of her room.

"I thought—" Nicole started, but Maria shushed her.

"Not so loud, Nicole, you'll wake up my mom," she said.

"Fine," said Nicole. "Whatever. I'll see you in the morning."

She followed the other girls downstairs.

"Thanks," said Kimi. As the girls had shuffled out, a couple cast jealous looks back at her. In a few short weeks, she had gone from outsider to getting the best spot in the house. Not bad.

As she lay down on Maria's couch, she found an old blanket at her feet and pulled it up over her body.

"Hey," she said. "This is the one I used to use when we were little."

"I can get you a newer one if you'd like," said Maria.

"No, no. It's great," said Kimi. "I used to love this blanket. I guess some things never change."

"Or...things do change...and then they circle back," said Maria.

At first the words made Kimi smile, but as she tried to go to sleep, they began to haunt her. Had Maria been talking about their friendship...or something else?

The next morning, Kimi woke up groggy. She looked over to see Maria's bed empty. From downstairs, the sounds of laughter, forks scraping on plates, and clinking glasses filled the air.

She padded down the steps to find the other girls in the kitchen. As she entered, silence filled the room, and she suddenly had the distinct impression that the girls had been talking about her before she walked in.

Maria turned and smiled when she saw Kimi, and so did Amanda, but the rest of the girls stared coldly. Lindsay wore an expression of pure envy, and Shannon, always in agreement, looked exactly the same. Nicole, for her part, looked equal parts jealous and sad.

"Waffle?" asked Maria as she pulled a perfect golden Eggo from the toaster.

Kimi's stomach grumbled. "Sounds great," she said. The waffle smelled like pure bliss. Kimi took an empty plate from a stack and set it down in front of her place at the counter, next to Amanda.

Lindsay snickered.

"A *whole* waffle?" Lindsay whispered to Shannon. "Why am I not surprised?"

Kimi looked down at herself, shame flooding through her.

"So...how'd everyone sleep?" she asked, hoping to dull the awkwardness.

"Great," said Nicole, eating a big bite of waffle. "The couch downstairs was actually *way* more comfortable than the one in Maria's room."

She smiled at Kimi and took another bite of waffle.

For months, Kimi had fantasized about a sleepover like this—all the most popular girls at school getting together for late-night talks and gossip and food. But this morning she didn't *feel* happy, and looking around the room, she didn't think the rest of the girls did, either.

Nicole, Shannon, and Lindsay clearly didn't take kindly to being on the outside looking in. To an outsider, they might have seemed to be on top of the social ladder, but the truth was that Maria was one rung higher, stepping on all of them.

CHAPTER ELEVEN

The next few days after the sleepover went by without conflict, and Kimi's thoughts turned to her upcoming date with Marcus.

Thanks to salads without dressing and hours on the elliptical, she was feeling a *little* more comfortable in her new clothes (albeit a little light-headed from hunger) as she got ready on Thursday night. Whatever. It was like she'd been saying all along: Pain was the price of beauty.

"You look sick," said Lily from behind her.

Kimi checked herself briefly in the mirror. "I'm fine."

"I never knew you wrote music," said Lily, refusing to leave.

"I guess it never came up."

"I'm working on a song, too," said Lily. "On the piano. Maybe you can help me with the lyrics."

"Sure," said Kimi. "Just not right now. I've got a date."

"With Kevin?"

"No. Kevin and I are just friends. This date is with Marcus. He's a model."

"Like on *Project Runway*? I thought they were all girls. And Kevin *is* your boyfriend. He told me so."

"He did?"

Lily nodded.

"Well," said Kimi, "if he ever was, he's not anymore."

Marcus showed up at sunset. He drove a red classic Mustang, and the roar of the engine was enough to let Kimi know he'd arrived. She peeked out the window and spotted him idling at the curb in front of her house.

"I'm headed out!" she called to her mom. "To the movies!"

Drying her hands on a dish towel, her mom walked out of the kitchen.

"What movie are you going to see? Nothing R-rated, right?"

Kimi smiled. She *was* hoping that her night with Marcus was heading in a PG direction—maybe even PG-13.

"Nah. It's uh—some animated movie," she said. "Kid stuff."

"Well, you have fun," said Kimi's mom, looking slightly concerned. "Be back by ten. It's a school night, remember?"

"Rightokaybye!" said Kimi, running to the front door. She paused there to smooth her top, and then calmly opened the door to find Marcus leaning against the side of his car, waiting for her.

"Hey," he said when she walked up. "Good to see you."

She leaned in to hug him. He smelled of expensive cologne and aftershave, and the light cotton of his shirt felt soft against her cheek. Holding on to him for an extra second, she also smelled the leather of his bomber jacket. She had to force herself to let go.

"Is that a new jacket?" she asked.

"Bought it just for tonight," he said. Then, looking her over, he added, "Aren't those your jeans from Monday?"

Kimi cringed. She'd assumed that, being a guy, Marcus wouldn't notice. Only Kevin noticed stuff like that. And *whatever*: You were allowed to wear the same jeans twice in a week, right?

"No, no. They're just, uh, really similar," she said.

Marcus nodded. "Got it. I do the same thing. Like I'll buy a shirt in both medium gray and dark gray, just to give myself options."

"Right," said Kimi. "That makes sense."

Marcus nodded, still eyeing her jeans with some suspicion.

"We should get going," he said. "There's no such thing as fashionably late to a fashion show."

Twenty minutes later, Kimi and Marcus pulled up to the main entrance of the downtown Four Seasons. The building, lit up with purple lights, seemed to glow from within like a massive amethyst plunging into the heart of the city's skyline.

"We're a long way from Motel 6," said Kimi, almost by reflex. Her parents had never been the types to spend extravagantly, preferring to save for a "rainy day," and Kimi had never stayed at a hotel that cost more than a hundred bucks a night.

Near the main entrance, a line of Benzes, BMWs, and limos were pulling in one at a time, dropping off well-dressed guests as photographers snapped pictures.

"Parasites," said Marcus. "They're always begging me for a photo. Lucky for them, I'm in a generous mood today."

As Marcus turned off the engine and handed his keys to a red-coated valet, Kimi felt like an impostor, a peasant trespassing in the king's palace. For a moment, Kimi waited in the car, wondering if Marcus would walk around and open the door for her like Kevin did.

"Miss?" said the valet, who had taken a seat next to her. Kimi looked out the window. Marcus was standing with his back to her. "Miss? I think your boyfriend is waiting for you."

Kimi opened the door herself and walked up to Marcus, who was posing for several uninterested photographers who stood on the other side of a velvet rope.

"Is that kid someone famous?" asked a small, portly man with a mustache, who was holding a camera almost as big as he was.

"Nah. Just some wannabe model," said a tall, bearded man next to him.

Marcus frowned and turned to Kimi.

"The paparazzi aren't exactly known for their intelligence," he said. "Or their taste. Come on. Let's head inside."

"Wait!" said someone else. "That girl next to him. That's Kimi Chen, right?"

"Are you sure? Her hair looks different."

"I'm telling you. It's her!"

Suddenly, a thousand camera flashes went off at once, completely blinding Kimi. She staggered back...and landed right in Marcus's arms. He held her close—and his body felt good against hers. But once her eyes readjusted, Kimi could see that he wasn't looking down at her, but rather at the cameras.

"You should turn your head a little to the left and up," said Marcus through his pearly-white teeth. "That's your good side."

Kimi wasn't sure whether to be flattered or offended. Didn't that mean that she had a *bad* side? Was there something gross about the right side of her face?

Behind them, Kimi heard another car pull up and saw tall, redheaded triplets step out. The photographers turned their attention to the new arrivals.

"This is our chance to escape," said Kimi, tugging Marcus toward the hotel lobby.

"Wait," said Marcus. "Just one more..." He looked hopefully over at the photographers. "Okay, fine."

And with that, he followed her inside.

*   *   *

In the lobby, Kimi and Marcus walked along a red carpet toward a pair of gold elevator doors, which parted as they approached. A short man dressed in a red-and-white military-style uniform pressed the button for the penthouse, then stood silently at attention as the doors closed.

"That was...unexpected," said Kimi.

"Being a celebrity is hard work," said Marcus, turning his head slightly to examine his reflection in the elevator's steel interior. "Wait. That isn't a zit, is it? Tell me I'm not breaking out."

"It's just a little piece of fluff from my coat," said Kimi.

"Let's hope it doesn't show up in any of the pictures," said Marcus, worried. "A model's entire career can get derailed thanks to a single blemish." He looked over at her warily. "What were you thinking? Didn't you lint-roll before you left the house?"

"I, uh, didn't think I had to," said Kimi, feeling embarrassed. She was starting to regret this date with Marcus. Yes, she'd always wanted to date a hot guy, but she'd never *really* thought about the maintenance cost associated with constant perfection.

A few seconds later, the elevator doors opened, revealing the domed ballroom at the top of the hotel. The large room's glass walls gave it the feeling of a roof garden looking out over the glimmering city below.

In the middle of the room, a long glass runway lined with sapphire lights stretched out to a pair of blue velvet curtains. Kimi couldn't believe it—she'd fantasized for years about going to a fashion show. Of course, in her daydreams, it had always been one featuring *her* designs.

Still, she was glowing with excitement already. The well-dressed crowd thrummed with energy. Silks moved like water in the light. Diamonds and pearls sparkled on necks and wrists and fingers. Perfumes and colognes mingled in the air, and Kimi seemed to catch a new scent with each breath she took.

"It's…" she started. "It's…"

"Boring, I know," said Marcus, shaking his head. "Halfway through winter, and everyone's still wearing last fall's looks. I guess this is what we get for living outside of New York or Milan."

"Oh…yeah," said Kimi. "I've always wanted to go there. To either of those places."

"You haven't been to New York?" asked Marcus, incredulous. "But how do you—? How did you—? How did you even learn about fashion?"

Kimi shrugged. "The Internet?"

Marcus shook his head. "As far as anyone here is concerned, the Internet is just a place where fat people go to shop."

"I thought you said you saw my video," said Kimi, feeling slightly defensive. "*That's* on the Internet."

"Maria just held up her phone for me to watch you," he said. "Anyway, it doesn't matter. The point is, you're here now.

You can finally see what *real* fashion is about. Now come on. Take my arm as we walk to our seats. I want people to see that we're a couple. One of the best ways for celebrities to get coverage in *Us Weekly* is to date other celebrities."

Kimi was becoming more convinced that this date was a bad idea. Marcus was a *little* more interested in Kimi's fame than in her personality. Come to think of it, had he asked her a *single question* really worth answering since the date started?

Marcus took her arm and smiled at several tall blond women as he and Kimi walked to their seats. The blondes eyed Kimi with suspicion. Apparently there were still some people in the world who hadn't seen her video.

As she got to her seat—an uncomfortable folding chair at the side of the room—Kimi looked out at the empty runway and imagined walking down it. She'd spent plenty of nights practicing her model walk down the hall at home. For a second, Kimi closed her eyes and daydreamed about a harried assistant running through the audience looking for a last-minute replacement model and then plucking her out of her seat.

Opening her eyes, she looked over at Marcus, who had a hand on his stomach.

"Are you okay?" she asked.

"Yeah," he said. "Just feeling my abs. I was looking at myself in the mirror last night, and it almost seemed like my eight-pack was down to a six-pack."

Kimi laughed. "I think most people would be pretty happy with that."

"Don't laugh," he said. "This is my career. It's not like they want my *face* in the JCPenney catalog. I'm an eight. Maybe a nine. All my gigs lately tend to just be for shirt modeling. Strictly neck-down work."

Kimi studied Marcus's face. He had a muscular neck, a strong jaw, perfect white teeth, clear skin, manicured eyebrows, and perfectly trimmed hair. If there was room for improvement, she didn't see it.

"Why are you looking at my face like that?" asked Marcus. "Is there something wrong? Did you get another piece of jacket lint on me?"

"Nope," said Kimi, crossing her arms. "I think it's a blackhead. You should really wash your face better."

Freaking out, Marcus reached into his pocket and took out a compact. Flipping it open, he studied his skin in the tiny mirror.

"Where?" he asked. "Where is it? Don't just sit there looking stupid. Come on! This is an emergency!"

"Relax," said Kimi. "I was just joking. You look fine."

"*Fine* isn't good enough around here," said Marcus, taking one last look at himself before he put his compact away.

Kimi turned from him, hoping he wouldn't see as she rolled her eyes. Yes, it was probably awesome to be here on a date with Marcus, but did she really want to go out with someone prettier than she was? And what kind of dude kept a compact in his pocket?

Well, she shouldn't judge too harshly. She definitely had plenty of quirks herself. Maybe it was *refreshing* that Marcus was confident enough in his masculinity that he could unabashedly carry a—

She turned back to see him applying concealer.

"What are you doing?" she asked in a loud whisper.

"I'm pretty sure I *did* spot something," he said. "Maybe it was just the overhead lights, but I think I saw a light spot, and I wanted to even out my skin tone."

He still had the mirror out and kept examining himself.

"You look fine," she said. She realized she hadn't caught him checking her out once since the date had begun. Even when he'd first picked her up and made a few comments on her clothes, he hadn't really been staring at her body—just at her outfit.

Weird. Most guys checked her out—Kimi had become pretty adept at catching them. Like, sometimes she'd leave the nerds' table at lunch, then glance back quickly to catch Kevin staring at her hips.

As for Marcus...he just seemed interested in staring at himself.

The lights dimmed and music started to play. Whatever song this was, Kimi definitely hadn't heard it before. At first she thought the singer was just mumbling, but eventually, she realized the lyrics were just in French or Italian or some other language she didn't know.

A few seconds later, the first model came out. She wore an outfit consisting mostly of peacock feathers. Kimi laughed softly.

"Try to take *that one* to the dry cleaner," she whispered.

"Why would you do that?" asked Marcus.

"No, I mean—it's a joke—like, how could you possibly…"

A large woman dressed in a way-too-small-for-her pink dress turned around and shushed Kimi. Marcus, for his part, no longer seemed to be paying attention.

For the rest of the show, Marcus leaned away from Kimi, as if dissociating himself from her. Unable to talk without fear of getting her head bitten off, Kimi had no choice but to watch fashion after miserable fashion as a series of models pranced down the runway.

For whatever reason, this particular line's designer had chosen some kind of zoo theme. Peacock Girl was followed by a model in leopard print. Then came a series of fur coats paired with flesh-colored leggings, crocodile-skin boots that went up past the knee, and even a pair of giraffe-print unitards that made the too-tall, too-skinny models look even more stretched out and skeletal than usual.

Flipping through copies of *Cosmo* and *Vogue*, Kimi had looked enviously at models like these, but seeing them in person, she felt bad for the girls. They all looked so fragile, as if a single fall might shatter every bone in their bodies. Once or twice, Kimi shuddered when she saw a model waver in her heels.

Finally, half an hour later, the houselights came on. The show was over.

Marcus smiled. "Great. That's done. Now we can get to the real excitement, aka the after-party."

He opened his compact again and checked himself out.

"I started getting paranoid halfway through the show that I had something in my teeth," he said. "I don't, right?"

"Given the fact that we haven't eaten anything since you picked me up, I'd guess no," said Kimi.

"Oh, I just assumed you were dieting," said Marcus.

Okay, that was the last straw. Kimi stared at him, her eyes burning with rage.

"And why would you assume that?"

For the first time since the date had started, Marcus actually seemed to register the expression on her face.

"Forget I mentioned anything," he said. "I know everyone's weight-loss journey is a personal thing."

"I think I want to go home now," said Kimi.

"But...the after-party," said Marcus. "There's a rumor that they're giving away bottles of the new CK fragrance as party favors."

"What am I supposed to do with cologne?"

Marcus smiled. "I was thinking you could give me your bottle."

"Sure," said Kimi, taking a step toward Marcus. "Take my bottle. And I'll tell you *exactly* where you can shove it."

Just then, a flash went off, and she turned to see the mustached photographer from earlier.

"What are you looking at?" she asked.

"A fight, I hope," he said. "Nothing sells better."

For just a moment, Kimi considered charging the man and throttling him. Then she imagined how *that* would look in tomorrow's edition of some gossip magazine.

She let out a deep breath, then turned and walked straight for the elevator.

"I'll, uh, talk to you later?" shouted Marcus as she left.

"Good luck with that," she muttered as she wandered through the crowd.

A few minutes later, outside the hotel, a doorman approached.

"Shall I call you a cab, madam?" he asked.

Kimi checked her purse and found three dollar bills. She shook her head.

"Just point me in the direction of the nearest bus stop."

The doorman smiled and shook his head.

"One of those days, huh?"

"Yeah," she said. "One of those days."

Kimi Chen: Shoot me now.

Emily Kessler: Oh no! Bad date with Marcus?

Kimi Chen: Let's just say I would have been better off watching *Troll 2* with Kevin.

Emily Kessler: Ouch. That is bad.

CHAPTER TWELVE

"Friday Night Showcase?" asked Kimi's mother as she set a pizza box down on the dinner table the next night. "I thought that was a comedy show."

"It is...mostly," explained Kimi. "But they also have special musical guests...and this time it's going to be me."

She tried not to let the smell of the pizza get to her. After the trip to the mall, then the sleepover and Marcus's comment on their date, she'd been dieting all week, still struggling to fit into her new jeans. For the last six days, she'd had coffee for breakfast, celery for lunch, and as little dinner as possible.

Now, the pizza in front of her smelled like the freshest dough, covered in the freshest cheese, covered in...heaven. Either Domino's had just updated its recipe or she was *hungry*.

She took out a slice and put it on the plate in front of her. Trying not to eat, she stared it down.

Kimi's mother looked at Kimi's dad as he picked a piece of pineapple off his pizza and ate it with his fingers.

"Do you have time to go with her?" she asked. "I've got about a thousand documents to review before we go to trial this Wednesday, and the lead prosecutor is going to bite my head off if I can't deliver."

Kimi's father shook his head.

"I'm already buried under work myself, and I'm taking Lily to her SAT prep course."

"I'm sure Lily will be fine if she misses *one* study session," said Kimi, trying desperately to ignore the increasingly tantalizing aroma of the pizza slice in front of her. "She's not even in high school yet!"

"Yeah!" said Lily, perking up. "Let me go to the dress rehearsal. I want to hear Kimi sing!"

Kimi's parents looked at each other nervously.

"We're starting to get a little worried about all this publicity," said Kimi's mom. "I caught some of the women at work watching your video the other day. They were laughing."

"Because it's funny!" said Kimi, starting to feel overwhelmed. She couldn't fight both her parents and the urge to eat pizza at the same time. She couldn't take it anymore. She reached down and took a massive bite of the pizza. A pleasurable, satisfied feeling radiated from her taste buds and out through her body.

"Everyone in middle school thinks Kimi's video is awesome," said Lily. "Except for Matt Larsen. So I spread a rumor that he has lice."

"Come on, Mom," said Kimi. "You've taken Lily to a hundred recitals. How is this any different?"

"It's not that we don't support you—" started Kimi's mom.

"Great," interrupted Kimi. "Then you'll come."

Her mother sighed. "I guess I can always bring some documents to review during the drive. Your dad can still take Lily to her study session."

"Great," said Lily, glumly setting down her pizza crust. "Perfect."

Kimi looked down at her own plate and realized it was empty. Oh well. She'd won the war with her parents but lost to the pizza. One out of two wasn't bad.

Half an hour later, Kimi met up with the cheerleaders at the mall, where they immediately bombarded her with questions.

"Okay. In one word, describe your date with Marcus. Go."

The cheerleaders went silent as Maria's words hung in the air of the food court, mingling with the scent of cinnamon rolls and pretzels. Every eye at the table fixed on Kimi. She thought about it for a few seconds before she answered.

"Disaster."

Maria laughed, and a couple of the other girls giggled in solidarity. Any trace of the previous weekend's drama seemed to be gone.

"Tell us all about it, sweetie," said Nicole. "Did he get all grabby or something?"

"Are you kidding?" asked Kimi. "He seemed more interested in himself than me. He spent half the date looking in a mirror, the other half talking about himself, and, uh, the rest getting mad at me for saying the wrong thing."

"I should have warned you," said Nicole. "I made out with him a couple times last year... until I caught him checking himself out in the mirror while he was kissing me. That was the last time. Well, actually, it was the second-to-last time. But the point is, it creeped me out."

"Right," said Kimi. "Thanks for the heads-up."

"New brainstorm!" said Maria. "We've got to make up for this. Who else have we got? I want names, people."

"You mentioned Cameron last time," said Lindsay, never taking her eyes off Kimi. "But I think you also said something about him being too much for Kimi to handle. Maybe she really was better off dating the nerds."

"I told you, Kevin and I were never dating," said Kimi. "And don't tell me what I can handle."

"Girls," said Maria. "There's no need to argue. If Kimi wants a date with Cameron, we can make it happen. But Lindsay raises a valid point. Cameron does have a little bit of a reputation... and Kimi, you seem pretty... inexperienced."

"Maybe I'm not as innocent as you think I am," said Kimi. Though of course she was. Sure, she'd kissed a few guys... even had a steamy make-out or two. But that was always where she'd drawn the line. Still, she wasn't about to admit that in front of Lindsay and Maria.

"I see," said Maria. "Very interesting. Okay, then. Marcus is out. Cameron is in. I'll talk to him later tonight."

"But are you sure he'll go out with me?" asked Kimi.

"Oh yeah," said Maria, smiling ever so slightly. "You're definitely his type."

Late that night, Kimi got a call from a number she didn't recognize. Since taking her phone number off Facebook, she hadn't received any more random texts, so she figured it was probably safe to answer.

"Hello?" she asked.

"Hey, sis."

"Daniel?" she asked. Her brother had literally not called her once since he'd left for college.

"I heard from Mom that you're going to be on *FNS*. Congrats. You're Internet-famous. I checked out your video."

"Great," she said. "Thanks."

"Look," he said, "it's not usually my place to be, you know, concerned about you, but I've dealt with plenty of trolls from my World of Warcraft days, and I was reading through some of the comments under the video and on blogs and stuff.... It looks like you're getting a lot of flak. I wanted to make sure you're okay."

"Basically, yeah," she said. "Of course, if this Diamond-Girl22 who keeps posting embarrassing old photos of me *happened* to die in a plane crash, I wouldn't be too broken up about it." As much as Kimi hated to admit it, she kept checking the site every once in a while. A new picture from her awkward elementary and middle school days was posted every day, and the site had almost as many followers as Kimi's video itself. Unfortunately, some of the images had also made their way into other coverage of Kimi and "Three O'Clock" around the Web.

"Sounds like you're handling things okay, then," he said. "So..."

An awkward silence hung in the air.

"Bye, I guess," he said quickly, and then hung up.

Now Kim *knew* she was getting big. Even Daniel had finally noticed her—he hadn't done *that* when they lived in the same house.

Early Saturday morning, Emily sat on Kimi's bed, flipping through a magazine while Kimi tried on various outfits. Kimi was trying not to hyperventilate. Outside of her wedding gown, this might be the most important dress she wore in her life.

She checked the clock. Alan would be by in twenty minutes to pick up her and her mom.

"So we haven't really had a chance to talk since the texts the other night," Emily said. "How was your date with Marcus? It's your turn to fill me in on all the gory details."

"It, uh, it was bad," said Kimi distractedly as she pulled a black-and-white polka-dotted sundress off a hanger and tossed it to the floor.

"That's okay," said Emily. "I know for a fact that you can

do better. Marcus is hot and all, but honestly…that guy is self-obsessed. Ben and I went to a party at his place once. His room is *completely* full of pictures of himself. He even cropped his mom and dad out of some old family photos."

Kimi laughed. "I'm not surprised, actually. He's kind of a tool. A hot tool, but still a tool. I'm sure I'll find someone new."

"Ben's friend Spencer is still single," said Emily. "And what about Kevin? I know he wasn't exactly coming on hot and heavy, but some guys are shy like that, and he's a total sweetheart."

For a second, Kimi thought about telling Emily about her upcoming date with Cameron Clark. Sure enough, Maria had texted to confirm that he was interested and would be asking Kimi out at lunch on Monday.

But Kimi wasn't ready to have that talk. Bringing up Cameron would mean stirring up old feelings: According to Emily, Cameron had once been in love with her sister, Sara, who had tragically died in a car accident not long ago. It seemed better just to avoid the subject. He hadn't even officially asked Kimi out yet anyway.

"Uh, I don't know," said Kimi. "I can't think about boys right now. I've got to concentrate on this performance."

Emily laughed. "You're starting to sound like me. Before Ben came along."

"Just help me pick a dress, Em. I'm going crazy here!"

"What's this for, again?" asked Emily. "I thought it was just a rehearsal."

"Yeah," said Kimi. "A *dress* rehearsal. As in, I'd better have a nice dress, or people are going to think I'm a total amateur. I will *not* be one of those wardrobe-malfunction stories that people gossip about the next day!"

"I don't think that's what a wardrobe malfunction is," said Emily. "But I know you want to look good. What about that Marilyn Monroe–style billowy white dress that's kind of loose on you. You look *so* pretty in that."

Kimi shook her head.

"I've got to look *normal*," said Kimi. "Not like some friendless dork girl with overprotective parents who watches way too much *Project Runway!*"

"But you *are* that girl! Minus the friendless-dork part."

"But I don't have to be." Kimi pulled down an eighties retro skirt and tossed it onto the growing pile of rejects. "This is about . . . managing my image, you know. It's not about what I think looks good. It's about what people out there watching are going to think."

Finally, she pulled her new jeans out of a dresser drawer and started squeezing into them. They weren't as tight anymore. Kimi would have felt *great* if she wasn't so hungry.

"I . . ." Emily seemed lost for words. "I guess you know more about this stuff than I do."

Just then, a car horn blared outside, and Kimi spotted Alan sitting in a blue Corvette in the driveway.

"Nice car," said Emily. "He must be pretty successful."

"Yeah," said Kimi. She didn't remember seeing a car like this parked outside of Alan's studio.

"Who's that with him in the passenger seat?" Emily asked.

It took a second for Kimi to recognize the passenger. When she did, her stomach tied in knots: Kevin. She hadn't spoken to him since ditching him for Marcus. What was he doing here?

"Well, this should be an interesting trip," said Emily. "Have fun, I guess."

"Yeah," said Kimi. "Fun."

The road trip to LA epitomized awkward. For six hours, Kimi and Kevin sat *way* too close together in the cramped backseat of the Corvette while Alan sang along to the radio. In the meantime, Kimi's mom read legal documents in the passenger seat, trying to ignore Alan's bad karaoke.

"I didn't know you were coming," whispered Kimi.

"Don't worry," Kevin said. "I'm just helping Alan with some technical stuff. Hopefully Marcus won't be jealous."

The words stung. She hadn't meant to hurt Kevin, canceling on him like that. But what could she say to make things better?

"I'm not going out with Marcus," she said. "It was just a onetime thing. He had tickets to a fashion show."

Kevin went quiet for a second, processing the information.

"So... you went because it was a fashion show?" he asked.

It was true. Kimi had at least *partially* gone because of the fashion show.

"Yeah," she said.

"So…it wasn't, like…a date?" he asked.

Great. Now what was she going to say? One misplaced word, and this was about to turn into a *very* long ride. She didn't want to lie to him, not exactly, but there *were* ways of being selective with the truth.

"We didn't kiss or anything," she said. "And I'm *definitely* not going out with him again."

Kevin smiled.

"You should have told me about the fashion show earlier. I was pretty bummed on Thursday. I had to take Dex to *Troll 2*, and he wouldn't shut up through the whole movie. He kept poking holes in the plot, you know, and laughing in all the wrong places…."

"Sorry," said Kimi. "Next time, I'll come with you."

"I'm going to hold you to that," he said, grinning even wider, and Kimi couldn't help but smile back. She *did* like Kevin. Sort of. Probably?

Now she just had to hope he wouldn't find out about her upcoming date with Cameron Clark.

Or see her possibly flirting with Ethan White at the dress rehearsal.

Ugh. She was starting to understand why Emily had sworn off boys for so many years. It was way too much drama.

CHAPTER THIRTEEN

Since 1993, *Friday Night Showcase* had been filmed on a large stage in downtown Los Angeles, just a few blocks from the Staples Center. After parking in a massive garage, easily large enough to hold every car at Twin Branches High ten times over, Alan, Kevin, Kimi, and Kimi's mom walked in through the main entrance, marveling at the twenty-story glass UBC Studios building towering above them. Still stiff from the long drive, Kimi stretched her aching legs as Kevin pushed open the front door.

"Welcome to the big leagues," said Alan. Kimi wasn't sure if he was talking to her or to himself.

Inside, a secretary sat behind a massive oak desk as a stream of men in suits and well-dressed women strode in and out of doors behind her. She looked up at Kimi and her companions with suspicion.

"Can I help you?"

Kimi had heard that line before, universal code for "You shouldn't be here."

"We're here for the *Friday Night Showcase* dress rehearsal," explained Alan, but the woman shook her head.

"Dress rehearsals are closed to the public," she said mechanically, as if repeating a line she'd said a thousand times before. "Please feel free to apply online for tickets to Friday's show, which is filmed in front of a live audience."

"No, no," explained Kimi. "I'm *in* the show."

The woman eyed her curiously.

"Who are you again?"

"I'm Kimi Chen."

"Who?"

Kimi cleared her throat. Then she started to sing.

"Eight in the morning it's chemistry.... Nine and I take another SAT...."

The woman's eyes went wide, and a smile crossed her face.

"Kimi *Chen*!" she said. "You changed your hair! I love the video. Love, love, love it! *So* funny! I'm not supposed to do this, but... can we get a picture together? And maybe you could pretend to be roller-skating in it? That's my favorite part of the video!"

"I... guess so?" said Kimi. The roller-skating bit was becoming her signature move.

"Just be quick," said Alan. "We're already late."

A few minutes later, a handsome intern (whom, for Kevin's sake, Kimi tried not to stare at) guided them up an elevator and down a maze of hallways until they entered a small auditorium barely larger than the Twin Branches school theater.

Onstage was a familiar set, a family living room used for a recurring sketch about Becky the Crazy Dog Lady, who thinks that all her dogs are cats. On TV, Kimi had always imagined it as a real-life living room, but now she could see that just beyond the borders of the camera's view lay exposed particleboard and black-painted walls.

"Smaller than you imagined, huh?" asked a thin, wiry woman with thick black glasses framing intense eyes. A name tag hanging around her neck read LARA. "The cameras make things look bigger. People, too. But you must know that already. You're much prettier in person than online."

That was blunt, thought Kimi, smiling nervously.

"Thanks," she said, trying to sound confident. "I've been trying to watch what I eat."

Lara looked concerned. "There are snacks in the greenroom. I can have them removed if you want."

"That won't be necessary."

Lara nodded.

"Right. Okay." She checked her watch. "It *does* look like we're a little behind schedule, but I think we can still get you into hair and makeup. Ethan is in there now, but as soon as they're done with him we can get to you. Let's see...anything else? Do you need a ready room to warm up your vocals?"

"I don't think so," said Kimi. "I—"

"We *will* need to talk with your sound guy," said Alan. "I called earlier about a couple of special audio requests."

"Yes. Of course. Right this way," said Lara. "Ms. Chen, head down that hallway over there. Third door on your left."

Kevin and Alan took off with Lara, leaving Kimi onstage with her mom, who just now seemed to be taking in the stage. Kimi walked up into the living room set, taking a closer look at one of the couches, which was actually practically brand-new—just cut with scissors to look frayed and dog-scratched.

"This is..." Kimi's mom started. "It's very impressive."

Kimi couldn't believe her ears.

"What?" she asked.

"I know I'm hard on you at times," said her mother, walking up a few steps to join Kimi onstage. "But it's because I want the best for you. But...look at all this. Most people never achieve something like this in their lifetime. And you, only fourteen and you've written a song that landed you on national TV. And...your singing is beautiful."

Kimi could barely look her mom in the eye. Here she was, finally giving Kimi some genuine praise...and it was for completely the wrong thing. Kimi hadn't written the song, and the voice on that recording was so Auto-Tuned that it barely sounded like her.

"Thanks, Mom," she said. "I, uh, better go. See you in a few."

"I'll be right out there in the audience, cheering you on," said her mom, smiling. "Break a leg."

On the way back to the dressing room, Kimi walked through a short hallway lined with doors decorated with star-shaped plaques featuring the names of the people inside. OWEN MCGRAW. ROY JAVELINA. JENNIFER SHVARTS. Comedians she'd grown up watching—they had been on the show for years. Peeking around an open door, she even spotted Laura J. Dean, practicing her famous Taylor Swift impersonation.

Kimi had to literally pinch herself to make sure she wasn't dreaming. And, yes, the pinch hurt. She was really here, really about to dress rehearse a song millions of people would watch.

Finally, she reached the door Lara had indicated earlier and peeked in to see a handsome blond guy waiting patiently as a large, middle-aged woman applied makeup to his face. With the rest of his body perfectly still, the boy's eyes moved to look at Kimi.

"Kimi Chen," he said, his voice excited. "So glad to meet you!"

Over the next few seconds, several facts dawned on Kimi, all in quick succession:

1. The incredibly hot guy sitting in front of her was Ethan White.
2. Ethan White knew her name.
3. Ethan White KNEW HER NAME!

"It's great to meet you, too," she said. "Uh, I didn't know people like you...used the Internet."

"Are you kidding?" he said, smiling.

"Try not to move your face too much, Mr. White," said the makeup artist.

"Right, sorry," he said, his expression returning to normal. "Anyway, I'm online basically all the time. Haven't you read my tweets? I just hit three million followers on Monday!"

"Impressive," said Kimi, not really knowing if it was. Ever since she'd launched her video on YouTube, numbers had lost all sense of meaning. What constituted "a lot"? A million people? A hundred million? A billion?

"I know, I know," he said. "For someone like you that might not seem like a whole lot. How many views has your video gotten? Ten times that? Probably more."

"I guess it has...."

"I haven't had a song go that big since my Superteam days," said Ethan. "And that wasn't even my own stuff. We were just the faces, you know? The record studio had professionals write the songs, choreograph the dances, pick out our clothes. They even gave us all personalities. Did you know I was supposed to be the 'bad boy'? Ha! Two years later, I'm the only one who *hasn't* been arrested."

He laughed softly, then added, "Ever since I went solo, started writing my own stuff, I haven't gone platinum on a single album."

"But at least they're your songs now," said Kimi.

"Definitely," said Ethan. "No regrets. And anyway, these days it's all about my film career. I'm here promoting *Under-*

cover Kid 3: The Next Generation. I even got my little brother a part costarring as my new partner!"

Finally done with Ethan's makeup, the older woman backed away from him to survey her work.

"How do I look?" he asked, getting up out of the chair. He tossed a towel that had been wrapped around his neck into a bin at the side of the room.

How much would some of the girls pay for that towel? Kimi wondered. *A towel that had touched Ethan White!*

The woman shrugged. "You're a little young for me. Ask her."

She turned to Kimi.

"Oh! Uh! Amazing!" said Kimi, meaning every word. Ethan seemed to glow from within, as if he were a cherubic angel that had wandered out of a Valentine's Day card. Looking at Ethan literally took her breath away. Even Marcus looked plain in comparison.

"You're not so bad yourself," he said, walking past her and out the door.

Kimi turned to the older woman.

"Did Ethan White just...flirt with me?" Kimi asked.

"Stranger things have happened," said the woman, taking a jar of foundation from a drawer. "Now get in the chair. Ethan White might say you're hot stuff, but the way I see it, we've still got some work to do."

Twenty minutes later, Kimi sat in a large room filled with couches, snacks, and televisions. As she watched, Ethan

White joined the various *FNS* regulars in a variety of comedy sketches.

In the first one, Ethan played a knife salesman trying to hawk his wares at Becky the Crazy Dog Lady's house. In the next one, he played himself, mobbed by various cast members pretending to be teenage girls, drooling over Ethan, and trying to steal articles of his clothing. The scene made Kimi cringe. She saw just a little too much of herself in this particular sketch. She'd had to fight with all her will to skip stealing his towel earlier.

Finally, after Kimi had watched Ethan for about forty minutes, a short, harried man dressed all in black and wearing a headset ran in to tell her to get ready. She was on after the next sketch. Kimi took one last look at the television. It was hard to believe, but in five minutes she'd go from watching TV to singing on it.

She followed the short man down a few narrow hallways, passing cast members, who smiled as they recognized her.

"Three o'clock!" shouted Roy Javelina as she passed. "This is your time, girl!"

Kimi reached the stage just in time to see Ethan and Jennifer Shvarts finish a sketch about a swimmer who keeps pretending she's drowning so that a hot lifeguard will give her mouth-to-mouth.

After Ethan finished the sketch, he leaped up, walked to the front of the stage, and announced, "Please welcome tonight's musical guest...the talented, the beautiful...Kimi Chen!"

This was Kimi's cue to enter. She walked to the center of the stage, where a mic stand awaited her. In the background, the opening chords of "Three O'Clock" were already starting to play.

As she looked out, the empty theater seemed suddenly bigger, and Kimi could only imagine how it would feel to sing when those seats were packed. As of now, only a few people who worked for the show sat there—along with Alan and Kimi's mom, who was watching her intently.

Kimi tried to remember the last time her mom had shown up to watch her do *anything*. Maybe a soccer match in elementary school? But then, when was the last time Kimi had actually performed something worth watching? She'd done a couple of embarrassing hip-hop dance routines in middle school that her parents had, thankfully, been unable to attend.

What had made her think that anything had changed since then? What if she just embarrassed herself again? Ten seconds until she was supposed to start singing, and her throat tightened like a fist. She could barely breathe, much less sing.

I'm going to blow this, she thought. *I'm going to stand up here and not sing a word.*

And then, in the distance, she spotted Kevin in the sound booth, a set of headphones strapped to his head; he wore a look of complete concentration.

He's up there, she realized. *Making sure everything goes okay with the Auto-Tuning. Making sure I'm okay.*

She let out a long breath and felt her throat relax. Kevin would be there to help her if she messed up. She could be off-pitch, even completely out of key, and the software would pick up the slack. It would be okay.

"Yeah! Yeah-ah! Yeah!" she sang, and the voice playing out through the speakers around her sounded crystal clear, nailing every note. The voice was hers—only better. In the distance, she saw Kevin smile.

She couldn't help but smile, too, as she sang the next line: *"Uh-huh! Yeah-ah! Uh-huh!"*

CHAPTER FOURTEEN

Despite feeling like the dress rehearsal had gone well that weekend, Kimi got the distinct impression that around school the novelty of her fame was starting to lose its luster.

As she passed a tableful of skaters on her way toward her spot at the center table, one of them coughed and said, "Poser," and a little farther along she overheard one of the band geeks say she wasn't a "real musician." Apparently, rude comments weren't only for the Internet anymore.

She took her usual seat next to Maria and opened the Tupperware container that held her lunch: a wilted, fifty-calorie kale-and-raspberry salad. Hungry as she was, she could barely force it down.

"...stupidest song ever..." she heard some random Goth guy say as he walked by with his pasty-faced friends.

What had she expected? People were going to be jealous. Even Taylor Swift probably had her enemies. Or at least people who hated on her out of pure jealousy. Still, it wasn't exactly fun to have random strangers making rude comments about her for no reason. It was almost enough for her to want to forget about the whole being-a-megapopular-celebrity-cheerleader thing. *I mean, why am I doing this again?* she wondered.

As if in answer, a voice filled her ears.

"Hey."

A waft of rich cologne filled her nostrils, and she turned to see Cameron Clark looking down at her.

He may not have been as handsome as Ethan White (though he *was* close), but Cameron was *definitely* sexier. His long, lean swimmer's body lacked an ounce of fat, giving him the look of a living, breathing Greek statue. Cameron's body was the kind people meant when they used the word "chiseled."

"Wednesday," he said.

Stupidly, Kimi repeated the word. "Wednesday?"

"Are you free? That night?"

Kimi looked across the table at Maria, as if she knew Kimi's schedule. Maria nodded as if to say *Yes, you are.*

"I...am."

"Good," he said. "I'll pick you up at five thirty."

He looked her up and down, and Kimi suddenly felt as if her clothes were transparent, like he could see right through them. And maybe Kimi *wanted* that. Her heart was beating like crazy.

Cameron smiled. "I'll look forward to it."

After school, Kimi headed to her first cheerleading practice, and Maria let Kimi go to the top of the pyramid.

"But this is her first year on the team," Shannon complained. "She's not...qualified!"

"She's a celebrity," Maria said. "Why would we bury her at the bottom? Besides, being on top isn't *that* hard."

Kimi wasn't sure if Maria was just insanely optimistic about how easy cheerleading was or if she was trying to be supportive, but Kimi fell twice on her way up before she finally wobbled her way to the top.

Below her, Nicole and Amanda seemed to be dealing with her weight just fine, but the next level down, at the bottom of the pyramid, Lindsay and Shannon looked absolutely miserable. Usually, Kimi wasn't the type to take joy in the suffering of others, but in this case she was willing to make an exception.

If Kimi had earned a little bad karma for enjoying watching Lindsay and Shannon struggling at the bottom of the pyramid, it didn't take long for the universe to pay her back. The next day before practice, Kimi was heading to the locker room to change when she saw the two girls with their heads bent over a cell phone, both snickering.

"What's so funny?" Kimi asked.

"Um, you are," Shannon said, tilting the phone toward her.

Kimi's jaw dropped. It was a video of her at cheerleading practice... struggling to get to the top of the pyramid! Whoever had edited the video together had looped the footage to show Kimi falling repeatedly and never quite making it all the way up.

The sound track of the video was a parody version of "Three O'Clock" titled "I Can't Count to Two"—*"One o'clock, what comes after one? Time for sun! Maybe fun? What comes after one?"*

Whatever, Kimi thought. *The lyrics are just as stupid as the original ones.*

Then the video cut to Kimi trying on clothes at the mall. She saw herself jumping up and down, trying to squeeze into her too-tight jeans.

"You guys were *filming* all of these things?" Kimi demanded, starting to feel creeped out.

"It wasn't us," Lindsay said.

"Yeah, we were *underneath* you on the pyramid, how would we even film that?" Shannon pointed out.

"Anyone could have set up a camera on the ground before practice started. Or you could have had one of your friends set up a camera to—" Kimi said, but she was interrupted by her own voice... coming from the video.

"Kevin. I'd kiss Kevin."

The screen flashed the words KIMI'S SECRET CRUSH!

She recognized the words she'd said.... It was just for that stupid Truth or Dare question of which nerd she would kiss, but taken out of context...

She grabbed the phone out of Lindsay's hands and scrolled to the bottom of the screen, where she read the words *Posted by: DiamondGirl22*. She couldn't believe it. Whoever this girl was, she was still out to get her. Not only had she posted those creepy middle school pictures before, but now she'd followed up with recent complete stalker footage!

Lindsay and Shannon were practically rolling on the floor with laughter. Kimi glared at both of them and then pushed past them into the locker room.

She shut the door but hesitated before changing. Who was DiamondGirl22? Was someone really following her around, filming her most vulnerable moments and posting them on the Internet? That was *beyond* stalker behavior.

Kimi grabbed her clothes and went into one of the shower stalls to change. That would at least give her a little more privacy. Right? She couldn't help but check around for cameras.

She briefly contemplated going to Principal McCormick or her parents...but what would she say? If DiamondGirl22 *was* just Shannon and Lindsay, they'd be overjoyed that they'd really gotten to her. Kimi would never hear the end of it.

No, she decided. Better to just ignore them. She was finally at the top of the social pyramid—literally. She couldn't risk that by having a paranoid freak-out in front of everyone.

The thing to do now was sit back, wait, and try to figure out the identity of her anonymous enemy...hopefully, soon.

CHAPTER
FIFTEEN

The next night, Kimi was in front of her mirror putting the finishing touches on her outfit. She was going out with Cameron Clark, so she had pulled on a tough-looking black faux-leather jacket over a flowered tank top and her good jeans, which were actually starting to fit. She ran her fingers through her short pixie cut, wishing there were more hair for her to work with.

Kimi had to admit that she was nervous, and not just because she was about to go on a date with Twin Branches' resident bad boy. She still didn't know where she stood with Kevin. On the way home from LA on Saturday, he'd leaned up against her, falling asleep as they'd driven home through the night.

"He was up all night, you know," Alan had said from the

front seat. "Learning the software. The guy who was supposed to be here flaked at the last minute. You should give the guy a shot."

I am giving him a shot, she'd thought. *He just isn't taking it.*

Kevin had definitely been upset when she'd canceled on him to go on a date with Marcus. She had no idea how he'd react if he knew about her date with Cameron.

He doesn't have any right to think we're dating, Kimi told her reflection. It was true. If Kevin wanted to date her, she'd given him plenty of time to ask. Sure, there was *something* there, but he'd never tried to make it anything more. At this point, she couldn't tell if he was just being friendly or if he actually had *intentions*. And what good were intentions if he never *did* anything?

Kimi turned away from her reflection. Kevin was the last person she wanted to be thinking about when Cameron arrived. Cameron at least had actually made it clear that he wanted a date—and possibly a lot more than just that.

Kimi closed her eyes and tried to imagine how Cameron would look when he showed up at her door. She'd often seen him in the pool at swim meets when Kimi went to cheer for Emily, but he'd probably be wearing a bit more tonight.

The subject of swimming made Kimi think about Emily. Kimi was pretty sure that even Emily didn't really know what had gone on between Cameron and Sara. As far as Kimi could tell, nothing overtly romantic had *really* happened between the two of them; they'd just had some weird flirty relationship.

And Sara was gone now. That didn't put Cameron off-limits forever after. They hadn't even dated.

Just then, Kimi's phone beeped. It was a text from Cameron—Kimi winced thinking about just how far over her text limit she was at this point.

Waiting outside, it read in Cameron's usual, terse style.

Kim glanced back in the mirror to check herself over once more. Rummaging through a drawer, she grabbed a perfume sample she'd gotten from Sephora and dabbed it on her wrists. Then she went to the door.

"I'm going out for a while," Kimi called to her parents over the sound of Lily's piano practice. "I've got a project to work on, and I need to meet with the rest of my group."

The music stopped for a moment.

"How are you getting there?" her mom called from the kitchen.

"One of the other kids in my group is giving me a ride. It's just a few blocks away. I'll be back in a couple of hours!"

"Be careful!" her mom called, and then she said to Lily, "Continue."

The piano music began again, and Kimi breathed a little easier as she slid her shoes on. She didn't enjoy lying to her parents, but it wasn't like they left her any other choice. If she told them she was going out on a date with a guy like Cameron, she'd be lucky if they ever let her leave the house again.

Kimi shut the door behind her and turned to see Cameron parked at the curb in a black BMW. For a moment, she'd forgotten how wealthy his family was. Suddenly, the possibilities for tonight's date seemed endless. Dinner at a French restaurant maybe? Or dessert at the top of a hotel, looking over the city?

She opened the door and climbed in. "Hi. Good to see you!"

"Hey," he said. He was wearing a gray hoodie and jeans.

Their eyes met and...silence.

Awkward! Kimi struggled to think of something, anything to say, but her mind kept circling around Sara, Emily, and Kevin.

"So. I thought we'd go to the beach. Is that cool?" Cameron said, shifting the car into gear.

"Oh, yeah. Cool. Cool." She tried not to sound disappointed. She'd hoped for something expensive and romantic. From the rumors she'd heard, the beach was a place Cameron just took girls to make out—and other things. Suddenly, the night seemed to be moving *very* fast.

Cameron started up the car and pulled into the street as Kimi slid her seat belt on. They sat for a moment in silence before Cameron flipped on the radio. Instead of the rock or pop music that Kimi would have expected, classical music came floating through the speakers.

"You can change it if you want," Cameron told her. "I know Bach isn't for everyone."

"No, it's...great," Kimi said, recognizing the piece from Lily's lessons. First Kevin with the jazz and now Cameron with the classical. Weren't there any guys at her school who just listened to Top 40 like normal people?

"I listen to it before swim meets."

"Ah."

"You must know all about swim meets," he said after a while.

Kimi stared at him blankly.

"You know, because of Emily. You guys are tight, right?"

"Yeah. Yeah, of course."

And back to silence. The scent of Cameron's cologne was overpowering and even in his hoodie, Cameron had an air of sophistication well beyond any other boy she'd met at school.

She imagined what it would feel like to have his strong arms wrapped around her. But what if he wanted things she wasn't ready to give?

She wished he'd say something. The silence was deafening. It gave her too much time to think, imagining what would happen when they arrived at the beach. And Kimi could imagine a lot.

By the time they finally got to the beach, Kimi was so desperate for a conversation topic that she started just talking at random.

"I love the ocean," Kimi said, inhaling deeply. "I love… sand."

Cameron looked out at the waves and nodded.

"So this is what you wanted?" he asked. "To come here with me. Right?"

He leaned over and looked deep into her eyes. For a

moment, she felt transfixed, as if she couldn't move her body. Then, instinctively, she leaned away from him, and he smiled at her curiously.

"Is something wrong?" he asked.

"I think...I need to take a walk," she said, reaching for the door handle.

She hopped out of the car and faced the ocean, breathing slowly to calm herself. There were other couples scattered over the beach, some sitting in the sand and others walking along in the surf.

"Sunset should be nice," Cameron said, looking slightly amused. "Do you want to head down to the water?"

"Sure!" said Kimi, relieved to be out of the car.

Kimi kicked off her flats and held them in her hand so she could dig her toes into the sand. Cameron did the same. They made their way toward the surf, stopping where the cold water brushed their toes.

The sun was beginning to go down, golden and pink light spreading over the clouds and the water.

Kimi let her gaze linger on the gorgeous sunset, then turned to Cameron. Out here, like this, she could feel excited to be on a date with him. The fear she'd felt back in the car was gone.

He was staring at her. What was she feeling? The excitement of being out here on the beach with an *insanely* hot guy standing next to her.

But was there anything else? She searched inside herself

for a feeling—the same feeling she got whenever Kevin gave her a compliment or hinted at feeling something more than friendship.

"Kimi...we should probably talk," said Cameron. "Maria told me what you said to her."

Kimi racked her brain. "What I said to her about...?"

"About me." Cameron sighed and turned to look out at the ocean. "Look, I don't want to make this awkward. I mean, *more* awkward, but..." He ran his hand through his hair.

"What is it?" Kimi demanded, a sense of dread starting to fill her.

"She told me how you were *so* into me, and that I should give this a chance, but...I just don't think this is going to work out."

"*She told you what?!*" Kimi squeaked.

Cameron took a step back. "Uh, that you were really into me."

Kimi's face burned with embarrassment. He hadn't been trying to jump her, she realized. He'd just been acting awkward because he thought she had a huge crush on him...and he was totally uninterested.

I'm on a pity date with Cameron Clark, she realized. *Maria completely oversold how interested I actually am. I'm never going to live this down.*

"Huh," he said. "Well..."

So. Awkward.

She didn't even know what to say. She prayed to the god

of all things cool that she'd somehow get out of this with her dignity intact.

"Well, I guess the whole thing was just a misunderstanding," Cameron said after a few seconds.

"A misunderstanding?" Kimi asked.

"Maria…" he started. "She still thinks I'm the guy I used to be. I dated a lot of girls. Anyone I thought was hot… I'd bring them here, you know. Ever since Sara died, though, things have changed. I'm not the guy I used to be. Or at least, I'm trying not to be."

"You really cared about her, huh?" she asked.

"I never got a chance to tell her," said Cameron. "I guess Sara made me realize… when you find someone worth loving a whole, whole lot, you've got to fight to be with them. All the rest of it—me coming here with all those girls—it was just a distraction."

Kimi nodded. "I think I know what you mean."

For some reason, her thoughts flashed to Kevin. He *was* someone worth caring about. But as a friend, or something more? She tried to imagine how she'd feel if he died in a car accident like Sara, and the thought sent a shudder through her. Yes, she realized, she'd have regrets.

"Let's just forget this date ever happened, okay?" she asked.

Cameron laughed. "You got it. This date is hereby annulled."

He held out his hand so they could shake on it. Kimi laughed and took his hand.

"Kimi?"

Kimi dropped Cameron's hand and turned to see Emily and Ben. From the picnic basket in Ben's hand, it was clear that they had also headed out to enjoy a romantic sunset on the beach.

"Oh. Hey, guys. You know Cameron," Kimi stammered awkwardly.

"Yeah," Emily said, her eyes flashing between Kimi and Cameron. "I didn't realize the two of you were...I mean..."

"Seems like this is a popular place," Ben said, smiling. "Nice running into you guys. Do you want to join us for—"

"Ben, we're going to be late," Emily said, pulling on his arm, a look of panic in her eyes. "Come on, we should go."

"We don't have to—" Ben began, oblivious to the look that Emily was shooting him.

"We were just leaving anyway," Kimi said quickly, cutting Ben off. "Good seeing you, Em." Kimi gave her a weak smile and fled, Cameron right behind her. She tried to keep her steps slow and steady, though her instinct was to run, to get out of there as fast as she could.

"Everything okay with you?" Cameron asked once they were safely back in the car.

"Yeah," she said. "Fine."

He shook his head.

"Emily looks so much like her sister. It always throws me. When Sara used to get upset, her eyes would do that same thing, narrow just a little. You could only tell if you were really paying attention."

Cameron had hit the nail on the head. Emily *was* upset... and Kimi wasn't even sure if Emily herself knew why. In the past, Emily had always told Kimi what she was thinking. But tonight, Emily had just wanted to get away from her.

Maybe Kimi should have told Emily about the date with Cameron. A few days ago it had seemed like a harmless lie— not even a lie, just a small omission. Now it felt like so much more. Through four years of friendship, Kimi had never deceived Emily like this.

She wished she could turn to Cameron and ask him what he thought of all this—but he was off in his own world now, eyes focused on the road ahead, his thoughts probably swirling around Sara Kessler.

Kimi wished, suddenly, that it was Kevin sitting next to her instead of Cameron. Kevin, who always listened to her. Kevin, who always seemed to know the right thing to say.

She would have given anything in that moment to hear him say everything would be okay. Instead, silence continued to fill the car.

Back at home, Kimi walked in the door to find her parents waiting for her.

"We want to know what's going on," said her father, and Kimi gulped. She started to get her lies in order. Cameron was just a friend. Maybe something about a science project? Or studying at the library? What had she told them earlier? She had to think fast.

"I was just—" she started.

"Eleven hundred dollars and eighty-three cents?" asked her dad suddenly. "How do you even spend that much at the mall?"

Oh right. That. They weren't upset about *guys*. This was about *money*.

"Uh...a nice pair of jeans, a few tops, some accessories, and a trip to the salon?" she asked.

"That credit card was supposed to be for *emergencies!*" said her mom.

"Yeah. And this was a fashion emergency," said Kimi.

"I'm starting to think this taste of fame is going to your head," said Kimi's dad. "Maybe this *Friday Night Showcase* thing is a bad idea."

"No," said Kimi. "Please."

She looked at her mom, pleading with her eyes. Finally, her mother sighed.

"You'll find a way to pay us back every penny," she said. "And you're grounded for the indefinite future. But we're not canceling your show."

Stupid credit card. Stupid money. It was fine, though, right? Alan had said something about selling the song online, making some profits. Surely some of those were coming her way? Right?

Strange that he hadn't mentioned anything about it since then. Or sent her any checks. Worry started to gnaw at Kimi's stomach. She hadn't even *read* that contract. What had she promised? What had she given up? Despite her best efforts to stop them, tears came to her eyes.

"It's okay, honey," said her mother. "It is a lot of money.... But we can handle a thousand dollars. Just don't do it again."

What if Kimi had lost *more* than a thousand dollars? She needed to talk to Alan and get this all sorted out. But it would have to wait for morning. She had the biggest show of her life coming up the day after tomorrow, and it was going to be hard enough getting to sleep as it was.

CHAPTER SIXTEEN

The day of Kimi's performance on *Friday Night Showcase*, her parents got permission for her to skip school. Around nine o'clock, as she sat at home agonizing over her final dress selection, she heard a knock on her bedroom door and opened it to find Emily on the other side. Her mother must have let Emily in.

"Em!" she said. "What are you doing here?"

"I figured I could skip *one* period of study hall," said Emily. "And I wanted to see you before you took off."

She looked at the simple black dress Kimi was trying on; it hung loose on her body.

"You look...skinny," said Emily.

"Thanks," said Kimi.

"Have you been eating?" asked Emily, sounding slightly worried.

"Not all of us need to eat eight thousand calories a day."

Kimi turned back to the mirror, feeling suddenly self-conscious. She was definitely skinny now. No more baby fat for her. In fact, the girl staring back at her in the mirror looked a little gaunt.

"I...never mind," said Emily. "I'm sorry I brought it up."

Normally, Kimi would have been thrilled to see her best friend, especially at a time like this. But today was the first time Kimi had seen Emily since their encounter on the beach, and she had no idea where they stood.

For a moment, they both waited quietly, not quite knowing what to say. Finally, Kimi broke the silence.

"About the other day, with Cameron—" Kimi started.

Emily sat down on Kimi's bed and looked at her hands, apparently choosing her next words carefully.

"Were you going to tell me about it?" asked Emily. "Ever? I heard Shannon and Nicole giggling over your little date the next day. Why is it that *they* knew about you and Cameron and I didn't?"

Kimi had been all set to apologize, but she suddenly felt defensive. Emily was barely around these days, always hanging out with Ben. It was like she'd been forcing Kimi to find new friends and a new life in the first place. "You don't own him," said Kimi. "He can date whoever he likes." She regretted the words almost as soon as they'd left her lips. Emily's face immediately hardened, and fire danced in her eyes.

"You knew about him and Sara," said Emily. "Do you have any idea how weird it feels to think that the same guy who used to be in love with my sister is completely over her now, hooking up with my best friend?!"

When Emily put it that way it *did* sound pretty bad. But Kimi hadn't even done anything with him. It was completely unfair—she was having to deal with all the consequences of hooking up with Cameron without actually having done it.

"Look, Em, I'm sorry if I hurt your feelings, but I just can't deal with this today. I'm leaving in, like, twenty minutes. A few hours from now I'm going to be singing in front of *millions* of people."

"So I guess those millions of people are more important than your best friend?" asked Emily.

"I'm just saying that *today* isn't the best day to bring up a bunch of drama."

"Oh, I'm sorry," said Emily. "In the future, I'll try to get upset at a time that's more convenient for you."

"That might work if you were ever even *around*," said Kimi. "I'm lucky if I see you once a week these days. Maybe if you'd been a better friend instead of hanging out with Ben all the time, you'd actually know what's going on in my life."

"Well, I'm sorry if I finally have a boyfriend," said Emily. "And maybe I haven't been the best friend lately. But it sure didn't take you long to replace me, either."

"Maybe it felt good to actually have some people pay attention to me for once," said Kimi. "Maybe I was tired of being your sidekick."

Emily sniffled a little, and Kimi could tell that she was about to start crying.

"You know," said Emily, "I was thinking of skipping all of my classes today, having Ben drive me down to see you sing. You've always been there in the audience, watching me when I swim. I thought I'd pay you back, but now—maybe I'd better just head to school."

With that, she turned and walked out the door, leaving Kimi alone in the room. For a second, Kimi wanted to run after Emily and apologize—but she couldn't, not today. There would be time for that tomorrow. Today, the performance came first. Everything else would have to wait.

Half an hour later, Kimi joined Lily in the back of the family minivan. In the front, her dad started the engine and her mom fiddled with the radio.

"Now you *know* this is a big deal," said Lily. "Mom *and* Dad skipped work. That hasn't happened since...ever."

The sound of soft jazz filled the radio, and Kimi cringed. It was the same song Kevin had played as they drove to Alan's studio a month or so ago. Had it really only been such a short time? Kimi could barely remember the girl she'd been back then—a shy little nerd who couldn't even sit at the center table.

"No offense, Mom, but could you play something else?" she asked.

"Actually, I have just the thing," said Kimi's mom, plugging her iPhone into the car's speaker system. A series of familiar chords began to play, followed by an all-too-familiar voice.

"Eight in the morning it's chemistry. Nine and I take another SAT. Ten and I want to climb a tree. Gonna be lucky if I get a C..."

"Mom," said Kimi. "Anything but this."

"How can you not like this song?" her mom asked. "It's *your* song."

"I guess I've just heard it too many times," said Kimi. Trying not to sound too dour, she added, "I never thought I'd get over the sound of my own voice...."

"Whatever you need today, sweetie," said Kimi's mom, switching to a playlist full of seventies light rock, which was at least tolerable. If nothing else, it lulled Kimi into a relaxed state of consciousness where she could watch the passing scenery and try not to think of her fight with Emily.

She had just settled into a nice Zen-like trance when her dad exited off 101 onto University Avenue.

"Are we out of gas?" asked Kimi.

Her dad shook his head and smiled.

"We have one more surprise guest for the road trip."

Daniel was waiting for them outside his dorm. As the van pulled up at the curb, he opened the door, threw his backpack onto the middle seat, and slid in next to it.

"I can't believe it," said Kimi. "Daniel Chen, skipping class to go to a concert. I never thought I'd see the day."

"Good to see you, too, sis," he said. "Of course, I *see* you a lot these days. You're a sensation. I can't even walk down the hall without hearing you singing out of someone's computer speakers."

"Looks like I made it into Stanford, then—" she said. "In my own way."

I should have known, thought Kimi. *The only way Daniel would ever pay attention to me is if I actually ended up on a computer.*

"The Auto-Tuning is really impressive," said Daniel. "You can barely tell it's computer-generated. Who helped you with it?"

"Auto-Tuning?" asked Kimi's mom.

"It's just, uh, a software thing," said Kimi as her dad started the van again and headed back to the freeway. "Technical stuff."

"They have no idea, do they?" Daniel whispered. "They actually think you can sing like that? You've had, what, three voice lessons in your life? Back in middle school. And wasn't there something about your teacher giving up on you because you *never practiced*?"

"I sing in the shower," said Kimi, glaring at him. "All the time."

"Funny, I've never heard you."

"Maybe you were too busy with your computer games," she said.

Daniel shrugged.

"I forgot that family time was so much fun," he said, pulling out his laptop and a huge pair of Bose headphones. "Let me know when we get to LA."

A few hours later, Kimi and her family walked into the UBC Studios building, where the woman at the front desk waved and smiled.

"Great to see you again, Ms. Chen!" she said. "They're expecting you inside. An intern will take your family to a waiting area while you head to hair and makeup."

"Good luck," said Kimi's mom. "We're so proud of you."

"We can't wait to hear you sing," said her father.

"Me, neither," said Daniel, flashing her a devious smile. He didn't know that Kevin and Alan's software would be Auto-Tuning her performance on the fly.

A few minutes later, she stood outside the hair-and-makeup room. Ethan White's voice drifted out from inside. Before heading in, Kimi gave herself a quick breath-check and straightened her skirt. It wasn't like she wanted to *date* Ethan, but she'd felt flattered when they flirted last time—and right now she could use a confidence boost.

She pushed open the door and walked in to find Ethan sitting at the side of the room, talking quietly with a tall, slender, dark-skinned boy. It took her a few seconds to recognize him as Paulo Moreno, one of Ethan's Superteam bandmates. It took a few *more* seconds for her to realize Paulo and Ethan were holding hands.

"Kimi Chen!" said Ethan, smiling up at her. "It's *so* good to see you again. Have you met Paulo?"

"I, uh, no. I mean, I've seen you together...in music videos."

"I miss those days!" said Paulo, excitement in his voice. "Not *all* of it. Touring was a complete nightmare, and a *few* too many screaming tween girls for my taste. But at least we had each other."

Kimi's stomach sank. She thought back to the last time she'd met Ethan, the way he'd complimented her.

He wasn't flirting with me, she realized. *He has a boyfriend.*

"Are you okay?" asked Ethan. "You look a little sick. It's not stage fright, is it?"

"I'm...fine," said Kimi, her confidence shattered. Suddenly, she realized all at once that over the last few weeks, she'd...

1. Dated a guy who was in love with his own reflection.
2. Gone on a pity date with the hottest guy at school...who had zero interest in her.
3. Mistakenly flirted with a gay celebrity.

A few days ago, the world had seemed like a buffet of guys, and she'd felt like she could have any one she wanted. Now it turned out that the entire thing had been an illusion. Internet-famous or not, she was still the same, undateable girl she'd always been.

"I just need a minute," she said, turning away from them and walking out into the hall, wishing she'd never have to deal with another guy again.

It was a wish that would not be granted: Kevin stood outside, waiting for her.

"Hey," he said. "How are things with Ethan White?"

"Fine," she said, slightly confused.

"Lindsay came over to our table at lunch the other day and mentioned that you were going to try to make your move on him tonight."

Stupid Lindsay, thought Kimi. *Why can't she just leave me alone?*

"I'm going to stop you right there," said Kimi. "I see what you're getting at, but the thing with Ethan is he's—"

"It's not just Ethan," said Kevin. "It's Marcus, too. And now everyone is talking about how you went on a date with Cameron Clark."

Kimi cringed. She'd known Kevin would probably find out about that at some point. She just hadn't thought it would be so soon. But so what if she'd dated a few guys? Kevin didn't own her. What right did he have to be angry?

"So what?" she said. "I can date whoever I want. I'm not saying you have to love it, but the thing is, you're not my boy-friend. I don't have to answer to you."

"You're right," he said. "I'm not. I'm just a guy who would have done anything for you. A guy you kept in the dark because—why? Because you didn't want to hurt my feelings? Or was it something else? Maybe you knew you needed me to be your tech support tonight."

"That's not fair," she said. "I'm not trying to use you. That's the last thing I want. Going on all those horrible dates with other guys, it's just made me realize how much I—"

"Save it," he said. "I'm through with it, through with you.

You say you're not using me, fine. Use someone else to Auto-Tune your stupid song tonight."

With that, he turned away and walked down the hall and out of sight.

Okay, this is bad, thought Kimi. *But how bad?*

She picked up her cell and called Alan.

"Kevin just stormed out," she said. "Tell me everything is going to be okay."

"What do you mean, stormed out?" asked Alan. "I've literally never seen the kid get mad. What did you say to him?"

"Who cares what I said? I'm asking you, is everything going to be okay? Can you run the Auto-Tuning software without him?"

"Sure I could," he said. "If I were actually down there. I'm up north, hosting a viewing party with a hundred of my closest friends here at the recording studio! I've got guys here from Epic Records, Universal, Columbia—all completely psyched to see your big premiere!"

"You mean you're not even down here?!" said Kimi.

"I'm *trying* to take us to the next level!" said Alan. "Now you'd better hope Kevin gets over his little tantrum and helps you out."

"I don't think that's an option," said Kimi. "I think he's gone for good. Got a plan B?"

"Yeah," said Alan. "Learn how to sing. Fast."

CHAPTER SEVENTEEN

Kimi paced back and forth in the greenroom, staring at her cell phone. In times of crisis, she liked to make calls. *Normally*, she'd start with Emily, then go to Kevin, then move down her contact list until she found someone who would help her out or at least say something comforting.

Of course, *normally* she hadn't just had huge fights with everyone she cared about most.

She called Emily. No answer.

She tried Kevin. Voice mail.

Kimi hovered over Maria's name on her contacts list. Maybe she'd have something comforting to say. Kimi hit Dial. A few seconds later, Maria picked up.

"Hey, Kimi, what's up? I've got the girls over, and you're on speakerphone! We're *so* excited to see you sing!"

"Woo-hoo!" shouted someone on the other end of the line.

"Maria?" Kimi whimpered. "I'm freaking out. I'm going on in like half an hour, and Kevin just threw a hissy fit, and the Auto-Tuning isn't going to work, and I'm going to completely blow this thing and—"

"Slow down," said Maria. "You're stressing *me* out."

"Just hang up," said someone in the background.

"Just say something comforting," said Kimi. "Please. Tell me I can get through this."

"Look, we'd better go," said Maria. "The show's about to start. I can't *wait* to see your performance."

The line went dead, and Kimi stared blankly at her phone. Great. Now she felt even worse.

For the next half hour, Kimi watched grimly as Ethan White and the *FNS* crew performed their sketches. The audience seemed to be in a good mood, quick to laugh, which was great as long as it was, you know, *on purpose*.

Kimi tried to think of a way out. Maybe she could cancel—or ask the sound guys to just let her lip-synch. But no. It was too late for that. Too late to pull out, too late to change all the sound cues. Like it or not, it was time to face the music.

The expression had never seemed so apt.

Finally, an intern stopped by and waved to her.

"You're on in five. You ready?"

Kimi shook her head, and the intern smiled.

"You'll be fine."

He couldn't have been more wrong.

Kimi stood in the darkness of the stage, a microphone in front of her, waiting for her cue. Then, high above her, a spotlight flickered on; it shone down on Ethan White, who stood a few feet away.

"Please welcome tonight's musical guest," he announced, "the talented, the beautiful... Kimi Chen!"

Light applause filled the theater as the spotlight shifted toward Kimi, nearly blinding her. The first few notes of "Three O'Clock" played from nearby speakers. She cleared her throat.

"*Yeah! Yeaaaaaaah! Yeah...*" she started, and the voice coming out through the speakers was not the sparkling, clean, Auto-Tuned one she'd grown accustomed to, but *actually her own voice*, creating a flawed, uneven bunch of sounds that barely resembled a melody.

Someone in the audience laughed. Maybe they thought she was joking, making fun of herself. But the laughter went dead as the song continued, and it became clear that Kimi was genuinely trying. Trying and *failing*.

"*...and I take another SAT...*"

Dead silence.

"*...Three o'clock! Three o'clock...*"

It literally sounded like she was strangling a cat.

"*...Noon and it's lunchtime. Wish I had some brunch time...*"

And then, just when she thought it couldn't get any worse, it did. Kimi couldn't, for the life of her, remember the next lyric. Her voice caught like a burr in her throat, unable to escape.

For a second, stupidly, she *hummed*.

Then she went silent altogether.

For what seemed like an eternity, the music continued to play as Kimi stood there dumb, trying not to tear up. The spotlight was too bright—overpowering. She could barely keep her eyes open, and the effort to simply look straight ahead was causing them to well up with tears.

Then, the music finally ended, and the houselights came on. As they did, Kimi's eyes adjusted, and she saw the audience sitting before her, their mouths open, their eyes wide in disbelief. They sat gazing at her, as if not comprehending the disaster they'd just witnessed.

The place was as silent as a graveyard—and Kimi felt like she was the corpse. Not even her parents clapped.

For one last moment, she stood there, staring out into the crowd. Then she ran offstage as fast as she could.

CHAPTER EIGHTEEN

A few minutes later, as Kimi tried to pull herself together in a bathroom stall, she got a call from Alan Delucca. He wasn't happy.

"Congratulations," he said. "Not only did you just destroy any chance you ever had of having a career, but also you made me look like a complete amateur in front of the entire record industry. I'll be lucky if I ever work again."

"I'm sorry everything worked out so poorly for *you*," she said.

"We could have been millionaires," he said. "Set for life. Now it's all gone."

"I thought you were already trying to—what do you want to call it—monetize the song?"

"Oh, I have. But don't think that I'm giving *you* a cent of it now," he said. "You should have read the contract more carefully. '*Profits from digital distribution of the song will be given solely to Alan Delucca.*'"

"You can't—" she started, but then she heard a voice on the other side of the stall door, a voice belonging to her mother.

"Kimi? Is that you? Who are you talking to?"

"My producer," said Kimi weakly. "Alan."

"I think it's about time I had a little chat with this producer of yours," said Kimi's mother, reaching her hand over the stall door. Kimi passed the phone to her.

"Now finish up in there, and go find your father in the hall," said Kimi's mom. "Alan and I are going to have a nice, long chat."

By the time Kimi's family had driven home on Saturday morning—a long, silent trip during which even Daniel didn't have the heart to joke about her epic failure—the *FNS* meltdown footage, which a fan had immediately posted on YouTube, was already set on a pace to eclipse Kimi's original video for "Three O'Clock."

Up in her room, Kimi sat at her computer, not even trying to fight off the urge to Google herself. What she found wasn't pretty. Not only were reddit and Boing Boing sending links her way, but even CNN had posted about the musical disaster, and the Associated Press had picked up the story. Headlines included:

THE REAL DAY THE MUSIC DIED

WELL PAST THREE O'CLOCK...IS IT MIDNIGHT FOR KIMI CHEN?

AUTO-TUNE FAIL: THE TRUTH ABOUT KIMI CHEN

But the worst thing she found was a response video posted by DiamondGirl22. It featured a remix of Kimi saying the most embarrassing things, all set to a horrible techno beat in the background. The video itself was just a series of humiliating pictures of Kimi—including several of her asleep at the cheerleading-team party at Maria's house!

I'm freaking out.
I'm freaking out.
I'm f-f-f-freaking out.
The Auto-Tuning isn't going to work.
Auto...Auto-Tuning isn't going to work.
I'm going to completely blow this thing and...
I'm going to completely blow this thing and...
Auto...Auto-Tuning isn't going to work.

It took everything Kimi had not to pick up her laptop and crack it over her knee. Wasn't it bad enough that she'd just had a complete and utter meltdown on national television? Why did DiamondGirl22 have to make it worse?

She was almost sure now that Lindsay and Shannon were behind this. Who else would have had the motivation to take pictures of her *while she was sleeping*? And she was sure they'd both been there at Maria's house during her frantic phone call before the performance. She'd been on speakerphone, which meant they could easily have recorded her voice.

Kimi picked up her phone, preparing to call them and deliver a nice long rant full of threats and obscenities, but then she thought better of it. No. That wasn't going to cut it. Something like this had to be done in person.

At lunch on the Monday after her *Friday Night Showcase* nonperformance, Kimi waited in the corner of the cafeteria, watching for Lindsay and Shannon to walk in. She wanted to make sure she spotted them before anyone spotted her.

As she waited, though, she felt a tap on her shoulder. She turned to see Dex looking at her dubiously.

"So, now that you've had your epic meltdown you're crawling back to sit with us nerds?" he asked. "Well, what if we don't want you back?"

"I'm not here to sit with you," she said. "I'm just waiting for a couple of people to show up."

"Well, maybe you should go wait somewhere else," he said. "I heard what you did to Kevin. Not cool. I may not have much social sense, but at least I know who my real friends are. And I don't use people like that."

"Yeah, well, maybe I—" She tried to think of some defense but came up empty.

"Lost for words again?" he asked, smiling. "Thank god we didn't get you to do the talent show. What a disaster *that* would have been."

Again unable to reply, Kimi decided to just ignore him. She turned her attention back toward the middle of the cafeteria, where the cheerleaders were taking their places at the center table.

Kimi saw Lindsay and Shannon sitting with their backs to her, laughing at something—probably something about *her*. Kimi's blood hit a full boil. It was time to show Diamond-Girl22 who she was messing with.

Kimi walked purposefully across the cafeteria and came to a stop right behind Lindsay.

"What's so funny, Lindsay?" she asked. "Or should I call you DiamondGirl22? You think it's funny to make videos of people when they're at their weakest? Huh? You like taking creepy pictures of people while they're sleeping?"

"You think *I'm* the one posting those videos?" asked Lindsay, turning to look up at Kimi. "How stupid are you? Whose *room* do you think you were sleeping in?"

All eyes at the table turned to Maria, who sat at the far side, calmly eating a bowl of fruit.

"Maria didn't put those—" Kimi started, but even as she began the sentence, Maria shot her a cold smile.

"Sure I did," said Maria.

"I—but—we're *friends*. Why would you—"

"I needed material," said Maria. "You may not realize it, but you're not the only celebrity at this school. Diamond-Girl22 is starting to develop quite a little Internet following. I did what I had to so I could get close to you."

"But...why?"

"Call it justice," said Maria. "You were skipping steps. I've worked every day since sixth grade to rule this place...and then you post some stupid video and everyone thinks *you're* a star? Imagine what would happen to the social order if nerdy girls like you were allowed to become megapopular overnight. It would be chaos."

"You were jealous."

Maria shrugged. "You had what *I* deserved. If you want to call that *jealousy*, fine."

"You lied to me," said Kimi. "Pretended to be my friend—"

"Oh, please. I used you just like you tried to use me," said Maria. "Have you ever asked me about who I am, who my family is, what I do with *my* time—any of it? You wanted an in with someone popular, someone to give you a little fashion advice. Don't pretend we've *ever* been friends. It was what it was: two people using each other to get ahead."

Kimi took a step back from the center table, and as she did, she realized that her desire to sit there had vanished completely. She'd sooner sit in a nest of vipers.

For a moment, she looked over the faces of the girls she was leaving behind. Amanda, who had been wearing a set of large headphones the whole time, seemed as oblivious as ever, but Lindsay and Shannon wore matching looks of sheer triumph. Maria maintained her usual cold smile.

Nicole, for her part, actually looked sorry. Maria noticed and her brow furrowed.

"Nicole," she said. "Come here. The seat next to me is free now."

For a moment, Nicole seemed to hesitate. Then she walked over and took back her old seat, never once meeting Kimi's eyes.

Without another word, Kimi turned and left, fleeing past the nerds' table and out the door.

That night, Kimi lay in bed staring at the ceiling, lacking the motivation to so much as turn on her computer. What was the point? All she'd find were a bunch of people making fun of her—people she'd never even met.

Why would people take so much time just to be mean to each other? How many hours had Maria spent at her computer editing together stupid photos and video clips of Kimi—and all for what? A little fame? Who even cared? Kimi realized now that fame was overrated.

What was the point of being a celebrity if it just meant everyone was secretly gunning for you, waiting for you to fail? Who wanted fame if it could vanish in an instant, leaving you lower than before your star had risen in the first place?

The door creaked, and Kimi looked up to see her mom looking in at her, a slice of cake in hand.

"I'm not hungry," said Kimi.

"Of course you are," said her mom. "You've never been this skinny in your life. Time to eat something."

She set the cake down in front of Kimi, who eyed it suspiciously.

"I have a pair of jeans that barely fit me as it is," she explained.

"Those new ones you've been wearing around that make your legs look all pinched?" asked her mom, wrinkling her nose. "I hate those jeans. And they're *loose* on you these days."

Kimi laughed weakly. "I hate them, too."

She examined the cake, wondering how many calories it contained.

"What about my baby fat?" she asked.

"I always liked your baby fat," said her mother. "And you're a long way from that now. I just want you...healthy."

Kimi took a peek in the mirror. It was true. She didn't look so good.

She picked up the slice of cake and took a bite. Nothing, ever, had tasted this good. She ate another mouthful. And another.

"Did you make this?" she asked between bites.

Her mom shook her head. "You know I'm a lousy cook. I got it from Safeway."

Kimi sighed and lay back down.

"I can't believe that actually happened...on national TV," she said. "I'm a joke. To everyone."

"Not to me you're not," said her mom.

"I just wanted...I don't know. To be special. But I guess I'm just especially untalented."

Kimi's mom smiled and put a hand on her shoulder. Outside the door, the sounds of a Chopin sonata filled the air as Lily resumed her practicing. For once, Kimi found it soothing.

"I've always thought you were special," said her mom.

"Right. Just not as 'special' as Lily or Daniel or Emily. You know, people who are actually *good* at things. People who have *abilities*."

Her mom nodded, thinking this over. After a few seconds, she asked, "Back in college, do you know how many times I switched majors?"

Kimi shook her head. "No."

"Me neither. Too many to count! First I wanted to be a doctor. Then a biologist. Then an artist."

"An *artist*?" Kimi asked.

"It was a phase," said her mom, shaking her head. "The point is, I didn't end up going pre-law until the last semester of my senior year! But you know what? I never regretted it. I'd gotten to wear all those different hats, to test out all those majors. And then, finally, I found something I was truly good at—and something I truly love, still, to this day."

"You were so proud, though, when I was going to be on *FNS*," said Kimi. "You must have really thought I was good."

"I was glad the world was finally recognizing you for the star you are," said her mom. "But who cares about that anyway? The important thing is what makes you happy. And if that's singing 'Three O'Clock'—"

Kimi smiled and shook her head. "I hate that stupid song."

"Then never sing it again," said her mom. "I know a lot of people are saying nasty things about you now, but they'll forget soon enough. Just be *you*. Be true to yourself. And after a while, whatever anyone else thinks will stop mattering."

Kimi laughed and wiped at her eyes.

"Does this mean you and Dad will stop giving me such a hard time when I get straight B's?" she asked.

Her mom shook her head and laughed. "I said 'Be true to yourself,' not 'It's okay to be a slacker.'"

Kimi nodded.

"Okay," she said. "I think I know what I have to do now. But first I'm going to need another slice of cake."

A few minutes later, cake in hand, Kimi went and tapped Lily on the shoulder.

"Hey," she said.

Lily looked up at her, fear in her eyes. "I can stop playing if you're freaking out right now or something. I bet you're megastressed that the Internet hates you, huh?"

Kimi shrugged.

"Mom actually gave me some really good advice."

"What?"

Kimi smiled. "Screw 'em."

Lily's eyes went wide. "*Mom* said that?"

"Well, not *exactly* like that. But that was the gist of it. Anyway, the point is, I'm working on a little plan. And I'm going to need your help. Are you in?"

Suddenly serious, Lily nodded.

"I'm in."

CHAPTER NINETEEN

The phone rang three times before the guy on the other end of the line picked up. As Kimi spoke, Lily's piano music resounded throughout the house. But this time she wasn't playing Chopin. This time she was playing something *new*.

"Who's this?" asked the voice on the other end of the phone.

"Kimi." As Kimi spoke, she woke up her laptop and opened Word.

"Kimi who?"

"How many Kimis do you know, Dex?"

"So Kimi Chen, then. How did you get this number?"

"You have it up on Facebook. Listen, I need a favor." As she spoke, she scrolled to the "recent documents" section of Word. Sad. It had been weeks since she'd written *anything*.

"Ha! That's a good one. You're the last person I'd offer to help. Hanging up now. Good-bye."

She had suspected Dex would be reluctant to help her. Luckily she'd kept an ace up her sleeve.

"Wait," she said. "I'm not asking you to help me for free. I can get you something you might want."

"What could you possibly do for me?"

"What if I said I could get you a date with a cheerleader?"

"Who cares?" he said. "Most of the cheerleaders aren't even that cute."

"But I'm not talking about just any cheerleader," said Kimi. "I'm talking about Nicole."

For a moment, the line went quiet. Dex was clearly thinking things over.

"I notice you haven't hung up yet," said Kimi after a few seconds.

"Nicole?" asked Dex.

"That's right."

"Okay," said Dex. "I'm listening. What do you want?"

Scrolling through the files on her computer, Kimi finally came across the one she was looking for. The file name was: OUT OF THE SHADOWS. It had been a while since she'd written it, but as she reread the lyrics, they seemed truer now than ever before.

There's a party at my house, and I'm standing in the corner. Everybody's dancing, and I'm here on my own.

"You know the talent show tomorrow?" asked Kimi. "I want in."

An hour later, Kimi crept up to Emily's house and surveyed the tree outside her window. From Emily's stories, Kimi knew Ben Kale had climbed this tree on several occasions, using it as a way to sneak into Emily's room undetected.

The only problem was that while Ben Kale had strong, thick muscles and ninjalike reflexes, Kimi had neither. Still, she was determined. Grabbing hold of a shoulder-high branch, she lifted with all her strength and barely managed to pull herself up. Already winded from the effort, she looked up to see half a dozen more branches she'd need to climb.

"Ben?" asked a voice from above. "Is that you?"

"Do I *look* like Ben?" asked Kimi, peering around to see Emily staring down at her from her open bedroom window.

"Get down from there," said Emily. "You're going to hurt yourself."

Ten minutes later, the girls sat next to each other on Emily's front porch, sipping hot tea.

"So," said Kimi. "First things first. Sorry. I'm really, really sorry."

"You don't have to be sorry," said Emily. "You didn't do anything wrong."

"I should have told you about Cameron," said Kimi. "I guess...I justified it to myself as being that you *technically* didn't have any right to tell me I couldn't date him. But friendship is based on a lot more than technicality."

"It's okay," said Emily after sipping her tea. "Everything—

and everyone—involved with Sara is just so—*loaded*, you know? I don't always know what I'm feeling when it comes to someone like Cameron. The emotions are like…all these threads tangled in a ball, and it takes me a while to untangle the knot."

"It's okay," said Kimi. "If I ever lost my sister—or even Daniel—I don't know what I'd do. I'm sure I wouldn't have dealt with it as well as you."

"Thanks," said Emily.

Kimi warmed her hands on her teacup and looked up at the sky, where a small pool of stars peeked through the gray cloud cover.

"I know I haven't been the best friend these last couple of months," said Emily. "I've just been way too busy with school, swimming, Ben, everything. But from now on, I'm going to try to see you more often—or at least hang out with you at lunch a couple of times a week."

"Not at the center table," said Kimi, flashing Emily a smile.

Emily nodded. "I never liked that place."

Though a gust of cold wind blew against her skin, Kimi felt good there, sitting next to Emily, the hot tea warming her from the inside.

For a little while, the two girls sat happily, quietly, simply enjoying each other's presence. Emily stared up at the sky, thinking. Then she looked over at Kimi.

"I wish I could have seen you sing," she said.

"No, you don't," said Kimi. "Believe me. But here's the good news. You'll get another chance tomorrow at the talent

187

show. It would mean a lot to me if you could be in the audience. Then I'll know at least one person out there isn't just rooting for me to fail."

Emily smiled. "I'll be there."

The next evening, Kimi stood behind a long red curtain in the school auditorium, waiting for her cue. For her outfit, she'd decided to go with the Marilyn Monroe–style white cocktail dress that Emily had told her to wear to *Friday Night Showcase*. Kimi was proud of the work she'd done in raising the hem of the old ball gown and carefully ironing ruffles into the skirt. It was definitely one of her best pieces: The cheerleaders were bound to hate it.

By her side, Lily sat at the school piano, her hands resting on top of the keys, ready to start. It had taken a little practice, but with Lily's music and Kimi's lyrics, the song had come together quickly.

On the other side of the curtain, Kimi heard Dex's voice: "And now, for our final act, I'm proud to announce a special performance from local celebrity and singing sensation Kimi Chen!"

Kimi detected a note of sarcasm in his voice. But whatever. She'd been expecting it.

At the sound of her name, the curtain began to rise, and the spotlight fell on Kimi. She felt a familiar blindness.

"Woo-hoo!" yelled someone in the audience. " 'Three O'Clock'!"

The rest of the audience started to chant, too.

" 'Three O'Clock'! 'Three O'Clock'!"

They were expecting her to try to sing it again, she realized. They probably wanted to see her fail in person. For a moment, she stared out at them, unable to speak. In the center of the crowd, she spotted Maria, her iPhone out, recording the performance. Lindsay and Shannon stared up at her, too, looks of glee on their faces as they anticipated a fresh train wreck.

And in the back, she saw Kevin operating the spotlight. With a steady hand, he kept it focused on her. He watched her every movement, making sure the beam followed her wherever she moved.

" 'Three O'Clock'! 'Three O'Clock'!"

Kimi cleared her throat.

"I've actually got something a little different to sing to you today. It's a song I wrote called 'Out of the Shadows.' "

Beside her, Lily began the song's intro, and as she played, the crowd quieted. Unlike "Three O'Clock," this song's melody was slow and haunting. Finally, it came time for Kimi to sing.

"There's a party at my house, and I'm standing in the corner. Everybody's dancing, and I'm here on my own."

This time, singing a melody that actually fit her vocal range, Kimi didn't miss a note. Sure, she didn't sound like Whitney Houston, but she wasn't *bad*, either.

As the song continued, and her nerves cooled, Kimi found her voice got stronger. And this time there was no chance that she'd forget the lyrics—she'd actually written them herself, after all.

"*Out of the shadows, I'll never be. The girl that you wanted, I'll only be me. And I promise you, you'll never see me go back in the shadows, back in the shadows....*"

As Lily played the final chord, silence filled the room, as if the crowd didn't know how to react. Maria turned off her iPhone and stared intently. Shannon and Lindsay shrugged and crossed their arms.

But in the back of the theater, Kevin began to clap, and then Emily joined him. Soon, others followed. Not everyone—certainly not Maria and the cheerleaders—but still there was enough applause to fill the auditorium and to make Kimi smile as she bowed.

"...and first place goes to...Amir Singh for Magic Is Believing!"

Lily sighed and shook her head. They were standing in the back of the auditorium listening to Dex announce the winners—a list that hadn't included Kimi.

"Are you kidding me?" said Lily. "He kept dropping his fake thumb during his whole performance!"

"It's okay," said Kimi. "I wasn't expecting to win, honestly. This wasn't a song that everyone was going to like."

"Well, I think everyone's stupid," said Lily, kicking a wall.

"Easy," said a voice from behind them. "What did that wall ever do to you?"

Kimi turned to see Kevin standing in the doorway to the auditorium.

"Nice song," he said. "Alan would not approve. No commercial appeal."

Kimi smiled. "There are more important things than mainstream acceptance."

He raised his eyebrows. "Who are you? And what have you done with Kimi Chen?"

"I'm, uh, gonna go," said Lily. "Over there." She pointed off in a random direction, then walked away in a hurry.

Once Lily was out of earshot, Kimi turned back to Kevin.

"I'm so sorry," she said. "I never meant to use you. And I should have told you about Marcus, Cameron—everything."

Kevin nodded. "It would have made things easier on me," he said.

For a moment, they stood in silence, and Kimi wondered if this was the last real conversation they'd ever have. Not that she necessarily deserved to stay friends with Kevin after the way things had gone down, but—

Kevin cleared his throat. "I'm sorry, too," he said. "I hung you out to dry when you needed me most."

Kimi shrugged. "I pretty much deserved it. Plus, have you seen how many hits the video of me screwing up on *FNS* has gotten? I'm bigger than ever."

"I just wish—" he started. "Well, that if you never liked me you would have said something. I still would have helped you. Even as a friend."

"I—wait. Who says I never liked you?" asked Kimi.

"It just seemed like—"

"Let me tell you something about girls," said Kimi. "And I hope you hang on to this for the rest of your life. We are never, *ever*, going to ask *you* out, kiss you, or tell you we love you first. Okay, well, some of us will. Maybe some of us should. But that's not me. If you want me, you can't just hang around waiting for something to happen. You've got to make a move."

"Kimi—"

"What?" she asked.

And then in one deft movement, he ran his fingers through her hair, brought his face in close to hers, and kissed her. For a moment, the auditorium, the students in their seats, the entire theater, all disappeared, leaving only the two of them, their lips brushing lightly against each other. After a few seconds, Kevin pulled back.

"How was that?" he asked.

Kimi smiled. "A good start."

CHAPTER TWENTY

The next night, Kimi's parents hosted Emily again for their monthly sleepover. This time, Emily had called Ben beforehand to make sure there'd be no surprises. This was strictly a girls' night.

Kimi was just about to head down to join Emily and the rest of her family at the dinner table when the door to her room opened and Daniel walked in.

"Hey, sis. Looking good."

Kimi looked down at herself. Forgoing her usual girls'-night pajamas, she'd dressed in a gold, vintage 1920s flapper outfit complete with silver fringe at the hem.

"I've gained three pounds in the last week," she said.

"Good," he said. "The skeleton look wasn't working out too well for you."

"Thanks. So, uh, what are you doing here? Don't you have homework you should be doing?"

"Are you kidding?" he said. "This quarter has been a cakewalk. I'm two weeks ahead. I figured a weekend at home wouldn't hurt."

"Only *you* would think Stanford is too easy."

"Listen," he said, "I know I haven't always been the best older brother—but I wanted to give you something." He held up a small flash drive.

"What's this?" she asked.

"Remember how you told me about DiamondGirl22?" he asked.

"Maria…"

"Ah, so you already know who she is. Well, it turns out *Maria* wasn't too careful about cloaking her IP address. What you've got there is a copy of every file on her computer. Sometimes having a computer engineer for a brother has its advantages."

"What do I do with it?" she asked, looking at the drive.

"Whatever you want," he said. "There's definitely enough dirt on that drive to make the rest of high school *very* unpleasant for your friend Maria."

She thought about it for a second. It *would* be pretty fun to let the entire world in on Maria's dirty secrets.

She took the flash drive and put it in her desk drawer.

"You're not even going to look at it?" he asked.

"Not tonight," she said. "But I'm going to let Maria know

I have it. And if DiamondGirl22 decides to post any more videos of me…there are going to be some consequences."

Daniel smiled.

"Did I ever tell you how much you scare me?" he asked.

Kimi pulled him in for a hug.

"Good," she said.

Kimi walked down to find the family and Emily gathered around a pizza box, grabbing slices. Apparently there would be no Chinese feast tonight.

"Sorry about the food," said Kimi's mom. "I've just been so busy on this new contract case."

"Are you kidding?" said Kimi. "Do you know how much I've been craving pizza lately?"

She was about to grab a slice and dig in when she noticed an envelope sitting on her plate.

"What's this?" she asked.

Her parents shared a smile.

"That contract case that's been keeping me busy," explained her mom. "I know you're probably not interested in a legal career, but the law can actually be *quite* fascinating. Did you know, for example, that a contract signed by a minor without parental consent is considered null and void?"

Kimi opened the envelope. Inside, she found a check. A massive check made out to her, from Alan Delucca, for a hundred and sixty thousand dollars.

"No way," she said.

"Let's just say I renegotiated for slightly more favorable terms," said Kimi's mom. "After we subtract a thousand for that little credit card fiasco, this should be enough to start a very nice college fund for you."

"Or to buy a couple of Ferraris," said Daniel.

"Or at least a used Honda," suggested Emily.

"Nice try," said Kimi's mom.

"This is exactly why we put the money in a trust that's not accessible to Kimi until her eighteenth birthday," explained her dad.

Later the following week, Kimi walked into the cafeteria. She gave a cursory look toward the center table. Maria and the other cheerleaders shot her cold glances, but that was fine. Maria couldn't touch her now. Kimi had no desire to sit down with them.

She blew past them and stopped by Kevin's table to grab him. He'd been sitting with Amir, who had his head in a book, ignoring the world. Dex was conspicuously absent. So was Nicole, now that Kimi thought about it. A few days earlier, Kimi had helped Dex compose a noncreepy letter to drop in Nicole's locker. From there, apparently, things had gone well.

Good, thought Kimi. *It looks like Nicole finally found a way out of that seat next to Maria. Good for her.*

Taking Kevin's hand, she led him out of the building.

"Where are we going?" he asked.

"You'll see."

She brought him over to a ladder leading up to the roof of the gym.

"After you," she said, kissing him lightly on the cheek.

On top of the gym, they found Emily and Ben sitting on a picnic blanket, looking out over the town.

"Nice view," Kimi said.

"Nice of you to join us," said Ben. "I know Emily's been looking forward to this little double date."

"So this is a date?" asked Kevin. "Officially? I thought I had to be the one to ask you out."

"Not all the time," said Kimi, taking his hand and leading him to the blanket.

"Didn't the Beatles once do a concert on a roof or something?" asked Ben. "Maybe this should be your next show, Kimi."

"I think I'm done with concerts for a while," she said.

"So then—what's next for you?" asked Emily.

Kimi looked out over the city. Each house contained a different life. Each car rushing past on the distant freeway contained another possibility. From up here, even their small town looked vast, endless.

She smiled.

"Everything."

ACKNOWLEDGMENTS

Many thanks to the Surviving High School writing team, who provided great feedback through the creative process: Eric Dean, Royal McGraw, Andrew Shvarts, Owen Javellena, and especially Jennifer Young.

Thanks also to everyone at Electronic Arts who believed in this series and helped make it happen: Pat O'Brien, Aaron Loeb, and Oliver Miao.

I'm very grateful, also, to our team at Little, Brown: Erin Stein, Pam Gruber, Sara Zick, and Mara Lander. Thanks again for all of your hard work on behalf of our book!

Finally, thanks most of all to Kara Loo, writing team leader, editor, and (by the time this book comes out) wife extraordinaire!

Wondering what happened to Emily Kessler's archrival Dominique Clarke? Want to know which clique *you'd* be a part of at Twin Branches High?

TURN THE PAGE TO FIND OUT!

DOMINIQUE'S STORY:
HOW TO GET BACK UP

Dominique Clarke pushed against the wall and flew back through the water, surfacing a few feet away and beginning her stroke. Only a few dim lights overhead illuminated the indoor pool, and she swam in darkness. As usual, she thought of Emily Kessler.

A surge of anger filled Dominique's chest as she reached back and cut through the water. Emily had taken everything from her. *Everything.* As Dominique swam, a thousand angry thoughts flew through her head like yellow jackets buzzing their rage.

She thought of the last few years, of everything she'd tried to build and everything Emily had stolen from her. Where had it all gone wrong? She turned over the facts in her mind, trying to find the moment when her life had taken this sharp turn—how she had ended up *here*—friendless, alone, and hundreds of miles from Twin Branches High.

The sounds of her splashes echoed through the darkness as she swam.

For some people, success came easy. Dominique, on the other hand, had worked for it.

When she moved to California in seventh grade, she had been cursed with an early bout of stubborn acne that had rendered her mildly unpopular and certainly undateable. Her teeth had been crooked, and though she'd been spared having to wear garish metal braces like some of her poorer classmates, the plastic mouthpiece she'd had to wear had made her self-conscious.

Then, in eighth grade, Dominique met Lindsay, and her luck started to change. Dominique had to wear her retainer only at night by then, and Lindsay let her try a special face wash that cleared up her acne. Best of all, Lindsay's mother, who worked at a makeup counter at Macy's, provided the girls with a seemingly infinite supply of free samples—not to mention discounts on designer clothes.

By the middle of eighth grade, anyone who didn't know Dominique would have looked at her and assumed she was one of the most popular girls at school. Gentle curves were beginning to take their place on her body, which was nicely toned, thanks to swimming, and her face was now flawless. She'd even started wearing cute flats when the rest of the girls in her class were still in sneakers.

And yet she still wasn't the most popular girl in her class. Her classmates' memories were simply too long. They still thought of her as the shy, pimple-faced kid whom they'd known from the year before.

High school, Dominique had sworn, would be different. Several local middle schools fed into Twin Branches High, meaning there'd be plenty of new faces in addition to all the older kids she'd never met. Dominique knew she could make a fresh start.

On the first day of school, she and Lindsay wore their cutest dresses and spent almost an hour making sure their hair and makeup were perfect. When they walked down the hall, she knew it had all been worth it. Wherever they went, heads turned. Guys whispered to one another, asking if anyone knew the girls' names.

But the real coup de grâce came at lunch. For two years, ever since Cameron had mentioned it in passing, Dominique had dreamed of taking a place at the center table. Now the time had come. When lunch rolled around, she and Lindsay walked fearlessly to the table and took their places.

"You're Cameron's sister, right?" asked a guy named Spencer, a beefy junior with the worst haircut Dominique had even seen. She nodded and smiled—but he wasn't the one she was paying attention to. Sitting next to him was the most beautiful boy she'd ever seen. He had short brown hair, just the right amount of muscle, and eyes that sparkled with intelligence. His name was Ben Kale, and from the moment she saw him, she knew he had to be hers.

"I'm starving," Spencer said. "I feel like I could eat half a pizza."

Dominique shrugged. Thanks to her aggressive swim schedule, she could eat practically anything and not gain an ounce.

"I could probably eat *two* whole pizzas."

She tried to meet Ben's eyes across the table, and he shot her a quick smile. *Good.*

"I'd like to see that," said Spencer.

Ten minutes later, a few of the senior guys had pooled their money to buy two full pies' worth of cafeteria pizza slices. Without a word, Dominique started eating, and with each bite she took, the guys around her got more excited. By the time she finished the last bite, they were chanting and clapping.

Everyone but Ben Kale. The smile had faded from his lips. If anything, he looked bored. A few seconds later, he got up and walked away, Spencer following behind him.

Dominique tried to put on a good show regardless. She bowed to the guys who remained, even gave out a few high fives. But she couldn't help watching Ben out of the corner of her eye as he walked toward the edge of the cafeteria…and stopped at Emily Kessler's table.

He lingered there for only a few seconds, but that was all it took for a wide smile to break across his face. And in that moment, Dominique's heart had crumbled. She'd spent twenty minutes choking down pizza, desperate to get Ben's attention. And Emily had made him smile just by sitting there.

The thought of Emily smiling at Ben brought forth a renewed surge of rage as Dominique's body sliced through the pool. It had been so easy for Emily to win Ben over. She hadn't even had to try!

Dominique couldn't help but feel as if that was how life always seemed to go for Emily Kessler. Dominique had known of Emily since elementary school; they were swimming rivals even though they'd never met. She had only started to despise her in day-to-day life since seventh grade, when the two of them began attending the same school and swimming against each other every day in practice.

Emily hadn't needed to work to become a great swimmer. She'd inherited the genetic gift of an Olympian's physique, *and* she had one of the world's best coaches (her dad) handed to her on a silver platter.

Growing up, Dominique had commuted to a pool two cities away just to practice with a second-rate swim coach who'd barely paid her any attention. Then she'd uprooted her whole existence, persuading her family to move here so that she could work with Emily's dad, who himself had ignored her as he concentrated on his own daughter's success.

The worst part was, Emily never seemed to appreciate anything she'd been given. She was always resisting her dad's orders in practice and walking around with an everyone-should-feel-sorry-for-me look on her face.

Sure, Emily had endured some hardships of her own. Losing her older sister must have been tough. But Emily's seemingly endless self-pity infuriated Dominique. Some people survived tragedy and became stronger. Other people wallowed. Dominique decided Emily was definitely one of the latter.

Still, Dominique might have forgiven Emily for those failings if not for Ben Kale. Things had all come to a head at his birthday party earlier that year. After a solid month of flirting her hardest with minimal results, Dominique had decided to step up her game. Lindsay helped her pick out the shortest, hottest dress at the mall, and then the two of them spent hours making sure their hair and makeup looked just right.

And then she went to the party, and everything was just... wrong. For the first hour, she couldn't find Ben, and she started to worry he was avoiding her. Then, to calm her nerves, she had a drink, something she had never done before. To make sure she would look perfect in her tight gold dress, she hadn't eaten a thing all day, and the alcohol hit her hard. Of course, it didn't help that the guy who had made her drink apparently had used *way* too much liquor. It took all of two minutes for her to start stumbling through the party, knocking into people.

From there, things just got worse. Much worse. She tried to track Ben down and ended up knocking on his door, calling his name like some kind of groupie. And when she'd finally found him, he'd been with Emily, swimming in the pool. Dominique had leaned over, trying to steady herself and warn Emily not to steal Ben away—and then Emily had knocked Dominique into the water.

It had been a social catastrophe, but at least Dominique still had her swimming. She even managed to set a record in backstroke, channeling her Emily-induced rage into raw power.

But then Emily had found a way to take that away, too. Out of nowhere, she'd shown up at Junior Nationals—completely unprepared—and still somehow, effortlessly, managed to destroy Dominique's record.

Yes, Emily had taken everything.

What had been left for Dominique to do but retreat? After her defeat at Junior Nationals, she'd begged her parents to find her another school, a place where she could concentrate on swimming with no distractions.

And so, for the last three months, she'd been here, in the Seattle suburbs, training day and night at Bellevue Athletic Academy, trying to get her lap times down. Three months, and the needle still hadn't moved. Emily's fifty-meter backstroke record still stood at 27.9 seconds. Every day, Dominique's coach timed her and told her the same thing: "28.0."

Just as Dominique's hand touched the wall, she heard a voice that brought her thoughts back to the present.

"Good technique."

Dominique removed her swimming goggles and looked over to see her brother, Cameron, standing nearby.

"What are you doing here?" she asked.

"Maybe you're not the only one who needs to get away from Twin Branches from time to time," he said. "I thought I'd pay my dear sister a visit."

Dominique grabbed the side of the pool and pulled herself out of the water, into the thick, humid air of the athletic center. She grabbed a towel and walked with her brother to sit on the stands off to one side. An awkward silence hung between them. They had never exactly been masters at communication.

What is he doing here?

"So . . . what's the latest?" she finally asked. "Any juicy gossip from Twin Branches?"

"I guess Kimi's music video is still the biggest news," he said.

"Video?"

Cameron smiled and did a search on his phone for *Three O'Clock*.

The video began to play. On it, Emily's best friend, Kimi, wore horrible clothes, looked worse than usual, and sang a stupid song. It brought a smile to Dominique's lips. Good. She wasn't the only one who had been utterly humiliated this year. Dominique laughed harder and harder as the video went on.

Four minutes later, Dominique was still catching her breath, trying to recover from a long, hysterical laughing fit.

"Thanks," she said when she'd finally recovered. "I needed that."

"I actually went on a date with her a few weeks ago," said Cameron.

"Ew," said Dominique. "Please tell me you didn't make out with *that*." She pointed to Kimi's face on the screen.

Cameron shrugged. "I didn't have the heart for it," he said. "I guess that's part of the problem. Part of why I needed to get away. The girl I want is gone. It's too late now."

He leaned back and stared up at the high ceiling. Dominique had rarely seen her brother like this. His usual mask of bravado was entirely absent.

"You mean...Sara Kessler?" she asked. She'd heard Cameron mention Emily's sister once or twice before, when Sara had been alive. It'd always been in passing, but often enough that it had aroused her suspicion. "Is that why you came up here?"

Cameron nodded.

"When she was alive, we'd talk and stuff, and...there were so many times when I just wanted to lean in and kiss her. It shouldn't have scared me at all to do it. I mean, I've kissed a lot of girls. And it was easy because it never meant anything. But with Sara, it was different. I was scared."

"Cameron—"

"There was a night," he continued. "This one night when we were all on a swim team trip, and I was *this* close to telling her how I felt. And then I just couldn't. And then—it was too late."

"So...what? You drove six hundred miles to tell me this?" asked Dominique, annoyed that the Kessler family was taking up so much of their combined headspace.

"Like I said, I just wanted to get away."

"Being up here in Seattle...I'm not running away, you know," she said. "I'm training. All the time. Getting ready to go back and win."

He shook his head.

"And how long is that going to take? It doesn't get any easier the longer you avoid something, you know."

Later that night, Dominique lay in bed, thinking about what Cameron had said. Again she ran through all that she'd lost. Her popularity. Her record. Ben Kale.

As much as she hated to admit it, her brother was right. Sure, she could go around telling everyone that she'd left to train, to build up her strength and come back with a vengeance...but it was all just a cover, an excuse.

She'd let Emily Kessler beat her. She'd run away. First from the center table, and then from Twin Branches altogether.

Her room's lone window looked out at the ocean and Dominique got out of bed to open it, letting in a cold breeze that blew against her skin. She shuddered for a moment, imagining how it would feel to walk back into that cafeteria, to endure the stares, the inevitable questions about where she'd been. It seemed impossible to ever return to that life.

And yet—and yet being here didn't make things any easier. If anything, each passing day made it harder to return.

*   *   *

Cameron awoke to a knocking on his car door. Squinting and still half asleep, he looked up to see Dominique staring down at him. He raised his seat back up and rolled down his car window.

"This may be the only time you ever hear me say this, but you're right," said Dominique. "Now help me put my suitcase in your trunk."

"Fantastic," said Cameron. "A little company for the car ride back. What changed your mind?"

"Because I want to win more than I'm scared to lose," she said after thinking about it for a few seconds. "And as long as I stay here, I'm just treading water."

"Actually, you're doing laps," said Cameron, a smile breaking across his face.

"You know what I mean," she said, throwing her suitcase into his trunk.

"It's good to have you back," said Cameron, throwing an arm around her. It was the first time he'd hugged her in years.

"I'm done running away," said Dominique as she hugged him back. "I'm going to take it back, all of it."

SURVIVING HIGH SCHOOL'S POP QUIZ

A BIG PART OF HIGH SCHOOL IS YOUR FRIENDS! ANSWER THESE QUESTIONS TO SEE WHERE YOU'D FIT IN AT TWIN BRANCHES HIGH.

1. ON THE FIRST DAY OF SCHOOL, YOU SHOW UP WEARING . . .

a. Sneakers and something comfortable.

b. Whatever you grab first.

c. A bright pink sundress or skinny jeans and a shirt with a funny slogan.

d. A collared shirt and khakis.

2. TIME FOR LUNCH! FOR YOU, LUNCHTIME IS ALL ABOUT . . .

a. The food! You need the right nutrients to fuel up for the day.

b. Relaxing! Finally, an hour with no one telling you what to do.

c. Seeing your friends! And being seen by the rest of the school.

d. Starting your homework! These math problems are going to take all night if you don't get started now.

3. WHAT WOULD YOUR IDEAL CLASS SCHEDULE LOOK LIKE?

a. Anything as long as it leaves you with enough free time for after-school activities.

b. You've managed to get two free periods in the morning so you can sleep in until lunch.

c. You're in all the same classes as your friends, of course!

d. The hardest advanced classes that you can take, plus a few extra community college classes for subjects your school isn't offering.

4. IT'S FRIDAY NIGHT! THAT MEANS YOU'LL BE . . .

a. Working out and then getting to bed early!

b. You've got no idea— but you and your friends always end up having a good time.

c. At a party with a huge group of people!

d. Playing board games or video games with your friends.

5. AT THE SCHOOL'S PEP RALLY, WHERE WOULD YOU BE SITTING?

a. Right in the front, paying attention so you can support your school's athletics department.

b. In the back, so you can spend the time playing a game on your phone.

c. Where all the popular kids are sitting—or at least close enough so you can hear all the good gossip!

d. Close to the exit, for maximum efficiency when leaving.

6. WHEN LEAVING FOR SCHOOL, YOU WOULD *NEVER* GO WITHOUT . . .

a. Your gym clothes. How could you work out without them?

b. A forged note from your dad about why you should be excused for getting to class late.

c. A mirror. You've got to look your best.

d. Your textbooks, homework, and extra credit.

7. WHEN THE BIG NIGHT OF PROM FINALLY COMES, WHERE DO YOU SEE YOURSELF?

a. Going to the dance, as long as it doesn't conflict with any athletic events.

b. Doing something outrageous! Maybe renting a bright green limo or pulling a prank in the gym— you'll figure it out the night before.

c. You and your perfect date are going to be crowned prom king and queen.

d. Playing a prom-themed role-playing game with elves and dwarves seems like the perfect way to celebrate.

Mostly A's:

You're athletic and focused! Sports teams will be clamoring for you to sign up. If you were a student at Twin Branches High, you'd be hanging out with jocks like Emily and Spencer.

Mostly B's:

You're all about being laid back and not agonizing over the details. Some might call you a slacker, but you see it more as avoiding a lifetime of stress. If you were a student at Twin Branches High, you'd be hanging out with Ben Kale.

Mostly C's:

You care about popularity, and you aren't afraid to be the center of attention. You'd be at home with the popular kids at any school. At Twin Branches High, Maria would recruit you for the cheerleading squad in no time, unless you're already hanging out with Kimi!

Mostly D's:

You're focused on academics, and you aren't going to let anything distract you. Some people might call you a nerd, but you're not afraid of embracing your studious side! If you were a student at Twin Branches High, you'd feel right at home with Kevin and Dex.

The
Kliptish Code

The
Kliptish Code

by

Mary Casanova

sandpiper

HOUGHTON MIFFLIN HARCOURT
BOSTON NEW YORK

Text copyright © 2007 by Mary Casanova

Maps by Stephanie M. Cooper

The text of this book is set in ITC Legacy Serif.

The Library of Congress has cataloged the hardcover edition as follows:
Casanova, Mary.
The klipfish code/by Mary Casanova
p. cm.
Summary: Sent with her younger brother to Godøy Island to live with her aunt and
grandfather after Germans bombed Norway in 1940, ten-year-old Marit longs to join her
parents in the Resistance and when her aunt, a teacher, is taken away two years later, she
resents even more the Nazis' presence, and her grandfather's refusal to oppose them. Includes historical facts and glossary. Includes biographical references.
1. Norway—History—German occupation, 1940–1945—Juvenile fiction [1. Norway—History—German Occupation, 1940–1945—Fiction. 2. Patriotism—Fiction. 3. Family life—
Norway—4. Fiction. Refugees—Fiction 5. World War, 1939–1945—Underground
movements—Norway—Fiction.] I. Title.
PZ7.C266KLi 2007
[Fic]dc22
2007012752

ISBN: 978-0-618-88393-6 hardcover
ISBN: 978-0-547-74447-6 paperback

Manufactured in the United States of America
DOC 10 9 8 7 6 5 4 3 2

4500366703

For my friend Johanne Moe,
who grew up in Norway
during World War II

ACKNOWLEDGMENTS

Many thanks to my editor, Ann Rider, who believed in this story, asked questions to stretch me further as a writer, and helped bring this story to fruition. *Tusen takk!* Our Norwegian ancestors would be proud of us.

No manuscript is complete without the fingerprints and feedback of others, including my family—Charlie, Kate, and Eric Casanova—as well as Hannah Riesgraf, Joyce Gazelka, Susan Gazelka, Lise Lunge-Larsen, Faythe Thureen, Johanne Moe, Tamara England, Mark Speltz, Mary and Andy Anderson, Huns and Marlene Wagner, Jim Hanson, and Hannah Heibel. And as always, a thanks to my local writers' group: Karen Severson, Sheryl Peterson, Shawn Shofner, Lynn Naeckel, Kate Miller, and Jessi-Lyn Curry; and the Oberholtzer Foundation, which has supported meeting on Mallard Island with writers Jane Resh Thomas, Cindy Rogers, Kitty Baker, Maryann Weidt, Phyllis Root, Alice Duggan, Lois Berg, Barb Santucci, Marsha Chall, Catherine Friend, and Janet Lawson.

A special thanks to the staff and curators at the Norwegian Resistance Museums in Oslo, Ålesund, and Godøy Island and for carefully documenting this period in history.

Finally, a heart full of thanks to Eric and Charlie for traveling with me to Norway to find Marit's story.

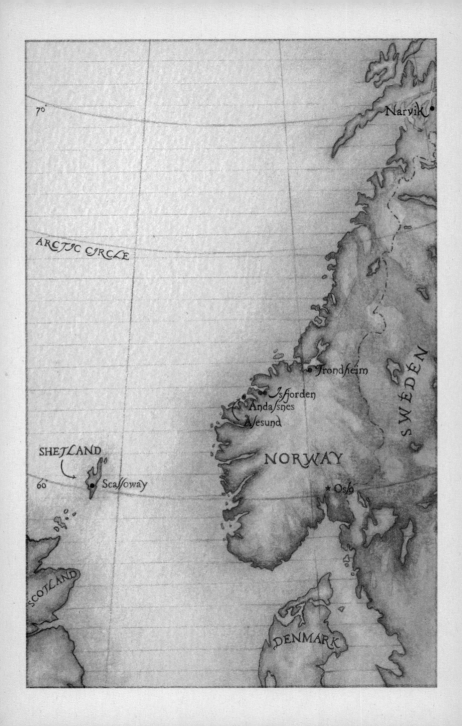

FOREWORD

*This story is based on events that followed the
sudden German invasion of Norway in the early morning
hours of April 9, 1940. Living under Nazi occupation,
countless ordinary Norwegian people—students, teachers,
pastors, fishermen—risked everything to keep
the hope of freedom alive.*

CHAPTER ONE

April 1940

In her dream, Marit raced Papa on her new wooden skis, farther and farther away from their *hytte*—their mountain cabin—and this time she was winning. Across the blinding whiteness, she pushed on, defying the mountains, said to be trolls turned to stone. She herringboned to the next peak, her thighs burning with the effort, then pushed off with her poles, and swooshed down through knee-deep powder.

An explosion wrenched Marit Gundersen from her sleep and shook her to her rib cage.

Wide-eyed, she bolted upright. Her skin prickled with fear. In near darkness, Marit flung back her feather-filled *dyne* and swung her legs over the bed's icy edge. What had startled her? Her mind darted back and forth. An early thunderstorm in the mountains? The train from Oslo—had it crashed? Had the steamer exploded in Romsdal Fjord?

Mama burst into Marit's room. "Marit!" she cried. "Get downstairs!"

"Mama, what's going on?" Surely there was an explanation and no need to panic.

But Mama's flannel nightgown swirled at her ankles as she turned to the hallway. "Come, Lars—you must wake up!"

Marit yanked a sweater over her nightgown, shoved her toes into her sheepskin slippers, and then stumbled from her room—right into Papa, his unlaced boots hitched over his pajama bottoms.

Marit squared her fists to her waist. "Papa, tell me what's going on—"

"Downstairs to the cellar!" he said, his hand firm on her shoulder as he guided her toward the stairs. "Questions later."

Mama dragged Lars through his bedroom doorway, but he pulled back against her hand and dropped in a heap on the floor.

"I don't want to," he moaned.

"Lars—wake up. I can't carry you!"

Shrill and piercing sounds whistled overhead, followed by a thunderous *boom-boom-boom!* Papa turned and scooped Lars over his shoulder—as if he had just turned three, not seven—and down the stairs they all flew.

The living room walls shuddered. Dishes rattled in the hutch, and the mantel clock and lamps crashed to the floor. Before Marit and her family had crossed the room, another explosion hit nearby—*boom!*—and the living room window shattered. Marit grabbed Papa's arm. "Papa, look." Beyond the empty frame, and under the questioning gaze of snow-topped mountains, strange planes wheeled through the dusky sky. The pounding continued.

"No time! Under the table!" Papa shouted.

They dived for shelter as an ear-ringing roar passed over them. Marit cowered. What in the world was happening? Though she was in grade four, old enough to brave many things—she was a fast skier, always the first of her friends to jump into the icy fjord waters in spring, the one who wanted to hike to the topmost peaks in the summer—now she barely knew herself. She clutched Mama's waist like a frightened toddler. With each explosion that shook the house, waves of fear rolled through her. Finally, a troubling quiet fell.

The house groaned with brokenness.

No one spoke until the last plane droned away.

Mama's blue eyes were set in an ash-darkened face, her normally blond hair now blackened with soot. "Marit, are you all right?"

How was she to answer? Nothing seemed real. Only yesterday they'd returned from skiing on their spring holiday. Only yesterday she'd left their grass-roofed *hytte* in the mountains. Only yesterday she'd laughed until her cheeks hurt. With a sunburned nose, she'd arrived home, ready to return to school. *Today*. She should be getting ready for school.

"Marit?" her mother repeated. "Can you hear me?"

Marit blinked dust from her eyes. "*Ja,* Mama. I'm all right."

Lars buried his face in the folds of Mama's nightgown and cried. "I'm scared!"

Her voice shaky, Mama comforted him. "We're fine," she said, smoothing his hair with the palm of her hand. "No one is hurt."

For several minutes they huddled beneath the table, as if the warmth of their bodies could protect them from what had happened. Marit pressed her head against Papa's chest. He wrapped his arm around her, his heart thudding against her ear. "We'll get through this," he said. Then he crawled out from their shelter and his boots crunched across glass to the broken window. He picked up his double-stringed fiddle from its fallen stand and shook out shards of glass. Holding it to his chest, he stared out the window. "Dear God—not Norway, too."

"Erik!" Mama said. "Get back—please."

He didn't move.

"But they might return any second."

"*Nei,* I think the Germans have done their damage . . . for the moment."

Marit's pulse thudded in her head and her stomach churned, but she finally found her voice. "Germans, Papa? Are you sure?"

"I'm sure. I saw the planes. Who else would invade us?"

"Invade," Marit ventured, "as in Austria and Poland?" Her parents had discussed the latest events throughout Europe every evening at the dinner table.

He was quiet for a long moment. "Marit, I don't know anything for sure yet. We need to find out who else was hit—what kind of damage has been done."

Limbs trembling, uncertain her legs would hold her, Marit crawled out from under the table. The hutch had hopped an arm's length from the corner, and Mama's teapot and porcelain plates lay in splinters. The potbellied cookstove tilted through the kitchen wall, leaving a gaping ragged hole.

Marit stepped closer and looked out. Dirt, boards, a bicycle wheel, and pieces of twisted metal littered the yard. Only yesterday four pairs of skis stood in fresh snow against the shed, but now they were scattered and broken matchsticks. More than once, her grandparents had boasted how Norway had avoided war for over a hundred years. They said Norway was a peaceful country that got along with its neighbors. This shouldn't be happening!

Village dogs began barking. Smoke rose above the trees and drifted in through the holes in her house's walls and windows. The wail of a woman came from somewhere beyond. Marit's hands fell to her sides and a vague numbness settled over her. Talk around the village had made her feel safe: "Norway stayed out of the Great War of 1914," someone had said. "We'll stay out of this one, too. Our king will see that we stay neutral." Everyone spoke with certainty that the Nazis would never invade Norway.

But now, it seemed, they had.

CHAPTER TWO
Leaving

Over the next few days, Marit refused to cry. Instead, she tried to be as helpful as possible—sweeping up glass, wiping down walls, scrubbing out cupboards, and restacking the woodpile. "Far better to stay busy," Mama said, "than to sit around worrying while we wait for news from friends and relatives."

When her best friend, Liv, who lived three houses away, had said she must go with her family to stay at a faraway farm, Marit asked, "But why? You can't leave. Can't you talk your parents into staying?"

"I'll show you why," Liv said, leading the way with a limp. After the bombing, the doctor had removed a splinter as big as a finger from her leg. It had flown through the air like an arrow and embedded itself in Liv's leg, leaving an angry red bruise behind. She picked a path through debris to where it looked like her dog had been digging a trench. "Here."

On hands and knees they peered beside the trench and looked under the foundation. A giant black bullet was wedged beneath the floor.

"It's a bomb," Liv said. "That's why we have to leave—just as soon as Mama's ready. Really, we shouldn't even be this close, but I wanted to show you—so you'd understand why I can't stay."

Marit cautiously eased away.

When it was time to say goodbye, the girls put their hands up and touched fingertips—a farewell they'd invented years earlier. "We'll see each other soon," Marit said, forcing a smile, though she doubted her own words. She didn't have an address to the farm where Liv was going. "It's a distant relative," Liv had explained. "My parents don't even know if he's alive. Haven't seen him in fifteen years—but we're going anyway." Once war started, how would Marit find her?

One day at dinner, Papa folded and refolded his hands, a certain sign he had something serious to say. "Marit and Lars," he began, "we contacted your aunt and grandfather and decided you'll be safer with them on the island."

Marit's forkful of potatoes stopped midway between

her plate and her mouth. She shouldn't be surprised. Everyone was talking of leaving, but leaving together—as families. "But we belong *here*—with you and Mama." Marit's voice rose. "You said, Papa, that 'we'll get through this,' remember? Why can't we stay together?"

Papa studied her, and for a moment, Marit thought he might agree. Then he said, "Cities and villages are targets for bombing. I know this is hard, but you two will be safer with Aunt Ingeborg and Bestefar. They'll take care of you, and, besides, you might learn something from them."

Through clamped teeth, Marit exhaled sharply. "But they're *not* you and Mama." She wanted to shout and cry all at once. How could she convince them? She couldn't be sent away. She needed to be with her parents. Didn't they understand? Only when she was with them did her fear begin to melt. Bestefar was as cold as fish scales! She'd never been able to do anything right around him, unlike her brother. "Then send Lars. Why can't I stay here?"

Mama reached for Marit's hands and held them in her own. "Your grandfather's not easy, I'll grant you that. But you'll be safe. That's our main concern. And you know Aunt Ingeborg adores you."

"I still don't get why *you* and Papa are staying here and sending *us* away." Marit squeezed back tears. "Why can't you come with us?"

Something in Papa's eyes told her there was no room for argument, that their decision was final. "Marit, right now," he said, "the less you know, the better."

That night, after Lars fell asleep, Papa motioned to Marit and Mama from his map-laden table. "I have news," he said. "And you must promise to keep this to yourselves."

Marit glanced at her father's maps. He always kept them neat and organized, but now many were ash-smudged and torn. She nodded, pleased to be invited in on his secret.

"Of course," Mama agreed.

"Boatloads of British soldiers have already landed in darkness at the end of our fjord. They've come because of Britain's own fight with Nazi Germany. They want to help Norway throw off the Germans."

Marit wondered why Papa was telling them all this. She glanced at Mama. The same question seemed to form in her eyes.

"We may have a British visitor sometime tonight. I don't want you to be scared."

"Who, Papa?"

"I don't know exactly."

"Will there be fighting here?"

Papa picked up his fiddle, rested it under his chin, and began to play a soft tune, as if to soothe her. "*Nei*, I hope not."

"What about your maps, Papa? Is the British visitor interested in your maps? Maybe that's why he's coming. If you need help with anything, you know I'd do whatever you and Mama asked, if only I can stay."

If she knew more, perhaps she could make sense of it all.

Later, a faint knock sounded downstairs at the back door. *Tap, tap. Tap, tap.*

Marit lay in bed, wide-eyed. Through her open door, she strained to hear.

"Come in," Papa said in a hushed voice. *"Velkommen."*

In broken Norwegian, a man greeted Papa and Mama, and then said, "Erik Gundersen, I'm told you know the mountains and roads better than anyone in this region."

Mama—who came from a family of teachers and taught English at the upper school—helped translate.

"What news have you heard of Oslo?" Papa asked. "Is the king safe?"

"King Haakon has fled. The Germans are eager to capture him, but so far he has eluded them."

The man went on to explain other events of the war, and Marit listened closely. He explained that the German attack was part of a full-scale invasion of Norway.

"I can understand their targeting Oslo and the larger cities, but Isfjorden?" Papa asked. "We're a village. It makes no sense."

Mama interpreted the soldier's reply. "You're at the

end of the fjord, right across from the Åndalnes port and train depot. That puts this region at risk. The Germans —they want to shatter Norway with one sudden and decisive blow."

"But we're Norwegians," Papa said, anger nearly crushing his voice. A moment of silence passed before he spoke again. "We won't fall that easily."

The man lowered his voice. "We hope not, and that's why we need to work together. I understand you might both be helpful. We need engineers who know the area and we need good translators, too."

Then the door to the staircase was closed, and their voices blurred.

But Marit had heard enough. She was right. Papa's knowledge of the terrain and his engineering skills were going to be used to fight the Germans. And if they needed translators, who could do a better job than Mama, who already taught English? Perhaps her parents would come to realize that they might need extra help. She could do whatever they needed—run errands, deliver messages, help around the home.

Marit was determined to stay awake until the man left, and then ask her parents about his visit. There must be something she could do to help.

But she never got the chance. When she awoke, everything happened with the speed of startled birds. Before she knew it, she was packing her suitcase, picking her path through her yard, and walking down the bomb-damaged streets to the harbor.

Together with her family, she passed neighbors still at work repairing homes and shops. Some homes were shattered beyond fixing. Before, she would have felt too old to hold Mama's hand in public; now she held on tightly. Everything had changed. It was as if she was watching a girl her age from a great distance—the blond braid that touched her waist, the red and white snowflake sweater, hiking boots and rucksack . . . the little brother in his blue wool jacket and the parents. . . . But nothing about them seemed real. This couldn't possibly be *her* family heading to the dock to wait for the steamer that would ferry her and Lars down Romsdal Fjord—away from home.

As they waited, Mama handed Marit a small basket filled with smoked salmon, cheese, bread, and a jar of milk. But Marit doubted she could eat anything. Her throat tightened with tears.

At the end of the fjord and protected by mountains, her village had always felt safe. Now, scraps of wooden boats filled the harbor and their charred masts poked up like old bones. Stone chimneys stood tall amid piles of burned boards. Wisps of smoke climbed from the rubble. How dare the Nazis invade them? She wanted to scream at the Germans who had dropped the bombs. Didn't they have families, too?

The steamer chugged around the fjord's bend, and Papa knelt and hugged her and Lars close. "Bestefar will meet you two in Ålesund—and then he'll ferry you with his boat back to the island." He paused, as if searching for something more to say. Finally, he stood and said only, "I promise—we'll be together soon."

"Then please," Marit burst out, "please—don't send us away!" She wrapped her arms around her mother. Her entire life was being ripped up by the roots.

Too soon, with Lars at her heels, Marit boarded the steamer. As the engine rumbled and the steamer pulled away and out of the harbor, she raced up the ladder to the stern railing. She had meant to wave goodbye; instead, she gripped the wooden rail and looked back through blurry eyes. Something larger and more frightening than she could possibly understand had been set in motion. Beyond the steamer's churning wake, Mama and Papa became smaller and smaller, until she could not see them at all.

Hours later, the steamer eased toward the landing. Fog thick as *risengrot*—Marit's favorite rice pudding—covered the city's harbor as the steamer slowed its engine. Marit kept a lookout for Bestefar's boat, which was like many other fishing trawlers with its two masts, open decks, wheelhouse, and the *tonk-tonk-tonk* of its engine. They were sturdy wooden boats that handled wind or calm, port or open ocean water.

In the fog, everything was gray and dull. On past holidays, she had loved looking at Ålesund's ornate and colorful buildings. She loved walking past the bustling wharves and fisheries where they turned dry, salted cod into klipfish and shipped it around the world. Once dried and salted, the codfish kept forever. She loved Mama's way of cooking it in butter and water. Though the fisheries used faster, more modern methods, some local fishermen still dried split cod on large boulders in the sun.

She spotted the trawler dockside. Two masts stood tall, the wheelhouse was empty, and Bestefar sat on the rail, his legs crossed in wool trousers, cupping a pipe. "There he is, Lars."

"Bestefar!" Lars called as he ran ahead down the steamer's rough planks, but their grandfather didn't hear. His head was bowed.

Marit followed behind, making her way slowly toward the fishing trawler.

Bestefar looked up and saw them coming. He held up his hand, probably the friendliest gesture Marit guessed she would see from him.

"*Hei*, Bestefar," Marit called, trying to force a little cheerfulness in her voice.

He nodded at them. "Hurry now." Beneath his fisherman's wool cap, tufts of white hair stuck out, matching his well-trimmed mustache. His steely eyes seemed harder than ever. Mama always said he was a happier man when Bestemor—Marit's grandmother—was alive. But she'd died when Marit was only three, too young to remember her. "It's as if your grandmother's long illness drained the life out of him, too," Mama had once tried to explain. "Not only did Ingeborg take over Mama's classroom on the island, but she stayed on at home to care for Papa. He wouldn't leave the house for days, not eating, not even tending his nets. It was your aunt Ingeborg who finally forced him from the house and back to fishing again."

Marit wished she could feel sorry for him, but the only grandfather she'd ever known was cold and short on words—except with Lars, of course.

"Lars," Bestefar said. "You're getting to be a big man now."

Lars jumped right into Bestefar's arms. "Not that big, Bestefar!"

Marit turned away. He hadn't even said hello to her or used her name. If he wanted to be that way, she could too. Let him be in his own salty broth, like herring in a barrel.

"Well, don't just stand there on the dock, Marit. Cast

off now. And no falling in this time. I don't want to fish you out again."

"Bestefar, that was a long time ago." She'd been four when she'd tripped and gone in, nearly drowning. Why couldn't he let it go? Swiftly, she moved to untie the line from the nearest cleat. In her haste, however, she managed to make knots in the rope where there had been none. She felt Bestefar's eyes on her, waiting. She was making a mess of things only because of him. It was the way he was. Nothing was ever done quite right. Never fast enough.

With the rope finally untied, Marit pushed off from the dock and jumped into the boat. The sails were down and secured. Her grandfather ran the engine for the short trip back to the island. He stood in the wheelhouse. Lars stood in front of him, a big smile on his face, hands up on the wheel, pretending to steer beneath Bestefar's large hands.

Seagulls swooped and cried mournfully around the boat as it crossed from the mainland to Godøy Island. Marit stood at the bow and clung to the rails. Salt water splashed up as the bow rose and fell. She breathed in the salty ocean air. She hated to leave her parents, but at least the island was a place she loved to visit. She loved combing the shoreline for treasures. There were the chickens and goats, and Big Olga, with her gentle brown eyes, the cow Marit had learned to milk years earlier. And Aunt Ingeborg. She was like a crab, hard-shelled on the outside, but soft on the inside. Strict, too, but she had to be. She was a schoolteacher.

Compared with her aunt, Bestefar was . . . Marit glanced back at the snow-crowned mountains. She had it. He was a stone troll.

CHAPTER THREE

Land of the Midnight Sun

On summer nights, the sun held fast to the sky, refusing to let darkness swallow the land. Whenever Marit opened her eyes, a hazy light covered the island and poured in through the open window. And this night was no different. She drifted on a sea of frustration, a rowboat tossed by every wave.

The bed she shared with Lars barely fit in the room. It may have been her mother's room when she was a girl, but it was never meant to be shared by two—especially with a younger brother. If Lars slept soundly, then he didn't wet their shared bed. If he slept fitfully and cried out from nightmares, then Marit hung sheets on the clothesline the next morning. Marit envied Aunt Inge-borg sleeping in a bed all by herself in the other upstairs bedroom.

She felt trapped, pushed up against the wall, but at least on her side of the bed, a window looked out toward the sea.

The pasture ended at the shore and rocky peninsula, and at the base of the lighthouse paced a German sol-dier, his rifle angled on his shoulder. Immediately after the first bombs fell, truckloads of German soldiers ar-rived and took control of every town in Norway. At first, they handed out candy, which she always refused. Every time Marit saw them, an icy unease settled in her belly. The Nazi soldiers patrolled everywhere, including the is-lands. And this soldier, guarding this lighthouse, came too close. As far back as she could remember, she'd loved walking out to the lighthouse. It was as much her own as it was every Norwegian's lighthouse.

Over two months had passed since the Germans had dropped bombs and invaded. It was already June. Though more bombs fell up and down Norway's coast, none had yet fallen on Godøy Island. And in all that time—since the day she and Lars had arrived at the is-land—she hadn't heard from Mama and Papa. *Not a word.* They were her parents. Why didn't they write? Or leave a message on the phone at the island's general store? Phone lines might be down, her parents were likely helping the British, but things still didn't add up. The British and Norwegians had failed to stop the Germans. The Nazis were rumored to make many unexpected arrests, and when they did, people disappeared. What if Mama and Papa were arrested in Isfjorden? What if she never heard from them again?

With a small kick, Marit untangled her legs from her nightdress. She checked on Lars, to see if he was twitching with nightmares. He slept stomach-down, burrowed in his pillow, his hair rumpled around his head. He breathed slowly, peacefully; otherwise—just to be safe—Marit would have nudged him to get up and use the night pot.

She flopped back down, shifting from her belly to her back. Day by day, there were more orphans in Norway. At least she wasn't one of them. She dropped her forearm across her eyes. But nothing worked.

Finally, Marit gave up and studied the buttery yellow slanted ceiling, the hand-painted chest that held her traveling clothes, and above it on the windowsill, the jar of daisies Lars had gathered alongside the dirt road. She rolled over, facing the wall. Papa had promised they'd be together soon. But when was "soon"? Two months, two years? *When, Papa?* They should never have left Isfjorden—no matter how bad things had seemed; they should have stayed together as a family.

Marit curled into a tight ball and finally slept.

"Frokost!" Aunt Ingeborg called upstairs, as she did every morning. Marit jumped up, emerging from a dream of searching for her parents amid bomb-shelled buildings, and bumped her head on the slanted ceiling. *"Uff da!"*

With a groan, she dragged herself out of bed. The sun was higher than usual. "Oh, no." By now, Big Olga's udder would be painfully full.

Lars's rumpled hair—the color of *kaffe* with cream—stuck out from under the fluffy *dyne*.

"Lars, get up. Don't keep Aunt Ingeborg waiting."

No sooner had the words left her tongue than the *dyne* flew off the bed. As Lars's feet hit the wooden floor, Marit hurried ahead down the steep stairs into the yeast-scented kitchen. She braced herself for her aunt's scolding, although the worst kind of scolding was Bestefar's stony silence.

Aunt Ingeborg turned away from her bread dough and wiped her flour-dusted hands on her apron. Her fingernails were trimmed short, her forearms covered with sun-bleached hairs and sprinkled with freckles from hours in the gardens. She pushed golden strands back into her tightly woven bun, then humphed.

"I thought you were going to sleep forever. The sun's halfway through its chores already, as you two should be." She had the same sterling blue eyes as Mama—only

Mama's eyes were glistening water, and Aunt Ingeborg's were melting ice.

At the back door, Marit pulled on her boots. "I'm sorry . . ." she began. "I'm going right now."

"No, I already took care of the milking. Boots off." Aunt Ingeborg patted Marit's shoulder and steered her to a chair at the table. It was set with plates of cheese, herring, bread, strawberry jam, and hard-boiled eggs and a pitcher of buttermilk. "Besides, you needed extra sleep. A girl of ten shouldn't have such dark circles."

"*Takk*. Tomorrow—I promise—I'll be up earlier."

"Tomorrow, *ja*, but today I need you two to pick rhubarb."

"For pie?" Lars asked, his dimples deepening in his rounded cheeks.

"And jam. I hope to trade some for flour and a little coffee. Now, bow your heads."

Later, they headed outside. Alongside the red barn, trimmed white like every door and window frame of her grandfather's goldenrod house, they found rhubarb leaves as big as elephant's ears. In the land of the midnight sun, the long hours of daylight helped crops grow fast—and large.

"Remember, Lars," Marit said, "pull them out like this." Without breaking its stem, she pulled on a long rhubarb stalk until it slipped free.

"I *know*, Marit," Lars said, shaking his head. "I heard

what Aunt Ingeborg said. You don't always have to tell me what to do, just because you're older." His bangs hung nearly into his eyes; Mama would have trimmed his hair weeks ago.

Marit put her hand on his shoulder. "I know you're smart. You finished grade one already."

Lars lowered his head.

"Well, maybe you didn't *finish* grade one, but close enough."

"See?" he said. "You said I didn't finish."

"Don't worry—we'll start school in the fall and you'll be in grade two."

He was two heads shorter, but sturdy. The island was a good place for him, and Aunt Ingeborg's cooking had helped ease the stomachaches he'd had when they first arrived.

Some things were the same. Her brother. Aunt Ingeborg and Bestefar. Three cows swishing their tails in the pasture. The island smells of kelp, fish, and salt water. Cries of seagulls and kittiwakes. Wooden trawlers and smaller fishing boats bobbing on a soft chop. The fairyland city of Ålesund across the harbor with its towers and turrets—or at least what was left of it. But when sirens rang across the water, the sound of bombs falling in Ålesund often followed.

She turned away and joined Lars in picking more rhubarb. Soon a pile of green leaves and red stalks reached Marit's knees. They brought their harvest to the back steps, cut off the stems, and threw the leaves behind the barn.

"Just enough sugar left to bake pies," Aunt Ingeborg said as they carried the ruby red stems into her tidy kitchen. "After this, I don't know when we'll see sugar again."

CHAPTER FOUR

Refugee

That afternoon—as they had every Monday, Wednesday, and Saturday since they'd arrived—Marit and Lars hiked the dirt road to the fishing wharf. They paused by the first boathouse, where a new propaganda poster had been tacked up overnight. The illustration showed a blond Norwegian and a blond German shaking hands, with *"Alt for Norge!"* written above it.

"Don't believe it," she told Lars. "*All for Norway* is a lie."

Such posters often combined Nazi swastikas with Viking boats and heroic characters, as if the Germans could convince Norwegians that the two countries were destined to merge. Norwegians regularly ripped down the pro-Nazi posters at night, but in the mornings, German soldiers tacked them back up again.

Beneath the gaze of Godøy Mountain, Marit and Lars walked on. They passed several island farms—narrow strips of land that stretched like piano keys to the shore. Fjord horses dotted a few pastures; more ponies than horses, their thick manes and golden coats caught the morning sunlight as they grazed.

Along the way, Marit's mind raced with worry that a letter from Mama and Papa might—or might not—arrive. At least there was one bright spot: her new friend, Hanna.

The day they'd first met, Marit had been waiting on the pier with other islanders for the mail boat to arrive. Someone had tapped Marit on her shoulder and asked, "Where are *you* from?" Marit turned to discover a girl her own height, with shiny dark hair and a smile that revealed a slice of air between her front teeth.

"Isfjorden," Marit replied.

"My name's Hanna Brottem. What's yours?"

"Marit Gundersen. I'm staying with my grandfather, Leif Halversen, and my aunt Ingeborg."

"You mean Miss Halversen. She's going to be my teacher next fall."

"Really? Oh, and this is my brother, Lars."

Lars glanced away shyly, but his dimples deepened. *"Hei,"* he said, without meeting Hanna's eyes.

Hanna told Marit about her family's new baby and two-year-old sister she looked after every day while her mother worked at the hospital in Ålesund. She pointed to a nearby red clapboard home facing the ocean. And Marit told Hanna about being bombed, how their cookstove had been blown partway through their kitchen wall, and how they hadn't been able to return home yet. That she wondered every day if her parents were all right.

"That's terrible," Hanna said. "Much worse than no flour or sugar."

"A lot worse."

Hanna's eyebrows bunched over her tiny nose. "Then . . . you're *refugees*."

Refugees. The word had an edge to it, like a fence meant to divide those who belong from those who do not. Marit wasn't sure if this girl was making fun of her. What had she meant exactly? She bristled. *"Ja.* I guess so."

Hanna touched her arm lightly. "That must be hard— to be separated like that from your home and parents."

Marit could only nod. Whatever doubts Marit had about Hanna instantly vanished. She knew she'd made a good friend.

As they waited for the mail boat to pull alongside the dock, Marit tapped her foot impatiently. Lars held

Marit's hand, and she let him. His small hand reminded her that he was only seven. Even at ten, she was having a terrible time being separated from Mama and Papa. More than once, she'd woken up from the same nightmare. Always, she was on a ship with her family and they were crossing the ocean, when out of nowhere, the legendary sea monster—the *kraken*—reached its terrible tentacles and suction cups around the ship and to the very top of the mast. Part crab, part octopus, it was enormous, and it finally found what it was looking for—Mama and Papa. It wrapped its slimy arms around their bodies and pulled them toward its pinching mouth, then sank out of sight, leaving a whirlpool behind. Marit clung to Lars as the ship twirled in dizzying circles, sucked slowly downward toward the bottom of the sea. That's when she usually woke up—terrified and sobbing.

"*Hei*, Marit!" Hanna ran toward them, her braids whipping in the breeze. Marit dropped Lars's hand. "Hanna!"

Soon after, the mail boat pulled up to the main dock.

"What do you have for us today?" called Mr. Larsen, grabbing a line and tying it off. Owner of the general store, with a head of short sandy curls and matching beard, he was taller than most men on the island.

"The usual," replied the captain. He tossed the leather mailbag to Mr. Larsen as a handful of passengers disembarked.

"Do you have a letter from the Gundersens?" Marit asked Mr. Larsen, following him step by step to his shop.

"Same answer, Marit. You'll have to wait—along with everyone else."

A new sign in the window stated: *Out of potatoes. Don't know when we'll get them.*

Inside, the shop's shelves of food, household, and farm supplies seemed to dwindle every day. Mr. Larsen stood behind his counter and began pulling letters and parcels from the leather bag. Villagers crowded around. "Ivarsen!" he called out.

"Here!" A young woman scurried forward, hand up.

"Riste."

"Over here." Marit recognized the fisherman who held his pipe in the air. He was a friend of Bestefar's.

With each name that Mr. Larsen called, Marit's dread grew that they would *never* get a letter, *never* again see Mama and Papa. To again hear nothing, to walk back along the road empty-handed, to be passed by truck-loads of German soldiers . . . A stone lodged in her throat and she chewed the inside of her lip to keep from crying. If she started, she'd never stop.

Hanna elbowed her. "Marit—he called Halversen. Raise your hand."

Marit shot her hand up and hurried forward. She suddenly couldn't speak.

Mr. Larsen looked over her head, waving the letter high. "Halversen?"

"Here!" She waved her arm back and forth.

Suddenly, the chatter in the shop died away as Mr. Larsen turned toward the window, the letter frozen in his hand. Everyone followed his gaze. Outside, a German officer dismounted from his bay horse, its coat as glossy as its rider's long black boots. When the Germans had arrived, they'd brought their own horses with them.

The officer stepped inside and frowned, as if he'd caught a group of children doing something wrong. "Too many," he said in halting Norwegian, his nose bent slightly at the bridge. He waved his arm through the air as if clearing unwelcome cobwebs. "A secret meeting?"

Mr. Larsen spoke up, waving the letter. "I was just handing out the mail. You see? This one goes to the Halversens." He pointed to Marit. "Marit and her brother are grandchildren of Leif Halversen."

The German studied Marit.

She held herself back from leaping for the letter like a starving dog after a food scrap. She kept calm—controlling herself—as if the letter meant nothing to her at all. But she had already noticed the handwriting. It was Mama's!

The officer took the letter from Mr. Larsen's hand and placed it in Marit's. "There you go, *Fräulein*."

She would rather spit in his hand than take anything from him, but she couldn't refuse the letter. It burned between her fingers. She wanted to rip it open, but instead she waited for the officer to leave. As soon as he was outside and turned his tall, ebony horse toward the street, Marit hurried to the door, with Hanna and Lars right behind her.

Once outside, she studied the letter.

"Is it from your parents?" Hanna asked.

"*Nei*. I mean, the return address says Siversen, not Gundersen. But the handwriting. Something's not right. I'm sure this is my mother's."

"Hanna! Marit!" came a familiar voice. The girls looked up from the envelope. Olaf, a year older and a friend of Hanna's, hurried from the docks toward them, all smiles. In his arms he carried a shaggy pup. The dog's eyes were mismatched—one was blue, the other brown—and its pink tongue lapped relentlessly at Olaf's face. "Look what my father brought back for me from Ålesund! It's a husky—the kind that pulls sleds."

He set the wiggly puppy down on the side of the road and combed the pup's thick fur with his fingers. The puppy's tail curved over its back. "He's going to be a fine dog, don't you think? And big. Just look at his paws."

The puppy was cute, but Marit could only think of the letter and getting home so she could read it with Aunt Ingeborg. "C'mon, Lars. We have to go."

But Lars dropped to his knees and hugged the puppy's neck. He was always quick to fall in love with animals. "*Hei*, little puppy—"

"What are you going to name him?" Hanna asked, squatting down alongside Lars.

Olaf's eyes flickered with mischief. "I was thinking of calling him Marit."

"*Nei!*" Marit tried to pretend outrage, but she knew Olaf was teasing.

"Actually, I'm thinking of calling him Kaptain."

"I like that," Hanna said.

At that moment, nothing besides the letter mattered. "Lars," she said, "we need to get back." She sounded as firm as Aunt Ingeborg and pulled him to his feet. "I'm sure we'll see Kaptain again soon. We have chores."

"Marit . . . but—"

"Now!" She nearly ran all the way home, but had to keep stopping along the road to wait for Lars to catch up. Past the school building, boathouses, and pastures, they followed the road as it curved northeast. As they turned down the dirt drive and raced past the barn, the goats lifted their heads in question.

Aunt Ingeborg met Marit on the doorstep. "Marit—what is it? What's the matter?"

Out of breath, Marit handed her the letter and stepped in. Aunt Ingeborg sat down at the kitchen table and stared at the letter in her hands.

"It's Mama's writing, isn't it?" Marit said.

Aunt Ingeborg nodded. "Sure looks like it, but . . ."

For what seemed like a decade, Aunt Ingeborg held the letter, and then she set it on the woven table runner. "We'll read it when Bestefar returns."

"But—" Marit started to protest.

"Bestefar will be home soon." Aunt Ingeborg set her jaw, as she often did when asked questions that were too personal or important.

"But I can't wait!" Marit said.

"You have to." And with that, Marit knew the discussion was over.

The cookstove and counter boasted jars and jars of rhubarb-strawberry jam and four pies with lightly browned edges, which Marit had shaped with her thumb and forefingers before they'd left to meet the mail boat. Aunt Ingeborg hung up her apron.

"*Tusen takk,* you two. Your mother would be proud of you for all your help today. Let's put all this away to keep busy until Bestefar comes home."

Finally, the door rattled and Bestefar stepped in, his face etched from the wind and sun. Before Marit could reach for the letter, Aunt Ingeborg grabbed it from the table. "It looks like Kirsten's writing."

Bestefar studied the print, and they followed him as he settled on the back steps. He read the letter aloud.

It was from his "old friend Mrs. Siversen," whose house had been bombed and who was working with her husband in the mountains.

> *We're keeping in touch with our new friends and working hard these days. We think of you always and hope you understand our need to work toward the best country possible for our children.*

"It's like a message in code," Marit said. "It's Mama, for sure, and Papa, but they don't want to use their real names. And the British—those must be the 'new friends.' The mountains must mean up at the *hytte*, or somewhere away from Isfjorden. And the children—that's me and Lars."

As Bestefar sat reading, Aunt Ingeborg stood aside; they maintained their usual distance from each other. "Marit and Lars," Bestefar said, "you must not say a word about this letter to anyone."

"But why? I don't understand why—"

"Marit." Bestefar's brows hooded his eyes like an owl's. "It's dangerous. The Nazis are opening mail before it reaches its rightful owner. If anyone involved in Resistance activities is caught . . . well, I don't expect you to understand."

She crossed her arms against her chest—and against

him. He treated her worse than he treated his farm animals. At least he talked to them. She was a smart, hardworking student, yet he spoke to her only when he had to, as if she didn't have a brain in her head.

A gray goat wandered over to the back steps. Lars grabbed a curved horn and scratched the tuft of fur beneath the goat's chin. "The letter means they're all right," he said.

This time, her little brother had been quicker to grasp the heart of things.

"That's right, Lars," Bestefar said.

Aunt Ingeborg smiled faintly, clasped her hands beneath her chin, and whispered, "Thank God they're alive."

CHAPTER FIVE

Turmoil on the Sea

The next morning, after milking, Marit let Big Olga out to pasture. As soon as Lars finished scattering feed for the chickens, they joined Aunt Ingeborg and Bestefar for coffee and a heart-shaped *vaffel* with a dab of jam. Marit loved coffee with lots and lots of cream and sugar, but now with shortages, she stirred only a spoonful of milk in hot water instead.

They couldn't afford to waste a crumb or drop of anything. In cities, even eggs and milk were hard to come by. At least on the farm, they could produce much of their own food.

The familiar rumble of a wood-fired German truck

engine rolled into the farmyard. Marit hated these visits the Germans made to collect their "daily donation."

Bestefar snorted, cup in hand. "*Ja*—produce for the Germans. They get fed first from Norway's food supply. We get the crumbs." Bestefar pushed back his chair. "Stay inside."

Marit jumped from her chair to the window. From the back of the canvas-topped truck, a soldier, not much older than a schoolboy, hopped out. He straightened his *jakke* and touched the gun in his holster. He spoke a word or two to Bestefar, who disappeared into the barn and returned with two baskets of produce.

Like a fog suddenly lifting, Marit's sense of caution evaporated. She bolted toward the door, turned the handle, and bravely stepped out.

"Marit," Aunt Ingeborg scolded, "what are you doing?"

But Marit was already closing the door behind her and walking straight toward Bestefar, who held out a basket full of strawberries and lettuce to the soldier. He tossed her a warning glance. The soldier waited as Bestefar went back into the barn.

Marit's feet became rocks. She was standing alone with the soldier, something she hadn't intended. Through his wire rims, he studied her. "Have you a name, *Fräulein*?"

She stared at the ground.

"You needn't be afraid," he said. "We're not monsters."

Nei, she screamed inside, *you're worse than monsters!*

Seconds seemed to expand into hours, and to her relief, Bestefar returned, this time lugging a basket of brown eggs and a milk can.

"Is that all?" the young soldier demanded, as if he were suddenly ruler and king. How dare he come and demand food, then act as if their hard-gathered donations weren't enough! She glared at the soldier.

"I'm a fisherman-farmer," Bestefar said evenly. "We have only a few chickens, goats, and cows—and only one milking cow."

"We ask the animals to speed up their production," Marit added with an exaggerated shrug, "but they just continue at their same slow pace." Then she shook her head side to side and kept a straight face, just the way Papa would after making a joke. Inside, she felt boldly triumphant.

Bestefar froze. Only his fingertips twitched at his sides.

The soldier glared at her, then turned on his heels and strode to his supply truck with the goods. He returned with empty baskets and an empty milk can to be filled again on his next visit. Then he jumped in the truck, rapped his knuckles on the door panel, and the vehicle rumbled on to the next fisherman's farm.

Marit waited, her shoulders tensed toward her ears.

"Marit!" Bestefar's voice carried the sting of a wasp. He pointed toward the empty road. "What in God's good heaven were you thinking? You could have been arrested and hauled away. Never, *ever* do that again! I told you to stay inside. You're not to speak a word to them. Such joking could get you—and all of us—in trouble."

Bombs had fallen on her village. The smell of smoke over Isfjorden had lingered for days. She had been separated for so long from Mama and Papa. The Germans were the cause of all of it. Yet Bestefar gave the Nazis everything they asked for. He almost made it *easy* for them.

"Walk with me," Bestefar ordered and headed into the pasture. Marit followed reluctantly, picking her path carefully between the cowpies. Grazing along the distant fence, Big Olga lifted her head and stared at them, chewing her cud. Finally, Bestefar stopped beside a large boulder that jutted out of the middle of the field. "Sit down."

She sat cross-legged on the sun-warmed, ancient boulder, her feet dangling. Bestefar clasped his hands behind his back. Marit followed his gaze. The field sloped and ended in a peninsula; from there, the breakwater extended to the lighthouse.

"In Oslo," he said, his voice low and matter-of-fact, "some young men bombed a bridge between the city and the airport. They thought they were hurting the Germans, but what did the Germans do? They posted threats. Anyone connected with the destruction of the bridge would be executed. Not only that, they warned that the local people would suffer as well." He paused. "It makes no sense to have a whole town suffer for the acts of a few." He turned and looked at her. "Do you see how complicated it gets?"

She couldn't believe he was actually speaking to her. She didn't know if he wanted an answer or not, but she gathered her courage. "But Bestefar, if no one fights back, the Germans will be here *forever!*"

"Perhaps it's better to keep the peace, no matter what, and not put family and friends in danger. We're a peace-loving, neutral country. We've stayed out of wars for many years and we need to stay out of this one, too."

She'd heard that kind of thinking before.

"No good can come of getting involved," he went on. "The Germans will respect our neutrality, you'll see. They're at war with the Allied countries, not with us. They want access to our coastlines, nothing more."

She didn't believe that for a second. Memories of whistling bombs pressed in on her, and she clasped her arms around her waist. Maybe Bestefar was living in a dream. *His* island, *his* home, hadn't been bombed. "And what about Mama and Papa?" she said. "They would rather be with us here, but they're staying in Isfjorden to help the British fight against the Nazis. Should they 'stay out'?"

Bestefar returned his gaze toward the lighthouse where the soldiers kept a constant guard. "Your father has always been a dreamer, Marit. An idealist. He's putting his life and your mother's in danger. It's folly, pure and simple. He's a fool."

Papa a fool? Nothing could be further from the truth. How could Bestefar say such things? *"Nei!"* she said, speaking to his back. "He's brave and so is Mama. At least they're doing *something!*"

Bestefar was silent; his fisherman's sweater rose and fell with his breaths as he looked off to sea.

Without a word or his permission to leave, Marit jumped off the boulder and ran back across the pasture, her throat on fire with all the things she wished she could say.

Chapter Six

The Lighthouse

Boathouses lined the harbor, their slate roofs matching the grayish blue sea. At the last boathouse, Bestefar was bent over nets and glass floats on the dock. After their morning argument, Marit didn't care to talk with him again, but Lars had asked if they could take out the rowboat. And rowing would help clear her mind.

The pea-pod-shaped rowboat was pulled up on shore. Marit ran her hand along the weathered gunwale. The blue seats were in need of painting soon. The ribs of the boat needed a coat of varnish. Still, the memory of rowing with her mother gave her a sharp pang. Mama had taught her to row when Marit was only five years old. They'd pretended they were floating on the water in the belly of a whale, and that she and her mother were, like Jonah from the Bible story, ready to be spat out onto the sands of a new land. And that's exactly how Marit now felt on this isolated island.

She inhaled the sea-scented air. She wanted to take out the boat—to get away, if only a short distance. But would Bestefar let her? Mama had once explained that long before Marit was born they'd lost Karsten—her mother's and aunt's younger brother—when he was swimming and pulled out by a tide. "Since then," Mama had explained, "Bestefar's been worried about children and water. First he lost Karsten and later your grandmother took ill. Sometimes life is too hard."

"Bestefar, may we take out the rowboat?" she called as sweetly as she could muster.

He lifted his head and didn't answer.

"I used to row with Mama, remember?"

Bestefar dropped his net and crossed his arms. His eyebrows gathered in watchfulness. He opened his mouth.

Before he could say no, she added, "We'll stay close to the shore and not go far. Promise."

He shook his head. "I'm afraid not. There are explosives—floating mines—in the channels."

Marit stood still, her hand stopped on the boat's bow.

"Bestefar," Lars called in his singsong voice. "Please? We'll stay close. We won't go far."

Marit glanced at Bestefar. *Unbelievable!* Lars's dimply

smile softened up Bestefar's stern face every time. That Lars was his favorite was more than obvious.

Bestefar looked to the water, as if considering the sun glinting off the softly rippled surface. "Well, it's a calm day, and if you stay close to shore, between here and the lighthouse, where I can see you . . . within sight! Marit, you're in charge."

Favorite or not, she smiled. Soon, she was straining her muscles against the oars as their rowboat furrowed through water.

From the stern seat, Lars faced Marit. With her back to the bow, she rowed, glancing occasionally over her shoulder to make sure she was staying on the course she intended. It would be easier if she could face forward and see where she was going, but rowboats didn't work best that way.

"Marit, look!" Lars pointed over the edge of the rowboat. "A jellyfish! A bluish green one."

"Don't touch it."

"I know, you don't have to tell me."

Jellyfish always reminded her of pulsing raw yolks, and Marit did her best to avoid them if they floated up onshore. She didn't want to get stung.

She leaned forward, oar handles meeting close, then pulled back hard, elbows out, back muscles flexing. Shimmery jewels dropped from the tips of the oars as they swept across the water. Over and over, Marit sliced into the ocean current, losing herself in the rhythm and occasionally glancing over her shoulder toward the lighthouse. For the first time in months she felt a little like her old self: without a care and ready for adventure. She strained against the oars while Lars faced her from the stern, smiling and humming.

She rowed past farms and toward the lighthouse and peninsula that marked the tip of their pastureland. When she used to row with Mama, they'd stop near the lighthouse at the cove to explore what the tide had left behind. Easing up on the oars, Marit let the boat glide forward onto the gravel shore. She hopped out and pulled the boat up higher on the beach; Lars stumbled out after her.

At the end of the breakwater, three soldiers manned the base of the lighthouse. Marit grabbed Lars's hand, trying to pretend this was like all the other summers— the summers before swarms of gray-green uniforms had descended on the island. With guns angled over their shoulders, the soldiers watched them.

"Remember the time we found that old chain?" she asked Lars.

"From the Vikings, right Marit?"

"Of course!" It was kinder to go along with his imagination. She doubted the chain they'd found was that old.

She knew the soldiers were watching them. She felt

their cold, constant presence—their eyes on every movement. In past summers, when her family had visited, she
and Lars always ran straight to the shoreline and
combed it for treasures. Once she found a small blue
bottle. When she poured out the seawater, a tiny crab
slipped out of its shelter. The bottle sat on her bedroom
shelf along with seashells she'd collected over the years.
She hoped it would all still be there when she returned
home.

Lars trailed her as she walked along the shoreline. At
the water's edge, a slick black film covered several pieces
of lumber and sticks. The smell was pungent, not the
natural odor of kelp, but of bombs and fuel.

"Marit, what's that slimy stuff?"

"Hitler's hair tonic."

"What's that?"

Some jokes were lost on little kids. "Oh, skip it. There
must have been an oil leak from a ship recently bombed
at sea."

A few meters away, a small mound moved amid the
seaweed.

"What's that?" Lars asked.

She picked her way closer. "Let's have a look."

Lars hung back. "Marit, maybe it's something poison-
ous."

A month earlier, when she'd walked from the pasture
to the shore, she'd found two dead birds—a puffin and a

cormorant. The same black deadly slime had coated their wings. She'd asked Bestefar and he'd said there was nothing they could do. He also explained that the Germans expected the Allied forces to invade along the coast, so they bombed any ship or fishing boat that looked suspicious, leaving fuel on the water. The Germans were shipping iron ore from Narvik in the north to keep their war across Europe supplied with steel. To foil the German efforts, the British also planted mines in the harbors to blow up German vessels. "Everyone," he'd said, "seems interested in our coast."

Marit squatted beside the barely stirring mound. "Oh . . ." Her heart broke. "It's a seal pup!"

The seal wasn't much bigger than a small dog, and it barked weakly, and then made a whimpering, mewling sound.

"We have to help it," Lars said.

The seal pup's coat was black with oil. Its whole face, even its eyes, were filmy. "Run across the pasture to the barn and grab an old blanket . . . there's a moth-eaten one in the loft. Bring that one . . . and I'll wait here. We'll wrap it up and carry it back to the barn. Maybe we can help."

But deep inside, Marit had her doubts.

Lars tore across the pasture.

Left alone with the seal pup, Marit talked to it softly for several minutes. She reached closer and gingerly touched the seal's fur. A sticky black layer clung to her fingertips. She shook her head. "Poor *vesla*."

"Poor 'little one'?" A deep voice startled her. "What have you found there?"

Marit jumped to her feet.

A lanky soldier with eyes as blue as Mama's stared down at her. How could the enemy look so much like a Norwegian? Around his waist, a leather belt was cinched tightly over his gray-green *jakke*. Along his chest a row of metal buttons sparkled, and above the top right pocket a metal eagle spread its wings.

She lowered her gaze to the seal pup. As angry as she was at Bestefar, she still reminded herself about his warning not to speak to the Germans.

The soldier bent closer and nudged the seal with the toe of his leather boot. The pup whimpered. "Ah, it's not only people who suffer. War has many unexpected casualties."

His manner was official, but beneath the uniform she sensed a human being, if that was possible. Then just as suddenly, he stiffened, as if he just remembered that he was in uniform, and adjusted the rifle on his shoulder. "And what are you doing here on the shore?"

She didn't answer, but glanced back toward Godøy Mountain, a backdrop of lush green that towered above the island's small farms and her grandparents' farmhouse and barn. In the distance across the vibrant green pasture, Aunt Ingeborg hung clothes on the line and seemed to be looking toward them, surely worried.

"You Norwegians. Can't speak a word, can you?"

Like a mountain goat, Lars suddenly sprang over the pasture's edge and onto the rocky shoreline.

"*Halt!*" the soldier shouted, spinning in Lars's direction and drawing the revolver out of his holster.

"*Nei!*" Marit cried.

"Oh, oh." Lars held out the navy wool blanket and froze. His eyes opened wide at the sight of the revolver pointed at him.

"I see you two can speak," the soldier said. Then he pivoted and aimed his gun at the seal pup. "It will die soon enough," he said. "Better to put it out of its misery."

"Please," she begged.

The soldier stepped closer and knelt beside the pup. Marit covered her eyes, bracing herself for the inevitable. Lars began to cry.

Then the soldier stood up and stepped back. "It's dead already. I don't need to waste ammunition." He motioned to Lars with his gun. "You. We need the blanket. It's cold at night. Bring it here," he commanded.

Marit had heard that soldiers often entered houses and "borrowed" whatever they needed. She had a better word for it. *Stealing.*

Lars's lips moved, but nothing came out. He had

frozen in place. The soldier stepped from one boulder to the next until he reached him. He took the blanket from Lars's arms, and then ambled along the breakwater to the lighthouse.

Before anything worse could happen, Marit pushed the rowboat back into the water and motioned for Lars to get in—and quickly. Halfway back to the pier, she stopped rowing and glanced back.

A line of black cormorants flew in formation over the peninsula. Seagulls filled the air with screeching as they circled and landed where the seal pup lay onshore. And in the distance, the soldiers kept a steady watch on the water.

CHAPTER SEVEN

Windblown

Marit passed the summer days by scrubbing floors; feeding the goats; cleaning out every corner of the barn; gathering blueberries, lingonberries, and raspberries; and carding wool from neighbors' sheep, which Aunt Ingeborg earned in trade for jars of jam. Only at the general store on mail delivery days did Marit have free time to see Hanna and Olaf, and Kaptain, his growing puppy.

Evenings, they gathered in the kitchen around the radio. Norway's radio station now broadcast only German propaganda. The only news worth listening to was the British airwaves—the BBC. Even though the Nazis forbade listening to it, everyone did. Marit learned that King Haakon had fled the country and was in exile in

London. She was relieved he was safe, but that meant the Germans were now unquestionably in control. What did this mean for Mama and Papa?

Names that had meant nothing to her before now made her shiver. Terboven was one. Vidkun Quisling was the other.

"Quisling—that traitor!" Bestefar nearly spat. "A Norwegian Nazi! How dare he declare that resisting German troops is a crime? He's nothing more than a puppet of the Germans—with Terboven pulling the strings." He mimed a puppeteer pulling strings. "Look at him dance. He thinks he's so clever."

Marit heard speeches by Winston Churchill, England's leader, and by their own exiled king. On the BBC, King Haakon told Norwegians to stand strong and never to give up. His words were immediately printed on illegal presses and spread secretly across Norway.

One day she found a flyer on the road, blown about by the wind, and she read the king's own words over and over:

The Norwegian people's freedom and independence is the first command of Norway's Law, and I will follow this commandment . . . the duty given to me by a free people.

Marit tucked the flyer in her blouse, as if the words were life itself. When a truckload of soldiers approached, the flyer burned against her skin as she pretended casually to pluck and eat the wild lingonberries and raspberries along the roadside. With the truck's gritty dust in her mouth, she ran back straight to the barn.

She passed Big Olga's empty stanchion and climbed the wooden ladder to the hayloft. Flecks of chaff floated in the ray of light from the open loft door. The gray tabby barn cat lay on her side in the corner, nursing five kittens in the straw, her eyes closed as if she didn't know Marit was there.

Marit pulled the flyer out. Such valuable words—words someone had risked his or her life to print and circulate. She couldn't toss them away. She found the loose board, pulled it from its base, and added the king's words to a few shells she'd stashed there years earlier.

The cat opened one eye, watched her, and then closed it again.

A strange mixture of guilt and pride welled in her.

"You saw nothing," Marit said to the cat, which ignored her anyway.

Symbols started to appear around the island. Marit found them scratched in dirt on the road, other times painted over a German sign. The most common symbol was a large *V*, with an *H* in its middle, and a *7* in the middle of that: *Victory for King Haakon VII*. Other times, she found the words "Long live the king" carved or written on road posts and trail posts.

Marit started to wear a paper clip on her collar, just as she had seen others do at the general store. When Aunt Ingeborg asked why she was wearing it, Marit answered, "Mr. Larsen said it's our way of saying 'Let's stick together.'" After that, Aunt Ingeborg started wearing a paper clip, too.

One evening, as they sat listening to the radio, Lars was playing on the living room floor with a tabby barn kitten. "Just for a little bit," he promised, since Aunt Ingeborg refused to keep a cat in the house as a pet. He broke into giggles as the amber tabby pounced on the ball of yarn hidden in the crook of his arm.

Marit watched Lars and wished she could forget about the war as easily.

"What shall I name you?" Lars laughed. The kitten reared back in mock combat, then dashed at the ball of yarn again with his front paws. Lars shrieked with laughter. "You think you're tough, but you're small enough to fit in a teacup!" And it didn't take long before Tekopp, as Lars named him, became a house cat.

One evening, Aunt Ingeborg held a rucksack out to Marit. "Would you bring this to the pier? Bestefar is having engine trouble and he may not make it back for dinner. A little kindness will do him good."

Marit studied her feet rather than meet her aunt's eyes. She was reluctant to do Bestefar a favor.

"Marit, I know you and Bestefar don't always agree on things. But he's a good man. I hope you know that. He's extra busy now that the cod season has started. And with the occupation—nothing is normal. Everyone is affected."

For her aunt, she would do anything.

Cheerlessly, Marit crossed the wooden plank to Bestefar's trawler. Harbor currents jostled the boat, even though it was tied up securely with three ropes.

Hands in leather gloves, Bestefar was hammering a poster beside the door of his boat's wheelhouse. He glanced at the bundle she held out to him and nodded.

Marit stepped closer and read the poster aloud. "You shall not in any way give shelter to or aid the enemy. To do so is punishable by death."

"What's that about?"

"Another warning."

With disgust, she watched him hammer the last corner of the poster. Nazis forced their way into their country, and his response was to do everything they demanded. "Bestefar," she asked, her voice shaking with anger, "it says you can't aid the enemy. But *who* is the enemy?"

He avoided her eyes and whispered through dry lips. "Marit, I don't expect you to understand. You're young. If I don't post this, my boat will be confiscated."

"They'd take your boat just because you didn't post the warning?"

He nodded.

"But if every fisherman refused to post it, then the Nazis would have to take every boat . . ."

He studied her.

". . . And soon they'd realize that there weren't any fish coming in to feed their armies. They'd have to let you go back to fishing then, wouldn't they?"

"It's not that simple," he said.

"Bestefar, you didn't even hear me." She'd never spoken so disrespectfully to her elders before. But how could she respect him when he had less backbone than a jellyfish? He made her want to spit on the floor of his deck. "What will they want next? That all the fish you catch raise their little fins and say 'Heil Hitler'?"

He didn't laugh.

And she wasn't joking.

Bestefar's face reddened as he raised one white eyebrow. "Enough. You have spunk, Marit. But remember"—he glanced toward the other boats tied up, as if to see if other fishermen were listening—"you *must* hold your tongue and keep your thoughts to yourself. Do you want something to happen to your brother, your aunt—do you?"

She stormed off his boat deck, knocking a bucket of salt water over in her wake.

Chapter Eight

The *Bunad*

When late-August mornings brought shivers, and yellowing birch leaves signaled the start of school, Marit made up her mind. She had to speak with Aunt Ingeborg. She and Lars had stayed on the island long enough. She refused—absolutely refused—to remain apart from her parents any longer.

Seated at her treadle sewing machine, Aunt Ingeborg worked the foot pedal. The little black machine with small painted flowers stitched rapidly through swaths of black fabric. Already hand-embroidered on the fabric were designs in threads as bright as flowering nasturtiums. Aunt Ingeborg bowed her head over the cloth, her fine eyebrows knit in concentration.

"Aunt Ingeborg, I'm sorry to bother you, but—"

"Good thing I bought all this fabric before the invasion. I've had in mind to start on a *bunad* for you, just as your grandmother did for me and for your mother."

Marit had always looked forward to wearing a *bunad,* the colorfully embroidered black wool vest and skirt with a white blouse worn at confirmation and on special occasions. Boys wore embroidered vests and knickers. Since she could remember she'd looked forward to the tradition. "Thank you, but . . ." Marit said sadly, "but I won't be staying that long."

The entry door creaked and footsteps fell in the kitchen. Bestefar peered into the living room.

"Ingeborg!" he scolded.

The whir of the sewing machine stopped.

"You know the *bunad* is forbidden."

Aunt Ingeborg sat straighter, lifted her chin, and turned to look at him. "In public, Papa, *ja,*" she said, "but those Nazis don't need to see everything we do or wear in private." Her gaze was steady. "Now do they?"

"You could be arrested," he said. "All of us could be."

Her grandfather and aunt stared at each other. Marit knew well enough to keep her mouth shut. The window curtains fluttered in the breeze. Lilting cries of seagulls filtered in with the low mooing of cows.

Then Aunt Ingeborg snapped her gaze away. Her sewing machine began whirring at a feverish pitch. They continued their disagreement the way they usually did—in silence. Marit would rather they kept talking through their differences—the way Mama and Papa did—until they came to some kind of understanding.

"Ingeborg," he said, "I *insist* that you stop work on that. You must hide it or burn it." His fingers tapped at the outer seams of his trousers.

Aunt Ingeborg tucked in wisps of hair at her temple, her chest rising and falling with deep breaths, and said firmly, *"Nei."*

His face reddening, Bestefar shoved his hands in his trouser pockets, took them out again, then turned and went back outside with a huff.

Working her foot pedal into a pleasant whirring, Aunt Ingeborg continued sewing. Marit was amazed that she'd stood up to Bestefar. But more than that, her aunt, in her own way, was standing up to the Germans, too.

Moments passed in silence, then Marit finally remembered the reason she had needed to talk with Aunt Ingeborg. "School's going to start soon, Aunt Ingeborg. Lars and I *need* to return to Isfjorden."

Aunt Ingeborg, two pins held lightly between her teeth, repinned a seam, finished, then looked at Marit with a slow shake of her head. "I don't think you'll return soon."

"But—"

"Marit, your mother and father would have written to tell you to come back by now. It must not be safe."

Marit felt herself crumbling over this—these few words from her aunt that represented so much more. Tears formed at the corners of her eyes. She'd thought that growing up was about being responsible and in control. Now when she wanted things to be different, she had *no* control at all. "We must go to school here, then?" she whispered.

Aunt Ingeborg nodded. "Folks have decided that students will meet at the church building. Church will be held there on Sunday, school will meet there during the week."

Marit had passed the regular schoolhouse everyday on the way to the pier. A large building, the Godøy School had become home to German soldiers and officers. Signs warned passersby not to gather in numbers outside the building.

Aunt Ingeborg's face turned stern, her blue eyes hard. "Do they think our Norwegian children aren't good enough for schooling? That they can just take over school buildings and toss our children on the street? They make me so—ouch!" A tiny drop of blood appeared on her fingertip. Aunt Ingeborg flashed a quick, determined smile as she held up her pricked finger. "The Nazis—it's all *their* fault."

Aunt Ingeborg laughed at her own joke. *Probably her first,* thought Marit. Then she said, "Oh, and I hope you don't mind, Marit, but I'm to be your teacher."

"I don't mind at all." This news softened the blow of not returning home. "But will I call you Aunt Ingeborg or—"

"At school, call me Miss Halversen. But everywhere else, you and Lars are the only ones in the whole world who can call me Aunt Ingeborg." She reached out and touched Marit's hand. "And I wouldn't give up being your aunt for anything in the whole world."

CHAPTER NINE

Iced Out

In September, the Germans ordered that every window be "blacked out" with dark paper so Allied planes would have a harder time hitting German targets at night. The slightest glimmer of light through a blackened window could lead to a knock on the door by the Gestapo—the dreaded Nazi police force.

By day, under the bell tower of the white octagonal church, Marit joined the other fifty-three students. They went from singing "A Mighty Fortress Is Our God" on Sunday to doing math, reading, and language lessons on Monday. At the island's makeshift school, the youngest children sat in the pews on the right, fourth- through seventh-graders met on the left, and the oldest students gathered in the balcony. Even with the war, each grade had to get through its own *pensum,* a series of required subjects.

At first, the teachers—Miss Halversen, her aunt; Mrs. Hammer, who had an irritating habit of tapping her pencil when she corrected papers; and Mr. Moe, who loved to sing louder than anyone in the upper grade—refused to let students wander through the adjoining cemetery. But as the month passed, their rules slackened.

Miss Halversen wore A-line skirts and cardigan sweaters and always started the day with a beaming smile, as if to lift her students' spirits. The smile and cheeriness were something Marit seldom saw at the farmhouse. When Miss Halversen's students finished their lessons early, she let them play board games, spend time outside, or read books of their own choosing. Marit enjoyed this new side of her aunt, as if she were more herself as a teacher than when she was living in the same house with Bestefar.

One day during free time, when Hanna and Marit were leaning against the apple tree, its ruby fruit hanging heavily, Olaf joined them. He sat cross-legged, took his comb from his pocket, and tried to tame the cowlick above his forehead, though it always twisted stubbornly upward as soon as he tucked away his comb.

"How's Kaptain?" Marit asked.

Up close, Olaf's eyes were as smoky gray as low-hanging clouds. "He's coming along. He loves to outrun me, and I'm teaching him to roll over."

Lars came running toward Marit, fell into her lap dramatically, and cried, "Save me, Marit! Save me!"

Two boys circled, sticks drawn like guns.

"Go on," Marit said, and waved them off. They ran away, and Lars bolted after them—stick in hand—around the church.

Hanna wasn't saying a word. Marit curved toward her and raised her eyebrows. "Hanna, are you still here?"

Her friend nodded, and then looked away at the gravestones.

"What's wrong?" Marit pressed. "We're friends. You can tell us."

Hanna refused to answer.

Marit gave Olaf a shrug.

"So what do you think of school here?" Olaf asked her. "I mean, compared to your school in Isfjorden."

"It's different having school at a church, but it's fine. I really like Miss Halversen." She laughed.

"Since you're her niece, she'll probably be easier on you."

"Or harder."

For a few minutes, they talked. He fidgeted with his leather shoelaces, and before long he said goodbye and walked away.

Marit turned to Hanna, whose eyes followed Olaf as

he left them. "Hanna. That was rude. You acted like you didn't even know Olaf. Why wouldn't you talk to him? It's as if he had head lice. I thought you liked him—as a friend, I mean."

"Ice out," she answered.

"What do you mean, 'ice out'?"

"Guess you haven't heard. We have to ice out Olaf Andersen. His parents are NS—the *Nasjonal Samling,* the Norwegian Nazi Party. Marit, they've *sided* with the Nazis." Her eyes narrowed and she whispered, "His parents handed a Norwegian over to the Germans!"

Olaf's parents? Quisling was a traitor, but Marit couldn't believe that any islander, let alone Olaf's own parents, would join the Nazis and turn in other Norwegians. She shuddered. "I can't understand how they . . . but that doesn't make Olaf . . . he wouldn't do that."

"Maybe. Maybe not. It doesn't matter. If anyone in the family is NS, a 'quisling,' then the whole family gets iced out." She nodded toward the tombstones, where Olaf was wandering alone. "It just happened. Yesterday. My parents told me about it last night. By now, most everyone on the island knows."

A wave of cold swept through Marit's body. What if someone turned Mama or Papa over to the Nazis? How could anyone do such a thing? *Why* would anyone do such a thing? Her heart went out to Olaf, but how could she ever understand his parents? "It's like he's dead then?" she asked. "Treated the way we treat the Germans?"

"Sort of like that."

"Like a dog?"

Hanna huffed. "My papa says we try to treat our dogs *much* better."

It seemed cruel, but if "icing out" was a means of uniting against the Nazis, then Marit had no choice but to take part.

After school that day, outside the church gates, steps sounded behind her and someone tapped her shoulder. She spun around, expecting to see Hanna. It was Olaf. His gray eyes were pleading, and for a moment Marit thought he might start crying.

"Listen, Marit," Olaf said, smoothing his hair back with his hand. "I know what Hanna probably told you, but listen—I'm *not* a Nazi. I'm *not* my parents."

Marit felt sorry for him, but in this war—a war in which *her* parents were risking their lives and *his* parents were turning in Norwegians—there was no middle ground. She grabbed her brother's hand and turned away. "Lars, let's go."

She hurried ahead, and Lars kept glancing back. "Why aren't you talking with Olaf?"

"I'll explain later."

That night, instead of cod stew, which seemed to get thinner each night it was served, Aunt Ingeborg served a feast: fish cakes in brown gravy, boiled potatoes, and small pancakes with jam for dessert. Bestefar spoke about his day's catch of herring, and Aunt Ingeborg talked about how the quality of flour was getting worse.

All Marit could think about was Olaf and the haunting words of the soldier on the shore months earlier.

War has many unexpected casualties.

CHAPTER TEN

If You Breathe

In late September, Marit learned from the radio broadcast that the German leader, Terboven, had stepped in and declared the Norwegian Nazi Party to be the official "New Order" in Norway. There would be no more voting.

One evening, Bestefar brought home a newspaper that was being illegally copied and sent all around the country. Before sharing it, he double-checked to make sure the black paper was tight against all windows.

"If any of us should be asked to trample ideals we cherish," he began reading, looking intently from Marit to Lars to Aunt Ingeborg, "to adopt a new way of life we scorn, there is only one course to take. If this is the New Order, our answer is: No Norwegians for sale. Several hundred Norwegians have sacrificed their lives for something they held sacred. It is also sacred to us."

When he finished, Aunt Ingeborg clapped her hands. "*Ja,* that's right. No Norwegians for sale! Let the Germans hear that loud and clear."

"Unfortunately, the author of these words has been arrested," Bestefar said. "With every day it's becoming clearer. The lines are being drawn. You're either a Nazi or a *jøssing.*"

"A *jøssing*?" Marit asked.

"A loyal Norwegian," he answered quietly.

After that, it seemed almost everyone was a *jøssing.* Even at school, where the red, blue, and white Norwegian flag was replaced with the German swastika flag, little signs of unity sprang up. Along with fishermen, everyone started to wear *nisselues,* red stocking caps like those worn by gnomes. And if not *nisselues,* then they wore red caps, scarves, or sweaters as a sign of unity.

When a German officer stopped by their school, they all pretended to have a scratchy throat and started coughing uncontrollably. Marit had heard that in Ålesund, when a Nazi soldier sat down on a bus, nearby passengers would get up and move to other seats. Nearly everyone, except Bestefar, started sporting a comb sticking out of chest pockets on coats, which meant "we Norwegians can take care of ourselves."

At school, Marit kept an eye on Olaf. Once, she

watched him arrive at the church gate. He paused, pulled a red *nisselue* from under his jacket, and when he thought no one was looking, he donned it. Then he walked around, his stocking cap matching those of the others. It didn't matter. Everyone ignored him. Marit wondered how he could stand coming to school. Many times she wished she could talk with him, but "icing out" was not only a punishment, it was also a warning—a way to remind others to stay loyal. Fair or not, Marit determined she would not cross the invisible line dividing loyal Norwegians from traitors, *jøssings* from *quislings*.

Yet Aunt Ingeborg still talked with Olaf. If he raised his hand, she allowed him to speak. In fact, all three of the schoolteachers spoke with him, one on one.

That evening at dinner, Marit blurted the question. "Aunt Ingeborg, if 'icing out' is a way of reminding everyone to stay loyal, then why do you and the other teachers talk with Olaf?"

Her aunt set down her fork. "Marit, I know it's difficult to understand. But you see, I'm a teacher first and foremost. My job is to teach, to help all students learn, no matter what their family background, their personality, or if they're eager or reluctant to learn. And to do that, I need to treat every student fairly. At school, I cannot 'ice out' Olaf."

"But it's not fair!" Marit said, pushing away from the table. "We were friends, and I *have* to turn my back on him. If I don't, then the 'ice out' doesn't work. I *don't* have a choice."

Bestefar kept eating, but was clearly listening.

Aunt Ingeborg sighed. "But you *do* have a choice, Marit." She reached for Marit's elbow, eased her closer, and then, just as Mama used to do, rested her hand on the small of Marit's back. "There are no easy answers these days. All I know is that you must do what you believe is right—and so must I."

Soon, warnings were posted all around the island, with notices such as "If you remove public notices, you will be severely punished." And the list of warnings grew longer every day:

- IF YOU RISE FROM A SEAT WHEN A GERMAN SITS DOWN, YOU SHALL BE SEVERELY PUNISHED.

- IF YOU WEAR SIGNS OF STANDING WITH THE ENEMY, INCLUDING WEARING PAPER CLIPS, RED HATS . . . YOU SHALL BE SEVERELY PUNISHED.

- IF YOU CLEAR YOUR THROAT WHEN A GERMAN APPROACHES, YOU SHALL BE SEVERELY PUNISHED.

On one such list posted on a dock pier, someone had boldly added in pencil: "If you breathe, you shall be severely punished."

CHAPTER ELEVEN

Christmas Eve, 1941

One Year Later

It was Marit's second Christmas Eve on the island, and she felt like a prisoner in her own country. Not only was every window on the island darkened with black paper or fabric, but now anyone caught trying to *escape* Norway would be imprisoned or put to death. This night, more than ever, she missed the cheerful flicker of the season's lights when candles filled everyone's windows.

But not even Nazis had stopped Aunt Ingeborg from preparing for *Juletid*. Since soap was scarce, Marit had helped wash the floors with water and sand. They washed the cotton and lace curtains on the scrub board and hung them to dry. Then they starched, ironed, and put them back up again. Aunt Ingeborg set out bright green, red, and blue table runners, while Lars and Marit polished a few pieces of silver and copper. Together they decorated a pine bush with paper-woven baskets, but this year they would have to skip the tree candles. Candles were too valuable. After the *requisition*—the fancy word the Nazis gave to making every Norwegian turn in their blankets, gum boots, tents, rucksacks, and the like to help the German army—it was surprising that anyone had anything left. Aunt Ingeborg had insisted that the children keep one *dyne* hidden away during the day and take it out only at night. "Paper blankets are not enough to keep children alive in the winter," she'd said angrily.

Unlike other years, when baking had filled the air, they merely talked about their favorite cookies: *sandkaker, krumkake,* and *fattigmann*. Herring and salted cod were stored in the cellar—Bestefar made sure of that—but sugar and white flour were impossible to come by.

"Christmas isn't the same without Mama and Papa," Lars kept saying, as if by saying so he could make them magically appear.

If he said it only their first Christmas apart, it wouldn't have bothered Marit so much. But this year, she couldn't stand it any longer. "Stop!" Marit blurted, turning on him. "If they really cared about us, they wouldn't have sent us away!" Her angry words flew out. "They don't even remember they have children!" She cupped her hand lightly over her mouth. To her own surprise, her words had come seemingly out of nowhere.

Aunt Ingeborg spun around, holding a wooden spoon in the air. It dripped batter. "They sent you away for your safety, Marit. Don't say such things!"

For a few long moments, Marit studied the floor. It seemed that lately every word and thought about Mama and Papa made her angry. Though they'd received a few vaguely worded letters in the past year—it was a comfort that they were alive—it would be so much easier to go through the hardships of war together with her parents than apart from them. If she were a parent, she would never send her children away to be cared for by others. In a time of war, didn't kids need their parents more than ever? And yet, beneath her burst of anger, she really *did* understand that Mama and Papa were doing what they had to do. On Christmas Eve especially, she knew they'd rather be together as a family, too.

"I'm sorry," Marit said quietly, glancing up at her aunt and then at Lars. "I know they care. It's just so hard sometimes."

Her aunt hugged her. "I know."

After Marit bathed with the last bit of soap, Aunt Ingeborg wrapped Marit's hair around narrow strips of paper, just as Mama would have done. That night, with knots all over her head, she struggled to sleep. She wanted Christmas to come, but another year without Mama and Papa made her almost wish away the holiday.

On *Julaften*—Christmas Eve—they sat down after their chores to the traditional dinner of boiled potatoes, brown goat cheese, mashed green peas, and *lutefisk*. Aunt Ingeborg had worked many days soaking the dried cod first in water and then in a lye solution to soften the fish, then in water to remove the lye. The fish filled the house with a nose-pinching odor, worse than Papa's socks after a long day of skiing.

"*Lutefisk* stinks!" Lars complained.

"Wouldn't be *Julaften* without it," Aunt Ingeborg replied.

Even without sweets—or Mama and Papa—Christmas was under way.

After dinner, they put on their cleanest clothes—no new outfits. Not even the *bunad*, which her aunt had apparently lost courage to work on. Marit brushed out her curls and tied her hair with the red taffeta ribbons Aunt Ingeborg had saved for her.

Although *risengrot*—the traditional porridge of white rice, cinnamon, sugar, and a little butter—wouldn't await them after church this year, Aunt Ingeborg had promised them something made out of millet. And whoever found the almond—this year it was a button instead—was assured a good year ahead.

"To church," Bestefar said, and held the door open.

In wool scarves and coats, boots and mittens, they trekked to church, each wearing a required "blackout mark." With the small illuminated tag on their coat lapels, the Germans could see them moving about after the six-o'clock winter curfew.

Nearly everyone on the island was at church and wished one another *"God Jul!"* and sang Christmas hymns. In the back, in a row all by themselves, sat Olaf and his family.

Though Pastor Ecklund's skin was splotchy red and his hair thinning and stringy, his voice was as soothing as dark honey. He spoke about God's love and the gift of sending His son to die for everyone's sins—a message Marit had heard many times before.

As they quietly stepped outside, the stars pierced the sky with a thousand lights. Marit listened to her breath as they walked along the snow-covered road toward home.

Halfway there, a set of car lights suddenly switched on, startling them. They jolted to a stop. Aunt Ingeborg squeezed Marit's shoulder, and Marit clutched Lars's hand.

A car door opened. *"Halt!"*

Marit blinked in the lights' blinding glare, unable to see. A wave of nausea passed through her. Was this to be one of those unexpected arrests she'd heard about? Would they all be hauled away—or shot? She braced herself for the worst possible outcome.

"Marit," Bestefar whispered, "not a word."

He didn't have to warn her. Even if she had wanted to, she wouldn't have been able to speak.

"Identity cards," the soldier ordered.

Aunt Ingeborg and Bestefar reached in their pockets and held out the mandatory identification cards. Anyone fifteen or older who was stopped without identification could be sent to reeducation camps in Norway or Germany—or worse. Executed.

The soldier turned his flashlight on the documents, studied them, and then waved them away.

"And these children?" His flashlight drilled into Marit's eyes, as if the car lights were not enough. Blinded, she looked at the snowy ground. Her hands trembled in her mittens.

"My grandchildren," Bestefar said. "And my daughter Ingeborg's niece and nephew."

"They live here on the island?"

"*Ja.*"

"And their parents? Why are they not with their children on Christmas Eve?"

"They were killed when their village was first bombed."

Marit squeezed Lars's hand tighter, trying to let him

know that Bestefar was telling a lie. Lars squeezed her hand in return.

Like a hound losing the trail of a promising scent, the soldier sniffed, seemingly disappointed. "I see," said the soldier. "On your way then." He snapped a salute, arm extended. *"Heil Hitler!"*

The car rolled on, crunching over snow and abandoning them.

The stars had dimmed and the darkness seemed menacing and endless. Could the Nazis not allow them a moment of peace?

With her heel, Marit carved a large *V* in the road.

CHAPTER TWELVE

Miss Halversen's Stand

January 1942

On the first school day in January, Marit watched through a stained glass window as a German officer approached on his black horse. He tied his mount to the gate, then eased open the entry door and slipped into the church. No one else noticed. Marit nudged Hanna, who sat beside her in the pew. "Look!"

His was like all the other uniforms, swaths of graygreen with moving limbs. Marit did her best to ignore them. But she remembered this one. He was the same one who had grabbed Mama's letter and put it in her hand at the general store.

Boots clicked across the floor—six paces—then

stopped. The officer passed his walking stick back and forth from hand to hand. From the back of the church, he watched Miss Halversen as she taught. Her sweaters and skirts curved softly over her tall frame. In the past months, her gray lisle stockings were increasingly ridden with snags. Everything, it seemed, was in shrinking supply or completely gone from store shelves.

After that, the officer started to show up nearly every day, sometimes on horseback, sometimes riding in the side wagon of a motorcycle, at other times in a vehicle, but always just minutes before lunch. Lately, when he visited, Miss Halversen had started to behave oddly. She dropped her pencil. Her hands trembled. She stopped in the middle of the lesson, told them to take out paper, and gave them an assignment. Then she would sit stiff-spined in the front pew beside her pile of textbooks and face the cross above the altar. The officer used to leave when she turned her back to him, but now, more often, he lingered to speak with her during the students' break.

One day, Hanna sat down next to Marit and cupped her hand to her ear. "Maybe he's in love with her."

Just then, Miss Halversen stopped speaking, crossed her arms over her buttoned sweater, and looked at them. "Marit? Hanna? Do you have something you'd like to share with the class?"

Heat surged to Marit's face. This was the first time her

aunt had scolded her like any other student. Along with Hanna, she shook her head and studied the open book in her lap.

In late January, they decided to spy. After lunch, when all the students trailed outside and only the teachers stayed in, they found their chance. The officer hovered in the foyer as students left, and when he was completely focused on Miss Halversen, they crept up the stairs to the empty balcony and ducked down. Marit felt giddy, tucked behind the banister with Hanna. They exchanged smiles. She hadn't done anything this daring in a long time. Her heart pattered as she peered over the top.

"Miss Halversen," the officer said striding up the aisle, his black riding boots gleaming and a small package tucked under his arm. "You look lovely today." His Norwegian was broken. "I must speak with you. Alone."

At the front of the church, Miss Halversen turned hesitantly toward him. Mrs. Hammer and Mr. Moe sat together on the opposite side, going through their lunch tins. Heads together, they appeared lost in their own conversation, though Marit was certain they were listening, too.

"I have told you, *Herr* Schmitz, I will *not* be alone with you."

"Very well," he said, and glanced over his shoulder at the other two teachers, then up toward where Marit and Hanna were hiding. "I would prefer discretion, but if you insist, then let everyone hear, including your two students spying from the balcony."

Marit was aghast at being discovered. She ducked down farther, shoulder to shoulder with Hanna, and froze.

She was sure her heart had stopped beating. What would he do to them? What would Miss Halversen say? She hadn't thought of getting caught. Neither she nor Hanna moved. They weren't going to stand up unless they were asked to. Maybe they could slip back down the stairs and outside before Miss Halversen saw them. But could they get past the Nazi officer?

Miss Halversen stood firm. "May I eat my lunch in peace, please?" Her voice strained with an anger Marit had seen only once at school, and that was when she'd caught Edvarg, the eighth-grader, with his hand in the cupboard. She'd shouted at him for stealing, but when Edvarg said he needed aspirin for his sick mother, she marched back to the cupboard and dropped something into his hand. "Here, leave a little early," she told him. "I hope they help. Next time, ask."

Below them, the officer removed his cap, his short, honey-colored hair combed back in waves. "There's an officers' party tonight. Perhaps you'd care to accompany me?"

Miss Halversen shook her head.

"Other girls and women, up and down the coast," the

officer said, "they've taken German boyfriends. I assure you, it will be all right." He paused, and then continued. "Perhaps a party is the wrong thing. A movie in Ålesund, would that suit you better? I could arrange it. Please." He stepped closer to her, as if to take her hand, but she backed up, out of reach.

"Very well." From under his arm he produced a shiny gold package. "I had to go through some effort to get these, but thought you might enjoy them." He lifted the box's lid, displaying its contents.

"Chocolates?" Miss Halversen's tone was one of disbelief. She looked at the box and then at him. A tremor crossed her face.

Marit's mouth watered. She hadn't tasted chocolate since her last visit with Mama to the milk shop in Isfjorden. Nearly two years! If only Miss Halversen would share the chocolates with her class after the officer left. Or better yet, bring them home to share.

"Everyone is sacrificing," her aunt said angrily. "Even milk is increasingly in short supply. You Nazis take *everything* and leave us nothing. And in the past weeks, many of the children are complaining of hunger." Her voice was quiet but powerful, as if she were holding back an ocean of injustice. "Do you know what it's like to teach when their bellies are rumbling for food? And you bring me *chocolates?*"

She knocked the box from the officer's outstretched hand. Chocolates scattered at his feet. Mrs. Hammer and Mr. Moe gasped, and a disquieting hush fell over the church.

Marit covered her mouth.

As if stunned, the officer didn't move. Then, almost in slow motion, he took two steps back. He snapped his officer's cap on his head and straightened his jacket. When he spoke, his voice was sharp. "You could be arrested for such talk," he warned. "I was trying to court you. I could have forced you, but I didn't. I'm doing you a favor."

Miss Halversen stood tall.

The officer turned away. His heels hit sharply across the floor, echoing stonily through the church building, and the door shut hard behind him.

As soon as he was gone, Mr. Moe hurried to Miss Halversen. "I can't believe you knocked the gift from his hand! You're so brave, Ingeborg."

"Or impossibly stupid," muttered Mrs. Hammer, her arms crossed squarely. "He'll make us pay for this, you can count on it."

Miss Halversen dropped to the pew and bowed her head in her hands. Her shoulders rose and fell with silent sobs. If she hadn't been spying, Marit would have rushed down and put her arms around her.

Hanna nudged her in the side and motioned toward

the stairs. Stealthily, Marit crept down the stairs after her. Once outside, they ducked snowballs, passed snow forts, and wandered through the gravestones without talking. A chill far colder than the winter air settled deep in Marit's bones. With her mitten, she swept the wind-blown snow off the headstones, as if learning the dates of every birth and death was more interesting than talking with Hanna about what had just happened to Miss Halversen.

CHAPTER THIRTEEN
Unspoken Thoughts

On February 1, 1942, Marit celebrated her twelfth birthday. Hanna came over for dinner and gave Marit a pair of multicolored wool mittens. "I knit them out of yarn from old socks."

The thumbs were a little lumpy, but to Marit they were the best gift in the world. "They're beautiful! *Tusen takk!*"

Lars gave her a tiny wooden gnome roughly carved out of wood. It wore a tall pointed hat—that much Marit could make out—and had two feet.

"Lars, for being only eight years old—"

"Almost nine. Only two months away," he reminded her. "April second, remember?"

"Right. Almost nine. You're an excellent carver!"

That night, as Lars drifted to sleep, she lay awake in the complete darkness of her bedroom. Another year had passed. Did her parents think of her and wish they could be with her on her twelfth birthday? If they were alive, she knew they would. Mama used to make *lefse,* Marit's favorite, and sprinkle the rolled potato pancakes with butter and cinnamon. After every birthday dinner, Papa always took out his Hardanger fiddle. With it rested under his chin, he'd tap his foot along with "Two Mountain Trolls" until she and Mama and Lars started dancing on the wood floor.

Months had passed since Mama and Papa's last letter. They had sent a letter every three months. Marit suspected they would write more often if they could, but that they didn't want to attract any extra attention that would in any way connect their efforts in Isfjorden with their children on the island. If one family member was found helping with the Resistance, the whole family was usually killed.

Still, they were due for a letter soon. As each third month arrived, the wait for their letter became unbearable, her worries torture. If Olaf's parents could side with the Nazis, then there had to be others, too. What if her parents had been reported by a neighbor for helping the Resistance? If arrested, they would face torture, re-education camps, or death. She wanted to believe that

Norwegians were quietly winning the war through underground methods. But were they? With each passing day, ordinary people seemed to lose more of their freedoms.

She whispered again to herself, "Mama and Papa are fine." Teardrops fell from the corners of her eyes and into her ears. She didn't bother to wipe them away.

Later that month, icy winds turned to gales as Marit walked with Aunt Ingeborg and Lars to church, their heads bent into the wind. Bestefar, who usually didn't miss a service, was away fishing for a few days.

Pastor Ecklund stood before his congregation. His usually blotchy red face was as pale as a peeled potato. He clung to the edges of his simple podium, as if to hold himself upright. His normally long-winded sermon ended abruptly. For a long moment he was silent, and when he started again, his voice carried determination.

"My dear friends, this will be my last service here. Bishops and pastors across Norway have decided to resign their posts, and I am resigning as well, as a matter of conscience. We will not be under the Nazis' authority—only God's. And I cannot in good faith lead you if I must bear a Nazi yoke."

A rush of whispering swept through the church, but Pastor Ecklund raised his hand, bringing quiet again.

"To agree to partner with the Nazis would mean to be puppets in their service. They would approve or disapprove of sermons. They would command us how and what to teach. And I know it would not be a message of God's love, forgiveness, and goodwill toward others. It would be to further their cause of racism, fear, and intimidation. Services here will henceforth be led by Nazi-appointed pastors. I will, therefore, not meet in this building," he said. "Rather, I invite you all to join with me in worshiping in the privacy of our homes."

Over the next week, snow fell and blew into drifts around the church building. During breaks at school, Marit and Hanna often took shelter from the wind in a snow fort they'd carved from a deep drift. The half roof and short walls glowed an icy blue and protected their secrets.

Marit clapped her birthday mittens together to warm herself. The sun barely traveled above the horizon, casting long shadows from the gravestones across the snow. From her squatting position, she rose to stretch. The wind, damp from the sea and stiff with cold, slapped her cheeks. She ducked back down, but not before spotting Olaf wandering toward their shelter, his stocking-capped head tucked between his shoulders.

"Olaf. He's coming this way. Do you think he wants to talk to us?"

Hanna shrugged and rubbed her mittened hands together.

In seconds, he was standing there. Wind teased the tufts of sandy hair jutting from his cap. He shifted from boot to boot, his gray eyes downcast.

"Marit, I must talk with you."

She looked at Hanna, whose eyes were determined, reminding Marit of their unspoken decision. Marit wished things were different. They rose in unison from behind their snow wall and walked away.

"I feel bad for him," Marit said under her breath. "Terrible—but we have no choice."

"I know," Hanna replied. "We have to."

That afternoon, before Miss Halversen excused them for the rest of the day, she stood in front of all the students. First, she called toward the balcony, then to the younger students. "I'm speaking for all of the teachers here at Godøy School," she began, a history book clasped against her yellow sweater. "We want you to know that teachers across Norway have been ordered to teach students Nazi propaganda." She paused, as if to make sure they had heard.

Marit couldn't imagine it. Miss Halversen was supposed to teach them how to be Nazis?

"Teachers across Norway are united. We have sent in

countless letters *refusing* to instruct our students in Nazi thinking. And do you know what Nazi philosophy is?" She didn't wait for an answer. "It means believing that you are of a superior race—an Aryan race—superior to anyone who is of Jewish ancestry, superior to anyone who is handicapped or different in any way. It means teaching you to identify and pick out those who don't fit in. It means that you are to follow orders and obey and not to ever, *ever* think for yourselves. We cannot and will not obey this request by the Nazi authorities. To do so goes against our training and conscience as teachers. We're Norwegians. We believe in the God-given worth of every individual. We believe in freedoms for everyone."

The students, like still treetops before an ominous storm, didn't move.

She inhaled sharply, then continued. "We don't know what will happen next. And so, I wanted to warn you. If anything should happen to teachers, should any of us suddenly disappear or be replaced, you will know the real reason. For now, teachers across Norway stand together."

Teachers disappearing or replaced. Marit's mind teetered at the edge of a possibility she hadn't considered. Would the Nazis stop at nothing? Marit drew a *V* in her notebook and followed the lines with her pencil—over and over until the paper ripped.

She was sick with worry for her goodhearted aunt.

That night, Aunt Ingeborg added corrections to a stack of papers. With school under way, she didn't have as much free time to knit or sew. Bestefar's disapproval must have stopped her from working on the *bunad*. Or maybe when she considered the risk of getting caught, she decided the *bunad* wasn't worth the price of Gestapo punishment.

Seated by the wood stove, like a tailor with an oversize needle, Bestefar pushed a metal fid through strands of thick rope, creating a loop for a mooring line. "For the teachers to openly defy the Nazis," he said, "it will cost many lives. The Nazis do not tolerate disobedience." He flashed Aunt Ingeborg a look of grave concern.

Her reply was resolute silence.

"But Bestefar," Marit said, taken aback by his response. "Don't you understand how brave the teachers are?"

He looked at her, but his blue irises were as unreadable as the sea, and his lips were closed maddeningly tight.

Of course he didn't understand! And now in his tight-mouthed way, he wouldn't say another word on the subject. She found her rucksack and settled at the table to do her homework. As she opened her mathematics book, the numbers on the page blurred. Her thoughts wandered, but slowly came into alarming focus.

In the past year, Bestefar had worked increasingly long nights. Once, he had been at sea for over a week. While he was gone, Aunt Ingeborg spent more time than ever embroidering the *bunad,* and often her eyes were red from fatigue.

"When will Bestefar return?" Lars asked after six days of their grandfather's absence.

Aunt Ingeborg cast her gaze beyond them. "Fishermen. They have minds of their own." That was all she would say on the subject.

Increasingly, though Marit hated to even think it to herself, Bestefar seemed less and less a *jøssing*—and more and more a *quisling*.

In mid-February, as welcome as the winter sun climbing above the eastern peaks, another letter finally arrived—three and a half months since the last one. Bestefar read it aloud. Like the previous letters, this one was written in Mama's hand, but signed Mr. and Mrs. Siversen.

> *Dear Ingeborg and Leif,*
>   *Months have passed and our hearts break with missing you, our most precious friends. You're lucky to have the company of grandchildren to help you on your farm. We hope they're a blessing to you.*

*Our work continues. Very difficult, but making prog-
ress. We trust the Lord to help us and everyone these
days. Difficult times, yet the mountains are as beautiful
as ever.*

*Hope your fishing is successful, despite the dangerous
activities at sea these days.*

> *Hearty Greetings!*
> *Mr. and Mrs. Siversen*

It wasn't much, but Marit clung to the words of the
letter, repeating them over and over to herself until she
had memorized them. Every night, Marit repeated the
letter to herself before asking the Lord to keep Mama
and Papa safe. And every morning, on her walk to the
church for school, she recited the letter in her head, trying to stretch the meaning of each sentence, trying to
hear Mama's voice in every word.

CHAPTER FOURTEEN

Distant Dreams

"Marit," Aunt Ingeborg called upstairs, "before you get dressed, try this on."

Lars was already up and feeding the chickens. But this morning, Marit was in slow motion. She didn't feel like getting dressed. Despite the recent letter, she didn't want to be helpful. Every chore was set against a hopeless, gray backdrop of never seeing her parents again, of a world where war never ends. In her nightgown, Marit peered from the top of the stairs.

Draped across Aunt Ingeborg's arms, brilliant threads of blue, red, and orange joined in flowers and swirls across the black fabric of the *bunad*. "Surprise!"

"Oh," Marit said, reaching for the *bunad*. "You finished it! I thought you had given up."

A smile flickered over Aunt Ingeborg's face before her stern expression returned. Marit knew her aunt was pleased but didn't want to appear boastful of her handiwork. Then she handed Marit a white blouse, a pair of silver-buckled black shoes, and red anklets.

Marit was stunned. "This is too much. When did you work on it? Where did you get—"

Aunt Ingeborg waved her concerns away. "I had a little savings. I worked on it when I couldn't sleep. We must *never* let some traditions die. And the *bunad* is much more than just clothing. Sorry it took me so long."

In no time, Marit slipped the white blouse over her head, pulled on the vest and skirt of the *bunad,* and adjusted the front ties. It *was* more than clothing. This particular embroidered design and style had been passed down from the Sunnmore region, east of Ålesund, and home of her ancestors. *Bunads* were worn with pride at every important event and celebration. She smiled as she pulled on the socks—red in color, because she wasn't married, of course—and then the shiny buckled shoes, which had been worn before but had recently been buffed to a high polish with cod liver oil, the only oil to be found.

Marit twirled until her skirt billowed.

She touched the neck of her blouse. A round *sølje* with dangly silver—that was all that was needed to make her *bunad* complete. Some things were too expensive, too much to hope for. She hardly recognized herself in the mirror. She saw less of the girl she had been in Isfjorden and—in the rise of her cheekbones, the set of her jaw, the arch of her eyebrows—more of Mama.

"Marit!" Aunt Ingeborg called up. "Are you going to take all day to show me how it fits?"

Embarrassed, Marit hurried down the stairs.

Aunt Ingeborg nodded. "Now turn around. It suits you and fits well, with plenty of room for you to grow. Now you'll have it to wear for your confirmation and for special events."

Though Marit knew she could never wear the *bunad* in public, she twirled again, too happy to contain herself. If Bestefar had been home, she wouldn't have dared to try it on, but he had left early and was fishing already, despite the pale rising sun of winter.

"Pack it away, Marit, in the chest in your room. Hide it at the bottom, underneath everything else, just to be safe."

Marit started up the stairs, then turned back and threw her arms around her aunt's neck. "*Tusen takk,* Aunt Ingeborg!"

That night by the radio, Aunt Ingeborg and Marit exchanged glances, sharing their own secret. Bestefar didn't need to know that the *bunad* was done. Let him worry about something else. When Aunt Ingeborg finished correcting assignments, she took skeins of undyed wool. "Lars, you need a bigger sweater. Dyes are impossible to get these days, but at least sheep are still in abundance on the island."

The radio crackled. Marit wondered why Bestefar listened so closely if he didn't believe in standing up to the Germans. These days, he spoke less and less.

The king's voice came in clearly for a moment. "All for Norway," she heard, but his words faded in and out. How long could Norway stay strong without their king, without more help from the Allies? Many German warships had been bombed by the Resistance when they entered Norwegian harbors, but the Nazis were always quick to react—sometimes burning whole villages in response. Hanna had complained that just that week Nazis had visited their house in the middle of the night without so much as a knock. They slammed open the door with the butts of their rifles. "I don't know what they were looking for," she said. "But when they took the one good piece of soap that my mama had hidden in a drawer, she couldn't stop crying for a long time."

CHAPTER FIFTEEN

New Orders

On March 20, a ray of sun fell perfectly on Miss Halversen, backlighting her golden hair. But this afternoon, her forehead was etched with lines, her mouth tight and strained, and her skin pale. "We have been informed," she announced to all the students, "that schools across Norway are to shut down for one month due to a 'fuel shortage.'" She moved her lips, as if to say more or to explain this strange statement to them. Instead, her eyes flitted to the back of the church.

Marit turned and her heart caught. She elbowed Hanna. "Look!"

The officer who had tried to win their teacher's affection hadn't been around for a year. Now at the back of the church, he towered in his uniform. She hadn't heard him arrive. The sun glinted off the eagle pin on his jacket and shot needle rays around the church. At his heels waited two younger soldiers, both armed.

"*Fräulein* Halversen," the officer said from the back of the church, as if he didn't dare get too close to her. "Come with us."

"You must all be brave," Miss Halversen blurted, rushing headlong with her words as the soldiers marched toward her. "Remember, you are Norwegians. You must be brave—and wise."

Within seconds, the two soldiers grabbed Miss Halversen by her arms. "I'm capable of walking on my own," she said. They released their hold, and walked on either side of her.

Whispers fluttered around the room. The soldiers looked neither left nor right, but straight ahead to the foyer, and Miss Halversen walked with them. Marit felt the blood drain from her whole body. She wanted to shout out, to tell them to stop. They couldn't take her aunt away! But along with everyone else, fear tethered her to her seat and sealed her lips. The moment they stepped out of the church, Marit jumped from her pew toward the open door, and the rest of the students followed her lead, pressing in around her.

She stared. The soldiers pointed to the back of an empty army truck, their breaths forming white clouds as they spoke. Without allowing her to take a hat or winter *jakke,* Miss Halversen—her own aunt—climbed in and sat on a bench.

The officer slipped into the back of the other vehicle, a sleek four-door car. Through the window, Marit watched him nod to the driver. The car gunned gravel, and the truck careened after it down the sloping road toward the harbor. From the rear of the covered truck, Miss Halversen stared back at the school, lifting her pale hand in silent farewell.

"Nei! Nei! Nei!" Marit wailed, her legs threatening to buckle beneath her. "They can't take her! They can't! That's my aunt Ingeborg! They can't!" But the truck was already gone.

A firm hand grasped her shoulder and tugged her backward. "Marit, Marit, come. Children, children. Inside now," ordered Mrs. Hammer. "Come, sit down."

A blizzard of thoughts and feelings left her numb as Marit walked blindly to her seat. Mrs. Hammer shored her up with an arm around her waist, steering her toward the pews at the front of the church. Marit slumped into the pew as Mrs. Hammer stood before the altar. "Quickly now. The rest of you—take your seats."

When everyone was seated, she explained. "This *is* terrible. I'm frightened and upset, too. We heard rumors that *one in ten* teachers would be rounded up across Norway and sent to concentration camps in our country. Now we know it's true. The Nazis want to scare us into obeying. They want us to bend to their ways." Her voice broke. "Now, go home and pray. Pray every single day for Miss Halversen and for teachers across Norway."

As other students gathered their things to leave school, Marit grabbed her *jakke* and rucksack and raced out to find Bestefar. Lars would have to catch up with her. Bestefar had to find some way to get Aunt Ingeborg back! She had to tell him what had happened.

Breathless, she arrived at his boathouse. But he wasn't there. And his fishing trawler was gone from the bay.

When Lars caught up with her on the road, Marit couldn't speak. In the past two years, with constant worries about the war, Marit had leaned on Aunt Ingeborg. Her kindness. *Her being there.* She'd become more than an aunt. She was like her second mother. Hot tears ran down her cold face. She wiped her nose on the sleeve of her *jakke*. Everyone she loved was being taken from her.

"Marit," Lars said, his voice wavery. Marit noticed his mittens were clumped with snow. "Aunt Ingeborg will come back," he said, patting her arm. "You'll see."

That night, when Bestefar stepped into the farmhouse, he went right past the thin soup on the stove that Marit had made and turned on the radio.

"I heard what happened," he said, spinning the knob until the BBC came in fairly clearly.

Marit listened intently to learn about the Nazi roundup of teachers across the country. The news went from bad to horrible. Not only were teachers sent to concentration camps for "reeducation" but also, to set an example, five hundred of the one thousand arrested teachers were crammed into the hold of a boat and sent from Trondheim up the frigid northern coast.

Bestefar raked his hand through his hair. "The *Skjaerstad* is a small coastal steamer—meant to carry one hundred fifty or so passengers—not five hundred!" His eyes were rimmed red and Marit was sure he'd been crying. "Ingeborg! How could they take her from us? What's becoming of the world when good teachers like my Ingeborg can be treated like livestock?" Head bowed, he said, "God protect her."

That night, before bed, Marit stopped at the threshold of her aunt's upstairs bedroom. It was tidy. Her sheepskin slippers were lined up neatly under her bathrobe, which hung from a peg beside the door. On her pine dresser, her pewter set—hand mirror, comb, and hairbrush—waited for her return. Marit considered sleeping in her aunt's bed. She wouldn't have to share with Lars.

But she couldn't. That would be the same as saying her aunt would never come back. Besides, only a large sheet of paper draped her aunt's mattress. After the requisitioning of all blankets, the only warm covering in the house was the *dyne* that she and Lars slept under every night. Before bedtime, they always pulled it out from under their mattress, shook it hard to fluff up its feathers, then hid it again in the morning. Marit turned away from the doorway. Without Aunt Ingeborg, the house felt cold and hollow.

After that day, Bestefar fell into a rock-hard silence. The cooking and cleaning fell to Marit. Lars tried to help, but he was better at tending the goats and chickens. When he tried to cook, he made more of a mess than it was worth.

Over and over Marit replayed the image of her aunt being taken away, trying to imagine if there was something she could have done to stop the soldiers. With dread, she thought of Aunt Ingeborg being tortured. Or being crammed with other teachers like slaves into a crowded boat. Marit couldn't help but scan the sea, wondering if brave teachers were out there, floating through mine-laden waters. Though the hours of daylight were lengthening, the darkness over Norway seemed only to deepen. Bestefar said he would try to find out what he could about Aunt Ingeborg, but as no news of her whereabouts came, the week passed like a year.

The morning the "donation" truck pulled up to the barn, Marit watched from the window, hiding behind the curtains. The soldier read something to Bestefar from a piece of paper, and then left with his milk and eggs.

Stepping inside, Bestefar brushed white flecks of snow from the shoulders of his wool jacket and sat down heavily at the table.

Marit stopped sweeping. "What is it this time?"

He rubbed his forehead with the back of his hand until his skin turned red as crab legs. "All radios must be turned in by the end of the day. This evening, they will do a house-to-house search. Anyone caught with a radio will face a firing squad."

Lars sat cross-legged on the living room floor holding Tekopp. He looked up, his eyes blank, then returned to playing with his cat. Without the radio, they would not hear any news from Britain. No news about teachers or other efforts by Norwegians—like Mama and Papa. Bestefar's radio was their lifeline to the outside world. It meant hope. He simply couldn't give it up.

"Bestefar, what will we do?" Marit asked. "Hide it?"

He circled his hands around an empty coffee cup and answered in a faraway voice. "I must turn it in. The price is too high."

The broom she'd been clenching dropped from her hands and clattered on the floor. Her eyes filled with tears. She could never know for sure what her own Mama and Papa were doing. But she believed they had sent their own children away so that they might work actively against the Nazi occupation. Her own aunt Ingeborg, her own teacher, had stood up and refused to do as the Nazis commanded and instruct students in Nazi propaganda. She'd risked her life on it—and now she was somewhere, probably in a reeducation camp. Yet Bestefar sat there, playing it safe, unwilling to take a chance on a hidden radio.

She yanked on her boots and tore her *jakke* and hat from the wooden peg by the door. She couldn't stand to be in the same room as her grandfather. Without thought as to where she would head, she stomped out and turned northeast.

Past several narrow farms and along a footpath that wove up the hills, Marit ran and ran. The top of Godøy Mountain called to her, and maybe she was angry enough to keep going until she had reached the top. The past month had brought rains and snow, leaving a thin crust of snow-covered ice over the path. She stomped through it, gulping the damp air as she slowed to a walk. It wasn't safe to be alone, a girl in the woods. But she didn't care. Nothing was safe anymore. School wasn't safe. Not even Aunt Ingeborg had been safe.

The path was familiar and brought back memories. Once at Lake Alnesvatnet on the top of the mountain, she'd caught her first trout, its scales iridescent as it flip-flopped on the shore.

An irritable cawing sounded overhead. Two ravens sat in the top branches of snow-laced cedars. Marit passed beneath them, ignoring their squawking complaints and fluffing of feathers.

At the next clearing, she stopped and looked back. Godøy and the surrounding islands rose like humpback whales from the sparkling sea. Sun glinted off distant peaks and melted the snow into icy waterfalls and streams that emptied into the ocean. So much had remained the same. The same sea, the same deeply carved fjords, the same towering mountains beyond. Nearly two years had passed since she'd last returned home from skiing in the mountains with her family—two long years since bombs fell and her world collapsed.

Marit pushed on, keeping the coast in sight. At the base of a low-sweeping cedar, something red caught her eye. She stopped. At first she thought it was a pine grosbeak with its fluff of rosy-red feathers, but a shiver went through her. It wasn't a bird at all, but a spot of blood.

Had a rabbit or squirrel been caught by a predator? An owl or wolverine or lynx? Stepping closer to investigate, she saw no signs of a struggle. No paw prints from a preying animal. No feathering of wings in the snow from a hawk or owl. Fresh snow from last night covered everything.

She inhaled sharply, looked closer, and saw that the blood extended under the thick branches. Her stomach lurched. She tripped backwards, away from the tree and whatever might be lying in its shadows. Suddenly the distance between this lonely place and the farmhouse seemed enormous.

Through the cedar's low branches, a man whispered, "Don't move."

CHAPTER SIXTEEN

A Desperate Plea

Run, her instincts told her, but she froze. If this were a Nazi commanding her to stop, the price of fleeing would be death. Yet something about the voice . . . This man's Norwegian was perfect, not the broken Norwegian of a German soldier.

"Please," he said, a desperate plea rather than his earlier command. She couldn't see movement beneath the tree's branches. The man was well concealed. She expected to see the barrel of a gun pointed toward her.

"Please," he repeated. "Help me."

Marit opened her mouth, but her throat had gone dry.

Branches rustled and a gloved hand pushed away the lowest snow-covered branch. A man rose up on his elbow from the ground, just enough for her to see his face. "I'm N-n-norwegian." Beneath a navy wool cap, just like Bestefar's, his cheeks were tinged white from frostbite. As he spoke, his teeth chattered. Certain now that he was in no condition to harm her, Marit pressed closer so she could better make out his words. As she did, he flopped back, groaned, and disappeared beneath the branches.

With a quick glance around to make sure no one was coming up the path from behind her, Marit pushed the branches aside and gasped. The man's right leg ended in a mass of mangled leather and flesh. Above his injured foot, a leather belt was cinched tight around his shredded and bloody pants leg.

"Oh—what happened to you?"

"They shot . . . our boat. Sank us."

"Us? Who?"

"Resistance. F-f-ive of us," he stammered through bluish gray lips.

"And the others? Where are they now?"

His nostrils flared and he looked away.

She couldn't get involved. *Turn. Run away now.* If he was indeed a Resistance fighter and the Germans found her helping him, Marit would be taken away. Perhaps Lars, too. "I need to go home."

The man opened his eyes. "I've been here . . . since . . . since last night. Help me . . . finish."

"Finish what? What do you need to finish?"

"Mission—f-for Norway."

Every moment that she lingered drew her into his fate. And if she helped him, she would be putting not only herself at great risk. Stories she'd heard from the islanders flashed through her mind. Whole families removed in the middle of the night, whole villages bombed beyond recognition, simply because one person was caught helping the Resistance. She remembered the warning posted on Bestefar's boat: "You shall not in any way give shelter to or aid the enemy. To do so is punishable by death."

Marit shook her head. "*Nei*, I'm sorry. I can't. I can't. It's too dangerous."

Trembling, she backed onto the path, turned, and began retracing her steps. Sunlight glinted off the sea and snow-crested mountains, piercing her eyes. She stopped. If she left him, he would die. If she helped him, others' lives would be at risk. She remembered Pastor Ecklund's pale face when he chose to step down from the pulpit, and his words: "We will not be under the Nazis' authority—only God's."

Her own words to Bestefar taunted her. "If no one fights back, then what will happen?" How easy it was to accuse Bestefar of being cowardly. How easy words were!

She could almost taste the bitterness of risk.

In war, nothing was simple.

Head down, she studied her leather boots and her red

wool socks protruding through the toe holes. Another reminder of the war. With leather so difficult to come by, she hadn't been able to replace the boots she'd outgrown. She'd cut the holes so her toes had a little more room. It was either that or Aunt Ingeborg's jam money to buy boots made from fish skin, and Marit had refused to let her aunt waste her money on such things. "I would rather wait until times get better," Marit had said. And when would that be if Norwegians didn't fight back? Her toes were damp from the melting snow and turning numb with cold. If her toes were cold, he must be nearly frozen.

The path wound down at an angle in the direction of the farm, but from where she stood, the ocean was only a stone's toss away. Below her, the rocky beach was empty. The man was badly wounded, and she doubted he could walk all the way to the road. If he could slide down the short slope to the water below, she might be able to meet him and row him somewhere safer.

With a deep breath, Marit turned.

Snow crunched beneath her boots as she headed uphill again to the soldier. She scanned the empty trail, pushed back a cedar branch and found him.

His eyes were half-closed and his breaths rose and fell in wheezes. Frost lined his jacket collar and the rim of his cap. If his boat was shot at, then he must have swum to shore and climbed here.

Marit cleared her throat, hoping to draw his attention. "How can I help?"

He didn't answer.

She knelt closer to his shoulder until the branches swooped back over her, hiding them both. She kept her eyes on his face, trying to avoid his mangled foot. She tapped his chest. No answer. She tapped him again. "I'll help you, but you must tell me what to do."

He lay there, unresponsive.

First, she needed to get him warm. But how would she move him? She would ask Bestefar. *Nei.* She shook her head. He'd likely report the Resistance soldier to the Nazi headquarters—just to play it safe.

Marit considered her options. She could hide the man somewhere near the farm and tend to him in secret until he recovered. The root cellar, or the loft, perhaps. But she couldn't possibly move him by herself. Hanna? Maybe she could help. But then Marit would be involving her friend and putting Hanna's whole family at risk as well.

With the force of breaking ice on a water trough, she thumped the man's chest. "You must—wake—up!"

He moaned. *"Mor..."*

"No, I'm not your mother. And I'm going to need your help."

She removed her mittens, reached for his closest hand, worked off his frozen, bloodstained gloves, then placed his icy hand between her warm bare hands. His teeth began chattering again. After a time she put his hand back in his glove and placed her palms on either side of his face and held them there until his eyes opened in panic. "Compass," he said, "I need . . . to get—"

"First, you have to survive. Now sit up. Can you do that?"

Face contorted, he rose to his elbow. Marit felt horrible, for making him suffer more pain. "Can you get down the hill to the shore?" She pointed at an angle to where the distance between the tree and water was shortest. "You could lie on your back and slide down much of the way."

He nodded, but his eyes were glassy and distant.

Marit was formulating a plan as she talked, and tried to sound confident so he'd trust her. "The sun will be down soon, in less than an hour. There's a house-to-house search going on for radios sometime today, so I doubt the waters will be watched as closely. If you can manage to get yourself down to the water, I could row by—"

"You'd attract at-t-t . . ."

"Attention?" She shook her head. "I don't think so. I've been rowing before. The soldiers at the lighthouse don't even see me anymore. Just be there. Somehow, I'll help you to a place where you can hide. You'll have to crawl a short distance to the barn."

He answered by shutting his eyes. His life, it appeared, was a skiff drifting farther and farther out to sea.

"Don't die on me! I can't carry you, and I refuse to get anyone else involved. Just be there, near the shore, just after the sun sets. You'll have to climb in the rowboat. I'll bring a *dyne* to cover you."

"*Dyne?*"

"*Ja.*"

"Warm."

"That's right." Marit peeked out through the branches. The trail was free of other hikers. She slipped back onto the path and started toward home, behaving as naturally as she could, trying to calm her flurry of emotions. She hoped no one would notice her tracks, but there was no way to hide them now. She would steal the rowboat from the boathouse, row past the lighthouse as the shadows deepened, and meet this wounded soldier on the shore.

If he was there.

She would wait no longer than a minute. One minute—she'd count it out—and not a second longer. After that, if he wasn't there, she would be forced to leave him to his own fate.

CHAPTER SEVENTEEN

The *Kraken*

Marit shouldered the farmhouse door, and removing her mittens, headed straight to the washbasin. Her bloodstained hands tinted the water pink.

"You're back!" Lars said, skipping from the living room.

Marit glanced over her shoulder.

Under his arm, Lars carried Tekopp, who by now was far larger than his namesake and struggled to break free.

"Where were you? You were gone so long! Bestefar wasn't happy that you were gone."

"I had to take a walk, that's all." She deftly dumped the washbasin water down the drain and dried her hands on a towel.

A pot sat on the cookstove and the room was filled with the smell of cod, thinned milk, and potatoes. Marit lifted the lid. "Bestefar made stew?" she whispered, amazed.

"*Ja,* and I helped cut the potatoes," Lars said, hands on his hips. "We ate already."

"Huh. And Aunt Ingeborg thought he couldn't cook for himself."

"Don't worry. She'll be back, Marit."

Her heart stuck in her throat. "I'm sure she will."

At the smells, Marit's stomach grumbled. But the soldier must be far hungrier. And he needed something hot in his belly. If she could manage to hide him, then she could sneak warm food to him. She ladled a bowl of soup for herself, sat down, and ate quickly.

"You shouldn't hike alone," Lars said. "That's what Bestefar says."

She had no time for small talk.

"He said it's dangerous with so many soldiers on the island."

Marit refused to meet his eyes. If Bestefar only knew. "Where is he?" she asked.

"Fishing. He said he'd be back before dark."

"I-I want to row before it gets dark, too."

Lars slid in his socks across the wood floor.

"Careful," Marit warned. "You might get a sliver."

"Marit," he said and slid again, "I want to go, too."

"*Nei*, Lars. You stay here. Take care of Tekopp."

He planted himself in the center of the kitchen and crossed his arms over his chest. His chin puckered. Marit knew the look. "Marit," he said, holding his voice firm, "please!"

Marit moved to the kitchen window, eased back an edge of the room-darkening paper, and gazed outside. The sun was low. She must leave soon, before her grandfather returned. She struggled to think up an excuse to keep Lars from coming along. "It's pretty cold, Lars. Are you sure?"

"I've been inside all afternoon. Aunt Ingeborg always said it's good to get fresh air."

She pushed the paper back in place. "All right then—a short trip before it gets dark. There's safety in numbers, right? Isn't that what she said, too?" Marit told him in a rush, pushing away from the table.

He smiled and nodded vigorously.

She was uncertain about the outcome, but she was forced to take Lars along. "Let's go!" Before they passed the barn, Marit had an idea. "Let's get that wool blanket from the loft."

"But the soldier took it, remember?" He scrunched up his face at her as if she'd lost her mind.

"The soldier? Oh, right. The German soldier at the lighthouse . . ."

Her mind was tangled. Too many lines in the water.

"Besides, why do we need a blanket?" Lars asked. "Did you find another seal pup?"

She thought of the Resistance soldier. Hardly a seal pup. "No," she said. "To help you keep warm."

He shook his head vigorously and stood taller. "I'm fine. I won't get cold. I'm not a baby, Marit. I don't need a blanket."

"Oh, no, I was thinking, um, for Tekopp. Maybe he wants to go for a boat ride with us. You could go find him and bring him along. He'd like that, don't you think?"

His eyes widened. Without a word, he ran back to the house and returned with Tekopp, wrapped up in their puffy *dyne*. "Aunt Ingeborg wouldn't want this outside."

"I know. We'll be careful."

The Resistance soldier would be a fool to climb into a rescue boat with two kids and a cat. But she had promised she'd be there. She had no choice, and she doubted he had other choices.

In the lengthening shadows, they headed down the road to the boathouse.

To Marit's relief, Bestefar's trawler had not yet returned. She poked her head into his boathouse and was met with the smells of oil, decaying rope, old barrels, and fish. Assured that her grandfather was nowhere near, Marit stepped to the rowboat.

The sun shot a fireball of red across the water. Marit breathed in deeply, hoping for courage, then she lifted the rowboat's bow and pushed. The stern eased onto the water as she held the bow. "Climb in."

Carefully, with his overly bundled cat, Lars crawled over the middle seat to the stern, a big smile on his face. "Let's be Vikings! Let's hunt down the *kraken*!"

"Why would we want to find a sea monster?" Marit asked, hoping to keep his mind occupied.

"We could tame it. Make it our pet! And then it would protect us, even when Mama and Papa are far away." Perched on his seat, with the *dyne* covering his knees, Lars snuggled his face into Tekopp's amber fur.

"Sure," Marit said. "We can pretend."

The water glittered dark with rubies as Marit rowed. They headed from the harbor to the lighthouse, but this time she kept rowing past the end of the peninsula. Two German soldiers huddled beside the lighthouse, out of the wind, their cigarettes glowing.

One of them looked up as they rowed past. He must have decided they looked harmless, and shaped carefree smoke rings that floated up, circle after circle, and disappeared in the air.

"Marit," Lars whispered, "we're not supposed to go past the breakwater. Are we really looking for sea monsters?"

"We are."

Off toward the open water, porpoises arced, diving in and out of the gray waves. "See them?" she asked.

As Lars turned, the porpoises skimmed the surface, dived, and were gone. His jaw slackened. "Sea monsters!" he whispered, with enough awe in his voice that Marit didn't know if he was playing along or truly believing in impossible creatures.

"*Ja,*" Marit said, leaning toward him. "And they may have injured a Viking long ago somewhere along the coast. If we find someone, we must be very quiet and help him."

"A Viking?"

Marit nodded. "He may not look like a Viking. They don't always wear their metal helmets or carry long swords. But he would speak Norwegian, just like us."

"Keep watch, Tekopp," Lars said, "a Viking."

Beneath the water, boulders lay visible and some broke from the water. Marit rowed closer to shore, careful to avoid rocks that could rip open the bottom of their wooden boat or hold it fast in place like a beached sea turtle. They rounded a bend and reached the beach where trees met the shoreline.

Marit began to sing aloud, "Oh, Viking, Viking, where are you?"

Lars looked at her with an expression of wonder and respect.

Rowing parallel to the shore, well beyond the lighthouse and its guards, Marit sang out again, "Oh, Viking, Viking, where are you?"

A flock of oystercatchers worked the beach, poking their orange pencil beaks in and out of crevices. Again she sang out and glided forward. A few of the birds, their black-and-white feathers sharply contrasting with the gray light, scuttled away from her approaching boat.

A haze of movement caught her attention. Onshore, easing from behind a boulder, the injured Resistance soldier stumbled toward them, his face milky white. Bent nearly in half, he hobbled toward the water with the use of a stout stick.

Lars gasped but—thankfully—didn't scream. "Marit! He's hurt!"

"Don't say a word," Marit ordered. "That's our Viking . . . injured many years ago by the *kraken,* and now we must rescue him."

Lars stared at the creature hobbling toward their boat. "He doesn't look big enough to be a Viking."

"Well, not all Vikings are huge."

Marit rowed quickly—pull, pull, pull—until the bow just touched the shore. The soldier tumbled headfirst into the boat with a grunt, and then curled into a ball on the floor between them.

"We must hide him," she said.

Lars put Tekopp beside him on the seat, and then spread the *dyne* over the soldier. "His foot. He's hurt bad," he whispered.

"*Ja,*" Marit replied. "And we must keep him a secret."

Marit studied the mound and looked at Lars. This wouldn't work. If they rowed back like this, the soldiers would know they'd picked up something, or *somebody,* along the way. How stupid could she be? Why had she ever agreed to help?

"Lars, the *kraken* is still searching for this Viking—and for little boys—to gobble up. And right now, it's very important that you hide under the *dyne,* too."

He made a face and shook his head. *"Nei."*

"Don't worry, this man won't hurt you."

Lars pulled in his lower lip, a sign he was getting ready to debate.

"I'm serious, Lars!" she cried, and then tried to act less demanding. "Please," she begged in a softer voice, "do as I ask, and if anyone stops us, don't say a word. Pretend you're sleeping."

Reluctantly, with Tekopp, he crawled under the edge of the *dyne* and disappeared. The mound at the bottom of the boat was large, but Marit hoped it would go unnoticed.

Then, with a silent prayer for their safety, she began rowing back. The rowing was harder now, and though the breeze had died, the sea worked against her in swells. She pulled her elbows back against the darkening waters. Sweat formed on the back of her neck and down her spine. As she neared the lighthouse, she glanced over her shoulder to stay on course. She didn't want to get closer to the lighthouse than necessary, but she didn't want a current to sweep her farther out into the bay, either.

"*Fräulein,* where is your brother?" a soldier called out, startling her to her toes. Marit recognized his voice. He was the German soldier who had come to investigate the seal pup onshore. She hadn't expected the soldiers at the lighthouse to think it was out of the ordinary for her to be rowing. His question unnerved her, but she forced herself to remain calm.

She let go of the oars, pointed to the mound at her feet, and bent her head against folded hands, hoping he would get her silent message.

The soldier nodded. "Oh, sleeping!"

She nodded and returned to rowing, but the guard held up his hand and motioned to the cove beside the breakwater. "Stop. No farther tonight."

Marit held the oars above the water. Her heart stopped.

"Soldiers are searching the island. You could get shot on the water. Pull your boat to shore and walk home from here."

So that was why he'd commanded her to stop. Her heart started beating again. She knew she couldn't argue. She pointed the boat into the cove. Would he come and take the *dyne*? Her plan to help the Resistance soldier was unraveling. She was a fool, and not only had she put herself in danger, but now she risked her brother's life and the Resistance soldier's, too. It was just a matter of moments before they would all be found out. She was practically delivering the wounded soldier into Nazi hands.

The boat nudged against the shore. The sun had set, and shadows and darkness merged. Shaking, sweat running along her spine, she climbed from the bow and with more strength than she knew she possessed, pulled the weighted boat onto the shoreline.

At the lighthouse, the German soldier faced the shore, watching them.

"Come, Lars," she said, pretending to shake him awake. "Climb out of the boat." He emerged, his face full of questions. She held her forefinger to her lips.

A risky idea came to her. Extremely risky, but the only thing she could think of. Earlier, the soldier had said they needed more blankets. If she could distract him, then the wounded soldier might have a chance to escape without being seen.

"Lars, wait here by the boat for me. And don't say a word."

Lars nodded, with Tekopp nestled under his chin.

Marit pulled the *dyne* off the wounded soldier, whose eyes widened in alarm. She whispered, "In a moment, I'll distract the guards at the lighthouse. When I do, head north to the pasture. You'll see the barn and you can hide in the loft. It's dark enough—they may not see you cross the field." Then she pointed with her head toward the barn. At first he didn't move. Had he lost his hearing? If he couldn't get out of the boat, then what was she to do?

To her relief, he nodded.

"I'll meet you there when I can," she said, then turned to Lars. "Wait here for me."

"But Marit—it's getting dark!" With the situation so confusing and alarming, perhaps that's all he could think to say.

She gave him a kiss on the top of his head, something Mama would have done to reassure him. "I'll be right back."

The fluffy *dyne* filled her arms and she carried it along the shore, across the narrow cement breakwater—careful not to slip into the freezing waters on either side—all the way out to the lighthouse where the two soldiers watched. With each step, her legs weakened. Was she walking into her own trap? She wanted to run and get away from the soldiers, but she willed herself to slow down and walk calmly—stretching out time as much as possible to help the Norwegian soldier escape. Her whole being quaked, yet Marit held out the offering. She hoped that it wouldn't be bloodstained from the soldier's wounds. That might lead to another round of questions. She forced an outer calmness and vowed to keep her mouth shut. Not a word.

The Nazi soldiers stepped toward her. The one who

earlier had aimed at the seal pup took the blanket and smiled. "Eiderdown!" he exclaimed. Then he continued in rough Norwegian. "For us?"

Marit nodded, and then lowered her eyes.

"The Gestapo," he said, and pointed toward the farmhouse.

What? What could he mean?

"They're gone now," he said. "It's safe. You can come back for your boat in the morning."

She almost felt she could trust him.

He lifted the blanket again and smiled. *"Tusen takk."* She was turning to leave when he held up his hand in command.

A panic filled her. Had he figured out her scheme? Did he know that she was trying to create a distraction? She studied his face and tried to read his meaning.

He removed his glove, reached into his jacket pocket, pulled out two chocolate hearts—the kind Papa used to buy her at the milk shop in Isfjorden—and patted them into the palm of her mitten. She stared at them, not sure how to respond. He chuckled as he turned away.

Again, Marit forced herself to walk casually—rather than sprint—back along the wall to the shore. As she looked back, her German soldier had rounded the lighthouse, the *dyne* wrapped around his shoulders. Another soldier said something in German, and they laughed. Perhaps they thought the *dyne* was a real gift, that she was in love with them; or that she was feeling guilty about not having turned it in earlier; or that she was thanking him for warning her about rowing farther. Or perhaps they laughed at the simple mind of a Norwegian girl giving up something so valuable.

With Tekopp in his arms, Lars waited beside the boat, thankfully now empty. Darkness nearly swallowed it whole. Marit pulled the boat higher onto the shore, tied the bowline around a boulder, and hoped it would hold when the tide rose. The lighthouse sat eerily dark, permanently turned off now so that Allied ships and planes could not see the island.

Clouds hung low and covered the evening sky, eclipsing moonlight and starlight. Tekopp meowed, and Lars put him down and let him run free. As they crunched over snow patches in the pasture, Marit kept watching for the wounded soldier. She reached into her pocket.

"Here," she said, handing Lars a chocolate. She popped the other chocolate in her mouth, startled by its unexpected sweetness. Marit reached for Lars's mittened hand and kept walking. "You did a good job," she said.

He squeezed her hand. *"Takk."*

"But Marit, why did he sneak away?" he whispered.

"I don't know."

"Vikings fight—they're not afraid of anything. Not even the Nazis."

"No more talk," she said. "Remember. It's our secret."

Tekopp pounced on anything that moved as they crossed the field. The injured soldier was nowhere in sight. Her stomach rolled with nausea as she thought of the risks she'd just taken, of what she might have set in motion. She put one foot in front of the other and kept walking. In spite of Gestapo orders to darken every window, a sliver of light escaped from the farmhouse—enough to guide them.

Chapter Eighteen

In Hiding

When they slipped into the farmhouse, Bestefar had not yet returned. Without the *dyne* to cover them, Marit and Lars slept with sweaters on over their pajamas and two pairs of wool socks each. In the middle of the night, Lars tapped Marit on her shoulder. "Marit?"

"*Ja?*"

"I'm freezing."

The damp chill of March had crept into their bed, clung with icy fingers, and refused to let go. Marit hadn't slept either. "Me, too," she said. "Follow me."

Quietly, they slipped downstairs and put on their *jakkes,* mittens, and hats. She debated about putting on her boots and going out to the barn to see if the soldier had made it there, but she didn't dare open the door, which creaked worse than an old mast in the wind. She'd have to wait until morning. Tiptoeing, they climbed back upstairs and curled up, back to back.

"Marit," Lars whispered in her ear.

She cupped her hand over his ear in return. *"Ja?"*

"Where's the Viking?"

"I hope he made it to the loft. I'll check in the morning."

"Let's check now."

She had to admit, that was exactly what she wanted to do. But if she waited until just after dawn, Bestefar would be gone. "Better to wait. And remember—"

"I know, you've told me a thousand times. Not a word."

"That's right. You know, you're pretty smart, Lars."

"I know. That's what Bestefar tells me."

Before the sun rose, Marit was in the kitchen, pulling on her boots to milk Big Olga.

"You're an early riser today," Bestefar said, startling her. He stepped from his adjoining bedroom, pulling his suspenders up over his shoulders. Ashen half-moons lay beneath his hollowed eyes. He was growing thinner, and the arrest of Aunt Ingeborg—his daughter—appeared to be wearing on him. "Already dressed and ready for chores, I see."

"*Ja,*" she replied and headed out.

Big Olga stomped her foot when Marit entered; she was clearly not in the mood to wait. Marit would milk her first, and then search for the soldier. She listened for sounds of movement above her or from the corners of the barn but heard nothing.

In the warmth of the barn, surrounded by the comforting smells of manure and animal sweat, Marit sat on the wooden stool beside Big Olga. Tied in her stanchion, the cow chewed hay and stood still for Marit as she worked. *Ting, ting, ting.* The foamy milk hit the side of the metal bucket. Aunt Ingeborg had taught her how to milk when she was quite little. As the milk rose in the bucket, steam gathered around Marit's bare hands. The barn cat strolled in, a new batch of barn kittens racing ahead of her. Marit angled one of Big Olga's teats and shot a small stream in their direction. They pawed and licked at the air, catching a bit of the milk on their tongues. Such generosity. War made sharing even a few drops of milk an extravagance.

When Marit finished, Big Olga craned her neck and looked back at her with grateful brown eyes. Marit poured the fresh milk into the milk can, then patted Big Olga's neck before turning her out with the other cows.

The German soldiers had started weighing the milk on a scale when they came to collect their "donation."

And Marit knew she shouldn't remove even a cupful of what they expected. But today she would take a chance. With a wooden ladle, she scooped out some milk, and then put the cover back on the pail. She would add an equal amount of water to the container later, and hope that the soldiers couldn't tell the difference. Stealing from the Germans. It felt good.

Carefully keeping the ladle upright, she scaled the ladder one-handed to the loft, praying that the soldier had found his way there. She pulled herself to the loft floor and scanned expectantly. He was nowhere to be seen. The cats, in hot pursuit of the scent of fresh milk, scaled the ladder after her and began purring and winding their way in and out of Marit's legs.

"Sorry," she said. "Not for you this time."

A mound in the corner rustled with movement. Fully buried beneath the straw, the soldier lifted his head, his skin colorless and his hair tangled with straw.

"*God morgen,*" she said, trying to sound like Mama on the icy mornings when Marit hadn't wanted to get out of a warm bed. She knelt next to him with the ladle of fresh milk and pushed away the eager barn cats.

He eyed the milk hungrily and reached for it, his hands trembling so hard Marit thought he might spill every drop.

"Here," she said, "let me." She brought the milk to his

chalky lips. Greedily, he gulped the milk down. Then he dropped back into the straw. "And water," he said. "I'm so thirsty."

"*Ja,*" she said. "I'll get some."

Rather than bring water from the hand pump in the kitchen, which was risky, Marit scooped a bucket of water from the animals' trough outside. A thin covering of ice was already melting in the early rays. Though snow stayed for a long time on the mountain, the island's farmlands rarely froze over, and the snow usually melted within days of falling.

The soldier drank three ladles of water before he said, "Enough."

"That's good," she said, trying to sound cheery. "Before long, I'll bring you something to eat, too."

"*Takk,*" he said, and burrowed beneath the straw again without another word.

When Marit entered the kitchen, Bestefar was busy ladling porridge from the cast-iron pot into bowls. "Marit," he said, his voice serious. "I just went upstairs to wake Lars, and your *dyne* is missing. Missing!"

Marit's heart dropped. She had hoped to come up with an excuse for its disappearance, but she was too late. Pinpricks shot through her. Could Bestefar read the guilt on her face? "I know. I should have told you."

Lars sat at the table, spoon in hand. Marit stared at

him, hoping to remind him that he wasn't to say a word about the soldier—or Viking.

"And that's why you came downstairs fully dressed this morning?"

She nodded.

"And you and Lars slept in your hats and *jakkes*?"

That part was true, too. *"Ja,"* she said quietly.

"They're worse than lice!" he growled.

Marit wasn't sure what he was talking about. She remembered how much Aunt Ingeborg hated lice, how she had treated and combed the heads of two school kids to help them get rid of the pests. But that was last fall—months ago. What was Bestefar talking about?

"Yesterday," he said, "when I returned briefly from fishing, soldiers were here at the house. You two were gone. They told me, 'Enemies on the island' as they jabbed pitchforks in the hay, tapped on walls, and even searched upstairs. And then they stole your *dyne*! Wasn't it enough to requisition all our blankets last fall? They say they need *everything* for their soldiers fighting throughout Europe and Russia. We held back only one. Only one! *How* do they expect children to stay warm? They are heartless!"

Marit breathed out relief. Her deception was covered by the Nazis themselves. *Let them take the blame.*

After breakfast, just as Aunt Ingeborg would have done, Marit and Lars washed clothes and sheets on the washboard and hung them on the line to freeze-dry in the breeze. When a quiet moment came and Bestefar was gone, she sneaked out with Lars to the barn.

They'd both saved a bit of their breakfast porridge and a little cheese for the soldier.

"How come you're so young," Lars asked the soldier as he ate the food with his hands, "when you've lived so long? Are you really a Viking that the sea monsters hurt?"

The soldier looked at him quizzically.

Marit nodded encouragingly.

"It's a secret," he said, his hands trembling. A deep crimson brightened his cheeks. Marit touched her hand to his forehead, as Mama had done to her so many times, and felt the soldier's fever travel through her fingers.

"You're burning up. You must rest."

He finished the small bit of food, and then lay back again.

"What's your name?"

"Henrik."

"We'll let you rest then, Henrik." She started to her feet as Lars climbed down the ladder.

"Wait." The soldier's face was guarded.

Marit couldn't see his face; he was hidden so completely. Only his arm stretched through the straw, a metal compass dangling in his hand. "I can't make it. You must take this to the fishing village—north side of the island. I was to have landed there."

The village he spoke of boasted the largest lighthouse on Godøy and was not an easy jaunt down the road. It would take a full day of hiking to get there and back—or a boat ride halfway around the island.

"But why?"

"No—no questions. The less you know, the better."

She remembered Papa telling her the same thing. She reached for the compass, and as soon as she lifted it from his hand, his arm flopped down beside him, as if he'd been holding a great weight. He lay there, his arm in full view. Marit covered it with straw again and leaned closer.

"Who . . . who do I take this to at the fishing village?"

"First house in the village," the soldier said, struggling for air between phrases. "Farthest house from the lighthouse. Ask for Astrid. Say, 'Do you have any klipfish for sale?'"

"Klipfish?"

"*Ja.*"

Then she repeated his instructions back to him.

"Good," he said. "And when she asks you how many, you say, 'A bucketful.' And make sure you show her an empty bucket. Can you remember this?"

"Astrid and klipfish," she repeated. "And I must bring an empty bucket."

"*Ja*, that's good. Go . . . please," Henrik whispered from beneath the straw, "before it's too late."

And then he was silent, completely hidden and completely still. Marit left him and joined Lars below. She held the compass in her hand. Lars scooted closer. "What's that for, Marit?"

"For telling direction. North, south, east, or west." She didn't want to involve Lars in this, but she would look more suspicious acting on her own. And she would risk a scolding and too many questions from Bestefar if she left Lars behind. It was early in the day. If she took off with Lars, they would appear as two bored kids trying to fill their unexpected days off with something to do. With school temporarily shut down, this would seem believable.

Marit paused, reminding herself of the risk, another choice filled with *unthinkable* consequences. She'd heard stories about the Gestapo: the woman who had her fingernails pulled out, the fisherman from Ålesund taken away for questioning and returned with cigarette burns across his body, the numerous bodies found floating in the sea . . . Norwegians . . . and no one knew what terrible things they'd suffered before drowning.

Compass in hand, her palms slippery with sweat, she examined the silver object and the simple carving of a ship on its cover. She flipped open the lid, expecting to find a note, a piece of paper, something secretive. But it looked like an ordinary compass. She turned toward Godøy Mountain and the needle pointed north. It worked like an ordinary compass. What could possibly be so important about it that this man, Henrik, would travel the sea, have his boat shot out from under him, lose his companions, and entrust her with it? There had to be more to it.

Marit forced a smile and feigned enthusiasm. "Lars," she whispered, "are you ready for another adventure?"

CHAPTER NINETEEN

A Bucket of Klipfish

Though the hike over the island's peak to the fishing village on the other side was daunting, Marit thought she could make it. She was less certain about Lars, especially if they ran into snow at the top. And she doubted he'd be strong enough to hike back again. Unlike Papa, she certainly wasn't going to carry him over her shoulder if he got too tired. That left only one other choice. They would row to the island's north side.

Marit packed a chunk of cheese, two slices of coarse bread, and a jar of water. Over their *jakkes,* they pulled on dark, canvas raincoats. Marit sniffed. *"Uff da!"* Beste-far had bought the raincoats for them in Ålesund, but they were not soaked in regular linseed oil, which had disappeared; these raincoats reeked of cod liver oil. Putrid smelling—but better than nothing in such weather.

A light drizzle misted the air. Shades of deep gray blanketed the sky above the sea and pasture. They hiked toward the lighthouse shore where the rowboat waited, nudged higher onshore from tidal currents.

"Help me push," Marit said, throwing her weight against the bow.

Lars's face reddened as they edged the boat slowly over the kelp-covered rocks. From the corner of her eye, Marit saw a German soldier trot across the breakwater toward them, gun over his shoulder.

The compass around her neck turned weighty as an anchor.

"*Hei! God morgen!*" he called with a wave.

Marit froze.

In a few long strides, the soldier was at the boat's side, pushing alongside her. Marit looked at him questioningly, and he smiled in return. It was the soldier she'd given the *dyne* to yesterday. She could not understand his motivation, but inside, she breathed a prayer of gratitude.

Within seconds, the boat eased into the water. Fast as rabbits into their burrow, she and Lars slipped into the safety of the rowboat. Lars sat in the bow so he could look ahead; Marit sat in the middle seat, facing their wake as she rowed. With a wave, she thanked the soldier, and then pulling quickly on the oars, glided away from shore.

She'd come to feel completely at ease in the rowboat, the oars familiar in her hands—the only thing left in life over which she had control. The task of rowing to the north side of the island would not be easy. She pulled hard, stroke by stroke, and they rounded the lighthouse and peninsula and skimmed over boulders that lay dangerously close to the surface.

"Keep a lookout for sea monsters," Marit called, just in case the soldiers could hear. "We're off on another adventure!"

Lars gazed at Ålesund to the east. Marit hoped that Bestefar's trawler was nowhere in sight. He would be furious to see them go beyond the lighthouse boundary, and he'd stop them.

To blend in and be less visible from the water, Marit kept the rowboat close to shore. If she strayed too far, they could end up wrestling ocean currents. Fortunately, morning waters were fairly calm. The rowboat crested over the tops of small waves and pulsed them toward the northeastern point of the island. The shoreline drifted by quickly. They passed farms, a single red boathouse, the wooded shoreline where she'd found Henrik, and another pasture where sheep grazed on patches of last year's grasses. Snows had begun to melt.

Drizzle drenched her face, but Marit didn't mind.

Perhaps this mission would be easy to accomplish after all. With a breeze at their stern, they glided easily. She understood the risk, but to be doing something to help the Resistance was exhilarating. For two years she had not been able to do anything to help fight the Nazis. Just a week ago, she'd stood mute and helpless as Nazis hauled her aunt away. Finally, she was doing *something*.

Unlike Bestefar, she chose to fight back.

"Are sea monsters related to trolls?" Lars asked, keeping watch.

"No, sea monsters live in the ocean. And trolls, they live deep in the mountains. They're all scary, but no, I don't think they're related."

"And they eat children."

"Oh, I don't think trolls like the taste of children. But they sure like mountain goats." She glanced over her shoulder at him, not sure if he really believed in such things anymore. Either way, at least he was willing to play along.

"Oh," Lars said, sucking on his lower lip. "And Henrik, did he really hurt his leg by fighting the *kraken*?"

"*Ja,* he's very brave."

"But then why did he hide from the soldiers in our barn?"

"Sometimes Vikings get hurt and they need to heal before they can go back to battle."

"Did the *kraken* bite his foot?"

She nodded.

"Marit," he said, his dimples forming tiny crevices in his rounded cheeks. "Are you telling me the truth? Are there really sea monsters and trolls? Is he really a Viking? Are you sure? Do you swear on the Bible?"

She drew a breath. This wasn't the time to tell him the truth. If she just played along, she lessened the risks for him should they be stopped and questioned. She remembered Papa's words: *The less you know the better.* In war, she now understood, this was often true.

"Lars," she said, "this is serious. Just keep a lookout. Better to keep watch."

That was all it took. Lars turned his gaze back to the sea, ready to resume his post. Marit was relieved. She needed to have him work with her, even if he didn't know the real reasons why.

She rowed on. Drizzle soon turned to plump raindrops. Her thoughts drifted with the current. She wondered about her old friend Liv. What was she doing at this moment? Marit pictured her on a distant farm, helping with chores, maybe reading a book in the hayloft in a patch of sunshine. Liv loved to read.

At the most eastern point of the island, their luck changed. Waves struck boulders and sent sheets of white spray into the air. Marit rowed hard as they veered into a wind that swept toward the island's rocky northern shore. She leaned hard into the oars.

"Watch for boulders!" she called.

"But I can barely see," Lars whined. "I'm getting rain in my eyes."

"Try!" she shouted. "I don't want to look over my shoulder and lose ground. Call out, 'keep left' or 'keep right.' Help keep us headed toward that lighthouse ahead. Do you see it?"

"*Ja!* Red and white striped."

"Good."

Only a fool would try to row into the wind here. But she *was* a fool, just like her Papa. If Bestefar thought such heroic actions were foolish, then let him. She pulled harder against the oars, straining her back against the bitter wind.

Icy salt water sprayed over the bow, pelting the back of her slicker. Lars whined. "Marit! We should turn back," he called. "I'm scared."

"If we make it to the village, then the sea monsters will be afraid of us. Right now, they're stirring up the waves. They're trying to scare us away from our mission! Be brave!"

Gasping for breath, lungs and throat on fire from the effort, Marit heaved on the oars, stroke after stroke after stroke. Her shoulders pinched in painful knots. Despite sprays of freezing water, she removed her mittens to get a better grip on the oars' handles. Blisters formed and soon broke in the crook of her thumbs, and she winced with each splash of salt water. She tried to think beyond her pain. Think of Aunt Ingeborg, she told herself, who might now be in a "reeducation" camp, or crammed with other teachers in a boat, journeying up the coast as a mine finder for the German boats that followed behind. This was one of the rumors she had heard. Think of Henrik, wounded and feverish in the hayloft, just because he was trying to help Norway. Marit clenched against the pain, against the burning of her muscles, and against the Nazi occupation—and rowed all the harder.

Abruptly, the shore rose to steep cliffs. If Marit couldn't hold them on course, the waves would seize their little rowboat and toss it against the rocks the same way seagulls drop clams to crack their shells.

Under a sky of slate drizzle, minutes turned to endless hours. Wave by wave, spray by spray over their bow, they began to take in water. Marit checked over her shoulder, uncertain that her raw and blistered hands would hold out much longer, but ahead—to her relief—two breakwaters beckoned like arms and offered protective harbor. She kept rowing.

As they drew closer, she looked again. A lighthouse towered above a slope dotted with sheep and houses of red, green, and gold and a row of boathouses perched on the shore. Through the mist, two German trucks traversed the road toward the lighthouse.

The rowboat finally rounded the breakwater. The

waves settled. A sea otter slid off a rock, floated on his back, then dived.

"See that?" Lars said.

Marit rowed past docks, where a fisherman, head bowed under his rain hat, unloaded lobster creels from his boat to the docks, but he paid them no attention.

"Lars, you need to wait here and watch the boat. Eat the cheese and bread we brought. Maybe that otter will show up again. Keep watch, Lars, and I'll be back soon. I promise."

She jumped from the boat, tied it up, and left Lars. The compass was tucked safely next to her chest, and beneath it, her heart pounded like a trawler's engine. She passed idle nets and strings of small fish drying beneath boathouse eaves. Under her breath, Marit repeated Henrik's instructions. "'Do you have any klipfish for sale?' When she asks you how many, say, 'a bucketful.'"

With haste, she headed beyond the boathouses to the first house on the edge of the village—a white house trimmed green. It was closest to the harbor, and farthest from the lighthouse that towered above the fishing village. It had to be the one.

Darting across the muddy road, Marit turned into the yard. With its stone foundation and slate-covered roof, the house was ordinary. Nothing about it hinted at Resistance activity. Had she remembered the instructions?

She swallowed hard, marched up to the door, and knocked.

Footsteps pattered inside, then paused. Finally, the door edged open.

Through the crack, a man with an unshaven face and the expression of a tombstone stared at her. One of his thick arms hung in a sling. If he was trying to discourage visitors, his manner was definitely working.

"I-I thought a woman lived here. I'm sorry." She turned to leave.

"What do you want?" he demanded.

Halfway down the steps, Marit turned. Could she trust this man? It was the right house, she was sure of it. But wasn't she to meet with a woman? Had something gone wrong? "Is Astrid here?" she finally asked.

The man didn't answer for some time. Finally, his voice softened.

"*Ja.* Do you have a message for her?"

Was she to wait for a woman to appear or carry on with her part? But the man knew the name, and maybe that was enough. She plowed ahead. "Does she have any cod—" She caught herself. "I mean, klipfish for sale?"

"I see. And what will you carry it in?"

"Oh, no! Wait, I can go back to my rowboat. I have a bailing bucket."

His face showed no expression as he waited for something more.

"I need a bucketful," she stated firmly.

He nodded. "And in return for klipfish?"

Her fingers trembled as she reached inside the top of her sweater and found the compass and its chain. She removed it from around her neck and handed it to the man.

He glanced at its cover. *"Ja,"* he said. "This will do. *Tusen takk,"* he added, then turned away and closed the door behind him.

Marit stood there, alone on the doorstep, bewildered. Was there more she was expected to do? Had she completed her part of a code? Should she have something in exchange to take back to Henrik—klipfish or something to prove that she'd done as he'd asked? But the door remained closed.

The man's message to her became clear: *Leave. And leave quickly.*

CHAPTER TWENTY

Ancient Walls

A truck rolled past Marit, splattering her with puddles of freezing mud. In the back of the truck, German soldiers huddled under a canvas top, heads down, shoulders hunched in the cold. Beneath her raincoat, she shook violently. Eyes lowered, she kicked at a clump of melting ice that lingered at the edge of the road and waited till the truck bumped away before she moved.

In the rain, she sprinted across the road and along the breakwater, hoping Lars had stayed put as she'd asked.

"I saw the otter again," he said, his voice wobbly, his face ashen. Was he chilled to the bone?

"Good," she replied. She fumbled with the lines, and finally untied them. Then she jumped in and took up the oars. The faster she could get them back to the farm-house, the better.

The wind had kicked up small whitecaps in the shel-tered harbor. It would be much easier returning with the wind at their backs on this side of the island. Her shoul-ders tensed as she eased past a couple of fishing trawlers. Two fishermen watched her with curiosity. She didn't have klipfish to show them. And no good excuse for be-ing there, either. She hadn't thought that far ahead.

Pulling against the oars, she nudged the bow past the breakwater walls and into open water. As soon as they passed the sheltering cement arms, a wave slammed up against their stern and pushed them forward. They rode swiftly up the crest of a frothy wave, slipped down to its base, then rushed ahead to the top of the next swell.

Wind hissed in Marit's ears and stung her face. Her vi-sion blurred with sheets of raindrops and salt water. Still, with her oars in the water, she held the rowboat steady and kept its bow pointed straight into the waves. A slight twist or turn, left or right, could tempt a wave to reach out and swamp them. She couldn't risk that. She also couldn't leave guiding the boat to Lars's judgment, so she kept glancing over her shoulder to make sure the bow was cutting straight through the powerful waves. In no time at all, they approached the farthest edge of Godøy. Somehow, she'd have to cut quickly to the is-land's eastern point, but the waves had grown wild.

"I'm getting sick," Lars moaned above the wind. "I can't stand going up and down!"

"Put your head between your knees," she offered, without turning to look at him. "Maybe that will help."

"Nooo," he wailed. "That makes it worse."

"Try looking out and breathing lots of fresh air! If you get sick, use this." She skipped a beat with her oars, grabbed the metal pail at her feet, and tossed it over her shoulder to Lars behind her at the bow. Rowing again, she shouted, "Don't lean over the side! I don't want to lose you!"

Suddenly, out of the corner of her eye, Marit saw him. He was on his feet, wobbling, and he tottered toward the edge of the boat.

"Lars, no! Sit down!"

She let go of the oars, jumped forward, and pulled Lars back to his seat. He held the bucket between his knees. Head down, he retched.

Marit slid back on her seat and glanced around. One moment, that's all it took. They'd gone too far past the calmer lee of the island. They'd lost their only chance to cut south. Instead of heading home, they had been pushed by large, deep rollers northeastward—straight for Giske Island.

"Nei! Nei! Nei!" Marit protested against the power of the wind and current. She had no choice but to row with the cresting waves, to do what she could to prevent them

from turning sideways. They were in open water, rushing headlong to the nearest island. She let the waves push them toward Giske. When the winds died down, she'd row them back to Godøy.

Lars finished using the bucket and looked around. "Marit!" he screamed, his eyes wide with fear. "Floating mines, remember?! What are you doing out this far?"

"This wasn't planned!" she shouted. "I didn't *try* to get us out here. If you hadn't gotten sick—" And then she stopped herself. That wasn't fair. He didn't need her yelling. It wasn't his fault—or hers—that they were adrift.

"I'm sorry," she said, looking over her shoulder to Lars. "I'm sorry you don't feel well. Are you better?"

He nodded, though his skin matched the greenish gray of the sky.

"Keep a lookout for anything floating that could be a mine."

She expected him to whine, but he didn't. He perched on the bow seat like a carved figurehead on a Viking ship's prow. They drifted on.

"There, on the right!" he said, and Marit veered the oars and shifted the boat to the left slightly. "No it's not—it's a killer whale!"

Marit shot a glance over her shoulder. "Oh, my!"

The head of a black and white killer whale floated several meters from their boat, its huge eye watching them.

It dived and then came arcing up out of the water before going under again, this time sinking like a submarine. They'd seen killer whales in the fjords before, but never so close up.

"Marit—right! Go right!"

"Whose right?" Uncertain, she pulled to her right and Lars screamed.

"No, not that way!"

She pulled hard on her left oar.

In the next second, on her left, a bobbing round metal object paralleled them, floating beyond the tip of Marit's oar.

A mine.

She eased both oars out of the water and brought them in closer to the gunwales. Bestefar had said that if you so much as brushed into a mine, it could explode. She froze, waiting as the distance grew between the floating mine and their little boat, centimeter by slow centimeter.

When they were clear of the mine, Marit rowed again, leaving it farther and farther in their wake. She felt sick about what might have happened. She glanced over her shoulder to Lars, perched on the bow. "You saved us," she called, her voice tremulous. *"Takk."*

He nodded but didn't turn from his duty.

Waves pushed them closer toward Giske Island. Ahead, a church steeple pierced the heavy sky. "See that church?" She tried to sound calmer than she felt.

"*Ja.*"

"Mama and Papa told me it's a few hundred years old, but the smaller chapel is even older. It was built by a powerful Viking family a thousand years ago."

"Really?"

"I'd swear on the Bible." This time, she was telling the truth. She tried to imagine people living on these remote islands so many years ago. Somehow thinking about them gave her hope. The Nazis seemed to have taken over her whole world, but even they couldn't stay in power forever.

Sooner than expected, their boat slammed forward, jolting them off their seats. She fell backward onto the wet floor of the boat, banging her shoulder. When she scrambled to her feet to look around, Lars had disappeared.

Marit scrambled over the bow of the rowboat. On the sandy shore, face down, lay her brother.

"Lars! Are you all right?"

He sat up slowly and brushed wet sand off his skinned nose. His lower lip quivered. "I'm cold."

"Then we'll find someplace to get warm." The white beach merged with gray pastures. Clusters of sheep stared at them, round and fat in their dirty white coats. "Let's try the church."

They pulled the rowboat onto the sandy shore. There

was nowhere to tie it, so they left it there. Then they ran across the pasture to the red-roofed stone church beyond. Unlike Norway's many octagonal churches, this one was rectangular, with a two-sided pitched roof; it was surrounded by a thick stone fence, which ended in two stone pillars. They passed through, hand in hand.

Ahead, a red and black Nazi flag hung above the door. Marit stopped, reluctant to move any closer.

But they needed shelter. Gusts of wind turned to torrents of rain. Her teeth chattered with cold. Lars's skin had gone from greenish gray to gray-blue. He needed to get out of the foul weather, to be dry and warm. Maybe they'd be lucky. Maybe the church was empty. They would stop for a short time, then hope for the winds to change so they could row back.

"Come on." She darted to the heavy wooden door, knocked, waited a full ten seconds . . . and then stepped in. Straight, ornately carved pews waited beneath the carved pulpit, off to the left.

Marit motioned to Lars to sit down beside her in the back of the church. She pulled off her slicker and hung it on the back of the pew. It was cold in the church, but warm compared to the wet, howling winds beyond its walls.

Her arms were heavy anchors. If she curled up in a ball and let her clothes dry out, and slept . . . just a short nap . . . She closed her eyes. She'd never felt so tired before. Rain pounded on the roof, pelted the paned windows, and created a sense of coziness, even though the building was cool.

Lars stirred in the pew beside her, but she gave in to exhaustion and slept.

CHAPTER TWENTY-ONE

Troubled Mission

Marit awoke to the deep voices of men. She was in a church, she remembered quickly, but why?

"A sister?" said a man in a melodic voice. Then it all flooded back. Rowing to the fishing village, asking for klipfish and leaving the compass in the hands of a strange man, and then getting swept by southwesterly winds to Giske Island. "Where? Show us."

Footsteps approached. It must be a pastor, someone who would help them. Expectantly and with a sense of relief, Marit opened her eyes. Lars stood at the edge of her pew, pointing. Behind him glowered the faces of two men: a Nazi soldier and an officer.

Marit jumped to the worst conclusions: They'd been found out, caught as part of the Resistance. But she tried to hide her fears. She rubbed her eyes, faked a wide yawn, and blinked.

The officer said something in German, and the soldier interpreted it in Norwegian. "What are you kids doing here?"

Lars's chin began to quiver.

No, Lars . . . not now! Marit thought. *Please don't tell about our trip.*

She debated if she should remain silent, as always, but decided to risk speaking. "School's closed," she started and cleared her throat.

Lars began to whimper, and his whimpers turned to crying.

Marit talked faster, hoping her brother would hold his tongue. "We were bored," she continued, "so we went rowing this morning and the wind was so strong it blew us off course." She pointed to the weather outside the windows and told him that they came from Godøy. "I couldn't row back, so we came into the church for shelter. I hope we didn't break any rules. We weren't trying to be trouble for anyone. We don't want to be a problem."

She surprised herself at how easily the words rolled off her tongue. She had never been good at lying. The war was apparently changing that.

The soldier related her story to the officer, and then asked, "What is your name?"

"Marit Gundersen. And this is my brother, Lars."

The soldier raised his voice above Lars's snuffles. "The enemy may try to attack on this coast and we want to keep you safe. You seem like smart kids. Tell us, have you seen anything on your island that seems unusual?"

"*Nei.*"

"Think harder. Anything out of the ordinary—visitors, perhaps? Faces you haven't seen before. Five men, perhaps, wearing oilskins and sea boots? Anyone with anything to hide? Anything unusual?"

She tilted her head, as if seriously considering his questions. She pictured Henrik's oilskin boots, one in shreds around his badly injured foot. He had said his boat had gone down. Had the other four all died? This question about anything *unusual* was almost laughable.

With a casual shrug of her shoulders, she replied with amazing outward calm. "*Nei.*" For extra effect, as if she were genuinely trying to think hard, she paused. Then, hoping to persuade Lars to not add a word, she slowly shook her head at him, then at the soldier. "Nothing unusual."

She hoped she'd convinced him.

He spoke again in German with the officer, then turned to her, his face revealing nothing. "Gather your things," he ordered, "and come with me."

In the pouring rain, Marit and Lars followed the soldier to the nearest house. He knocked—*bam, bam, bam, bam*. Behind them in the distance, in the shelter of the church doorway, the officer smoked a cigarette.

The tallest woman Marit had ever met opened the door. To her chest she held a crying infant. *"Ja?"*

"By orders of the Reich, give these children shelter and return them to Godøy where they belong."

"Return them? But my husband—"

The soldier snapped his arm straight toward her head. *"Heil Hitler!"* he shouted, then walked away.

The woman stood board stiff. Her baby bawled harder. Then she turned her attention to Marit and Lars, as if seeing them for the first time. Her shoulders relaxed and she exhaled. *"Vel,"* she said. "You'd better come inside. It's a foul day." Once the door was closed and locked, she added with scorn, "But for the Nazis, compared to the hell that awaits *their* souls, this weather will someday seem like heaven."

Marit smiled. She liked this woman.

"My husband is fishing, and you'll have to stay here until he returns. I have no way to get you back to Godøy before then."

A small fire crackled in the cookstove. As she placed her baby in a basket on the counter, she motioned with her head to a bench at the table. "Sit," she said, "and hand me your wet clothes." They removed their layers, right down to their thin wool undergarments, and she hung their clothes on a line that stretched from one end of the kitchen to the other. Bright yellow dishes decorated the open shelves. A red runner graced the simple wooden table. Marit enjoyed the comfort of being in this home. She thought of the many times she'd sat at her own kitchen table in Isfjorden with Papa and Mama. The scents of fresh coffee, wood smoke, and homemade flatbread, fresh from the oven. She'd give almost anything to go back to those times.

The woman added a birch log to the cookstove, and before long, heat billowed, warming them and drying their clothes. She poured mugs of hot water. "Something to warm you," she said. Arms across her chest, she studied them, then turned to her nearly bare cupboards and icebox. Soon, she laid out a few pieces of pickled herring and two pieces of bread.

"Takk," Marit said, knowing that with food increasingly scarce, this was a generous gift, a banquet. She and Lars huddled side by side and ate hungrily.

They soon learned that the woman's name was Johanne, and that she was originally from Bergen on the mainland. "With this war, I'm beginning to wonder if anything is left standing there anymore." The Allies, she said, had hit several German targets, including ships.

"And the Germans bomb any building that they think is connected with Resistance activities. The world has turned upside down."

What would Johanne think if Marit told her she was helping the Resistance and hiding a soldier? She had an impulse to tell this woman everything, but she held back. Because of her actions, she must be extra careful to guard her secrets so no harm would come to Johanne's family.

Johanne told them a joke. "A knock came at the door," she began, "and the old woman asked, 'Who is it?'

"'The Angel of Death,' came the reply. The woman opened the door and smiled. 'Come in, come in! I thought you were the Gestapo!'"

Marit laughed, but Lars scrunched his forehead in confusion.

"The Angel of Death," Johanne explained, "even *that* looks good compared to the Gestapo—the Nazis' secret police. Get it?"

He nodded. "I knew that."

Johanne told them how when the radios were recently turned in on Giske Island, the villagers put their radios on a horse-drawn cart, draped it in black, and followed the cart like a funeral procession. "We even sang hymns," she said, "accompanied by fiddle."

Marit told Johanne about the bombing of their real home at Isfjorden, about staying with Bestefar on Godøy

Island, and about Aunt Ingeborg being taken away in the middle of the school day.

"Oh, dear." Johanne's shoulders rose slowly. She looked at them with sympathy. "And your parents, are they alive?"

"They've sent letters," Lars said.

"Good," Johanne said. "That's good. With this war, you never know."

What Johanne said was true. Marit's parents could be killed any day—any second—by air attacks, or found out by the Gestapo. But her parents were still in the mountains, Marit tried to console herself, tucked safely away from harm. At least, that was her prayer.

"My husband won't be back until later. Read or rest, whatever you like. He'll get you home. Not that I like the idea of his crossing the waters at night, mind you, but we've been given no choice, have we?"

"*Nei,*" Marit replied.

The baby started to fuss, and Johanne moved to a corner rocker to nurse.

From a shelf, Marit pulled down a book called *Kristin Lavransdatter: The Bridal Wreath*. She opened the novel and began reading aloud about a Norwegian girl in the Middle Ages and her struggle to survive in difficult times. Marit knew Lars loved to be read to. And she had loved it when Mama had read to them every night.

That afternoon in the living room, sitting shoulder to

shoulder with Lars on the braided wool rug, Marit read until her voice grew hoarse. Before long, Lars stretched out his legs, lay his head down, and fell asleep. And still Marit read, partly because Lars's body, snuggled against hers, was comforting. And partly because she couldn't put the book down. It took her away from the present and everything her world had become. It silenced her concerns about returning to Godøy. It helped her pretend they could stay here with Johanne instead. What would Bestefar do when he learned of their misadventure? And the soldier in the loft. What if Bestefar found him? Would he stay quiet and hidden while she was away? It was easier to keep turning the page of the book than to answer such questions.

By late afternoon, to their fortune, the wind and rain had eased. When Lars stirred, Marit put the book back, went to the kitchen, and talked with Johanne. "The wind seems to have died down. I think I could row back."

"It's too far, and it's growing dark."

"But I'm a strong rower," she said, her arms and shoulders aching.

Johanne shook her head. "That may be, but you were put in my charge, and I'm not going to let another wind toss you back up on our shore. For your sake and for mine. The less often those Nazis come to my door, the better. You'll stay and wait until Rollo returns. He'll motor you back."

Marit didn't have to wait long. Within the hour, Johanne's husband returned, and then wordlessly he bade them to follow. In the thickening darkness, he towed their empty rowboat behind his trawler.

At considerable risk, they slowly crossed the water between the two islands and rounded the peninsula of the familiar lighthouse. Marit was told to watch for mines, but how was she to see them in such dark waters?

Suddenly, a shot rang out and water sprayed before the bow. She screamed.

From the lighthouse, rays of light swept across the boat.

"Halt!"

Rollo idled the motor. "These children," Rollo shouted, "drifted in their rowboat to Giske! We were ordered to return them here, where they live!"

There was no answer, just lights washing back and forth over the deck, illuminating them. Water lapped against the boat and rocked them from side to side.

Marit held on to the boat's mast with Lars. "Just stay calm," she whispered, "don't talk."

"Proceed!" the soldier shouted.

Rollo shifted from neutral to forward, and they made their way slowly from the lighthouse to the wharf. In the distance, shadowy shapes looked increasingly familiar.

"There's the pier," Marit called. "Up ahead."

Without a word, Rollo eased the boat slowly into the

harbor and pulled up beside an open dock. "Stay home," he said, almost the only words he'd said the whole way. "You put others in danger."

"*Takk,*" Marit said.

He motioned to their rowboat tied to the stern of his trawler. She and Lars hopped down into it as he untied it from his boat and pushed it away.

Marit picked up the oars and rowed the short distance to the dark silhouette of Bestefar's boathouse. As she pulled through the black water, her shoulder muscles, back, and hands protested in pain. She was more sore than she'd ever been in her life.

They touched shore, hopped out, and pulled up the rowboat. Marit almost wanted to kiss the stones beneath her feet. They had made it back. They were safe! As they passed the boathouse's side door, it creaked open.

They jumped, and Lars seized Marit's arm.

"Marit!" Bestefar spoke harshly.

She took in the figure darkening the door frame. He would never forgive her for being gone so long with the rowboat, no matter what excuse she tried to come up with now. He'd spoken one word, and by his tone, she understood clearly where he was placing the blame.

CHAPTER TWENTY-TWO

Infection

"Straight home!" Bestefar ordered. Without another word, he marched them down the road. Marit glanced at the barn as they passed. She needed to check on Henrik, to bring him food and water and tell him that she'd delivered the compass. All that would have to wait until Bestefar went to bed.

In the warmth of the kitchen, Bestefar paced, his eyebrows meeting in a white, furrowed *V*.

"It wasn't Lars's idea to row out so far, that much I know. Marit, I think it's best you go to bed early tonight."

"But I'm starving!"

"You'll survive until morning. No, your punishment is

to head straight upstairs. You've caused me enough worry. You need to ponder your foolishness."

Marit drank a cup of water from the hand pump at the sink, and then paused at the first step, wondering about Henrik. He needed food. He needed water. Perhaps if Marit told Bestefar the truth, he'd help her care for him. Maybe call a doctor. But she came to a quick decision— the same one she'd come to earlier. To tell Bestefar was to risk Henrik's life further.

"Marit!"

Her anger toward Bestefar burned all the hotter as she stomped loudly up the stairs.

"That's enough for one day," Bestefar called after her. "Not another word, not another foot stomping, do you understand?"

She refused to answer.

Stretched out on her bed, she listened to her stomach rumble with hunger. She'd never felt more tired. Every muscle in her body was filled with lead. And she was really, really hungry. But she would not beg. She was too proud to plead for something to eat. Still, it wasn't fair that Lars was allowed to eat a bowl of cod stew. Far from the wood stove, her bedroom was cool; Aunt Ingeborg's homemade wool socks and her own sweaters barely warmed her.

Even Lars made her angry. His voice flitted up the stairs, chatting on and on to Bestefar about being on the water and the wind blowing them straight to Giske and spotting a killer whale. "And we nearly bumped into a floating mine," he added, "but I told Marit to turn right."

She held her breath and waited for him to tell every bit of their day and get her in real trouble.

"But she turned fast," he said, "and we missed it completely!"

To her relief, Lars didn't mention anything about the fishing village or the church on Giske or the Germans. "A nice woman named Johanne gave us food and I fell asleep."

From what she could hear, Lars was intentionally steering clear of telling everything. "We're safe and that's what matters," he said, sounding just like Papa.

Bestefar humphed. "We're in the middle of a war," he said, seeming to talk more to himself than to Lars. "I have enough to worry about without my grandchildren wandering off—across open water, no less."

Her mind replayed her long day. What had the German soldier on Giske Island meant when he said "The enemy may try to attack on this coast"? Did that mean the Allied forces were planning to land somewhere on Norway's western coast? She wondered if delivering the compass was part of such a plan. Did it carry codes in the engravings or, somewhere inside its case, a small note of importance? Had anyone seen her on the doorstep of the house in Alnes?

Before she knew it, she had dropped into a fathomless sleep.

Lars's moaning and leg-kicking woke her. He was sound asleep, and she was grateful that she no longer had to wake him to use the night pot. From the main floor, Bestefar's snoring whistled through the house—a good sign.

She slipped into her boots, *jakke,* and hat. Then, silent as a mole, she grabbed a half loaf of something that passed for bread—as Aunt Ingeborg had said, the flour was more like ground sand these days. She broke off a chunk of cheese from the wheel in the icebox. She poured a glass of milk, ate quickly, then stuffed Henrik's half of the cheese and bread in her pockets. This time, Big Olga would have to wait.

Climbing the ladder to the loft with a half bucketful of water, Marit was met with air so foul she nearly tumbled backward.

"Henrik?" she whispered, then clasped her hand over her nose.

She should have left him an empty bucket to use, but that hadn't occurred to her. He was in no shape to climb up and down the ladder. He surely couldn't have hiked to the outhouse. She was a foolish child taking on tasks far larger than she could possibly handle.

If the Gestapo returned to the farm to search again—and especially if they brought search dogs with them—

the smell in the loft would flash a signal brighter than any lighthouse. She knelt beside the soldier.

"Henrik?" No answer.

He was dead—there could be no other explanation. Panic built in her legs. She wanted to run away but forced herself to stay calm. She reached into the pile of straw and touched his chest. Beneath her palm, she sensed breathing—breaths as shallow as a parched riverbed.

Marit brushed straw from his face. His eyes were sunken behind shadowed lids. A white crusty film covered his cracked lips. She touched his forehead. He was burning with fever.

"Mor," he cried weakly, like a child calling out for his mother.

"Oh—you are alive!" She brushed more straw from his body. Careful not to bump him, she examined his injured foot. It was swollen to three times its earlier size, and the open wounds oozed. She didn't know much about medicine, but she knew that his foot was dangerously infected. His fever was possibly high enough to kill him.

She lifted a ladle of water to his lips, but it dripped across his face. Some of it fell into his parted lips. She tried to give him more, and he opened his mouth wider but choked, spitting water, which dribbled down his neck. If he was too weak to drink . . .

"Don't die on me, Henrik," she whispered. "I delivered

it—the compass—just like you asked." She didn't know if he could hear her or, if he did, whether he understood.

The sky was growing hazy with a dusky morning light. Bestefar could be leaving for his boat at any moment, and Marit needed to be milking Big Olga when he stepped from the farmhouse, just in case he checked on her. She gently placed more fresh straw over Henrik, hoping to hide the foul odor, and then headed down the ladder. "I'll get help, I promise."

From her stanchion, Big Olga studied Marit as she skillfully eased the cow's full udders with her hands. The barn cat and her kittens showed up, right on schedule, and waited for their taste of warm morning milk. Before foamy milk had covered the base of the bucket, the barn door opened.

"Marit?" Bestefar stepped in.

She didn't answer, even though she knew it was rude not to do so. She was afraid that if she said a word, her true feelings—about him, about his unwillingness to take action, about brave Henrik lying overhead, whose life was quickly unwinding like a skein of yarn—would all come out of her mouth and she would say too much. She bit the soft, fleshy inside of her lips.

"*God morgen,*" he said, his voice softer than the night before. She sensed him moving closer, standing behind her as she leaned over the bucket, sheltered by the steady breathing of Big Olga. Marit tensed, hoping that he wouldn't notice the smell from the loft.

"Marit, it's not that I don't—" he began, then stopped. "I was terribly worried last night when you two were not at dinner. And then the rowboat was gone."

She kept milking—*ting, ting, ting*—aiming the white stream against the side of the can. Though he was apologizing in his own way, and she felt she should at least acknowledge him, she held herself in check. She wasn't ready to let go of her anger.

From the corner of her eye she watched him. He slid his hands into his trouser pockets and filled his lungs with one deep, long breath. When she didn't turn or say anything, he exhaled in a huff, stepped away, and headed out through the barn door, most likely to his boat.

With hands trembling from anger and fright, Marit continued milking. To her relief, the smell from the loft hadn't sent him up the ladder to investigate.

After turning Big Olga out to pasture, Marit knew what she had to do.

"Lars," she said, calling into the house. "Wait here. I'll be back soon!"

Then she dashed down the road, cutting over paths from the general store to Hanna's home, a red clapboard with a porch overlooking the water. Marit banged on the door, trying to catch her breath, and waited.

"Marit!" Hanna said, still in her pajamas. "It's early, but come in. I've missed you, with school out."

Marit stayed on the porch and shook her head.

Hanna's cheerful expression faded. "What happened? Marit, are you OK?" She glanced across the water toward Ålesund. "Oh, no. Did you get bad news about your parents?"

"I need your mother," Marit said.

"She's still at the hospital in Ålesund. The war keeps her busy. She should return in an hour on the first boat. Why?"

Marit didn't know what to do. She had nowhere else to turn. "He made me promise not to tell anyone about him. But if he doesn't get help, he's going to die."

"Who?"

She couldn't return alone. Not without a plan, without help. In a whisper, she told Hanna about the soldier hidden in the loft. "You must not say a word about this. Not to anyone, Hanna."

"I promise."

Marit waited for Mrs. Brottem at the wharf, and when the mail boat chugged into the harbor, she looked for a red scarf and navy wool coat, just as Hanna had described. Since Marit had seen her last, Mrs. Brottem had gathered deep lines across her forehead.

As passengers stepped from the boat, Marit stopped her. "Mrs. Brottem?"

"Why, Marit," she said, a tired smile turning to concern. "Is everything all right with Hanna and my babies?"

"They're fine," Marit said. "It's my brother, Lars." She lied. "Could you please come check on him? He's in a bad way with a fever."

"Of course."

Chapter Twenty-Three

Warning

With Mrs. Brottem walking alongside, Marit headed toward the barn. Lars was outside, petting the gray goat.

"Your brother certainly seems fine now," Mrs. Brottem said, pausing on the dirt drive.

"It's not really Lars," Marit said in a rush. "I'm sorry. I had to say that because of the other passengers. Please. I'll show you. In the barn."

"I don't know anything about farm animals, Marit."

"Lars," Marit said, pushing open the barn door. "Keep watch and let us know if anyone is coming. Can you do that?"

"*Ja,*" he said. "I'm good at that."

For the next hour, Marit assisted Mrs. Brottem, supplying her with buckets of warm water. Tucking her strawberry blond hair back into her scarf and washing her hands, Mrs. Brottem set to work. She didn't fret and she didn't smile, but she held the edge of her lower lip between her teeth as she examined the soldier.

She cut the pants right off the soldier's legs. "Don't worry," she told Henrik, who slipped in and out of consciousness. "I promise to sew them back up after they get a good washing."

Marit took his clothes down to where a wash bucket waited, then scrubbed and cleaned his torn and soiled pants. When she returned, wet cloths covered Henrik's forehead and Mrs. Brottem ladled water into his mouth, sometimes smoothing his throat with her fingers to help him swallow.

"It's your foot that's causing all this trouble," she told him. "It's badly infected. I'm going to use some hot compresses, and it will hurt, but you must be quiet. Marit, hand me a clean rag."

Marit handed her one from the pile she'd gathered.

Mrs. Brottem put the cloth in the soldier's mouth. "Bite on this if you must."

Then, she faced the twisted and raw stump of his foot and shook her head. "We should get a doctor here to you, but there isn't one on the island. Marit, your grandfather will have to ferry one over from Ålesund—and they're very busy there, too."

179

"*Nei*. We can't tell Bestefar!" Marit pleaded.

"Why not? This soldier needs help."

Ashamed of her grandfather, Marit felt heat rise to her face. "I'm worried he'll report Henrik to the Nazis."

Finally, Mrs. Brottem spoke. "Oh. I see." She examined the soldier's foot further. "I'll see what I can do first, but if his foot must be amputated, then we'll have to risk telling him."

Eyes tight with pain, Henrik bit down on the cloth and moaned as Mrs. Brottem swabbed his infected foot. Marit couldn't stand to see anyone in such pain and looked away. But it was either pain or certain death.

"Let's hope that by cleaning the infected wounds he'll take a turn for the better. I'll return tomorrow morning before heading across to the hospital. You must make sure he drinks plenty of water so he doesn't get dehydrated. And if he's warm, use a cold, wet cloth to keep the fever down. When I return, if he's not better, I will speak with your grandfather myself."

Marit nodded.

As Mrs. Brottem lingered to stitch up the other pant leg as Marit watched Henrik. His eyes were a little brighter, his breathing deeper.

His gaze met Marit's, and she guessed his question. "Did you . . ." he began.

She nodded with a smile. "*Ja*. Just as you asked. It's done."

"Tusen takk," he said. "I owe you a great debt."

Mrs. Brottem must have thought he was speaking to her, for she answered, "Marit—she did the most. But don't thank us yet," she said, her voice stern. "You're not well yet. *Rest.* And do your best to use this pot when you must."

Later, as they headed down the loft ladder, Mrs. Brottem whispered, "This war. None of us can handle it alone. But this boy . . . Henrik . . . without the risks you took to save him, Marit, he'd be dead by now. He owes *you* his life. You've been very brave."

They stood by the cow stanchion as Lars continued his lookout.

"Nei." Marit shook her head back and forth. "I've been terrified, scared to death that—"

"Marit," Hanna's mother interrupted. "You didn't let your fears stop you from . . . doing what needed to be done. *That's* bravery."

That afternoon, Henrik's fever dropped, and he drank water greedily from the ladle Marit held to his lips. He managed a bowl of thin cod stew, which Marit fed him spoonful by slow spoonful. Then he dropped back, exhausted.

At supper, Lars carried on with Bestefar as if the day

had been just like any other. He talked about missing school, how cold he was at night now without the *dyne*, and about becoming a fisherman someday. Marit was glad for his chatter. She could stay tucked within her silence. She wouldn't have to try to lie about her day.

A knock—so light that she wondered if she'd imagined it—sounded at the door. She dropped her spoon against the edge of her bowl, and cod stew splattered across the table. What if Henrik had managed to climb down the ladder? Maybe he was feverish again—possibly delirious. She had warned him about Bestefar, and that it wasn't safe to come to the house.

Or worse, the Gestapo had returned to do another search. Worse than the Angel of Death. Marit remained statue-still.

Bestefar was at the door, easing it open, clearing his throat. Marit stared at her nearly empty bowl and listened. Whatever bravery she might have shown earlier was no longer in her grasp. She was certain of that.

"Mr. Halversen, my name is Olaf," the voice came. "Olaf Andersen."

Marit jerked her gaze toward the door.

"I need to talk to you."

On the doorstep stood Olaf, with Kaptain at his side, his tail curved over his back. Olaf removed his cap, ran one hand through his untamable hair, and turned his cap round and round between both hands. Why was he here? It made no sense. And to be out after dark was to risk getting stopped by the Gestapo. But his parents were NS—traitors. Maybe that's why he was free to roam about despite the curfew.

"I came to warn you," he said, looking beyond Bestefar to Marit. "I heard my parents talking with a German officer. I . . . I hear more than I should. But I came to tell you that there will be a crackdown on the island. 'A severe crackdown,' the German said. I thought you should know."

A surge of fear zinged through her body. Was it possible that Olaf knew about her helping the Resistance soldier? Did he know about her having delivered the compass? But how could he? He had always acted as if he wanted to be friends. Had he been spying on her all along?

Bestefar said quietly, "They've searched here already! What more do we have to worry about? Maybe you're trying to trap us." He stepped closer to Olaf, towering over him.

Olaf glanced questioningly from Marit to Bestefar, then took a step back.

"Go," Bestefar said icily, his hand clamped on the edge of the door, ready to close on Olaf's shoes. "Now."

Olaf yanked on his cap and backed down the steps. "I . . . I'm only trying to help."

"Bestefar," Marit pleaded. She suddenly felt sorry for

Olaf. If he was forced away so soon, they would never know more about his warning or what he actually *knew* about her efforts to help Henrik. "Wait, um, shouldn't we hear him out?"

"*Nei.*"

Before Bestefar had closed the door, Marit slipped outside and flew down the steps after Olaf. "Wait!"

The damp ground soaked through her wool socks. Beyond the barn, a crescent moon hung low in the night sky. She made out the shadowy figures of Olaf and his dog as they headed toward the road.

"Olaf, wait!"

He stopped and slowly turned. Then he walked back, his face mostly in shadow, lit only by a hint of moonlight reflecting off patches of melting snow. Kaptain sat down immediately at his side.

"I'm sorry," she said, tilting her head toward the farmhouse, "for what happened in there. Thank you for warning us, even if I don't understand."

"Your grandfather doesn't want to hear the truth, does he?"

"He wants peace," she said. "He thinks if he avoids trouble—" She stopped. She had no excuses for Bestefar.

The night air was icy with mist. Marit wrapped her arms around herself. Her breath hovered in tiny clouds. "At school," she started, not sure exactly what she was going to say, "I'm sorry I never talked with you. I hope you understand. I can't. It's not you. I don't believe you're one of them."

"Them?" He sounded bitter. "Who, my parents?"

"*Nei,* I mean . . . NS . . . you're not a Nazi."

"Marit," he said. "You don't even *know* me."

She thought of the day he'd carried Kaptain, just a puppy, from the wharf—so proud, so excited. His father had brought back a puppy for Olaf when most people were worrying about the cost of eggs. She didn't know everything about Olaf's parents, and she didn't know everything about Olaf, but she knew him well enough. "I know you're good, Olaf. And I know I'm sorry for so much. You tried to warn us. What can I do?"

"Just believe me." His voice softened to a plea. "I've heard talk. When one family member is taken away, the others look more suspicious. I'm worried you might be at risk."

The door opened and Bestefar stood in the doorway. He cleared his throat. Before he ordered her to come inside, Marit said quickly, "It's the war, Olaf. Maybe someday things will be different."

"Maybe," Olaf said. Then he turned his back and hurried away, absorbed into the damp night.

CHAPTER TWENTY-FOUR

At Risk

Marit couldn't sleep. Bestefar's snoring rose through the floor vents like the snorting of a hibernating bear. As much as Marit tried to stay angry with him for the brusque way he had treated Olaf, her own conversation with Olaf bothered her more.

"Your family is at risk," Olaf had said. In her heart, she believed Olaf was good, but how could she know for sure? How long could anyone be "iced out" before they turned bitter and angry? He *had* risked much by coming to warn them of a crackdown. But was Bestefar right? Was it possible that Olaf had sided with the NS and was warning them as a ploy, a way of getting them to confide in him and to reveal something secret? Or had he come to warn them as a friend would? What exactly had he overheard? In a world where all the rules had changed, she couldn't know anything for sure.

Just as she learned by listening to the sounds around her, and paying attention, she would listen with her heart. And her heart told her that Olaf had meant only good.

She drifted in and out of sleep. Sometime later, she awoke. Outside, a storm was gathering. Waves rushed the shore beyond the farmhouse. Sleet pelted the windowpanes. Wind taunted the farmhouse, and overhead slate shingles trembled.

Footsteps sounded up the stairs.

"Marit?" came Bestefar's deep voice. "Lars?"

Bundled like a bear in foul-weather clothing, he ordered, "Get up. Put on your warm clothes. Hurry now and come with me."

"Is your boat loose?" Marit asked. A thousand possibilities came to her. He'd found the soldier in the loft. The Gestapo were here, beginning their crackdown. Maybe there was a fire. Bombing—it had started again. She sat up, trying to get her bearings. She didn't feel like getting out of bed if she didn't have to. It was the middle of the night and the air was icy. "But why?"

"Just follow. Do as I say. And for God's sake, hurry." Then he headed down the stairs.

She thought of the morning when bombs first fell and

Mama and Papa insisted they go downstairs. Like then, this wasn't a time to delay. "Wake up," she said, shaking Lars's shoulder. "Bestefar said we have to get up and follow him." He moaned.

Marit pushed him to a sitting position, swung his legs over the side of the bed, and helped him to his feet. They didn't have to worry much about adding warm clothes, since they were already dressed in nearly everything they owned. They made their way downstairs and found their boots beside the door. She helped Lars, who was more asleep than awake.

For a moment, they waited at the door, ready to go. Lars leaned into her.

"Bestefar," Marit said, sure he'd discovered their soldier for sure. "Just tell us—"

"I'll tell you soon enough," he said. "But Marit, just this once," he said, his voice full of pleading. "Don't argue with me!"

Moments later they were following him out the door. "Not a word," he said, his hand raised up to them as they crossed from the house toward the barn. Marit braced herself for questions about Henrik. But he walked right past the barn without a glance. Instead, he hurried through sleet, rain, and wind to the road. In a night as dense as peat, they could easily lose him. Marit grabbed Lars's hand and scurried to keep up. Freezing rain lashed her face. Never had she seen Bestefar move so fast. He was nearly running.

Then, in her stomach, the reason for this strange leave-taking struck. Olaf's warning. This had something to do with his visit. But what?

Her whole body tensed, filled with questions and apprehension. They had no excuse for being out in the middle of the night. If a Nazi soldier stopped them, they would all be in terrible trouble. They could be shot on sight.

They skirted the ditches on the way to the boathouse. Bestefar paused, waiting for them to catch up. Then he pulled them into a huddle so that their heads touched. "Not a word," he whispered. "Not a sound until we're inside. Do you understand?"

They nodded. With the Nazi headquarters in the schoolhouse just down the road, Marit wasn't about to protest. Still, this whole thing was crazy. Maybe that was it. Bestefar truly had gone crazy.

Ahead, the boathouse beckoned like a fortress. They followed him through the side door. One step, two. She stopped, waiting. Surely he'd light a candle or help them see somehow. There was a scratch and the smell of sulfur, then the flicker of a candle glowed in Bestefar's hand. And there, coming toward her from a cluster of huddled shapes in the corner, shedding a blanket as she drew closer, was a face that sent Marit's heart on wings.

Aunt Ingeborg!

Marit wanted to cry out loud, to scream with joy. She expected the vision would vanish like a dream, but Aunt Ingeborg, dressed in oversize men's clothing, drew her and Lars into a tight hug, the scratchy wool of her *jakke* against Marit's face. This was no dream.

"Oh, Marit! Lars!" Aunt Ingeborg whispered.

"How did you get here?" Marit asked, her voice hushed. "I saw them haul you away! I thought I'd never see you again." A hundred questions tumbled within her.

"Our German truck was ambushed—soon after we left Ålesund. Three of us teachers were in hiding, until yesterday. Our guide received a signal—brought us here to wait for the next bus."

"What bus?" she whispered. There were no buses on the island.

"Not a real bus," Bestefar interjected. "We'll go from here to Scotland's Shetland Islands. The fishing boats that ferry back and forth—we call them 'The Shetland Bus.'"

CHAPTER TWENTY-FIVE
Valuable Cargo

"Everyone, listen!" Bestefar said, his voice commanding, even at a whisper. He spoke not only to them but also to five people in the shadows. In the ring of the candle's faint light, Marit noticed three men (one with a dark beard, one with a rifle slung across his shoulder, another with a bandage over both eyes) and two women (one whose cape stretched across her protruding belly, the other older, in a calf-length coat). Marit could not understand why Bestefar seemed to be in the middle of this. And how could he know of this plan to take "The Shetland Bus"?

"You will hide quietly in the hold, shoulder to shoulder, tight as sardines," he began.

Not only could Marit barely see, but she struggled to grasp the meaning of what she was hearing.

"Me, too?" Lars asked with excitement. Aunt Ingeborg pulled him close. *"Shhhh."*

Marit was completely stunned. The man she had turned her anger toward, whom she had accused of being as spineless as a boiled potato, was part of the Resistance?

"You won't be comfortable," he explained to everyone, "but whatever happens on deck, you must all remain below—and absolutely silent. Am I clear?"

Marit tried to catch up with all that was coming to light.

"There's no time to waste. Let's board the bus," he said. "We'll ferry out in the dinghy to the trawler."

The Shetland Islands were over three hundred kilometers away. It was stormy, the worst kind of weather and the wrong season to make that kind of voyage.

Marit's mind buzzed with questions, but this wasn't the time to ask them. She understood the risk of making any more noise than necessary. But what about Mama and Papa? Was she to leave Norway and leave them behind? Then she remembered. She grabbed Bestefar's sleeve.

"There's a soldier—a Resistance soldier—in the barn loft. He's wounded. I've been hiding him. If we don't go back for him, the Gestapo will find him."

"In the loft? *Our* loft?" Bestefar said. His silence was filled with foreboding. "If we go back for anyone now, we risk the whole mission."

"And if we don't, he'll die. We can't leave him!" Marit headed toward the door. "I'm the one who told him to hide there. I'll go."

Bestefar glanced around, as if weighing the value of his cargo. "Not alone," he said. "It's better if I join you. We must hurry. The rest of you—row out and take your places in the boat's hold. Ingeborg, guide them. We'll return quickly, God willing. If anything should happen to us, get word to Einar. He'll know what to do." Einar, Marit knew, was another local fisherman—apparently working, too, for the Resistance.

Marit forced herself to leave Aunt Ingeborg and Lars. She had to help Henrik.

Heads tucked, she and Bestefar braved the pelting sleet.

"Shouldn't we stay in the ditches?" she whispered.

He shook his head. "They're accustomed to seeing me at this hour. If we're stopped, let me do the talking."

No sooner had they rounded the first bend than lights bore down on them from behind. Marit scuttled out of the way, but not before a truck splashed past her, then squealed its brakes to a stop. She and Bestefar continued walking until they were alongside the vehicle. Its window opened, and a flashlight blinded them.

Marit covered her eyes with her mitten, hoping to keep from giving away her dread.

"What are you doing out past curfew?"

"I'm sorry, sir," Bestefar said. "I had to check on my fishing boat. The bilge pump has not been working, and I had to make sure she wasn't taking on water."

The light fell squarely on Marit. "And you?"

"She's my granddaughter."

"Nei!" the soldier shouted, and with a swift motion through the open window, hit Bestefar across his face with a pistol.

Bestefar stumbled back. Marit gasped, but held herself still.

"She must answer for herself," barked the soldier.

If she didn't speak up this time, Marit was certain the soldier would hurt Bestefar far worse than he already had.

"The night is so awful," she said, "I didn't want Bestefar to be out all alone. He didn't want me to come, but I followed him."

The soldier humphed. "To have such devotion, old man. You're lucky."

"Ja," Bestefar said. "Marit is my pride and joy."

Despite the bleak situation, she tucked away his words.

"Get home quick, before your luck runs out." Then the Nazi soldier motioned to the driver, and the wheels churned forward, kicking up a spray of freezing water. The wind whined and churned up the sea so that it roared against the shore below. Marit and Bestefar pressed home, nearly at a run, without a word. Some encounters were too close to even speak about.

The barn and farmhouse sat dark and lonely. Marit opened the barn door, and Bestefar followed her inside. She clambered up the loft ladder. "Henrik! We must get you out of here."

The loft was silent.

"Henrik?"

She fumbled in the darkness and found him. She removed her mittens and reached out to touch his face. The moment her hands touched his nose and forehead, she gasped. His skin was stiff and cold. Lifeless. She leaned forward and touched her head to his chest, hoping for the sound of a faint heartbeat, the slightest breath of air. But she was too late. Her efforts to save him had not been nearly enough.

She had failed him.

She eased his stiff eyelids shut with her fingertips. Though her throat ached, she whispered, *"God natt."* Good night.

Then she nearly stumbled down the ladder, her chest shuddering.

"Marit," Bestefar said, catching her.

The low moan of a wounded animal rose from her

core. Her legs buckled, and as she slid to her knees, Bestefar pulled her into his arms and held her up. Though she had barely known this soldier, his death seemed to embody all the losses, all the sacrifices being made across Norway. Somewhere, Henrik had a mother and father who would cry when they learned the news—*if* they ever learned of their son. Maybe he had a brother, or a sister, or even a girlfriend. "I tried—but it wasn't enough," she cried, her tears flowing into Bestefar's wool jacket. "I should have asked you to help, but . . . he's dead."

For a hurried moment, he wrapped her in his sturdy arms and whispered rapidly in her ear. "How could you have known? I've done my best to keep you unaware. Even scared off your well-meaning friend. You did what you could."

"Oh, Bestefar." She cried harder. "But we can't leave his body to rot or be found by the Gestapo."

"We can't bury him, Marit. There's no time."

"We could take his body with us and give him a proper burial."

"No. A dead body in tight quarters puts the living at risk."

He was right. Face wet with tears, Marit brushed past Bestefar. "I'll be right back."

"Marit!"

She raced past him out of the barn and into the farmhouse. Without taking off her boots, she flew upstairs and straight to the storage chest. The moment she lifted the lid, the sweet cedar filled her nose as she tore through tablecloths and runners to the soft wool of her *bunad* at the bottom. She couldn't let the Gestapo find it and burn it. She'd take it for Aunt Ingeborg's sake—for her own sake.

She flew down the stairs, stuffing the *bunad* inside her *jakke*.

In the kitchen, a meow startled her.

"Tekopp!" Marit cried. She wanted to bring the cat along, for Lars's sake. She could tuck him in her jacket to keep him quiet, and besides, even if he got loose there was nothing unusual about a cat roaming the harbor. She reached down, scooped him up, and tucked him in her *jakke* along with the *bunad*.

With a sense that hours had passed instead of seconds, Marit hurried down the stairs with her cargo, said a silent goodbye to the old farmhouse and her brave soldier, and fled.

CHAPTER TWENTY-SIX

The Shetland Bus

Marit caught up with Bestefar outside the barn, and without a word, they hurried toward the road, ducked low, and sped through the water-filled ditch. If they were stopped this time, there would be no second chance.

As they neared the boathouse, the gleaming eyes of headlights swung toward them from the Nazi headquarters. Bestefar grabbed her arm and pulled her with him to the soggy earth. Breathless, Marit rolled onto her back, careful not to squash Tekopp.

Lights cut a hazy path through the darkness and drew closer with the slow approach of wheels rolling over the wet road. For a moment, lights lit the air just above her nose. All she had to do was lift her hand and she would give them away. She remained motionless in the ditch's shadows, trying not to breathe.

Wind swooped down on them. Sleet stung Marit's face. Water seeped through the back of her *jakke* and sweater and iced the small of her back. Tekopp began to squirm and wiggle. Marit held him more tightly. But the tighter she gripped him, the more he dug his claws into her skin and struggled to escape.

"Yeeoooow!" he complained, but Marit held him harder.

The light and wheels stopped, and then the vehicle backed up in their direction.

"Let him go," Bestefar whispered fiercely.

Marit released her grip and Tekopp sprang from her coat. He bounded over her chest, his claws raking her neck as he fled.

A door opened. *"Halt! Was ist los?"* A second door opened and boot heels sounded on the road above. Another light swept back and forth.

Her heart thudded louder with each passing second.

Up on the road, a set of boots pivoted, then stopped.

The light paused in its sweeping search.

The soldier laughed, then said something more in German.

Footsteps sounded, the door shut, and wheels splattered mud as the vehicle moved slowly forward, dragging the light away with it.

A welcome darkness covered them, and their only companion was once again the wind. They held still. Silently, Marit chastised herself for trying to bring Tekopp. Finally, Bestefar stirred. In haste, they closed the remaining distance.

Aunt Ingeborg waited behind the boathouse door. "The soldier?" she whispered.

Bestefar shook his head, and Aunt Ingeborg seemed to understand.

Life vests on, they piled wordlessly into the rowboat. Bestefar rowed quietly to the trawler, and Marit hoisted herself up the rope ladder behind Aunt Ingeborg.

Once aboard, Bestefar motioned to the hold and whispered, "The rest are below?"

Aunt Ingeborg nodded.

"Good," he said. Then he pointed Marit to the wheelhouse that sheltered the steering wheel and controls. Teeth chattering, she was wet clear through and colder than she'd ever been. From the shelter of the small wheelhouse, she watched Bestefar as he secured the dinghy to the line, lifted anchor, and single-handedly hoisted a sail to half-mast.

The wind howled outside the wheelhouse and whined through its cracks. It couldn't be a worse time for leaving. Then she realized, on the contrary, maybe this was the best kind of weather. The Germans wouldn't want to be out on the water in such a storm.

As soon as the sail rose partway up the mast, the wind turned on the canvas and pressed the trawler toward the waves. Marit hung on to the handholds inside the wheelhouse as the boat tilted. Bestefar squeezed in beside her, his slicker rain-drenched.

"We can't afford to start the engine in the harbor," he whispered. "Someone could hear—even in this wind."

They skimmed out of the safety of the breakwater. When they crossed into open water, Bestefar gave her the wheel. "Keep it steady. See where the compass is? Just hold it there on course."

Then he bustled outside again, dropped the sail, and returned to join her in the wheelhouse. He throttled the engine forward. The engine caught and hummed, but out of the sheltered harbor, the wind drowned out the trawler's usual *tonk-tonk-tonk* noise.

Like a madman, the wind rocked their cradle. Rain drenched the wheelhouse windows. Now, finally, it would be safe to talk.

"I'm sorry, Bestefar," she said, certain that the wind drowned her voice to anyone onshore. "I didn't understand you. When you turned in your radio, I thought you'd given up completely."

"I lied," he said heavily. The lines and creases in his face had multiplied, and beneath his eyes, his skin was dark with worry. "I gave up the one radio, but I still have another disguised as a tackle box—here on the trawler."

"Oh, but I thought . . . I was so angry at you for—I'm sorry."

Then he explained how he'd initially intended to stay clear of getting involved. But when the Resistance came to him and asked him to fix a boat engine, he did what he could, and his involvement grew. He'd helped transport shipments of arms for the Allies and captained a boatload of agents and soldiers *into* Norway, "right under the noses of the Nazis," and this was his third trip of transporting refugees.

"So that's why you were gone so long at times."

He nodded. "And your soldier?"

In turn, she told him how she'd stumbled across Henrik, hid him, and tried to finish his mission by delivering the compass. "On the way back, that's when the wind caught us—"

"All the more reason to get you off the island. People have a way of talking, especially when under pressure by the Gestapo. This war, it changes people—and not always for the better."

Outside the wheelhouse, boat lines that should have been secured suddenly danced in the darkness like angry white snakes. "Bestefar, look!"

"Stay here," he ordered, "and keep your hands on the wheel. Keep us pointing southwest." He stepped out again into the night.

Shivering, Marit watched the compass and turned the

wheel back and forth to counter the force of waves and wind. The compass needle careened west, then south, but each time, she brought it back halfway between the two points.

Waves crested higher than the gunwales. Maybe this whole trip was a suicide trip, an escape from the Nazis only to be swallowed by the sea. Finally, Bestefar returned again, dripping wet. His wrist was chafed and bleeding.

Bestefar took the wheel. "*Takk.* Now get below with the others." He pointed to the hatch midship, which usually held a full day's catch of fish. "And hold on to something as you cross that deck!"

Blinking back blowing rain and salt water, Marit bent low and steadied herself by gripping the boom, which was now secured, its sail down. At the hatch on deck, she knocked and the square door opened.

"Quickly. Don't let in rain," Aunt Ingeborg called.

Arms caught her and directed her feet. She squeezed down alongside two bodies—Aunt Ingeborg's and Lars's —and the rest, sitting or lying down in the hold.

"I brought the *bunad*." A chill had settled deep in her bones. Her teeth chattered and her mouth had grown stiff with cold. "I wouldn't let the Nazis have it."

She couldn't see her aunt's face, but in the few seconds of silence that followed, she knew Aunt Ingeborg was pleased. "Oh, Marit." A hand reached over—a welcome comfort of softness and calluses.

"You have so much to tell me," her aunt said. "But not now. We should try to sleep."

Silence enveloped them and the air reeked of fish. Later she would explain everything to her aunt, but for now, Marit was drenched and bitterly cold. Wedged between bodies, she closed her eyes. Eventually she warmed, and lulled by the rumbling engine, she slept.

More than once during the night the pregnant woman retched in the darkness. Someone must have found her a bucket, because the hatch opened, something clunked on deck, and then the hatch closed again. "I'm sorry," the woman said.

"No need to apologize," Aunt Ingeborg replied.

Marit tucked her nose inside her sweater, which helped only somewhat, and managed to go back to sleep. Though she didn't know the stories of the other passengers or why they were fleeing, she understood they were all in danger—and that they were drawn together as close as family in the belly of the boat.

Sometime around dawn, Marit guessed, Aunt Ingeborg woke everyone. "Listen!"

Before Marit opened her eyes, she jumped up and bumped her head.

"Everyone—stay below," Aunt Ingeborg ordered, then lifted the hatch slightly.

Through the crack, Marit glimpsed the dusky gray sky

and a low-swooping plane coming from the north. It droned closer and dropped lower until it was nearly upon them. If the boat was shot to pieces, it would become their coffin. God would have to protect them. They were only a fishing trawler alone on a vast sea—no match for Nazi bomber planes.

She and Aunt Ingeborg watched as Bestefar slipped from his wheelhouse and ducked beside an overturned wooden barrel, its lid askew. "The barrel doesn't contain herring or extra fuel oil," her aunt explained, "but guns and rifles."

"How do you know?" Marit asked.

"I know."

Droning low, the plane approached, drawing closer and closer. As it did, Bestefar reached into the barrel. But to Marit's relief, the plane turned sharply away and then flew off into the charcoal sky until it was no longer visible. The pilot must have thought they were a simple fishing boat.

"Thank God!" Aunt Ingeborg shouted. She dropped the hatch, and darkness and the damp, sharp smells of fish, fuel oil, and vomit engulfed them again.

"I can't stay down here," Marit said. She pushed open the hatch and scrambled onto the deck. "And Bestefar needs help keeping watch."

"Marit!" her aunt warned.

"I'll stay out of sight in the wheelhouse," she called over her shoulder. She didn't want to disobey her aunt, but this time Bestefar needed her.

All morning and afternoon, Marit helped Bestefar keep watch for approaching German planes. If one were to come too close and open up on them with gunfire, he'd be ready beside the gun-filled barrel. He might be able to inflict some damage in return, and Marit would keep the boat on course.

The storm had passed, settling into a steady drizzle. Winds blew across giant swells, and their mood grew more confident as they traveled southwest. When a spray of water shot into the sky, not far from their boat, Marit panicked. From her nightmares, her first reaction was— *kraken*! But she knew she wasn't being logical. It was far worse. "Submarine!" she yelled to Bestefar.

"Marit!" He laughed beside her in the wheelhouse. "Have you forgotten where you're from? Look again!"

A pod of humpback whales spouted from their air holes, then arced . . . rising, rising from the surface—one, two, three—until their mighty tails swept upward, revealing light-patterned undersides as they dived. For a time, the whales paralleled the trawler, as if keeping watch over them. All too soon, they veered away, and gulls followed in their wake.

"Marit, until we reach Scalloway, I need an extra set of eyes."

Long after sunset and late into the night, eyes straining with fatigue, Marit kept watch for planes, boats, or mines that might have drifted off course into open water. Several times, Bestefar motioned for her to go below, but she shook her head. She refused to give up her post. Bestefar couldn't navigate and keep watch for so many hours all alone.

A full twenty-four hours later, they'd covered over three hundred kilometers to Shetland, the islands off the northern tip of Scotland. Out of the vast darkness, a few lights flickered in the distance, and Bestefar steered straight for the British base in Scalloway. At his direction, Marit opened the hatch, and one by one, everyone came up on deck. The pregnant woman was pale and unsteady with sickness. Lars held fast to Aunt Ingeborg's hand.

As they entered the harbor, Bestefar slowed the engine and sounded the siren several times.

"A message in code?" Marit asked.

"Morse code," he said. "The letter *V*, for *victory*."

Like gathering fireflies, lights flickered on in the harbor. Soon, a growing crowd of men—and a few women—gathered at the wharf, waiting to greet them.

Marit stepped to the stern, gripped the rail from the back of the trawler, and gazed out.

Beyond the black ocean, her parents waited.

Her country waited.

CHAPTER TWENTY-SEVEN

Homecoming
Three Years Later

"Will all the Germans be gone?" Marit asked as the fishing trawler neared the humpback island of Godøy. The city of Ålesund lay beyond, framed by mountains crowned white.

"That's our hope," Bestefar replied.

She worried, along with everyone, that with 350,000 Germans lingering on Norwegian soil, they might try for a last stand and leave the country in ruins. Over the radio, the king and Resistance leaders kept advising Norwegians not to take revenge, but to be patient—and wait.

Marit stood outside the wheelhouse, its door ajar as Bestefar steered the fishing trawler into the familiar wharf. Lars, Aunt Ingeborg, and several other passengers stood watching from the bow. Morning sunlight danced off the sea as the boat rode its gentle swells. As they passed island farms, Norwegian flags flew proudly from every flagpole. Marit breathed in the saltwater air. They were actually returning home.

When the news had come to the world—and to the village of Scalloway on Shetland—Marit was in the dining hall gathered with others around the radio. It was May 8, 1945, and Winston Churchill officially declared that peace had come at last to Europe. The room filled with cheering, then singing and dancing that went on for hours. Marit danced with Resistance soldiers, with Lars, with Aunt Ingeborg and Bestefar. She felt herself return to a semblance of who she once was: a girl without fear. But she was hardly the same. She was ten when the first bombs had fallen. Now she was fifteen.

For the last three years, thousands of refugees—including the men and women who had journeyed with them on the trawler—passed through Scalloway and on to England, the United States, and other Allied countries. Some went where they had relatives, some had no family left and decided to start over, some received special training and returned to Norway to help the Resistance. Some stayed on in Scalloway, a compact village of a thousand people, including Marit, Lars, and Aunt Ingeborg, who helped in the base's kitchen and boarded with a blind, elderly woman at a nearby farm. Bestefar made numerous trips with his trawler between Shetland and Norway's treacherous coast, and each time he returned to Scalloway, Marit hugged him fiercely. Now, with the news of peace, the German occupation of Norway—five long and bitter years—had finally come to an end!

As soon as they could ready the trawler, they once again made the long crossing. Seagulls circled the trawler, expecting scraps from a regular fishing voyage. Marit's stomach fluttered. She longed to touch shore. The engine slowed, its reassuring *tonk-tonk-tonk* reminding her that some things had not changed.

She studied the crowd, bracing herself for the sight of grayish green uniforms. But she didn't see a single German soldier anywhere. Friends cheered as their boat docked in the harbor. She could see tall Mr. Larsen, Mrs. Brottem, and a young woman with dark hair held back in a scarf who cried out, "Marit! You're back!"

"Hanna!" Marit raced across the deck and didn't wait for the plank. She squeezed under a rail and jumped onto the dock. Hanna's face was thin, and when Marit hugged her, knobby shoulders spoke of food shortages. But the slice of air between Hanna's front teeth was still the same, and her smile belied the years of hardship. "There's so much we need to talk about," Hanna said, then she turned. "Miss Halversen!"

Beyond the crowd, Marit caught sight of a new large sign on Mr. Larsen's general store that read "Closed for joy!" She smiled.

Soon after, when they neared the farm, Marit stopped abruptly. Above the door of the goldenrod farmhouse hung a red and black swastika flag. What if a few Germans remained? She couldn't move. But Bestefar didn't falter. He strode ahead, ripped down the flag, threw it to the ground, and spat on it.

Then he searched the house, chicken coop, and barn. Though the Nazis had taken over their farmhouse, they were gone now. "At least," Bestefar said, "they didn't burn everything to the ground in their retreat."

That day, Marit helped scrub every room from top to bottom. On her hands and knees Aunt Ingeborg declared, her face red from scouring, "I want every trace, every scent of them gone forever!"

Marit happily ripped down the paper that had covered the windows and blackened the landscape. Despite the long summer hours of evening light, she lit candles on every windowsill—along with the rest of the islanders. No more darkness. No more occupation.

With each day that followed, Marit waited for news of her parents. While in Scotland, they'd heard rumors from others working for the Resistance. Someone saw them arrested by the Nazis. Another said they were living in Oslo. But with no letters or messages, she could not know if they were alive or dead, and in her memory, their faces had dimmed. But from her time at the base, she'd come to better understand the workings of the Resistance. They had waged war against the Germans by slipping soldiers and ammunitions into Norway; by blowing up German ships, trains, and supply trucks; and by helping countless refugees—teachers, pastors, dislocated families, Jews and non-Jews—anyone, adults or children, escape.

One morning in late May, when raindrops fell sideways, Marit and Lars waited for the mail boat to arrive. Not only did new supplies arrive daily, but each boatload brought returning islanders—some who had escaped, others who had joined the underground militia, and still others who had simply disappeared.

In a light rain, Marit and Lars took shelter under a boathouse eave. Once the mail boat docked, a thin couple made their way down the plank. The man limped badly and used a cane, and the woman, whose hair was shorn, carried a small rucksack. They were like leafless trees, angular in form, their limbs unsteady in the breeze. But when they glanced out at the crowd, Marit recognized their eyes immediately. Her throat closed and she couldn't find her voice. She thought her heart would explode.

Finally, she screamed, "Mama! Papa!"

In a few long strides—in one fierce embrace—they were reunited. Laughing, crying, hugging, examining one another.

On their slow walk to the farmhouse, Papa explained that they needed to build up their strength before—or if—they returned to Isfjorden. Their home there had been bombed again, this time to splinters. For now, Papa would help Bestefar fish and Mama would help at the school in the fall.

"We met there for school," Lars explained, with a nod in the direction of the church. The wind caught his sandy hair, and for a second, with his growing frame, he reminded Marit of a fjord horse—sturdy and dependable. "But this fall," he continued, "the schoolhouse is ours again." He spoke as if the island had always been his home. "Aunt Ingeborg made us study while we were at Scalloway so we wouldn't fall behind. I'll be in grade six this year."

That day at the table, everyone had stories.

Mama told how she worked as a translator from their

hytte in the mountains. She worked alongside a Briton and a Norwegian—both radio operators. "But the British soldier," she said, shaking her head, "turned out to be German. His accent was so good he fooled even me. Many died because of him. Dozens of us were arrested."

"Papa," Lars said. "What did you do?"

Papa stirred his *kaffe* slowly, seemingly lost in his thoughts. At first Marit wondered if he'd heard Lars's question. Finally, he spoke. "I mapped out bridges, train trestles, tunnels, and highways for destruction—the very things I helped design and build, I helped blow up. We had to handicap the Nazis, whatever way we could."

Marit told about Henrik, and how she'd delivered his coded message about klipfish and his compass by rowboat with Lars, to the north side of the island.

"We'll never know for sure," Aunt Ingeborg added, "but the compass Marit delivered just might have been the same compass our host received as a signal to move us on. All I know is that we were sent from our basement shelter to take the Shetland Bus. I thought it was going to be a real bus."

In the rhubarb patch, Marit worked alongside Mama and Aunt Ingeborg, harvesting the sturdy, bittersweet red stalks. Now that the first Allied food shipments were arriving, they could count on sugar and flour, and they planned to make jams, jellies, pies, and sauces to store, sell, and trade. Since she'd returned to Godøy Island, chores had never felt so good.

As Marit pulled out the tender pink stems from the moist, rich earth, she spotted a few slimy gray slugs clinging to them. Disgusted, she flicked them off, one by one. But rhubarb was hearty. It endured droughts and heavy rains, bitter winters—and war. What were a few slugs? Before moving to the next plant with its massive green leaves, she stood up, stretched out the knot in the small of her back, and gazed toward the pasture and sea.

Papa and Lars worked at repairing the fence. Sweat marked a *V* on Papa's shirt between his jutting shoulder blades as he dropped a cedar beam into the ground. Then Lars tapped dirt around the new fence pole. She hated to think about how Papa and Mama had been held at the Grini concentration camps outside Oslo. Papa refused to discuss the treatment he was subjected to, but when they'd all gone swimming, the pale scars on his legs and back made Marit wince. Separated at a men's camp and women's camp, her parents had each done hard labor, and the food portions were, according to Mama, "never, never enough."

"Mama?" Marit asked, glancing over at her mother, who was bent over a rhubarb plant. "Do you want to take a rest?"

Mama looked up, her eyes still bright as crystal blue fjord waters. "Rest? Why would I want to rest? This is play!" She laughed, but that started up the cough that she'd brought back from the camp. Sometimes she coughed up blood. Her face, gaunt and sunken, barely resembled that of the woman who had smoothed Marit's hair and had said goodbye five years earlier at the ferry.

Her parents' work in the Resistance had come at a high price. Did they feel their efforts had been worth the sacrifice? Marit wondered. And her own efforts of delivering the compass and the klipfish code, even though her role had been small—had she made any difference at all? She remembered her aunt's words: *You must do what you feel is right, and so must I.* And so had poor Henrik, at such a terrible price. Would she do the same if she had the chance to do it all over again?

She expected so.

"I'm surprised the Germans left this rhubarb patch," Mama said between coughs. "They certainly didn't leave anything else."

"From the bottles we found in the barn," Aunt Ingeborg said, her long braid hanging over her shoulder, "they were probably drinking more than eating these last months. They must have sensed the end was coming."

The goats and chickens were gone. Only Olga

remained. Earlier, Olaf had come by to explain how he'd asked the German soldiers if he could milk Olga for them, and in return he was allowed a weekly pail of milk for his family. It was his way, he'd told Marit, to help out until Olga's real owners returned. Unfortunately, only days after their return, locals asked Olaf's parents to leave the island. They sold their home and left to start over somewhere else. Marit never had a chance to say goodbye to Olaf.

Across the pasture, no soldiers flanked the lighthouse. Only seagulls, oystercatchers, and terns frequented its nearby shore. Now that Hitler was dead and the Nazis had lost, now that Germany was in ruins, she wondered about her lighthouse soldier—the one who gave her two chocolates in exchange for her *dyne*. Did he question the teachings of Hitler and the Nazi propaganda now? How had the war changed young men like him?

Marit turned back to gathering rhubarb. The sun pressed its warmth along her bare arms. A sea breeze cooled her back and neck. Her family was together again. The war was truly over. A deep joy coursed through her from head to toes. She was only picking rhubarb behind a barn. A simple thing. She was only doing chores on a piano key of farmland off the western coast of Norway.

On Godøy Island.

She was home.

My research for this book included a trip to Norway, a country rich in history, landscape, and the character of its people (some of whom I proudly call my ancestors). With my husband, Charlie, and our son, Eric, we visited several World War II museums and combed the region where this story is set. The more I learned about the Resistance efforts, the more in awe I was of the bravery of ordinary Norwegians.

The Nazi occupation of Norway lasted five years. All major events of this story are historically true.

When I asked my friend Johanne Moe about her experience growing up in Nazi-occupied Norway, she replied, "I lived in constant fear." She also told me about a bomb that was wedged under the floorboards of her house, and also how Nazi soldiers would enter the house unannounced anytime of day or night, taking what they wished, including the last piece of her mother's precious soap.

Two months after the Nazis bombed Norway on April 9, 1940, they effectively defeated the Norwegian army, which had known peace for 125 years. The Nazis attempted a "friendly" occupation, regarding Norwegians as a kindred people that should preferably be led into the fold . . . through persuasion, eventually to side with the Germans. When Nazi propaganda, however, failed to win over the hearts and minds of the Norwegian people, the Nazis resorted to harsher tactics, including house raids, interrogation, and torture by the Gestapo. As a way of coping, Norwegians resorted to humor and Resistance symbols, such as wearing red hats and paper clips. German-run concentration camps existed in Norway, too, and many Norwegians eventually were sent to these camps. Who was sent? Anyone who openly opposed the Nazi occupation or was caught helping with Resistance efforts.

Though this story focuses on life under Nazi occupation, it is important to note that throughout Europe the Jewish population was treated most severely. In Norway, the property of Jewish citizens was the first to be confiscated, and all Jewish males over the age of fifteen were sent to the brutal concentration camps in Germany, never to return. According to one author, the "Norwegian Jewish community suffered the greatest losses of all Scandinavian countries."

Despite the Nazis' terrorizing presence and demands, Norway's pastors and teachers rallied together and took bold stands. Lutheran pastors refused to stay in their churches under the new banner of Nazi authority and preach as they were instructed. Instead, most left their pulpits and took risks by meeting with church members in private homes, much as Pastor Ecklund chose to do.

When Quisling's new government passed laws to establish a Nazi teachers' association, as well as a national youth organization, similar to the Nazi Youth in Germany, both were met with great protests. The Nazi Youth organizations in Germany had been highly successful in molding young minds toward a Nazi philosophy. By making every Norwegian boy and girl between the ages of ten and eighteen attend such meetings and activities, the Nazis hoped to have similar success in Norway. The Church of Norway objected. More than 200,000 parents wrote letters refusing to allow their children to participate in the "Nazi Youth" organizations. The teachers, too, rallied together in this struggle to protect the freedoms of teachers and students. In short, when the Nazi leadership ordered teachers across Norway to instruct students in "the new spirit" of Nazi philosophy, the teachers refused.

The retaliation toward teachers was severe.

One out of every ten teachers—just like Miss Halversen —was rounded up and sent to a concentration camp. To make an example of them, the Nazis crammed five hundred of these teachers in a ship in nightmarish, slavelike conditions and shipped them sixteen hundred miles up the frigid northern coast to a concentration camp. Some did not survive the voyage.

Despite such harsh tactics against teachers, the teachers who remained behind stood firm and refused to give in to the Nazis' demands. Eventually, the Nazi leadership relented and said the teachers had "misunderstood" their earlier demands. Though I do not know of any individual teachers who escaped en route to the camps or from them, it is certainly plausible that a teacher such as Miss Halversen might have been helped by the Resistance. In the end, the teachers won this battle against the Nazis and were left to teach according to their conscience.

Roughly 50,000 Norwegians were arrested by Nazis during the occupation. Of these, some 9,000 were sent to Nazi concentration camps in Norway that offered woeful living conditions: lack of decent food and drinking water, and hard labor. Some died and many became sick. About 9,000 Norwegians were sent to German concentration camps in Czechoslovakia, Poland, Austria, France, and Germany, where conditions were inhuman. Fourteen hundred Norwegians died at these camps—half of them of Jewish ancestry, and of these, most perished in gas chambers.

"The Shetland Bus" was the term used to describe the efforts of fishermen and boat captains who ferried refugees *out* of the country. The term "refugee" could have included almost anyone fleeing for safety: families whose homes might have been bombed in a Nazi reprisal, individuals suspected of aiding the Allies, Jews and non-Jews, or anyone who went against the Germans in any way. The bus also helped bring Allied weapons, supplies, and agents *into* Norway. Scotland's Shetland Islands lay roughly two hundred miles away from the middle of Norway's western coast, and boats traveled these waters at great risk in the dark arctic months. Ålesund and its surrounding islands, including Godøy, harbored numerous Shetland Bus operations.

Some 3,300 people escaped from Norway via small boats—with heavy losses—and close to 50,000 people crossed the border on foot, largely into Sweden.

After five bitter years of German occupation in Norway, Winston Churchill declared over British radio that peace had come at last to Europe. On May 8, 1945, bells rang out joyously across Norway. The Norwegian flag shot up every flagpole. Radios came out of hiding. On May 17, children marched throughout Norway in their annual Children's Parade on Independence Day, which had been banned since the occupation. Finally, on June 7, fireworks filled the sky as Norwegians celebrated their greatest symbol of freedom—the long-awaited return of their exiled king.

GLOSSARY

Norwegian Words:

alt for Norge (ahlt forr nor-geh) all for Norway

Bestemor (behss-tah-moor) Grandmother

Bestefar (behss-tah-faar) Grandfather

bunad (boo-nahd) traditional costume of Norway, consisting of blouse, vest, and skirt for women and girls; and shirt, vest, and knickers for men and boys

dyne (dee-nah) a down-filled quilt, or eiderdown filled duvet

fattigmann (faht-tih-mahn) twisted and fried dough flavored with cinnamon and cardamon seed

frokost (froo-kost) breakfast

God Jul (goo-yewl) Merry Christmas

god morgen (goo-maw-ern) good morning

god natt (goo-nahtt) good night

hei (hay) a greeting; hey there

hytte (hit-ah) cabin

ja (ya) yes

jakke (yak-keh) jacket or coat

jøssing (yuhs-sing) a Norwegian patriot

Julaften (yewleh-ahf-tern) Christmas Eve

Juletid (yewleh-teed) Christmastime

kaffe (kahf-feh) coffee

Kaptain (kahp-tayn) captain

klippfisk (klip-fisk) klipfish; split, salted, and dried cod

kraken (krah-ken) a sea monster of Norwegian folklore, an enormous octopus/crab creature said to pull ships down with its tentacles

krumkake (kroom-kah-keh) a cone-shaped cookie baked on an iron, similar to a waffle iron

lefse (lef-sah) a thin potato pancake

lutefisk (loo-teh-fisk) a type of dish made from air-dried whitefish, prepared with lye, soaked many hours, and served with butter

Marit (Mahr-it) a first name

Mor (moor) Mother

Nasjonal Samling (NS) (nah-shoo-naal sahm-ling) national gathering; or Norwegian Nazi Party

nei (nay) no

nisselue (nissah-luah) red stocking cap

Norge (nor-geh) Norway

pensum (pen-summ) syllabus of classwork

quisling (quiz-ling) a traitor; a term used for Norwegians who collaborated with the Nazis, so named because of Vidkun Quisling, a Norwegian who worked with Nazis during the occupation

risengrot (rees-ehn-gruht) warm rice pudding sprinkled with cinnamon and sugar

sandkaker (sahn-kaa-ker) almond cookies in fluted tins

sølje (suhl-yeh) type of Norwegian silver broach

takk (tahkk) thank you

tekopp (teh-kopp) teacup

tusen takk (two-sehn tahkk) a thousand thanks, or many
thanks

uff da (oohf-dah) an exclamation of dismay

vaffel (vahff-ell) waffle

vel (vehl) *well!*

velkommen (vehl-kom-mehn) Welcome

vesla (vehs-lah) "little one"

Norwegian Places:

Ålesund (ohleh-sunn) city on the western coast of Norway

Alnes (ahl-nes) fishing village on the north of Godøy Island

Åndalnes (ohn-dahl-nes) a city at the end of Romsdal Fjord in
west-central Norway

Giske (gih-skeh) an island off Norway's western coast near Ålesund

Godøy (goo-dey) an island off Norway's western coast near
Ålesund

Isfjorden (ees-fjorh-ehn) a village at the end of Romsdal Fjord

German Words:

Fräulein (froy-leyen, or froy-line) girl; miss

Gestapo (Geh-stah-poh) Germany's secret police

Halt! Was ist los? (Halt, pronounced as in English; Vahs ist lohs)
Stop! What's the matter?

Heil (heyel, or hile) Hail

Herr (hehrr) man; mister

Reich (rahyk) empire; German Nazi state

Was ist das? (Vahs ist dahs) What is that?

For Further Reading

Folklore Fights the Nazis: Humor in Occupied Norway
by Kathleen Stokker
Madison: University of Wisconsin Press, 1995

Norway 1940
by François Kersaudy
New York: St. Martin's Press, 1990

Norway 1940–45: The Resistance Movement
by Olav Riste and Berit Nokleby
Oslo: Tanum-Norli, 1970

The Shetland Bus
by David Howarth
New York: Lyons Press, 1951

Snow Treasure
by Marie McSwigan
New York: E. P. Dutton, 1942

War and Innocence:
A Young Girl's Life in Occupied Norway
by Hanna Aasvik Helmersen
Seattle: Hara Publishing, 2000

+- ❀ -+